THE MONARCH PAPERS: VOLUME TWO

THE MONARCH PAPERS: VOLUME TWO

Cosmos & Time

Cosmos & Time

CJ BERNSTEIN

Ackerly Green Publishing
90 Broad Street
2nd Floor
New York, NY 10004
www.ackerlygreen.com

Quantity sales. Special discounts are available on quantity purchases by corporations, associations, and others. For details, contact the publisher at the address above.

Orders by U.S. trade bookstores and wholesalers. Please contact Ackerly Green Publishing.

Cover Design: Xavier Comas

Publisher: Ackerly Green Publishing, LLC

Editor: Nick Eliopulos

ISBN: 978-0-9990387-5-8

1. Fantasy - Contemporary 2. Magical Realism 3. Alternative History

10 9 8 7 6 5 4 3 2

CONTENTS

PART I
COSMOS

1. Cold   3
2. Remains   6
3. Kemetic Solutions   13
4. Artifacts   23
5. No Constants   38
6. Misplaced Memory   53
7. Teatime   78
8. Whistling   87
9. The Eye   101
10. Firefighter   114
11. Forewarned   123
12. May 31st   139
13. The Well   147

PART II
TIME

14. A Month like a Year   157
15. Wake Up   171
16. Separations   179
17. Traveling   195
18. Stories In A Dream   235
19. Windows and Doors   287
20. Figuration   299
21. Housekeeping   310
22. The Lodge   320
23. Time for Tea   342
24. The Lantern of Low Hollow   352
25. Myth and More   364
26. The Little Red House   376

27. The Wishing Well   387

28. Dr. Brightwell   397

29. The Day of Change   408

30. Sacrifice   428

31. The Mountain's Will   434

32. Mirumagiqum   447

    Epilogue   460

    Explore The World of Magiq   465

    You Can Make A Big Difference   467

    About CJ Bernstein   469

PART I
COSMOS

March-May, 2017

CHAPTER 1
COLD

"Magiq does not run according to science. It runs
on intention and emotion."

— ROBERT

I dreamed about snow. Tall white drifts suffocated the world, the bitter winds shaping them into familiar forms only to morph them again into something alien, something other. The city buildings that rose around me were the only landmarks I recognized, but even they looked different somehow, like distant relatives I hadn't seen in years. Their dusted faces glowed in the moonlight, and their black, empty windows looked down on me like mournful eyes.

I was naked, trudging through snow up to my hips, my legs numb, my exposed skin burning in the cold. The wind picked up and I saw her, Lauren, her snow-body coalescing inside a tiny whirlwind that drifted down a forgotten alley. I followed, pushing my way through the ever-thickening drifts. She turned and looked at me, looked through me, as if I were the one made of snow.

I ignored my blackened, frostbitten fingertips, my tears frozen and heavy on my cheeks, and burrowed my way to her. She hovered atop a drift before me, the moonlight caught inside the snowy matrix of her body. It lit her from within, the blue glow waxing and waning like the winking of a pulsar, like a falling and rising tide, like breathing.

Like a heartbeat.

She watched the snow swirling around her, as if every flake was a new world of discovery finally opened to her. I shivered uncontrollably at her feet, blinking at the wind and struggling to keep my eyes from freezing shut. The snow grew deeper, pressing my folded arms harder against my chest. I was immobile; only my head remained above the snow.

Lauren bent to one knee and cradled my face with an ethereal hand. She pointed out across the silent white city, to a house that sat far off in the distance, untouched by the snow. Its deep red shingles were a defiant patch of warmth in the blinding white. There was a fire flickering in one of its windows, and a shape looking back at me from inside. I wanted to feel that warmth so desperately, but I wasn't going to make it there. Too far. Too cold. The tears I shed turned to ice in an instant.

She turned back to me, said nothing, only stared at me with eyes that twinkled like cold, unfiltered starlight until the snow finally covered me completely and I was frozen in the dark.

I woke confused. I couldn't see, and my arms were still pinned to my chest. Panic rose swiftly until I realized I was cocooned in blankets. Somehow I had managed to roll off my bed and was hanging off the side by a tangle of thick sheets. When I was finally able free myself, I changed out of my sweat-soaked undershirt into something dry. I shivered violently. Ever since the night of the performance, I couldn't get warm. Even the unseasonably warm weather did little to help.

The glow from the digital clock on the dresser filled the room with a jaundiced haze. The numbers burned like cigarettes in the dark. Three on a match. Crimea. Russia. Cold. Snow.

My mind bounced from thought to thought, unable to calm itself or focus on any one thing for very long. I stumbled to the bathroom and splashed cool water on my face, not bothering to turn on the light. I was too frightened to see what might stare back at me. I could still feel her hand on my face, that impossible cold on my cheek when the rest of my body was too numb to feel anything.

Numb. *Comfortably Numb.* Pink Floyd. Madison Square Garden. Sneaking in liquor. No ice. Ice. Snow.

I let the hot water run over my fingers, wishing heat back into them, but they wouldn't obey. I had to be coming down with something. The chills, the shivering, the fevered delirium, every random thought always bringing me back to snow. To her, and that impossible night when the universe cracked open and the abyss gazed into our world.

Nietzsche. College. Kissing Christine Baylor in the dark room. Fumbling in the dark. Falling. Twisted ankle. Bag of ice. Ice. Snow.

Snow.

Outside, a blanket of snow lay across the city and I could see the fluorescent welcome sign of a liquor store shining into the night like a lighthouse tempting lost souls to crash upon the rocks. My hands were shaking, either from nerves, the cold, or simply a bodily reminder of alcoholic detox to deter me from falling off the wagon. I pulled the blankets from my bed and sat in the corner beside the radiator.

I wept until the sun rose.

CHAPTER 2
REMAINS

"As a wise tree once said, "Don't be hasty."

— RIMOR

W hen I finally found the will to move, I caught my reflection in the bathroom mirror. I was never easy on the eyes to begin with, but now I looked almost feral: red, puffy eyes, sunken cheeks, wiry stubble cracking through dry, leathery skin. The last time I had looked so bad had been at the height (depth?) of my drinking days. I needed to get my act together. Fast.

Oddly enough, my nerves calmed halfway through my second pot of coffee. My skin buzzed with caffeine, but the unnatural chill was finally beginning to dissipate. Outside, the city moved as it did every day, oblivious to the impossible truth I was still having difficulty admitting to myself:

Magic was real. Not just in the abstract. Real. Physical. Alive.

I was first introduced to "The Low World" decades before while investigating the Brandon Lachmann story. The Low was a loosely connected network of secret organizations, quiet societies, and subcultures all looking for proof of something outside our world, specifically the Lost Collection. Groups like the Mountaineers. Early on, I gave their talk of magic little credence. I assumed their belief in magic was much the same as that of Wiccans and their druidic brothers. The pagan concept of magic mostly manifested itself as ritualistic prayer to the Moon or Sun, to Nature itself. Deasil and widdershins, the symbol of awen and pentagrams, robed or sky-clad —all working a magic we find in ourselves to better connect us with one another and the world around us. But that is magic of the mind, the heart, perhaps even the soul. Whereas this . . .

Magic was real. Real, bona fide, honest-to-goodness Dumbledore-and-the-Elder-Wand sorcery existed. I had spent my life searching for verifiable facts and the journalistic Who, What, When, Where, Why, and How. And as much as my left brain demanded rational, logical explanations, I could no longer deny what I had seen with my own eyes, heard with my own ears, felt with my own hands: a human being, warm, solid, turning to snow in my hands.

Admitting this terrified me. But I felt solace, too, because I knew I wasn't alone. There were others who knew what I knew, who at least partly understood this incredible truth. Had it not been for the existence of the Mountaineers, I have little doubt I would have found myself searching for solace at the bottom of a bottle.

I wished I had known all this in '94. I could have been a bigger help to the original Mountaineers, to their search for the Lost Collection. And I wished I had gotten to know them better.

There hadn't been very many back then, but I remembered some of them, friends I only knew by their hackeresque aliases: Ascender, Augernon, and Knatz. Tinkerdown and Saberlane. In 1998, they all disappeared. I had heard through the Low that the Mountaineers had gotten close to something that scattered them "to the six corners." I hadn't been able to find out what that "something" was or why they needed to disappear. Did it frighten them? Threaten them? Or did the frustration of not being able to find what they were looking for finally get to them?

I didn't encounter the name Ascender again until the new Mountaineers posted the Magiq Guide in the summer of 2016, in what I assumed was a bulwark against whatever or whoever had wiped them out in the 90s. Ascender was back, but the others were still unaccounted for. I was saddened to learn, through a post written by Ascender, that Augernon had been long ago hospitalized, having lost his mind when the original Mountaineers fell apart. I guess, whether there's magic in the world or not, life will always intrude in its brutal and inevitable ways.

If Revenir hadn't contacted me about the Cagliostro, I may never have dove back into the forums. That's probably not true, but who knows? Perhaps I'd still be fruitlessly looking into bureaucratic corruption. Part of me wished that I was. Ignorance is bliss, after all. But overall I was glad Revenir had drawn me back in. Because of the Mountaineers, I'd found the one thing all reporters search for: the truth. And as unlikely or impossible as this truth was, it only emboldened my sense of purpose. I'd resolved to continue working to expose those in power who took advantage of others. What difference did it make if some of those "powers that be" possessed magic? Abuse of power was abuse of power.

The Lost Collection was erased from history, and with it most knowledge of magic, to the detriment of the world. So was Brandon Lachmann. I wanted to know why. The Mountaineers' cause had become my own.

I needed to keep moving, keep busy, to try and fend off the cold— never mind that the cold was something inside of me. After I brunched on coffee and cigarettes, I readied myself to venture out into the world, to see what was left of Lauren and the Cagliostro.

It took two days, but I tracked down the Cagliostro's loft. It was in ruins. Shattered glass littered the floor, and not a single piece of furniture stood intact. The walls themselves were torn open, the drywall ripped away to reveal a complicated nest of wiring. Lauren had mentioned that he had hidden artifacts in the walls. Whether it was her, the Cagliostro's manservant Carfax, or someone else, whoever had been here had taken whatever treasure the Cagliostro had secreted away.

As I was leaving, I noticed the faintest smell of incense. Not the cloying scent of a head shop or a cheap massage parlor, but the incense I remembered from my youth. It was the smell of churches, of ritual, of reverence. Of power. That lingering scent was all that was left of the immortal man.

I tracked Lauren's parents to Florissant, Missouri. I gave them quite a scare when I called and asked if they had heard from her recently. They demanded assurances that Lauren was okay. I had no idea how to explain what had happened, so I lied and told them I was simply doing background on a story about rural migration to urban centers and thought she would be someone worth talking to. I don't know what made me feel worse: lying to them, or that the ruse worked.

Eventually, I went online to catch up on what the Mountaineers had been up to while I'd struggled to process everything I had seen. Robert had found a fresh link on the Cagliostro website that led to a message from Lauren—a message written *after* she had dissolved in my arms on the floor of Grand Central Station. Just seeing her words on the screen sapped the heat from my bones.

She had found something she believed was meant for the Mountaineers. It was an envelope, hidden inside the book she had taken from the Morgan Library; Cole had evidently missed it when the two of them had been racing to find the spell that protected Deirdre. The envelope contained another entry from the mysterious journal from 1889, this time chronicling the writer's disbelief upon finding himself in a new and magical land. I could relate.

THE 1889 JOURNAL:

 I could not return home. Though wonder had kept its unspoken promise and once again visited me, called me to its heart to witness the world of dreams, I dare not leave it. Not for fear of trusting it would visit me another time, but for fear of casting myself out to the cold world, the world in which I do not belong. I am a wandering man. Unshackled. Free from all that sent me from civilization to hide in the untamed country. Free from judgment and sidewise glances. Free from whispers about the man who cannot remember. I believed that I was escaping the false comforts and trappings of this modern existence, to live an unfettered life. But in truth, I was running toward the heart of wonder. Running back as if I'd been asleep there all my life and only temporarily awakened.

My whiskers unshaven, clothes worn through and tattered, I wash myself in teal-blue streams by light of glowing vines like fairies perched on swaying swings. I eat fruit that joyfully stings my tongue and fills my belly for days at a stretch. At times there are baskets of sandwiches on the paths I follow, filled with gold-speckled cheese and purple, squashed-flat tomatoes. The edible vines of the tomato still attached, coiled around the soft sliced bread as if they were holding their hats to their heads in a gust of wind. The things I've seen. I've followed the lilting sounds of children giggling and instead found five moons circling one other playfully in the sky.

Ah, the sky. What is black and cold in the old world is teeming with untold forms of life here in the wondrous dream. Eddies of stars swirl and loop like schools of fish. I am not without moments of doubt however. I recall the visions that infrequently overwhelmed me in the city. Visions of other worlds. Another life. Of all manner of unbelievable machinery and towers piercing the sky. I wonder, am I simply wandering the backroads of the farmland I claimed as home, imagining all I see now, deserving of all the terse whispers and fearful looks given me? Did I long ago lose my faculty and have since simply stalked the gray world, imagining all that lay before me? Even if it were true,

would I want to leave this lie? No. I venture deeper.
Alone, yes. Missing kind faces, a familiar wave of a hand
calling me on. Everything here is soaked in wonder, but
distant. Sumptuous to see, but not in need of me. I am
enraptured, but useless. In my old visions I was in a
strange, unfamiliar world, but yet I felt purpose. Here, I
am simply a wanderer. This will all go on without me
when I'm gone. A mad man's vision of heaven, that need
neither his eyes nor mind to continue on in existence.
But is that not life in summary? I decide I will continue
my writing, my sketches. My purpose here is not to
affect this world, but see it. Suppose it. I find a tree
whose bark peels away into thin sheets of paper, whose
leaves are tipped in ink-like sap of many colors. I find a
berm beneath the dark, open sky. And I see what no else
will look up to see.

Additionally, a passage was written on the outside of the envelope:

> Thirteen volumes, the foundation of our universe
>   until a revolution changed our position.
> At the whim of the master clock, Shepherd Gate
>   shows all time. And in the courtyard the
>   Astronomer Royal observes from here.
> Because of the tenth there now are eight. When
>   Xena fell, discord rose in her place.
> What sees what we cannot? A giant, a Titan, a
>   dragon, and all great light combined?
> Three ancient stones mark the midwinter's
>   sunset, their faces toward Cora Bheinn and
>   the mountain of the sound.
> Borne from Ida to serve the wine, who waits in
>   the celestial court between the whale and
>   the eagle?

This is where the Mountaineers excelled. As their numbers grew, their collective intelligence grew as well, and they were well positioned to find the answers to these mystical riddles. They'd learned to go with the flow of these challenges, these puzzles. With them, we were not only unlocking the Book of Briars, but also learning more and more about the world, and the power still tucked away in its hidden corners. I could do the legwork with the nosiness and tenacity of any reporter worth their salt, but solving puzzles created by a magical, truth-telling book struggling to make its way into our reality was most certainly not my forte. So I decided to help them by doing something that was a little less magic but a bit more up my alley: sticking my nose in places it didn't belong.

I still had the RSVP list for the performance that had ended with Lauren becoming the new Cagliostro, and I thought it might be worth digging into some of the names. They were all big fish when it came to morally and financially questionable business dealings (it was the corruption of a select few that put me on the Cagliostro's path in the first place), but judging from their reactions on the night of the performance, none of them had been prepared to swim with sharks. I'd bet a Tony Luke's Philly cheesesteak that many of them were nothing more than rich LARPers who'd thought they'd be slumming with Mina Crandon. If I hadn't been too busy soiling myself, I might have even enjoyed seeing the looks on their faces when they realized just how big the shark was.

But I had already barked up several of those trees already, so I knew most wouldn't lead anywhere. Or, if they did, they would only lead me into the shallows. I wanted to go deep. I wanted to find Leviathan's lair and have a good snoop around.

CHAPTER 3
KEMETIC SOLUTIONS

"We just do not know, we can't build a full
scenario with the information we have."

— ARCCHILD

The one lead the Mountaineers had but weren't able to follow very far was the tech firm providing the Cagliostro with email servers and cloud storage: Kemetic Solutions. Bells even did an image search for the logo and came up dry. That struck me as odd. If there's one thing tech companies want, it's high-profile branding. If a company has a digital footprint so small that their logo never sees the light of day, it's because they're being run by a pack of teenagers too busy surfing to do any actual work . . . or because they don't want to be seen. My cheesesteak was on the latter.

After a few hours spent contacting some old friends in the telecommunications business, I found a phone number for Kemetic Solutions, but it just sent me to a call center somewhere in Nebraska. Even though the number was pretty much bogus, it *was* an American phone number. Which most likely meant the business was operating in the States. And if that was the case, Kemetic would have had to provide the IRS with a physical address. So I put in a request to the IRS and waited.

Hunting down leads, following up with sources, researching even the most frivolous clues . . . It felt good to scratch these old itches. This was what I knew. What I was born to do. Find the story, no matter how deeply hidden it was. Thing was, I always had a pretty good idea where a story would take me, whether it be underneath a forgotten overpass or into a boardroom atop a high rise. But this was something new.

Maybe it was this renewed focus on the job, but I was sleeping a little better. I still dreamed about snow and more often than not woke up shivering, but the chill I felt on waking would fade after a few hours. I started brewing pots of hyper-caffeinated coffee using some local brand of beans with a skull and crossbones stamped on the black bag. Pumping that much caffeine through my veins probably wasn't helping with my sleeping problems, but it certainly helped with the chills. Some steaming coffee in my stained and chipped NYT mug and a pair of tattered slippers got me feeling about as back to normal as I was likely to get.

While I worked on Kemetic, the Mounties were making some serious headway into finding the next fragment, four of which were required to unlock each corner of the Book of Briars. Apparently, the strange passage Lauren had found on the envelope referred to various astronomical concepts.

New Mountaineer Gryphon believed the first clue—"Thirteen volumes, the foundation of our universe until a revolution changed our position"—could be a reference to Euclid's *Elements*. But Kelsey suggested Ptolemy's *Almagest*—which Brendon noted put forth Ptolemy's geocentric view of the universe, an idea that remained popular until Heliocentrism began to find favor during the Copernican Revolution. Yeah. That's how the Mountaineers rolled.

And thanks to Leigha bringing some Olympian insight into the mix, the Mounties also knew that "Aquarius" was the answer to the question: "Borne from Ida to serve the wine, who waits in the celestial court between the whale and the eagle?"

As the Mounties worked their way through the strange clues, something interesting began to happen to the journal pages. The text of those pages had been set around circular areas of blank white space. A couple of those circles were now filled with illustrations of planetary objects, which were marked with strange abbreviations and symbols arranged in lines that emanated from the centers of the circles. The imagery reminded me of an old, circular star map I had as a child during my brief flirtation with astronomy.

It was certainly fun to watch them work. Veterans like Robert, OracleSage, Brendon, Kelsey, and Leigha worked alongside new and clever recruits like Hannah and aTomic to crush the puzzle at hand. In no time, all six circles were filled with the strange letters and symbols. Also of interest was the appearance of what seemed to be "craters" randomly spaced in each circle. Kelsey figured out how to punch out the craters and use the holes of one circle to align with another in a way that gave a series of letters. Brendon rearranged those letters into a series of celestial names that, when entered into the Book of Briars website in a specific order, revealed a constellation called "Galifanx."

They had found another fragment. Great news, but I was getting restless and wanted to feel useful. Now that I had a night or two of decent sleep under my belt, it was time I got cleaned up and put on some adult clothes.

It was strange, but I had a hard time remembering the last time I showered. The hot water always took forever to heat up, and I must have forgone the idea of soaking in it to warm myself for that very reason. Better to wear half a dozen sweatshirts and hibernate under the covers for warmth than wait for an aging boiler to rescue me.

Washed, shaved, and wearing relatively clean khakis and a button-down, I made my way to a deli down the street. Spring hadn't officially arrived yet, but it was warm enough that most people only wore light jackets. I, on the other hand, wore a peacoat and a Scottish wool scarf to keep warm. The icy grip of Lauren's Grand Central transformation was slowly loosening its hold, but there was still a desperate chill inside me, coiled like a hungry snake that would strike the second it felt the slightest rise in temperature.

I pulled out my laptop while I spooned down a steaming bowl of soup and saw that Deirdre had only published two posts on her blog since I'd last checked. I had been so lost in the aftermath of the Translation that I had forgotten that Cole had finally told Deirdre about the Mountaineers, the Lost Collection—everything. It had obviously been a lot for her to process. Her first post after learning the truth was a poem titled "The Sea."

DEIRDRE: FEBRUARY 2ND, 2017:

 To learn at last why I have always felt adrift and wanting.
   Why my efforts always left me lacking, lost.
   It was you, after all, the one I didn't know I was chasing.
   The one who built a box and packed me up inside it.
   Wrapped tight in the lies you wrote for me.
   I'm going to do you one last favour, one mad deed I do for you.
   And then I cast you out to sea.
   I'm going to write a new story and see what it can do.
   One where I'm no longer blind. One where light can get inside.
   One where all of what I could've been can be dusted off and made to be.
   Possibility. Possibly.
   Where you have no more reign on me.
   I pray the truth is brighter than the lie that was your gift.
   I pray I wake tomorrow and I see the curtains lift.
   Then I will set you out to sea and meet the girl you wouldn't let me be.
   A girl who doesn't need to know you any longer.

A daughter that can see.

It was the story she had to write to break the spell that her father had cast on her. She'd done it. She'd decided to walk the path.

Cole hadn't been back to the forum since coming clean with Deirdre at the train station, but he confirmed Deirdre's spell-breaking in a post on his Tumblr blog a couple weeks later.

COLE:

 I texted with her on Valentine's Day. (It was a coincidence, calm down.) She knows everything now. She's read everything. She knows about the Mountaineers, the Lost Collection, King Rabbit, the other volumes of her dad's journal, every time we talked about her, everything . . .

And I told her everything about me too. The night I brought her the spell.

And then she left the country. Back to Ireland. She didn't say how long she'd be gone. Hell, who knows if she's ever coming back. I don't know if I would.

I haven't been back to the forum. I think it's best like this. If you ever need anything though, I'm here.

What a mess, huh?

But . . . we did the right thing. And we did it as soon as we could, right?

Hope you guys are doing alright. Not getting into too much trouble.

Deirdre's next post was over a month later. It was a direct message to the Mountaineers.

DEIRDRE: MARCH 22ND, 2017

 To the Mountaineers,

I haven't posted to my blog in a while because it feels, well, compromised? But it's not like I'm trying to cut you all off.

I'm all caught up on what you've been up to since I got to New York. Yes, it's weird. Yes, it's unnerving. Yes, this is all waaaaay too much. I mean, I was stalked by a talking rabbit who'd possessed a human body to steal my dad's pocket watch.

But as hard as all this is to get my head around I realise that you saved me. You tore the plaster off, which is good, but right now it's painful and raw and I feel very exposed.

I read everything on your forum but I don't go there anymore. It's too weird to read people talk about you like you're a character in a book. But I get it. That's your space to figure out what's going on.

Meanwhile, here's what's happening with me . . . I can read my dad's journal now. Most of it still doesn't make sense, in that it's rambling and disjointed, but the words are words now, not jumbles of headache-making blobs.

Whatever my dad did to me protected me from the truth. From "magiq." So his journal, *The Monarch Papers*, must lead to the truth, or some part of it, because now that his spell is broken, I can read parts of it. It's all I have to go on right now.

So that's what I've been doing for the past few weeks, following my father. He talks about a trail that was left behind hundreds of years ago. A trail that leads to the buried truth. A trail of paintings and sculptures and tapestries and books, all around the world. And as I follow the trail, more appears in the journal. I don't know what I'm doing or why, but starting a publishing company doesn't seem like my prime imperative right now, right?

Strange to ask a question and realise there are people on the other side of this with help, advice, maybe even answers for the first time in a long time.

Magic is real. My father learned how to perform it. And he left a trail for me to follow him. Maybe it'll lead to the lost books, maybe it'll lead me to learn magic, or maybe it won't lead anywhere. Maybe back to a warren in Central Park where he died, alone.

I don't know. But I'll stay in touch. You deserve that.

To Cole:

I had a hundred reasons to walk away from New York City. What you confided in me wasn't one of them. I promise.

When Deirdre said she was following her father's trail, she meant it literally. She'd started posting images to Instagram from her travels: Ireland, Amsterdam, Spain . . . I could only imagine what she must be feeling as she tried to work through all of this. And I was sure that Cole was having a difficult time as well. He told her the truth, and she left to go on a global walkabout. My heart ached for those two kids. Sue me, I'm a softy.

By the time I got back home, the mail had arrived. And there, in the midst of a stack of credit card offers and coupon booklets, was something from the IRS. My first instinct was to panic—it was quite possible my financial diligence wasn't up to Uncle Sam's snuff. But when I got inside and opened it, I was doubly relieved. It was the information I'd requested on Kemetic Solutions.

Sadly, there wasn't much there. A phone number (to the same call center), a business ID number, and a physical address. Someplace just outside Boston. On a whim, I headed up the following morning.

The drive wasn't too bad, all things considered, but my constant need for coffee's warmth left me no choice but to make a few pit stops along the way.

I wasn't sure what I was expecting, but the ordinariness of the place was a letdown. It was a small office park set back just off the highway, nothing more than a couple of bland, rectangular buildings surrounded by several copses of trees.

I drove through, keeping an eye out for anything unusual. But there was nothing. And that was what I found so strange. The nothingness, the blandness of it all was suspect. There were no placards on any of the buildings, no signs indicating what businesses lay inside; even the lone trash can outside what I assumed were the front doors was so pristinely clean I'd swear it had never been used.

Perhaps strangest of all was the empty parking lot. It wasn't very large; there were about twenty spaces or so, but not a single one was filled. It was completely clean of any garbage or debris, without even an errant oil stain marring the pavement. It looked more like a movie set than a business park.

I assumed Kemetic Solutions had given the IRS the address of some unused and abandoned offices. If that were true, I could probably blackmail them into speaking with me. Defrauding the IRS is no small thing, not even for secretive tech firms with ties to magic. Of course, I still had no idea how I'd get a hold of them. This was looking like a dead end, and I wagered the call center was a facade, too.

But if this place were truly abandoned, it should have fallen into disrepair. Yet the park was clean, the lawn well manicured. And there were no "space for rent" signs anywhere, which meant that the upkeep wasn't for the sake of attracting new tenants. Someone had to be using the place.

The windows were all opaque and reflective. There was simply no way for me to get a good look at what was behind them, and what little I could see was the uniformity of closed, beige blinds.

I parked the car and made my way to the front doors. Sunlight glared off the glass of the double doors, so I pressed my shading hands against it and peered inside. I saw an empty lobby with a marble floor and a hallway that faded into darkness. There was nothing else: no furniture, no lamps, no legend on the wall to indicate which business resided on which floor.

I pulled at the doors. Locked.

"May I help you?"

The voice came from a call box on the brick wall next to the oddly clean garbage can.

"Sir?" the voice asked again.

Sir? That meant they could see me, but I didn't notice any cameras anywhere.

"Uh, yeah. I'm Martin Rank with the *Globe*. I'm doing some background on a story. Electronic security protocols, voting machine vulnerabilities, that sort of thing. I was told someone at Kemetic Solutions could help."

"You'll have to make an appointment."

"I'm just looking for some basic info, a couple of quotes, shouldn't take more than a few minutes."

"Make an appointment and someone will be more than happy to speak with you."

"Appointment, okay. Can I confirm your number? It's . . . Ma'am? Ma'am, are you still there?"

Silence.

"Ma'am? Hello? Hello!" The call box was dead. I peered inside once again, thinking I might see a security camera or maybe even a person hiding in the shadows. But there was nothing.

I tried the call box for a few more minutes, but whoever had been on the other end either didn't hear me or was ignoring me. And since I was confident that they knew their number was bogus, I figured they had no intention of ever talking to me.

On a hunch, I pulled out my phone. I wanted to see if they had a Wi-Fi hotspot and what kind of protections they were running. But right away, I saw there was a problem. There was no Wi-Fi signal at all. None. Kemetic Solutions was looking less like a tech company and more like a CIA-funded black site every minute. I'd never been one to have truck with conspiracy theories, but then again, I'd never been one to believe in magic. I knew this wasn't really a government operation, though. If it had been, security would have escorted me from the premises. But there was no security. There wasn't anyone.

I was getting frustrated, and my steady intake of coffee was wreaking havoc with my bladder. I toyed with the idea of testing the "no security" theory by relieving myself against the wall, but decided against it. They could just call the cops and have me hauled off to jail for indecent exposure and never have to interact with me at all. And given how shabby I was looking even after a shower and shave, there was a good chance the police would tack on a charge of vagrancy for good measure.

Instead, I went back to my car and got my camera. It was an older Nikon Coolpix that I had held onto since the *Baltimore Sun* had brought me on as a photojournalist for all of a week. I snapped a few quick pics, hoping security would finally materialize to confiscate the camera, but no one came.

I thought I'd hit another dead end, until I got home and checked the photos.

CHAPTER 4
ARTIFACTS

"Well, after about an hour or so of staring at these things my eyes are starting to glaze over and I haven't made any progress."

— THINGFROMTHEDEEP

The ride home was uneventful, which was problematic. I do my best thinking in the car, and I was hoping the trip back to the city would jar something loose in my subconscious. No such luck. Whatever was going on with Kemetic Solutions behind their bland and unremarkable facade, it wasn't going to be easy to find.

When I got home, I thought I should let the Mountaineers know about my little field trip. Granted, I didn't have much information to share, but if the Mounties were good at anything, it was taking a morsel of information and turning it into a meal.

I pulled the memory card from my camera and put it into my laptop, which was so old that the only things keeping it together were a wad of bubble gum and wishful thinking. I could actually hear the gears grinding underneath the weight of the squirrels running inside as I waited the requisite eon for the OS to boot up. When I was finally able to inspect the pictures I had taken, I saw there were strange digital artifacts bleeding into the images. Thin rectangular bands of black and red ran across the pictures, as if the camera was unable to fully process all of the digital information.

Something about the artifacts struck me as familiar, though I couldn't quite put my finger on it. I decided to post the pics anyway, hoping something in them might get the Mounties' hive mind whirring.

I WROTE:

 Place looks like every other corporate office park. Except it's ironclad. No way in without clearance. Windows are reflective. Not even a Wi-Fi signal leaking out of the building. Completely locked down.

I took a couple photos but was cheerfully encouraged to make an appointment (don't know how I'd do that) by a voice on a call box.

Got back home and checked the photos.

I mean, yeah, my camera's a POS, but I don't know . . . it's never done anything like this. Thoughts?

Right away, Robert and Kelsey saw that the mess of digital artifacts actually contained a few letters, "KS" and "NW," and what appeared to be the Star of David. I wanted to think that if I had the eyes of a man twenty years younger I would have noticed it too, but my vision had never been that good, even with the help of LASIK surgery and sobriety. When the Mountaineers started discovering clues in the artifacts, the Book reached out.

You've been searching far and wide

For keys to revolution
But something hidden deep inside
Will lead to the solution
Another fragment's reaching out
From the dark that means to bind it
And it might take all that you have
To heed the call and find it

Two of the letters, "KS," gave Robert the inspiration to search for a Kemetic Solutions website, which he promptly found. It was a rather lovely welcome page, an animated KS logo that exploded into butterflies every twenty seconds or so before looping back to the logo. Butterflies again. To go further into the site we would need a password.

I knew a couple of women who wrote for the *Sun* who liked to spend their time fishing for sites on the dark net and honing their hacking skills. I toyed with the idea of bringing them in to break the site wide open, but since magic was a part of the mix I doubted there was much they could do. Besides, with the Book of Briars being involved, chances were the password we needed was most likely hidden somewhere in my photographs.

I reached out to the few non-Mounties I still knew in the Low, but no one ever got back to me. It's always been difficult getting people to talk to a reporter, but recently it seemed that my contacts in the Low World had shied away from me. The sands beneath our feet were shifting, and the rules of interaction were changing with them. I didn't know if they were avoiding me because I was a reporter or because I had thrown my hat in with the Mountaineers. Either way, my sources were drying up.

Leigha was the one who recognized the star symbol was actually a reference to the elements. I'd seen alchemical symbols before, but I'd never known that, when combined into a star shape, they represent aether. This could have been a happy coincidence, but Robert remembered from the Call the Corners spell that "aether" was a word (and element) associated with the Gossmere Guild, which sits in the northwest direction of the chronocompass. "NW" again—even I had to admit that couldn't be by chance.

As I sat there watching the Mountaineers work their way through the clues hidden inside the images, I grew very tired, like all the sleep I had missed over the past month was now suddenly catching up to me. It was only late afternoon, but I felt like I hadn't slept in days. I'm not sure when or how, but I eventually crawled into bed and didn't wake until late the following morning.

By then, the Mountaineers had made more progress. Examining my photos, they had noticed a slight discoloration of leaves on a bush that somehow appeared as the letters "ZIP." From there, Revenir had found a file hidden inside the image file by renaming it with a ZIP extension. I'd had no idea such a thing was possible. This opened a password-protected file named "patience.rtf." And sure enough, the password was "aether." It was some rather nice teamwork from the recruits, though the fruits of their labor were a bit scarce. The only thing this newly found document said was "63 minutes."

63 minutes until what, we all asked ourselves.

The only lead they had was the Kemetic Solutions site, so we parked at the looping logo animation and waited for 63 minutes to pass. As we waited, Robert regaled us with the finer points of steganography (the art of hiding secret messages in images) and its Benedictine roots. Give me a bottle of rye and three hours to pick that man's brain and I'd be in heaven.

After one hour and three minutes, the Kemetic Solutions homepage redirected us to a two-minute video. I didn't see anything special, just your typical boilerplate business promo with inspiring images, corporate buzzwords, and a heavy dose of creepiness thrown in for good measure. It seemed that their mission was to make the world a better place through some technological wizardry that was never clearly specified.

VictorianFlorist was kind enough to transcribe the video, and the words seemed just as unsettling on their own:

PROMOTIONAL VIDEO:

 We are tiny creatures, living in an obscure corner of a
vast universe. Small, alone, alongside billions of other
planets just like ours and yet, we are different. This is a
special place with special inhabitants. Ours is a planet
full of life—life and freedom. Freedom to grow, to
evolve. Freedom to enjoy simple pleasures. Freedom to
connect safely. But to ensure that freedom we must
defend our world with advanced technology and
industrial solutions. There will always be threats to
freedom, but we are ready. For years we at Kemetic
Solutions have developed technology to keep this world
safe and free. But we didn't stop there. Our
technological advances now power discoveries in
physical well-being. We are helping advance the
research of rare diseases and the discovery of new cures
every day to help people live better lives now. But also
to help us understand where we come from and where
we're going. Our systems protect life and extend it into
the future. From research and technology, to industry
and commerce, Kemetic Solutions allows life to evolve.
Helping communities to function, knowledge to
flourish, and digital technologies to progress. Our
global communications help governments, media, and
organizations of all kinds stay connected. So we can
enjoy our lives in the sun, as our great and special world
keeps turning. Kemetic Solutions. Freedom. Safety.
Evolution.

Right away, I had questions. What technology, specifically, had
they developed to "keep this world safe and free?" Which rare diseases
were they studying and how close were they to finding their cures?

How, exactly, did their systems "protect life and extend it into the future?" Which governments, specifically, had they helped?

I had dozens more, but I knew it was useless to torture myself over such questions. It was highly doubtful I'd ever have a chance to corner a rep from Kemetic Solutions and get the answers.

Several of the Mountaineers, Bells especially, thought the video had a cultish vibe to it, and I wholeheartedly agreed. I've always found Mac enthusiasts and Xbox diehards cultish in the extreme, and this felt like Bill Gates and Steve Jobs invited L. Ron Hubbard to a mescaline party and woke to find "Kemetic Solutions" scrawled on a roll of toilet paper in the guest bathroom. Not to mention that whenever a company, government, or group of any kind throws the word "freedom" around that much, freedom isn't what they're selling. The mantra of "Freedom, Safety, Evolution" left me with a cold feeling —one as deep as any that Lauren's snowy ghost had given me.

As if the video weren't creepy enough, something odd was happening on the Basecamp forums. Someone using the handle xxxxaetherxxxx was going through old posts and changing them. Kelsey was the first to notice, as one of her older posts had been altered—though the change was subtle, and to my eye, pointless. In all, five posts, from five different people, had been changed. They seemed to have no connection to one another, until the Mountaineers noticed that each altered post mentioned a number. It took some fiddling, but they determined that this "Aether" character was giving us a date and time.

Oddly enough, Aether's account had just appeared two days prior and hadn't been approved by Bash, the resident Basecamp IT wizard. Whoever Aether was, they were either magimystically connected like King Rabbit or they knew their way around some code. But why alter posts and not just come out and say hello?

When the time Aether had given us finally arrived, Hannah discovered that the welcome video on the Kemetic Solutions website had changed. Or, more accurately, it had been intercut with snippets from another video: a car moving down a highway, a low-angle view of the sky, a car trunk closing. My first thought was that we were watching from the perspective of someone being shoved into the trunk of an SUV. There were also images of an IV in someone's arm, flashes of text on car windows, cards with strange symbols scattered on the ground, and a person leaving footprints in the snow. As the video played, an unfamiliar voice spoke. And it seemed to be speaking directly to someone named Aether:

 Meet us. Please. Just for a few minutes. We'd like to talk to you face to face. We have some questions and, uh, I think we could do some incredible things together. I'm going to show this card to the camera on my phone. And I want you to tell me what the camera sees. I want you to see through my phone. Does that make sense to you, Aether? I want you to try very hard and I want you to show me what you are truly capable of. I want you to reach out with your mind and into my phone. I want the camera to become your eyes. I want the processor to become your mind. I believe you could find a family with us. A family, Aether. Perhaps for the first time in your life. No, we have no interest in changing your mind, but with your mind, we will change everything.

The Mountaineers went through the video frame by frame and found a number of phases and words hidden in the video: "watching," "find her," "help us," "stumbled," "not much time left," "There Are No Constants."

Each of these Easter eggs held a world of threat and promise. Questions hidden within questions. Theories bounced around the forum but no one could offer any concrete answers, least of all me. The consensus seemed to be that Aether, with the help of some kind of technological power, was the one responsible for the intercut video, along with the hidden clues.

I'd found myself drawn closer and closer to the Mountaineers.

Maybe it was that I'd finally dropped the pretense of not being part of the story (that delusion ended the night of the Translation) or maybe it was just that I was allowing myself to seek the warmth of their community, their camaraderie in all this. Regardless, I wanted to share my thoughts with them on the forum.

I WROTE:

 For me, the outstanding questions are—
    The big one . . . Who is the "her" we're supposed find that can help us and "Aether?" I know some of you figure Lauren Ellsworth for the "her" but things like this rarely end up so circular. My money is on somebody we haven't met yet.
    How do we find her? Is there information still buried in the altered video we haven't found yet?
    Why isn't there, according to Aether, much time left? Makes me think if we don't figure this out bad things are gonna happen to him or "them" since the message said "Help us."
    Who is the "us" in "Help us"?
    How is Aether reaching out? I don't mean what kind of magic is he using, I mean how is he managing to do this under KS's nose? And why only now and then, the tweaked forum posts, the photos, the video . . . What if I hadn't taken those photos? Was Aether looking for us specifically, or anybody who could help?
    Where is all this coming from?
    We know The Book of Briars is at least aware of Aether and KS because it sent the frag 10 email after you all found information in the glitches. But the Book couldn't have planned on Aether being taken by this company, right? Is this an unintended detour it's sending us on? What would have happened if we'd

never found Aether, if we'd never looked into KS? (This
might just be navel-gazing . . . I can save this for my next
sleepless night. The questions I have about the Book,
what it is, and who's behind it could fill a whole
other book.)

I don't know if I'm adding to the discussion or
distracting you but figured I'd go back to journalistic
research techniques 101 and see what we can make of
this whole thing.

There was so much we didn't know and so much we needed to sift
through. Everyone was asking the same questions, but I was
compelled to get them out there for everyone to see. It was like I could
smell the bones buried in the backyard, tickling the back of my throat
like smoke, and the only way I could make it stop was to dig them up.
But with a backyard the size of a county, a pack of dogs is better than
just a lone wolf.

Brendon found something interesting in the video.

BRENDON:

 So I'm going through the video and making note of all
the phrases that appear, and I noticed something
interesting. At the 1:21 mark, the phrase "There Are No
Constants" shows up. And then at the 1:22 mark, a
different phrase pops up, which reads, "There Are No
Constance." More or less the same phrase, just altered
slightly. I just think that is a little peculiar. I am going
to keep investigating and will post if I find anything
more.

If there was anything we had learned from our experiences so far,
it was that such a little thing wasn't to be ignored. Kelsey found a
couple of Tumblr pages, one titled There Are No Constants and

another for There Are No Constance. The former was password protected, while the latter was not.

Robert reached out to the unprotected site, trying to establish contact, but the reply he received wasn't exactly what we were hoping for: "Who is this?" He then told the person who the Mountaineers were and a bit about our mission and was answered with, "Is this some kind of joke?"

Though in fairness, I could relate. I put on my curmudgeon pants every time a stranger tries to get friendly with me online, too.

Robert was concerned he might end up with a restraining order against him if he continued pestering the person behind the Tumblr site, so Revenir took a more direct approach and simply asked if they knew someone named Aether. It was a ballsy move considering how little we knew about everything. But Revenir's gamble paid off. "Constance" responded by telling us we needed to protect our site before they told us anything.

I always assumed that Bash was a competent IT tech and saw no glitches or obvious weaknesses in any of the Mountaineers' websites. But now that we were looking into a company touting "Freedom, Safety, Evolution" through unnamed technology, a little more protection seemed like a good idea. If Aether was able to get in and edit posts and possibly access user information, who was to say others couldn't, others with darker motives?

But there was a problem. Revenir asked Constance what sort of protection we needed to apply to the site, to which they replied, "The Safeguard at least, whatever the latest version is."

Bash had no idea what they were talking about.

It turned out that the Safeguard was magiq and other sites in the Low were already running it. Apparently, whoever was at the other end of the Tumblr account had access to an online library with an area devoted to magiq. The library's systems were protected by the Safeguard, and our contact was going to help us get set up, too.

The Mountaineers all seemed excited for the chance to do more actual magic, but I was nervous. The preternatural cold that coiled around my bones was a constant reminder of how magic could go wrong. We were tapping into a world we didn't fully understand, and we needed to be careful.

Revenir's contact sent him instructions for something called a "Joradian Non-Material Safeguard v. 42.06." I know that for old folks like me, the Internet is still a newfangled gadget bordering on witchcraft. But I'm also aware that many in the Low don't even remember a time before computers dominated every aspect of our daily lives. That there seemed to be at least 41 previous versions of the Safeguard meant that the merging of magic and technology had been going on since at least the days of dial-up. Somehow, that realization hit me hard. When you're in your forties, you can still pretend that you have just as many years in front of you as you do behind, but that fiction disappears in your fifties. Maybe the cold I was feeling wasn't a lingering effect from the night Lauren turned to snow in my arms. Maybe I was just feeling old.

Thankfully, younger and more elastic minds set to work on readying the Safeguard spell.

THE JORADIAN NON-MATERIAL SAFEGUARD V.42.06:

 The following enchantment is based in large part on the Jorad's Nordic Hearth and Home Protectory (originally published alt. 1741) but has been updated and tested extensively to ensure safe digital (non-material) spaces as well.

Its protection is based solely on visitor intent (only those with pure will/intentions may enter your home/site). The most recent version of the enchantment blocks all known methods of bypass.

Steps for Safeguard:
The likeness of the Joradian Wheel must be placed somewhere on the site. It must spend at least one day in

a place that is less than two links from the front page/door. Any deeper and it has been found to weaken the Safeguard (the Wheel's Eye must first learn what primary entry it must watch to reflect negative intention back on its source). You may teach the Wheel's Eye simply by visiting the site as you normally would. No formal instruction is required.

—Create six keeping vessels (request instructions), with each vessel containing one of the six elements.

—Before building the vessels, inscribe a pale (positive) memory of the place you intend to protect on the soon-to-be vessel's outer surface.

—Visual representations of the chosen pale memories must be added to the Wheel likeness in a protective hexagon before posting.

—Each vessel must have the corresponding elemental pledge (request instructions) spoken aloud to it. If performing the Safeguard with others, it is preferred to speak the pledges in the literal or virtual presence of the other vessel creators.

—A Fray Summoning Fraction (2 for every 20-25 who call the site "home") must witness this pledging as it happens, either literally or virtually. (Unlike the original Hearth and Home Protectory, the Safeguard may need to be reapplied periodically as your visitor count grows in number.)

—The Safeguard will remain in place as long as The Wheel is on the site and the keeping vessels remain intact.

Elemental Pledges

Ore- You are the rock all life is built upon. You provide the mount on which we build our homes and the tools we use to build them. You lift us up to reach

our true potential and receive us when our purpose
wanes.

The Tides- You are the never-ending call of time.
You cast your gifts upon the shore then draw them to
the cold and twinkling deep. You witness all life rise and
fall and rise again.

The Wild- You are the source of all things savage
and beautiful. You summon our primal urges and
soothe us with the cradle song of life. You are the howl
of our destructive instincts and the whisper that
responds when we need mending.

Light- You are the dawning rays of sun and hearth at
all days' end. You call us all to rise and seek, then lead us
safely home by firelight. All life begins and ends in your
embrace.

Aether- You are the breath

Thought-

Revenir's source addressed the seemingly incomplete instructions.

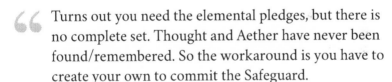 Turns out you need the elemental pledges, but there is
no complete set. Thought and Aether have never been
found/remembered. So the workaround is you have to
create your own to commit the Safeguard.

(Learning all this as I go.)

Do this ASAP so we can discuss Aether.

In addition to these instructions, Revenir's source included an
image of a strange symbol comprised of three intersecting lines that
created six branches, with each branch ending in a unique collection of
additional lines, circles, and crescent. According to the Mountaineers,
it resembled a Norse protection rune. There was also a schematic with
instructions on how to fold paper into a cube receptacle.

Though we needed to come up with some pledges of our own, the spell didn't seem too terribly difficult, which is something I never thought I'd write. A little origami and some appropriately timed recitations and it should work.

As for the missing elements, OracleSage and Hannah came up with lovely pledges for Aether and Thought, respectively:

> You are the breath that fills others' lungs, you dance through life in a song that is sung by the voice of many.

> You are our internal wishes and desires. You challenge us to grow mentally and emotionally. You help us to protect ourselves.

Now it was just a matter of finding Mountaineers to perform the spell. OracleSage stepped up to represent Gossmere, Hannah for Ebenguard, Revenir for Flinterforge, Leigha for Balimora, Furia for Weatherwatch, and Ricardo for Thornmouth. While the six Mountaineers set about making their origami boxes and deciding what to put in them, Endri created an online video Hangout where they could all interact during the spell.

I had to brew myself a fresh pot of coffee. Just watching them prepare for the spell sent Lauren's chill deeper, tighter around my bones. But as I sat with my coffee, watching them on the Hangout, I felt a sense of relief flooding over me. This spell didn't have the unnerving pall of doom hanging over it like the Cagliostro's tragic ritual. Magic could go very dark, but it was a joy to see it in the light.

An hour later, it was done, though we had no idea for sure if it was working. I tried reaching out to several of my contacts in the Low, hoping they could shed some light on the Safeguard, but again, no one responded. The Low was changing, people were going to ground, and it was making me nervous. I've always had pretty good instincts when it comes to finding a story, and every instinct I had told me that something big was coming.

In light of the quiet that fell over the Low, it was a relief to find Constance. At least someone with some answers was still willing to help us. But Revenir believed that Constance had taken a great risk in getting that spell to us. And as RootNotes mentioned, Aether's strange video message seemed to indicate that someone had been kidnapped. It was no wonder if people in the Low were scared and going to ground.

CHAPTER 5
NO CONSTANTS

"It seems like in the past all the clues we needed
were in front of us, it was just a matter of
deciphering what was there."

— RYVICK

That night I dreamed of disembodied faces in the dark, screaming at me. No words, just a constant, raging howl that I couldn't turn away from.

I woke the next morning in my web of tangled blankets and sweat-soaked sheets. I immediately checked to see how the Mountaineers were doing and learned some of those who'd helped perform the spell were suffering some adverse affects. Ricardo had a fever, OracleSage developed a splitting headache, while both Revenir and Furia came down with a rather nasty cold. It seemed that even a relatively mundane protection spell could have physical consequences. I could only hope that it all meant the Safeguard worked.

Deirdre was still posting to her blog, this time from Istanbul.

DEIRDRE: APRIL 6TH, 2017:

 Hey Mounties,
Still in Istanbul.
Lovely, yes, one of the most beautiful cities I've ever visited (though I haven't visited lots) but I am tired, in the throes of perpetual jetlag, and it turns out the Alhambra clue I thought I knew the answer to hasn't led me anywhere. So I was wrong. And no new clues, no new passages. Just stuck. And even if I wanted to leave (I don't, and won't) the idea of getting on another plane right this very moment makes my stomach turn.
Feeling :emoji for frustrated and jetlagged girl who is stymied by the magical journal her dead father left her:
I went back and read the story I wrote to break the spell on me. The one where I said I was done with my father and was never looking back, blah, blah, blah…
Here I am, still chasing him. Still stuck, lonely, frustrated.
Am I ever going to be out of his shadow?
Am desperately trying to get used to the idea that you've all been here the entire time and I need to just go with it.
I need a nap.

The Mountaineers all knew that she was, rightfully, having a difficult time. And to their great credit, they offered their support and recommended ideas on how to find some of the answers she was looking for. After all, they knew a thing or two about unraveling mysteries. In the comments of her post, they followed up:

LEIGHA:

> Please get some rest and take care of yourself. And if there's anything we can do to help, we're here.

DEIRDRE:

> Very much appreciated. Still at a loss. Still in Instanbul. Does Topkapi mean anything to you, besides the actual palace? I've scoured the place and haven't found anything, with the not-changing journal reinforcing the fact. I'm working on a bigger post (with all my free time) but the last clue in Alhambra led me to a pillar added in the 16th century, but no luck with the palace here. The clue that led me here reads "A line of lovers offer a sorrowful rest in Topkapi."

REVENIR:

> Hey Deirdre! We Mounties are looking into your clue. There's a location in/near Topkapi called the Palace of Tears – a place where a Padishah's harem would be exiled to when the Padishah passed away. It was said to be a sad and lonesome place, and the women were forbidden to leave it. Maybe you could look there?

Something must have clicked, because Deirdre soon responded with a post titled "Something's Worked":

DEIRDRE: APRIL 12TH, 2016:

> Not sure what. I spent the entire day looking into everything you guys recommended. The university, back to the palace, back to the museum there. There were a couple places/things that were definitely "sorrowful" including a painting with a harem and this chained-up monkey that was heartbreaking, but who knows . . . Regardless, #goteam
>
> The journal now says "return to the line of silver, the line of the craftsmen. Where Archemedes' cry shines brightest through its adoring cut." The "line of silver" bit has to do with the two paths my dad found (will explain as soon as I can put a big post together, hopefully on a long flight to somewhere else, no offense Turkey) but the rest seems like the clue for the next leg. Any ideas? My brain is scrambled.
>
> Cole: I got your messages. I was never able to get my phone working here. Write me?

I was glad to see her reach out to Cole. We all knew he was heartbroken, so it was good to know that some future mending between them was possible.

Mountaineer Nahemah replied to Deirdre with some of thoughts that had been percolating on the forums.

NAHEMAH:

> We think that the "Archemedes' cry" means the word "Eureka." We also found that it may relate to either the Eureka Diamond (the first diamond found in South Africa which is on display at the Kimberley Mine Museum) or a painting about a sort of death ray

Archimedes invented which is in the Uffizi Gallery in Florence. (I have personally been there and if it's not the place you are supposed to go for the next leg, go there some other time nonetheless because it is awesome!) We do believe that the diamond is the most likely choice, however, but since we do not know how they relate to the first part of the clue, we decided to send you both options.

These are our findings so far, but if anything else comes up we shall tell you.

Have a safe journey.

The Mountaineers were certainly doing their best to help Deirdre on her quest, but their own progress toward the next fragment had stalled when Constance stopped responding to Revenir. I wondered if maybe the Safeguard spell had failed. On the other hand, if she really had given us the spell at her own personal risk, then this could mean she'd been found out. By whom, I didn't know. Someone at Kemetic Solutions? The strange video narrator with the southern drawl who wanted to speak with Aether? One thing I knew, there were more players than we could see.

But the next day, Constance showed up on the forums. The spell had worked after all, I realized. The Mountaineers compiled a list of questions, which Constance did her best to answer:

M: Who are you?
C: Constance.

M: How did you get involved with the Low?
C: Aether found it. He was my best friend. It's a long story but he can look into machines and technology, like send his mind out of his body. He was having a hard time and his parents put him on stuff for depression. When he took it he found out he could do that. He used to stay over and we'd screw with people at school, mess with their social, check their email . . . then he saw a bunch of sites online when he was

looking for stuff about what was happening to him. It's when he started finding people talking about magic and stuff. That's how he found the Low. He showed it to me. I've always been obsessed with that sort of stuff. We kind of went crazy getting into it, finding a way in.

M: Do you know why the Low is so quiet?
C: Not really. There are sort of tiers of access. But a site I'm on started talking about "guidelines" and how talking about the Low to anyone who wasn't already in could get you booted. And people were saying people were getting kicked out for talking, but also suddenly forgetting about the Low. Nobody wants to risk getting booted or their memory wiped. I don't know.

M: Is there some kind of organization that controls the Low?
C: Not that I know of? I'm not sure, like I said.

M: Who is Aether and why is Kemetic Solutions interested in them?
C: He's my best friend. Aether's not his real name that's just what he was called online. I don't know who Kemetic Solutions is. There was a guy who was calling a while back before he "ran away" saying he knew what he could do and could help him. The guy kept saying he knew other people like him and wanted to meet him. Maybe that's him.

M: How do you know Aether?
C: We've been friends since we were eight. So, nine years?

M: Why are you concerned about Aether/why do you need our help?
C: Everybody said he ran away or killed himself. I knew it wasn't true. I'd been waiting to see something from him. But he found you guys. I don't know what to do but I know I can't really do anything by myself. I'm glad he told you guys to find me, but I don't know why. I don't have powers or anything.

M: How can we find Aether? If you don't know, where were they last spotted?

C: His mom said she dropped him off at my house, but he never showed up. That was back in November.

M: What do you know about Kemetic Solutions?

C: Nothing.

M: Do you recognize the voice in the Kemetic Solutions video?

C: No.

M: Is there anything at all that you recognize in the video?

C: I've watched it a lot (lurking) and I see his mom's truck at the beginning and the playground in the park behind our school. I see A's feet in there for a second, his shoes. His purple hoodie. I think he was just trying to tell me he's alive. I can't do anything. You guys can though yeah?

As I read Constance's answers, my constant chill disappeared, replaced by heated anger. It was Brandon Lachmann all over again. Another poor kid had gone missing.

I knew where he was. We all did: that damn, bland, godforsaken business park outside of Boston. I'd been so *close*. I realized Aether must have been behind the corruption on the photos I took during my visit. He'd been reaching out, desperate for help. If not for the Mountaineers, I would have never known. But I would be good and god damned before I'd stand by and let another kid get swallowed up by corporate malfeasance, magical or otherwise. We were going to have to bust him loose.

The Mountaineers were certainly up to the task, but no one was quite sure how to go about it. Constance had low-tier permissions to a few sites those in the Low frequented, including an online library. But she worried that if she started poking around and asking questions, she'd be locked out and we'd lose our only insider. She wanted to help—Aether was her friend, after all. But she was expecting us to provide her with the answers, not the other way around.

She did have something for us, however. Constance sent us to Aether's own secured Tumblr blog with the password: "TheCommonDrumCalls." A link on his blog led to a surprising discovery: Aether had co-opted the Mountaineers' YouTube channel and scheduled a live video five days hence.

In the meantime, I decided to do some digging. I had a good feeling that the Lost Athenaeum was the Low library Constance was talking about. It was known for its rare book collection and was a research Mecca for anyone fortunate enough to be given access to its sizable archives. I reached out to a low-ranking contact in the Low, a woman I'd had occasional communication with for nearly fifteen years, but, as was becoming too common now, she didn't respond.

My research into the Suffolk County high school system didn't bear any fruit, either. There were no students named Constance (obviously our secretive friend was using an alias). I called a few police contacts—they, at least, answered my calls—but none had any records of missing kids matching Aether's story.

More missing kids.

There's something about the burn of whiskey at the back of your throat, the way its warmth vines its way along your limbs until the numbness blossoms beneath your skin and the terrors of this world seem just a little bit farther away. I remembered the terror I felt finding Brandon Lachmann. I remembered the barrels of bourbon it took to dull the jagged edges of those years following that day in the library with Sebastian.

Impatience, bad memories, and the agony of ignorance was waking that old beast in me. I needed to stay busy, stave it off. I found respite when Deirdre posted to her blog. She was on the move again and wanted to catch the Mountaineers up on where she was going, as well as how her journey had started.

DEIRDRE: APRIL 14TH, 2017:

 I drafted this while on the plane. Now I'm in Cape Town, with Wi-Fi, the museum's closed for the day, and I'm going straight to sleep (I can't sleep while in midair.) Happy weekend, Mountaineers. (Am I a Mountaineer?)

I didn't mean to get involved in any of this once I left New York.

I was just going home. I had to. Not forever, but for a while. It wasn't until I realised I left my laptop charger at the brownstone and was scrounging for something to do on the flight back that I found I had my dad's journal in my big bag (hard to keep all my knock-off bags straight.) I cracked it open and suddenly some of it made sense.

And I was sitting there holding honest-to-god magic. A book that was until very recently hiding its content from me because I'd been hidden from the world.

In the journal he writes about how there are clues hidden inside it that will lead to a path paved with stones (artwork and other created objects) that come from two old "roads." The road of wool and the road of silver.

He says there were two groups of people who knew what happened to the world, or knew something worth knowing at least. Centuries ago they set two trails of clues, designed to be found by anybody with a strong enough desire to find them.

He travelled both roads, following clues he thought would lead him to the truth, but as he describes in the journal:

". . . at the end of both roads nothing but silence and ruin. Roads that, at one time in history, were walked by those who sought the truth. But when I walked them I found those who built them were no longer waiting at the end. And hadn't been for quite some time. It wasn't until years later that I found what I believe to be the truth and now I leave it safe at the end of this new road. For you."

I think he did what he could to protect me. But also wanted to give me the chance, no matter how slim, to wake up – if I wanted it badly enough. I think I did want it; I always felt disconnected from the world, drifting . . . But if it hadn't been for everything you all did, who knows? I like to think I would've got on track eventually. I did have the unwavering desire to find the damned books. I just happened to be looking for the wrong ones.

Anyway, I spent time with Mon, drank too much, ate too much, slept too much. Like when I used to come home from uni. But I was also catching up on everything on your forum and reading the journal. Processing it all. After a few weeks I thought I'd figured out where the trail started and I got itchy. I had to see. It took me a few days to work up the nerve, but I did and I was off.

I would like to say that I went to Amsterdam to find a magical trail of art. So let's say that. But it was there that I kind of figured out the first clue which ended up leading me to Barcelona's Sagrada Familia. I got back to the hotel and found a new clue that led me to the Alhambra ("Ferdinand and Isabella will meet your disapproval at the seat of the Sultan.") To be honest, I'm not sure what triggered the next clue, but I think it could have been Charles V's Pillar. Crafted by metal instruments (the road of silver?) I most completely disapproved of the carvings of Daphne being chased down by uber-rapey Apollo. The next clue led me to

Istanbul ("A line of lovers offer a sorrowful rest in Topkapi.")

And you know the rest.

I wasn't being cagey on Instagram. Part of me wanted to know that I could figure it out on my own. Which I did. That I wanted it enough. Which I do. And now I don't need to prove it to myself. It doesn't mean I'm not brutally lonely, perpetually tired, and sad to realise my stomach isn't quite as cast-iron as I once believed it to be.

I am going to follow this story to its conclusion. And though your help is much appreciated, if I have to do it on my own I will. I wonder what he left for me at the end of the road . . . ?

Oh, and yes, I'm an Ebenguard. Seems fitting.

ADDED:

In my haste and Turkish-fog I failed to realize that the Kimberley part of Kimberley Mine is the city of Kimberley, which is a nine-hour drive from Cape Town. HA! So . . . not visiting the museum today. I'm in the midst of booking a little baby hopper flight either tomorrow or Monday (the agent seems vague about the whole thing or maybe I'm just still in need of a sleep.) Ah the life of a completely inexperienced world traveller. (In these moments I can't help but think how David would react if he could see this. Anyone else do that? Imagine if your ex could peek into your life now? Or is that just me? Please don't be just me.)

There was no telling where her father's journal would lead her, but I found the idea of a "road of wool" and a "road of silver" very intriguing. How long had people been seeking the truth? These roads of silver and wool had been established long before the *Guide to Magiq* was published. It made my head spin wondering when everything changed, how it changed, and—assuming Sullivan Green was right and this search had been going on for centuries—if we really had a chance to figure out the answers.

Deirdre appeared to be in good spirits, anyway. I, on the other hand, was in a sour mood as I impatiently awaited Aether's "broadcast."

Finally the moment came. Aether's live broadcast on YouTube. I'm not sure what I was expecting, but what we saw was 53 seconds of the bizarre. The video comprised mostly a blank screen interrupted by a series of disturbing and surreal images that would flash onto the screen for a moment before slamming back to black. Disembodied faces, an eye, digital noise, all coalescing into what Robert accurately described as "nightmare fuel."

And there was sound, as if someone had butt-dialed with their smartphone while in an airport bathroom. There may have been voices, but they were distant and difficult to hear. A small clanking echoed intermittently. Whatever we'd been hoping for from Aether, this wasn't it.

Before I even had time to digest the utter craziness of what I had just watched, the Mountaineers began dissecting the video. Sellalellen found an interesting image at the 21-second mark.

It looked very much like the Galifanx constellation they had recently found. It sat on a background filled with digital artifacts similar to those found in the photographs I took of Kemetic Solutions. A recruit named Timidity heard the word "test" in the audio, and many theorized that this was Aether's way of testing the connection. A trial run just to see if whatever he was doing was working.

Several of the Mountaineers pulled other images from the video, some of which I instantly wished I'd never seen. One image was of a frightening face with glowing eyes emerging from a tree line. There was a close-up of a person's ear with an oily substance snaking its way inside the ear canal, and the image of a face created from a melting kaleidoscope of colors.

What was Aether trying to tell us with these images? Or was there any message at all? If this was simply Aether testing his ability to communicate with us, these terrifying images could have been snapshots of his raw subconscious—the static that ran through the mind of a scared, depressed, and lonely kid.

I didn't know which I felt more: revulsion or pity.

But this was only a test. The channel indicated that another livestream was going to happen within the hour.

Without realizing what I was doing, I walked to my cabinet to grab a bottle of rye and was both relieved and disappointed that it wasn't there. Instead, I brewed a fresh pot of coffee and lit a cigarette. By the time I finished the smoke, Aether's livestream had begun.

For the first minute, there wasn't much of anything: a black screen with the occasional flash of digital noise, like playback from an old VCR tape that needed its tracking adjusted. But the sound droning in the background reminded me of a beat poet's ride cymbal.

Then the voice came. When Aether spoke, he sounded a million miles away, as if his words had been broken down and reassembled until they were barely recognizable and not wholly human.

AETHER:

 Hello? Hello? Can anybody hear me? [Inaudible] Are you trying to reach us? Are . . . are you the Mountaineers? Are you the Mountaineers? [Inaudible] I found you.

I only have a few minutes. Once a month, they put us in these sleep studies. They medicate us. [Inaudible] I'll be asleep soon so I only have a few minutes. Right now I can communicate without them knowing.

I'm not sure where I am. We're at a facility. Underground. You found Constance. [Inaudible] How is she? I'm sorry, it's hard to keep this up. So . . . sorry . . . so . . . you have to save them.

We have to save them.

I'm not the only one here. There's a girl here, and . . . a Mountaineer. I need your help. I don't know. They . . .

They're trying to . . . They were testing us. Testing our abilities. But then they started using us to try and open a door.

[Static]

They want us to open a door.

Um, I don't—I've never seen her. I've never seen the Mountaineer. But she's a woman. I can hear her voice. She tells the girl bedtime stories. They want us to try and open a door, but it's not working.

The boy who did that . . . he was . . . special. They know but they're going to keep trying. I don't know. Sorry I don't know who [inaudible] is.

It's hard to communicate like this. She tells the girl stories. [Inaudible] They see the other side. They see through the veil. [Static] Well, it's going to take everything I have, but I've found a way to help.

[Static]

Next week they're going to try and make me open the door again. [Static] They're going to try and make me open the door, but instead, I'm going to leave here.

[Static]

But to do that, I have to leave my body behind. I think I can . . . I think I can get into their system. And break it open. Give you information that can help you [inaudible]. But I have to do that [inaudible]. Is Constance here?

[Static]

I don't know. I've never done it. And I know there's a chance that I might not be able to. But they've tortured us. They lied. It's horrible. And I don't want them to do that to the girl. When they're not here you can save them.

Tell Constance that I will be there to see her again. If not . . . agh. I don't know. Just tell her that I'll be all right. Next week. I saw the schedule. They're going to make me open the door again. And when they do, they drug me and I'll be under. I'm going to leave. I'll leave.

The Mountaineer said that you'd be able to help, that you'd know what to do. And so, I'm going to trust you with my life and theirs. They're very dangerous. You have to be careful. And protect Constance.

There's something else I have to tell you. There's a storm coming. Follow this [inaudible]. It's nice to talk to someone.

They're going to try to control everything. Me, this world, your minds. You have to be careful. They could be anywhere. I'm getting tired now. [Sigh] A part of me can't wait to be free of all this. No matter what it means. Even if I can't get back, I'm going to build a [inaudible]. We're going to bring them down. I don't know how much longer I can hold on. I can't hold on. So tired.

When the livestream stopped, I threw the pot of coffee against the kitchen cabinets. I stood there for a solid five minutes, screaming expletives as shards of glass and steaming coffee pooled at my feet. I didn't stop cursing until Mrs. Schaumburg came to my door and threatened to call the police if I didn't stop making such a racket.

The boy. The special boy who opened the door. Aether had to be talking about Brandon Lachmann. Kemetic Solutions was trying to open a door to the other side by kidnapping and drugging people gifted with magiq. Not just Aether, but a girl, too. And a Mountaineer. One of us.

CHAPTER 6
MISPLACED MEMORY

> "I love the fact that you never know what's
> happening until you get back on the forum."
>
> — PHANTOMPHOENIXFROST

Maybe this is why the world changed. Because this is what happens when humans have access to a sliver of magiq. They abuse it, manipulate it, hurt with it, kill with it, destroy with it. And *for* it. Maybe the world changed to this, this lie, because we didn't deserve the truth.

The coffee was cold by the time I was calm enough to take care of the mess I had made. Once the kitchen and my feet were clean, I listened to the audio again and read the transcript that Sellalellen was kind enough to provide. I wanted to bring Kemetic Solutions to its knees, to burn its very existence from the world and salt the earth behind me. Aether was right. We *were* going to bring them down.

One of our own was missing, trapped inside Kemetic Solutions. Panic swept through Basecamp as the Mountaineers tried to discern who had been taken. Some speculated that it might be Ascender, but

Endri had spoken with Ascender numerous times and confirmed that he's a man. Certainly not the woman we were looking for.

The one silver lining was that Kelsey noticed the word "Gladitor" in one of the video frames. It was the name of the next fragment, a sign that the Book was still there, helping us. Whoever was responsible for guiding us to these fragments had led us here, to Aether and the other abductees. Whatever lingering doubt I had about their motives was gone. They were leading us down dangerous paths in search of the truth, but if it meant helping the powerless and breaking the bad guys, well, our motives were fully aligned. But what should have been a joyous moment for the Mountaineers was instead somber.

As everyone tried to figure out what our next step should be, I saw that Deirdre had posted again.

DEIRDRE: APRIL 17TH, 2017:

 Sunday was a long day. Saw the diamond. It's diamond-y. (No photography allowed, which makes sense I guess. The museum is essentially an old department store with mannequins dressed in 19th century costumes ogling fake diamonds.) I took the journal with me. No new clue.

Based on the symbol in the front of this journal (Psyche) we've all assumed it's triggered by different emotional states. So I've figured out (assumed) I'm supposed to find these objects and while somewhere near them have a specific emotional response? The latest clue is "where Archemedes' cry shines brightest through its adoring cut." Which means I have to feel what, either revelation (Eureka!) or adoration? Infatuation? Love? I mean, I'm not really a diamond girl, so ... Blurgh. This all feels a bit like a parent's emotional manipulation from beyond the grave.

Revelation is something I feel pretty regularly but if it's love or adoration I'm supposed to feel, I might need to start looking at local real estate. The closest I've felt to any of that is, well . . . I won't be vagueblogging today, you've all had front row seats to that story.

I mean, yes, there are feels and loads of them, both simple and complicated. And that's the problem! Two people who want (for a lot of reasons) something simple, uncomplicated, transparent, but we're separated by a complicated morass of secrets and lies and magic and mountains (and mountaineers), and to get back to each other we have to wade into that world again, and wading into that world sometimes feels like drowning. To ask that of him, to come back to the girl with the spell and the father and the past and the road ahead of her feels cruel. It feels like I'm reaching out for help only to drag him under with me.

I've imagined the night I found out everything going a hundred different ways instead of me stumbling away like I'd just climbed out of a car crash. But it didn't. And I don't know if I could've done anything else.

So I'm here in Kimberely with the diamond and the mannequins and the empty mine. Revelations yes, but anything else . . . Maybe I'm not that girl.

Cole, it seemed, had thoughts about her post, as evidenced by his immediate response in the comments.

COLE:

 Funny, I seem to recall my life was already pretty weird and complicated. I'd had visions of magic flowers and missing kids who'd turned into poetic wizards even before I "met" you.

I know you're having phone trouble. I don't know if you're getting my messages or texts, but since you kinda opened up here, I'll do the same, and hope you see it. (Nice to know that you not seeing a text is just your hilarious and adorable inability to figure out your phone, not magic.)

Those words are hard. Adoration. Love. Those words are hard to offer if you don't know for sure you're going to get them in return. And you think you barely know the "real" me. You mostly know me pre BC33. But that guy is the same guy. The things I didn't tell you weren't about me (mostly) and . . . I don't know. You're not the Deirdre you were either, I guess, yeah? So maybe we can meet again and see if this Cole and that Deirdre hit it off the way the old ones did.

Thing is, I'm reaching out too, you know. And sure, there's a lot of weird between us, but I think we can juuust reach each other if we both reach together.

Cause the words I can (and am brave enough) to use are still really good ones. Like respect. And awe. And butterflies. And hope.

The truth is my life . . . the simple, uncomplicated one where I go to work and then I go home and back and forth and back and forth, it feels so much darker and scarier now that I know about this other world. The world where there's magic. And you.

I guess what I'm trying to say is . . . I'm willing to wade if you'll wade with me.

Two days later, she posted again.

DEIRDRE: APRIL 19TH, 2017:

 Thanks for the talk last night, Cole. It was so nice to

hear your voice again. And thanks Mounties for getting me here.

After Cole and I spoke, a new clue appeared in the journal (yeah, yeah, love and adoration . . . this journal is meddling.)

"The trembling light of ukioy-e is printed on the souls of the lost and the damned."

So the diamond's done. I know (from Google) that ukioy-e is a Japanese art style, but not sure where to start. And my hotel here is waaaay too sunny, warm, and lovely to leave unless I know exactly where I'm going (though . . . sushi.) Thoughts, Mounties?

Brendon responded in the comments with research the Mounties knocked out.

BRENDON:

 Hi Deirdre,

We haven't actually met, but I am Brendon, one of the Mountaineers. Now we could start this new friendship off right with the standard awkward small talk, talking about the weather, how your trip around the world is going, the usual. But I feel like we have more pressing matters.

Now that leads me to this, and I don't mean to be the bearer of bad news, but you may not be getting your sushi after all. What are your thoughts on falafel? The other Mountaineers and myself have been looking into your clue and we think it could be leading you to "One Hundred Stories of Demons and Spirits," a page from a ukiyo-e painted book by Kitagawa Utamaro. We looked where this particular page is being kept, and it seems like it is being kept in the Tikotin Museum of Japanese

Art, which is on Mount Carmel, in Haifa, Israel. Yeah, I know what you are thinking, I was thinking it too.

Hopefully this helps and we aren't leading you on a wild goose chase. As always, if you need more help, we are definitely here ready to help.

⚜

I finally got an email from a contact who had pull in Suffolk County. Attached was a sheriff's office police report regarding a teenage boy briefly thought to have gone missing, until police followed up with his mother and discovered it was a false alarm. The boy, Jeremy, had been missing from school, and the guidance counselor brought his absence to the attention of the local police. It turned out he'd been sent to a special school so he could receive treatment for his depression along with his education. Though, oddly, the name of this "special school" didn't show up in the report.

I called Jeremy's old high school to speak to his guidance counselor and see if I could find a name for this school, but he said he didn't know it. The conversation was awkward. The man clearly had better things to do than speak to me about someone who was no longer his responsibility. In fact, I thought he must have someone on the other line at that very moment, since I could hear a barely audible clicking sounding on the line. Unlike most people, I still made most of my calls with a landline, so the sound wasn't anything to do with digital interference. I figured it must mean that he had someone on hold.

I heard the same sound in the background when I called Jeremy's mother, though the conversation itself was less rushed and more disturbing.

"He's away at a special school," she said.

"Yes, ma'am. And which school is that?"

"It's a special school. He's doing very well. What's the day today?"

"It's Saturday, ma'am. Do you know the name of the school?"

"I'm sorry, I mean the date."

"It's April 22nd. And what's the name of the school Jeremy is attending?"

"Oh, Jeremy is doing very well. Sorry, could you tell me what the date is?"

We spoke for ten minutes like this. She was on a loop, asking the same question over and over again and never telling me the name of this special school, only that Jeremy was doing well. Though she could never tell me how she knew that, since she hadn't spoken to Jeremy or anyone else from the school since Jeremy left, nor could she tell me the name of anyone associated with the school.

It was similar to the way Sebastian behaved after the incident in the library. The only other time I had seen something like that was when I interviewed a diabetic man for a story about the quality of insulin covered by different insurance companies. During the interview, his sugar level dropped like a hammer and he started seizing. Luckily his wife was there and she was able to get a few glucose tablets down his throat. When he was finally coherent enough to speak again, he asked me who I was. He didn't remember me at all. Even scarier was that he kept asking me over and over again who I was and what I was doing there. The seizure had not only fried his short-term memory, but had kept it offline for almost an hour. It was the same with Jeremy's mother. Only this time I was pretty sure it wasn't because of low blood sugar but because of magiq.

Unfortunately, Jeremy's mother wasn't the only one suffering from memory loss. After Aether's livestream, Constance disappeared from the forums for almost two weeks before finally responding to Revenir's attempts to check in with her.

CONSTANCE:

 lol, ugh, I have the flu, out of school for another day or two. who's this?

Who's this? Unless there was an epidemic of diabetic seizures racing across the northeast, it was beginning to look like someone was mindwiping anyone connected to Aether.

Paranoia set in. I grabbed my notebooks and flipped through them, making sure I remembered everything I had written in them. Nothing was unfamiliar, which meant they hadn't gotten to me yet. I then jotted down the bullet points of the current situation, rough timeline of events, and relevant URLs. After all the notes, all the bullet points, all the clues, I wrote myself the following message:

> If you don't remember, head to Basecamp. Same name as Times: 733T snake plus favorite holiday.

It was enough information to lead me back to the forums with all the clues necessary to figure out the username and password I'd need to log in. At least the forums were protected now and were unlikely to be wiped. They could provide an accurate chronicle of events.

I wrote the message in every one of my notebooks, then created a doc with the same information, which I saved on both the cloud and several storage devices. I hid the physical drives throughout the house with the notebooks. Should something happen to my memory, I was bound to come across one of the information caches—and wonder why the hell I was hiding story notes behind the toilet.

There are certain protocols a reporter uses when investigating a dangerous story. She and the editor will come up with a plan for scheduled check-ins, code words, even secret digital drops for copy. But I didn't have that kind of infrastructure to help me navigate these waters. I was going to have to be very careful. Kemetic Solutions knew me. There was no way they wouldn't have kept an eye on me after my visit. If they caught wind of what the Mountaineers and I were doing, they'd surely come for me. I had Brightwell's token, but wasn't sure exactly how it worked. I'd never tested it, and frankly, wasn't keen to.

A few days later, I checked in on the forums to discover that Revenir had kept up his correspondence with the mindwiped Constance. He kept his answers vague and said he knew Jeremy.

Constance gave Revenir the same response Jeremy's mother gave me: *He's at a special school and doing really well.*

I knew from my experience with the diabetic that having the short-term memory cooked out of your brain isn't very good for long-term mental health, but I could only imagine what a magical mindwipe would do to a person. There were no case studies for this kind of thing. For all I knew, Constance could come down with Alzheimer's or a brain tumor because of this. We were all of us playing with fire, and there was a good chance that innocent people were going to burn.

Constance was no longer a viable avenue of information, and even if that weren't true, we were all hesitant to ask any more of her, for fear of putting her in further jeopardy. We were stuck in limbo. Our next break came when Brendon noticed that Aether had set up another livestream on the Basecamp channel. He had mentioned in his last transmission that they were going to try and force him to open a door in a week's time. This was it.

Once again, there was only a black screen with the occasional digital noise leaking through. This time, though, it wasn't Aether who spoke, but the man who had addressed Aether in the first video. The man—Teddy, he called himself—had sounded calming the last time I'd heard his voice, his genteel southern accent almost like that of a caring father figure. But here, that calm demeanor carried a menacing quality that was impossible to ignore. This was the man holding Aether against his will, and I despised him. I held onto his voice, imprinting it in my memory so that if I ever heard it in person, I would know whose throat to throttle.

TEDDY:

 All right, are we ready? Is he in there? All right. Aether, can you hear me? It's Teddy. I'm here with you. How you feelin'? Aether, I want to try something different today. I want to try a little experiment. You're

gonna help me. I want you to imagine a door. A door
that you can open to anywhere you want to go. I want
you to imagine that door as vividly as you can.

Now I want you to tell me a story about it. I want
you to tell me what it looks like, everything that
surrounds it. I want you to imagine what it would feel
like to hold that doorknob in your hand. What it feels
like to open that door. And then I want you to tell me
what's on the other side, Aether. And if you can, I want
you to use your abilities to reach out to that door.
Touch it if you can. Does that make sense to you,
Aether? It's just a little game I want to play today.

(Wha . . . wait, what?)

Aether, are you with us? They're telling me your
levels are high. Your heart rate's up, Aether. Just calm
down, it's okay. Nothing has to happen today, we're just
going to talk. Aether, can you hear me?

(What is going on? Well, bring him down. Increase
the dosage.)

Aether. Aether, listen to me. [fingers snap]

(What is going on?)

Aether. Aether! Can you hear me?

(You idiots, he's trying to get outta here!)

Aether, you stay right here, do you hear me? I know
you're trying to reach into the system. You have to stop.
Aether, you remember what happened last time, don't
you? Aether! Aether, listen to me! You come back here.
Back to this room.

(God dammit, pull it! Pull it!)

There was a constant hum, a droning in the background that grew
to a crescendo before the feed cut out, making Teddy's words difficult
to understand. Had Aether escaped? Though his body must still be
inside Kemetic Solutions, I fully believed his mind could be elsewhere
—if he'd been successful. But I had no idea what "reach into the

system" would look like. We were at a loss, waiting for a sign that Aether had escaped capture, or even survived at all.

Deirdre made it to Israel and updated us.

DEIRDRE: APRIL 25TH, 2017:

 In Israel. Sorry for not updating sooner. I've had a very weird experience. Let me back up though so you understand the maximum amount of weirdness.

There were a couple nights in Istanbul where I'd wake up to someone loudly knocking on my door. Not like, angry . . . just slowly pounding on the door. There were some guys in a room a few rooms down who could get rowdy and stumble back from wherever and sometimes not know where their room was so I figured it was them. I'd yell their actual room number and they'd go find their actual room.

So after the "Japanese" clue I flew back to Cape Town the next morning, got the same room in the amazing hotel I was staying in, overlooking Camps Bay.

Talked to Cole, emailed Mon, posted the letter I got from Orvin, ate, misplaced the contents of a rather lovely bottle of red, and went to bed.

Then two or three hours later someone started pounding on my door. Just like Istanbul, slowly slamming their fist into the door, over and over. In my stupor I yelled that they had the wrong room before realising I wasn't in Istanbul. I freaked out, sneakily checked the peephole, but it was just black. Like someone was covering it up. So I called the front desk.

After a few minutes the knocking changed. It was faster, quiet. And then someone on the other side of the door said, "Ma'am, it's the manager . . ."

I answered with the chain on. He said no one had been in the hall, but he heard the knocking too.

He said it was coming from my side of the door.

From inside the room.

Mmmhmm.

Okay.

Changed rooms. Stayed up all night. Got first flight out. Slept on the planes (three connections, fun.) And kept waking up thinking I heard the knock.

In Tel Aviv now. Will try and make it to the museum tomorrow. I've called ahead but I keep getting put through to a curator's voicemail when I ask about *100 Hundred Stories of Demons and Spirits* (a title which is very comforting right now, thanksverymuch.)

While I am thoroughly freaked out, I'm assuming this means I'm getting closer? I'm on the "path" he left me?

But why exactly did he have to make it so creepy?

Leigha and new Mountaineer Miss Evans replied, advising her on how to keep herself safe with some simple magic.

LEIGHA:

 Deirdre, Miss Evans had a few ideas about protecting yourself from dark magics on your journey. "I'd suggest Dee needs a lot of salt about her person. Salt lines across room doors, etc.

"And she needs to be so careful viewing that piece.

"Oh, and she's in Israel: quick cleansing dip in the Dead Sea? Salty as you like . . ." —Miss Evans

I personally always have a little baggie of salt in my bag, and regularly place black salt (salt mixed with charcoal) at the four corners of my house. Keeps the nasties away.

Also, when you go to your room for the night (every night, every hotel room), get the useless little bar soap from the bathroom and use it to draw a five-pointed star on the floor in front of the door, with one point pointing out, at the door. It will protect your room from any magical malfeasance. Stay frosty out there, Deeds.

Finally, Deirdre followed up:

DEIRDRE: APRIL 28TH, 2017:

 I've been here for what, a week, almost, and have left countless messages for the curator who "knows about that sort of thing." No response.

Magical Adventuring is not nearly as fun as it's made up to be.

Cole is concerned.

I have almost literally talked his ear off. He fell asleep on the phone yesterday (his 3am) while I droned on for ages about paths of silver and wool and what does it mean and who are all these people and how does this have anything to do with me, and why couldn't my father have just left a plainly legible letter explaining all the nonsense he's worked so hard to hide . . . I guess that question answers itself, but all the others!!!

I have jumped out of bed at every door slamming in the hallway outside my room, sure it's another ghost who's also so done hearing me ramble on and on that he's knocking from the inside of the room, trying to get out. (Though a big thanks to Leigha and Miss Evans (my fairy godmothers) who told me how to protect my doorways with salt. I went ahead and covered the room in it, took a bath in it, and have been eating my weight in chips since I got here so I think I'm covered for now.)

But ... BUT!

In all my free time I *have* been doing some reading. You know where this is going don't you? Did you guess mad speculation?

I was going through the posts about my father's other journal volume, the one Lauren had (SO happy the winged, fire-spewing lady wizard never discovered I owned a volume of my own) and guess what I came across ...

The story about the Unicorn Tapestries. The one about Anne of Brittany and her court of artists and her death and the objects her various parts were buried in ...

Gold and silk. Silver and wool. Does silver and wool sound familiar?

The road of silver and the road of wool. Two "roads" made up of art and crafted objects that my dad followed years ago, the two roads that led to nowhere, that he then upended and put together to make the road I'm on right now.

He wrote that there were two groups of people who knew some or all of the truth, and hundreds of years ago they set two trails of clues, hidden but built to be found by anybody with a strong enough desire to find them. A sort of recruitment tool.

The Anne of Brittany story mentions a secret guild of artists who were members of Anne's court and also the cult of collectors who eventually stole the objects from her grave(s).

Could those be the two groups my dad mentioned? Artisans and Crafters? The secret guild and the cult? Are those the people he was looking for?

Is that where he's got me heading?

Deirdre had connected two very interesting but ominous threads
—more whispers becoming solid connections. The clues in Volume
One of Sullivan's journals referencing lost histories in Volume Three.
It couldn't be happenstance. It seemed like none of this was. Even
Aether and Kemetic Solutions. They were all knots along the same
thread we were climbing. Where were Sullivan and the Book leading
her, the Mountaineers, maybe everybody?

Clueless where to go next, Robert arbitrarily typed "aether" at the end
of the Kemetic Solutions URL and found a page containing what
appeared to be excerpts from a personal log belonging to Theodore
"Teddy" Fallon:

> [DATE]
> What would this power have been in the time
> before?
> Telemancy? Telography?
>
> Could he be the first case we've seen of an adept
> evolution? A power adapting to its environment?
> Fascinating.
>
> If we could harness it, the technological potential would
> be staggering. Surveillance, communication . . . possibly
> the foundation for an organic-born AI.
>
> [DATE]
> He is a kind boy. Reminds me of [ ] It hurts to see,
> hurts to say. I hope I can do better by him than I
> did by—
> [DATE][DATE][DATE]

It was unclear whether Aether's mind had gotten out of Kemetic

Solutions, but he'd managed to release sensitive Kemetic information to us.

Littlbat did the same thing, using "lachmann" instead of "aether," and found a list of names. Several of those names led to other pages and snippets of information. Even the number 117-2, which Kelsey found hidden in a frame of Aether's most recent video, provided a link when added at the end of the Kemetic Solutions URL. Aether had hacked his captor's files and exposed them to us.

Going from the list of names, it was clear that the missing Mountaineer used the code name Climber and the captive girl was called Portencia. There was so much information to unpack:

LACHMANN ENTRIES:

 All individual therapies have been halted.

A piece of an Etruscan arch dating to the 4th century BC has been unearthed and all signs point to it being an emergent frame. It's been delivered on sub-level five.

The area where it was harvested (a powerful ley line) and etchings of the six elemental symbols on it suggest it was used ritualistically. They were trying to find a way through the veil even then.

We've been ordered to direct all adepts into the Lachmann project. It's believed that another door can be recreated using the arch (and the Chair), as Lachmann did with the City Hall station (though its intentional design as an emergent frame was ultimately the cause of its closing) but it remains to be seen how.

My entire staff has been reassigned. I have my doubts about all of this. The boy is the *only* one who's ever pierced the veil.

Our desire here has always been to better this world

. . . not clamber for the next, but it's not our decision in the end.

The other world waits.

[DATE]

The middle of the night.

I know Brandon was adept.

His unique ability to see the world as it should be combined with his preternatural creativity was a potent cocktail.

But I've had a thought. Perhaps the way to open another door is by using our subjects' abilities and funneling them into creative endeavors? Connecting "the spaces between" as Lachmann himself said?

CLIMBER ENTRIES:

 [DATE]

It's true. What a boon. She's able to recall the memories of her ancestors. She is immensely intelligent. Knowledge gathered over generations is at her fingertips.

We acquired her at her home. She expected us. Knew why we were there and what we wanted.

The gears are always turning. She knows more than all of us combined and is always ahead of us.

There will be challenges of course. Keeping her here when at times she's able to outthink our smartest . . . a thrilling challenge.

[DATE]

She is unwilling to share her experiences, as expected.

We'll begin coercion therapy in the morning.

[DATE]

We can ask her almost anything and she can answer

it, or at least extrapolate a possible answer.
Mathematics, physics, history . . .

[DATE]

Today was extraordinary. Under duress therapy she
finally revealed the truth I suspected (being the only one
here who's memorized the history and missives of the
Mountain).

She has been a "mountaineer" for generations.

Every ancestor she is descended from, and shares
her memories with, followed the path of wool.

The implications . . . Could she be a collector like her
ancestor? Or has she found herself at the crux of two
miracles?

It's only a matter of time until this revelation brings
a storm to our quiet little corner of the world. We are
always watched, always heard. She is now too valuable
for them to resist.

Everyone around me wants to use a hammer but I
believe we can use a more gentle touch and reap greater
reward.

I fear we could lose them all in the process. It's
dangerous to be in the same room with the Chair, let
alone sit in it. I am preparing myself for the darkest
possibility. Adepts are powerful, but fragile. They
shouldn't exist here and yet they do, despite everything
that's trying to prevent them from existing.

Those are the questions I want answered. But no one
else cares. They simply want more power.

And power waits beyond the veil.

Fallon had implied in his entries that not only had there been
"generations" of Mountaineers but that Monarch's Mountain and the
Mountaineers were synonymous with the "path of wool." That was a
long, long line of people working together to seek out magiq. There

were also entries about other Kemetic projects called "Wanderer" and "Sweeper":

PROJECT ENTRIES:

 [DATE]
It's not foolproof but we've had some breakthroughs in the past year.

I have to be honest, I don't understand the point of displacing those who risk what we're trying to do.

But here we are unhooking people who might've caused us irreparable harm, and possibly still could. Where they go, what they remember . . . none of it's proven. It's exhausting trying to argue the counterpoint. Sweeper has proven successful in 95% of use cases. Why we're using Wanderer when we have no clear overview of its effectiveness, or consequences, I don't know.

But there are machinations at work here that I'm not privy to.

I would like to say I'm proud of my work of the Wanderer project, that it was worth the cost, that he died for a cause. It's a monumental leap forward in power. But I'm so deep in the shadows I can't say anything we're doing is worth the price.

And entries about the young girl:

PORTENCIA ENTRIES:

 [DATE]
She cried for days. It nearly broke my heart.
Then I felt her in my mind . . . She was looking for a

way out through my senses, seeing if I was telling the truth about letting her go back home someday.

She looked back inside me and saw what we'd done to her fathers.

What we had to do. It haunts me.

She now knows it was a lie. She's seen an inevitability that I can't.

[DATE]

She can see the past and future of anyone she chooses.

Well, not see. She can *feel* their past and future, the smells, the sights, the feeling and sensations.

She can then extrapolate what they mean. It's extraordinary.

Her biological father was also adept. Another case of abilities passing on through genetics.

He taught her coping mechanisms to control the power. She won't share them yet.

[DATE]

Her power is immense. One of the most gifted adepts I've ever seen. But she's too young to wield it properly. Too young to have done to her what we've done. I have my regrets. I was the one after all who discovered her. But what's done is done. And now we have to find a way to pick up the pieces.

[DATE]

Couldn't sleep. Went down to my office and overheard [Climber] telling the girl stories about her own past. People her ancestors knew, places they saw. The girl could see them in her own mind. What a pair. She's become a parent figure to [Portencia].

[DATE]

Catastrophe.

Kendrick was unconscious for hours. He administered the coercion session that broke her. He finally came to, only muttering a street address over and over . . .

Her home address.

[DATE]

I believe she's been fractured. The best way I can describe it. Her mind has been shattered by the sessions. What defenses she had, the walls she'd built to stem the flow of stimuli, from both the past and future . . .
all gone.

Kendrick's condition has led me to believe pieces of her mind are now embedded in the minds of those she's reached into, now and perhaps in the past and future.

There is no conceivable way we could retrieve them.

What a devastating loss. Another miracle thrown on the heap.

Along with the entries, Portencia's page had one part of a child's drawing that looked like it had been cut into pieces.

Once we had discovered the entries, the Book emailed us with even more clues:

A malevolence as yet unseen
Means to gather power
By breaking the poor mountaineer
And crushing the young flower

It's time to dive deeper still
A mystery to test your will
A fractured mind, a vicious byte
Another fragment's taken flight

Nahemah made a connection between the Book's riddle and Portencia, who, if Fallon's entries were to be believed, had suffered "a fractured mind."

Finally, Aether reached out, revealing that his mind had indeed escaped Kemetic Solutions.

AETHER:

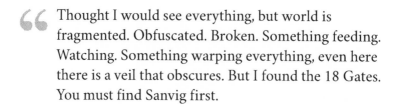

> Thought I would see everything, but world is fragmented. Obfuscated. Broken. Something feeding. Watching. Something warping everything, even here there is a veil that obscures. But I found the 18 Gates. You must find Sanvig first.

All the information we had was disjointed. Spiderweb on top of spiderweb. I couldn't see how it all fit together, how to decipher it, the paths of silver and wool, a girl's consciousness lost inside other people's minds, generational memories, eighteen gates, and someone or something called Sanvig. We were so deeply in the dark, all we knew for sure was that Aether, Climber, and Portencia were trapped and suffering. I was getting antsy, angry, frustrated.

The clues Aether left us were enough for the Mountaineers, however. They gathered a list of oddly highlighted letters in Fallon's entries, and Littlbat combined and reorganized them, creating a hyperlink containing the named "B. Sanvig" which led to an image of a doctor.

Kelsey ran a reserve image search and that same photo came up on a site for Lower Shore Mental Health Clinic in Maryland. Something about the clinic pulled at my memory. It took me a moment to realize why.

Ascender.

In his last post before leaving the Mountaineers, he'd spoken of visiting Augernon at a Maryland mental health facility.

I suspected Sanvig was Augernon and that, for some reason, Aether wanted us to reach out to him. I called the clinic and asked to speak with Mr. Sanvig, but the receptionist politely explained that unregistered people weren't allowed to speak with patients. I had to get on the list for that. With the little information I had, I tracked down Sanvig's family, hoping I could get more information about his condition, the facility, and maybe even worm my way into getting put on the registry.

I spoke with his wife on the phone. She was lovely, with a sweet, lilting mid-Appalachian accent. I wasn't lying when I told her that her husband and I had been friends, though I admitted that I'd never known his first name and only ever knew him as Augernon. His name was Bill. She had as many questions for me as I did for her. Hers were about what had really happened to her husband in 1998. I didn't know the answers, and what I *did* know she probably wouldn't believe. She'd been in a holding pattern for nearly twenty years, her voice still weepy, waiting to know why her husband sent her and their boys away and why, when they came back, he was physically there but gone in every other sense. In the end, she put my name on the registry.

I let the Mountaineers know that Aether wanted us to meet Augernon.

New Mountaineer Deyavi worked on focusing the Mountaineers on finding a solution to how I'd communicate with a near-catatonic man. Finally, they found one. Or, at least, a solution presented itself to them. Aether sent a few of the Mountaineers emails containing a username and password to the Lost Athenaeum, a digital library in the Low. When they gained access to the protected site, one of the things they found was a spell.

RITUAL SPELL 842, CONSOLATORY TEATIME FOR MISPLACED MEMORY:

 A Summoning Ritual v1.03
[Multiple Practitioners/Food & Beverage/Memory/Unperfected/Hearsay/Herbs]
Note: the original text of this spell involved two persons, the one who had lost the memory, and the one

who would summon the memory. As with most spells now, it may take more people to conjure the memory on this side of the veil.

REQUIRED:

—Several people must brew a cup of tea simultaneously. Any tea of one's choosing is appropriate as long as it's herbed in some way.

—One of the practitioners must be in the physical presence of the person with the misplaced memory.

—Sit with someone, have a warming cup of tea, and tell them something, a story, an anecdote about your day. Think calm and tranquil thoughts, allowing memories to swim in and out of consciousness.

—The act of sharing teatime around a "table" of any sort is helpful in summoning the lost memory, especially if the memory is particularly lost. In the mundane age, a conference call or video call might suffice.

—When you're finished, speak the summoning phrase:

"Now tell me something you remember, eyes are open, ears are hearing, something far away but nearing, something bubbling into view, something gone made now and new." The original ritual depicted the misplaced memory being summoned physically inside a spheroid shape, though it may have been an artistic elaboration. Modern practitioners have claimed seeing glimpses of memories in their tea but no such claims have been substantiated.

This ritual may bring a sense of comfort but has yet to be perfected as an actual spell here in the mundane.

Pieced together from numerous sources. As with all materials in the Athenaeum, you view and perform them at your own risk. There is no such thing as magic without consequence.

It would take several people to perform the spell, but if it worked, it could help Augernon recall who he was, and Aether seemed to think that was our best next step. But the spell required someone to be present with the person it was being cast on. A call wouldn't do. I was going to have to go to Maryland.

CHAPTER 7
TEATIME

"Just take everything with an ocean of salt."

— OMEGA12

After calling the clinic again and setting up an appointment to see Augernon, I coordinated with the Mountaineers. Calculating the drive time along with a bit of setup, I suggested they start the ritual at 3 p.m.

The morning came, and I stopped to pick up tea along the way to Maryland. I much preferred coffee, since it worked better at keeping Lauren's chill at bay, but since the memory ritual required tea, I thought it best to keep with the theme.

I'd had enough practice talking my way into various institutions that I wasn't too concerned about raising anyone's suspicions about the true purpose of my visit. I was concerned, though, about the ritual. Not that I doubted the Mountaineers' ability to perform it; no, they had proven themselves quite adept at such things by now. But I was concerned about what it would do to Augernon. If the ritual worked and his memories came back, would he be grateful or resentful? Was it cruel to play with a man's mind, even for a noble cause?

I had plenty of time to mull over the ethical issues during the hours-long drive, and by the time I arrived at the clinic, my stomach was a ball of guilty knots.

I checked in with the Mountaineers. They were ready. I headed inside.

The building was quite lovely. Fragrant lilies sat in vases on a number of shelves and counters, and the walls were painted a calming au gratin yellow.

I stepped up to the receptionist, a round woman with an infectious smile, and introduced myself. She handed me a number of forms to sign and said, "We'll bring Mr. Sanvig to the common room for you. If you'd step over here, please."

She motioned me toward a large man in baby blue scrubs. He pulled out a security wand and ran it over my body. It beeped when it hovered over my phone.

"No electronic devices, sir. They make some of the patients uncomfortable. Radio waves, radiation and . . . whatever. I'll return them to you when you leave."

Well, shit. I'd hoped to livestream our conversation, but that wasn't going to happen now. I told the man I had to make a quick call and stepped outside. On the forums, I let the Mountaineers know that I wouldn't have my phone and that I'd have to go old school. My shorthand was a bit rusty, but I was confident enough that I could do this with nothing but a pencil and paper.

Back inside, they led me to the common room and I sat at a table in the center. There were other people in the room, older, not really interacting with one another. But for Vivaldi playing softly over the loudspeakers, it was eerily quiet.

A nurse came into the room, pushing a man in a wheelchair: Augernon. His eyes were glassy, vacant, but the rest of him appeared almost vibrant. His gray hair was stylishly cut, and his handsome features were only enhanced by his short salt-and-pepper beard.

"Hi, Bill. It's good to see you," I said.

Augernon said nothing, only stared at me for a moment before turning his attention to something only he could see.

"How have you been?" I asked.

Nothing.

"I'm afraid Bill here isn't having a good day." The nurse sighed. She put an affectionate hand on her patient's shoulder and gave him a gentle pat.

I checked my watch. Quarter after three. "Do you think Bill and I could talk somewhere less crowded?"

"Of course." The nurse led us back to Augernon's room and placed his wheelchair near the window. "There's a call button there by the phone. Press it if you need anything." She smiled and closed the door behind her.

I sat at a small desk on the other side of the bed and pulled out my pad of paper. I drew hot water from the tap into a plastic mug and dunked a teabag into it. Augernon didn't react, didn't even notice I was there in the room with him.

I sipped the tea, worried that the Mounties' spell wasn't going to work. Then I remembered I had to speak a verse. I flipped back in my notepad to where I'd written it and said, "Now tell me something you remember, eyes are open, ears are hearing, something far away but nearing, something bubbling into view, something gone made now and new."

Nothing immediate happened, but after a moment Augernon sat up in his wheelchair as if something outside the window had caught his attention. He turned and gazed around the room, taking in the mauve walls, the landscape painting, the oak furniture. He seemed confused, unsure, but aware.

"Bill? Augernon? Are you all right?" I asked.

He looked at me, his eyes now focused. "What happened?"

"You just woke up."

Augernon leaned forward, trying to stand.

"No, please, don't get up."

"Where's Anne, my kids?"

"They're okay," I said. "Everybody's okay."

Augernon nodded and looked about the room again, taking it in like an animal studying its cage for weaknesses. The ritual was working, but I had no idea how long it would last. Normally, I would ease into an interview, try to make the subject comfortable, but I doubted I had much time. I had no choice but to dive right in.

"Can you tell me what you remember about the Mountaineers?"

He pulled his gaze away from the painting. "The . . . Mountaineers?" Confusion returned, but not the kind caused by senility—rather that of someone searching for a memory he had forgotten he had once possessed. But his confusion faded almost as quickly as it appeared. He nodded and spoke, more to himself than to me. "My other family. I tried to save them. I tried to buy them time." He brought his eyes up to mine. His were a fierce gray that, in another setting, could have commanded a board room. Or an army. "I sent my family away because I knew they'd come for me. And I thought I could . . . I thought I could give everyone a chance to hide."

"Hide from what?"

"The Storm."

The Storm. This wasn't the first time I had heard about it. Whatever it was, it was coming, and there were those in the Low who could see its clouds already darkening the horizon.

"What is the Storm?" I asked.

Augernon folded his hands across his lap. When he spoke, his tone was almost professorial. "The other side of the forked road," he said. "I don't know what they call themselves, but they've been here for centuries. The shadow cast on the world. They wiped out the originals. Monarch's Mountain. And when we got too close, they did the same to us."

"You met them?"

Augernon sat still for a moment before turning his gaze out the window. "I am an Ebenguard," he said. "I stood my ground so my friends could live."

He started crying.

What had been done to this poor man was cruel and unforgivable, but it was also a blessing in that he had not been burdened by

whatever painful memories returned to him now. I wanted to give
him a moment, to let him face those horrible memories in his own
way. He needed that, he deserved it, but there wasn't time.

"Augernon . . ." I handed him a tissue and then sat on the edge of
the bed.

"No one calls me that but Ascender. Call me Augie." He wiped his
tears and then smiled. "I remember him here. Ascender."

"Yeah. He's come to visit you."

"I recruited him, you know." The man's smile broadened.

"You did? What about Climber? Does that name sound familiar?"

Augernon's smile faded. He balled up the tissue in his hands, his
knuckles turning white. "The Book. Where's the Book?" he asked.

"What book?"

He closed his eyes and continued, "I can see the yellowing edges of
its pages. It was there. It *is* there . . ." Slowly, he opened his eyes and
really looked me over for the first time. "Who are you?"

"My name's Martin Rank. I'm a reporter."

"I don't know you." I tried not to take it personally.

"Not exactly, but someone told me you could help us. We're trying
to help some people. Maybe the book you remember could be useful.
What book are you talking about?"

Augernon looked at me as if I were daft. "The Book of Briars."

"How do you know about that?" I asked.

Augernon leaned forward, his voice almost a whisper. "It's almost
unlocked. But we didn't see the Storm coming."

"I don't understand. Are you talking about now? Or in the 90s?"

Augernon sat back, his wheelchair squeaking. His brow creased
and worry flashed behind his eyes. "What year is it?"

I was afraid that if I told him, it might send him down a rabbit hole
he'd never come out of. I hated myself in that moment. But as much as
I wanted to help this man, to ease his suffering, I wanted answers
more. "The Book of Briars existed in 1994?" I asked.

"The Book has always existed, Mr. Rank. The originals tried to
open it. Others in the unwritten times. Us. And now you, yes?"

"Yes," I whispered.

"You think it's going to tell you the truth, don't you?"

All my journalistic instincts flew out the window. I wasn't interested in conducting a carefully orchestrated interview anymore. I was desperate for answers, grasping for them like a drowning man grasping for purchase. "What is it?" I asked.

He didn't answer, only said, "I don't think we're meant to learn anything from it. I think it was put here for *us* to teach *it*. Shape it. I don't think it's a book at all."

"What do you think it is?"

"What do *you* think it is?" he asked me.

My words came out, unbidden by conscious thought, surprising me with their obviousness. "I think it's a spell," I said.

Augernon rose from his wheelchair, the leather seat creaking as he stood. He walked to a small screened-in patio off the bathroom and stopped, staring out to the pond in the distance. I followed him.

"What kind of spell is it, Augie?"

"They won't let anyone have it," he said. He took a deep breath, sucking in the fresh air through his nose. "They want the world the way it is. They want to enslave magic and keep it in the shadows." He turned to me and very matter-of-factly said, "I've been gone a long time. Haven't I?"

I nodded. "Yes."

Augernon turned back toward the pond and said, "But they've been here with me, always. I hear them whispering to each other from around the world. Feel them moving like they're under my skin. A splinter. A thing I can't remember but can't forget."

"Can you tell me anything else about them? Who they are. Where they are."

"Everywhere!" He threw out his hand, gesturing to the world beyond the screen. He took another breath, calming himself. "Everywhere. Because they rule this world from a palace made of doors."

He turned and looked at me again, but his eyes blinked, unsure and unfocused. "I don't know you."

"I'm Martin Rank, Augie."

He looked back out to the water, his shoulders sagging under some unseen weight. "I'm really tired."

I took him by the arm. "Come sit down," I said. I could tell the spell was failing, or perhaps fading. Either way, I was losing him. He was becoming the Augie I'd first met. Glassy-eyed, blank.

I led him back to his wheelchair and helped him sit. He looked up at me, his eyes struggling to find something familiar in my face, and said, "Ascender . . ."

"He's—"

"What are you doing here?" he asked, his voice rising in panic. "You can't be here," he said, glancing at the door. "I did this to keep you safe."

He thought I was Ascender. Whatever magic had corrupted his mind was now convincing him that I was his old friend. The friend he'd tried to save. Bile rose in my throat. There was still more I needed to know. And so I was going to let him continue to believe the fiction that was spinning inside his poor, corrupted mind.

"I don't know what to do, Augernon," I said. "What can we do to stop the Storm?"

He grabbed my hand and squeezed. "You need to learn all you can, Sender. How close are you? How many fragments do you have?"

"Ten."

He pursed his lips and nodded. "You're close. They came for us at twelve, remember?"

That's what happened to the '94s. The Book, the Storm, all of it. They got close to real answers, and then the danger came. Just like now. Some insane cycle we had no idea we were a part of.

When I didn't answer, his expression faded, his friendliness replaced by confusion. I was a stranger once again. "Who are you?" he asked. "How did you find me?"

It was heartbreaking to watch this strong, intelligent man reduced to such confusion. I didn't want to burden him anymore. Augernon had been burdened enough. I gave him a sad smile and said, "It's a long story."

I sat on the edge of the bed, staring at my notebook. I wanted to sit with him for a while longer, keep him company even if he wasn't truly aware of me anymore.

"All stories are long when it comes to magic," he said. I looked up at him and he was staring at me, a wistful smile on his face. The ritual must have brought him back.

Augernon stood and put his hand on my shoulder. "Remember what I told you, Sender. There are pieces moving on both sides of the board. Some are trying to hinder. Some are trying to help. Hide from hinder, you're too weak right now to fight, but follow help with all your might. It won't make sense. Until it does. Trust the flow of magiq. Trust whoever it is that wants us to open the Book."

Augernon then helped me to my feet and embraced me, as if I were the one whose memories had been taken and who was in need of comfort. He pulled back, saying, more to himself than me, "Trust whoever it is that wants us to open the Book."

He started wringing his hands, pacing back and forth across the room. He stopped in front of me, his eyes clear and focused. "Is my family safe? Tell me the truth."

"They are," I said. "Your boys are grown. They have families, too, now."

"Good. I'm a grandfather." His smile was full of pride. "The past is just a moment, Martin," he said, patting my shoulder. Parting advice from one old man to another. But Augernon's smile suddenly faded. He looked around the room, whipping his head from the door to the window to the patio. "They're coming," he said.

"Augie?"

The man froze for a moment. Slowly, he turned, his eyes fixed on mine, and whispered, "They're here." He was still Augernon, the original Mountaineer, with all his faculties. But the look in his eyes was no longer one of clarity. It was one of fear.

His spine went rigid, his arms tight at his sides. Then his stiffened body collapsed to the floor, falling against the wheelchair and sending it clattering across the room.

"Augie!"

I bent over him. He was seizing violently. White foam oozed from the corners of his rictus mouth. His limbs bounced against the carpet, creating a diseased cadence of dull and fleshy thuds. I stood momentarily frozen as his body danced to the horrific rhythm.

"Help!" I shouted. I ran to the call button and pressed it, over and over again. "Help, god dammit, help!" I ran back to Augie and tried to hold him, to keep him from breaking his bones against any of the furniture.

Two orderlies and the nurse rushed in. One of the orderlies grabbed me by the collar and rather unceremoniously tossed me aside.

And then I felt it. Something heavy, electric, and warm moved through me, flashing across the room like an aurora. All the hairs on my arms stood at attention, and I could smell the sickly-sweet scent of ozone and burning meat.

I stumbled backward, tripping over the wheelchair. I ran. I ran, snatching my phone as I moved past the receptionist, and didn't stop until I was at my car.

CHAPTER 8
WHISTLING

"Oh my gosh, there are way too many
resemblances!"

— SUPERNOVA

I don't remember how far I drove before I finally had the wherewithal to check in with the Mountaineers. I was terrified, I was angry, and I was sick with guilt. But most of all, I was determined. I worked to unpack everything I'd just learned, even as my hands shook from nerves, adrenaline, cold.

There was some mysterious group, some force, working in the shadows to prevent The Book of Briars being opened. They had someone or some *thing* called the Storm at their disposal. The Storm decimated the '94s. Brandon Lachmann, Aether, and somehow even Sebastian had warned about it. Hadn't he, when he told me he smelled rain? (I admit that could've been me trying to connect my son to the greater web, in the hope I could solve it all in one fell swoop.) If they hadn't shut me out, I'd have been wiped away by the Storm like the rest of them.

I found a cheap motel room just off the interstate and then let the

Mountaineers know their ritual had worked. I transcribed my conversation with Augie the best I could, but my hands were shaking so badly it took me forever to type it all out on my phone. I didn't want to be on the road until I was calmer, thinking more clearly. Best if I stayed the night.

The Mountaineers were reeling from everything we'd learned from Augernon. The '94s were trying to unlock the Book twenty years ago, (that's where the spells, rhymes, rituals, and strange devices must have come from) and Mountaineers had possibly existed even *before* the '94s but were always wiped out before they could open the Book by some dark, opposing force that waited at one end of two divergent paths. Wool and silver. The forked road, as Augernon called it. We had been unknowingly walking the same path as all the mountain climbers who'd come before. The path of wool.

A second piece of Portencia's drawing appeared on the Kemetic Solutions site after my visit with Augernon. It revealed part of a tree, a house with three people standing inside it, and the phrase, "The past is just a moment." Deyavi reasoned that Augernon may have held a piece of Portencia's fractured mind and by casting the spell on him, speaking with him, we'd somehow released it. A new Mountaineer named Augustus_Octavian suggested that Kendrick, the comatose employee of Kemetic Solutions who administered Portencia's last session, would be the most likely source of another piece of the poor girl's mind. Maybe that was Aether's play. Maybe he could see those pieces within the digital magimystic chaos and was leading us to them. But how we'd get to Kendrick, we had no idea.

I don't think I slept that night. But I did dream. I was lying on the bed, looking up at the ceiling, where thin lines of light from the street lamps bled through the blinds. And I could feel someone next to me. At first I thought it was Lauren again, but no. Whoever it was, she was younger. Much younger. She whispered in my ear so softly I couldn't make out what she was saying, only the faintest rhythm of her soft syllables tweeting like birdsong in my mind.

The following morning, the uneasy feelings of guilt, helplessness, and unending cold were still sitting in the pit of my stomach, but I was no longer shaking. I downed a pot of coffee and headed back into the city.

The first thing I did when I got home was call Augernon's family to see if he was okay, if they had heard anything. I couldn't get through to anyone. When I tried the clinic, the person who answered wasn't nearly as friendly this time around. She stated that no medical information could be released except to registered family members.

I had no idea if Augie was dead or alive. And after I'd thought that, somehow, I could help him.

Just like I'd thought I could help Brandon Lachmann.

As awful as it was, I wasn't going to let whatever happened to Augie stop me from helping Aether, Climber, and Portencia.

Portencia. The little girl's name fluttered through my mind on butterfly wings, and I could feel warm breath against my ear. Was she the girl I dreamed about? If so, what was she trying to tell me? A warning? A secret?

DEIRDRE: MAY 5TH, 2017:

 I'm in Montreal. Long story. Unpacking (literally and figuratively.) I've just landed, but I wrote this on the plane:

The curator finally called me back after a week of messages. She said she wanted to meet at her house, not the museum. It turns out it had taken her a week to get the page out without anyone noticing. She said she'd been following the page from museum to museum. She said she'd been expecting me, hoping I'd turn up someday. Oh. Okay. Nothing to worry about. Nope.

She brought me into her office when I finally got there (I had the cab leave me at the bottom of the hill so I could walk up and then I promptly got lost for an hour) where she'd laid the page on her desk, covered in a thin film.

The image of a pale demon. It was creepy, but I wasn't crawling out of my skin. I didn't want to pull the journal out in front of her so instead I asked what she meant when she said she'd been expecting me.

She told me she knew my father. And he told her to expect a call someday about this page. I was gobsmacked. I had a thousand questions that all revolved around *Why did he do all of this?*

She couldn't tell me. She said no one knew what "Sully" was up to in those last days. He was frantic, driven. She said I probably knew more than anyone else by now. (She would be incorrect.) She told me she could see him in my eyes.

She excused herself and while I was alone I looked through the journal, hoping for a new clue. I mean, I'm the one who knows the most about everything, right? I'm the one with all the information. Nope. Nothing. As far as I know not one single step closer to the truth. Or the point.

She came back and said she thought she'd heard someone at the door but when she opened it no one was there. I didn't think anything of it until something started knocking on the closet door behind her.

She turned to it and then back to me and the look on her face sent a chill running all over me. She asked me what I'd brought into her house.

She told me I had to leave, but I refused. I was essentially begging her to explain any of this, to help me, help me find the truth, but she pushed me out of the office, out of her house, every door knocking as we went. I walked to the main thoroughfare and the knocking followed me. Every door in every home. The faster I went, the louder they got until I screamed, and although I don't fully remember I basically collapsed in the street, dropping my bag, skinning my knee and frankly bursting into tears. I couldn't do it anymore. If this was a trial or a test, I failed it. I couldn't be whoever he wanted me to be. I couldn't find whatever he wanted me to find.

The journal had fallen out onto the pavement and I thought very seriously about leaving it there and going home. And then I remembered Mon.

Cole knows this, but I left NYC not only because of what happened, but also because Mon is sick. She has dementia. It came on suddenly. I mean, she was more and more distracted, forgetful . . . I thought it was funny when she misspelled her own name on a letter to me a few months back . . . but it's gotten much worse the past few months. But she didn't want to tell me. And then she couldn't remember me. A family friend had phoned to explain everything, so I'd rushed back home to her.

We were on the banks of the Ralty one afternoon— she still loves being outside as much as she always did— and she was holding my hand. She looked at me and said I looked different since New York. There was a light about me now. She said she'd had her doubts, but following my father had been the best thing for me.

That was a moment of clarity both for her and me. That all this, as tough as it was, was a positive thing, the right thing to do, and that moment with Mon set me pursuing the path in the journal. I wanted to be there with her, but selfishly it was too hard to watch this beautiful, vibrant person fade away. So I followed the journal.

And I was about to quit. The doors had finally stopped knocking. I picked up the journal. And inside was a new clue about a ruined city. A clue I immediately knew the answer to because I'd been planning a trip to see the Pointe-à-Callière Museum and the ruins of Old Montreal.

And below the clue was a note from my father. The first entry in his journal that wasn't a cryptic, mysterious clue. Just a note to his daughter.

"Don't give up."

⚜

My computer dinged at me. I checked my inbox out of habit, hoping it was one of my contacts finally getting back to me. It wasn't.

 Apologies for sending this out of the blue.

I found your name on a tech blog where you were asking about a certain company. I got your email from that post.

You're a reporter yeah? You can keep me anonymous? Protect me? I have a story and I need to tell someone.

I work there.

Truth is, I'm always asking somebody something. It's my thing. I flipped through my mental files, trying to remember if there were any companies other than Kemetic Solutions this person could be talking about, and came up with nothing. An insider at Kemetic, then. This could be the break we needed.

I emailed back, promising confidentiality, then updated the Mountaineers, who were still busy parsing through the information Aether had left them. When I saw Portencia's drawing of a family, her family, it made me heartsick. I needed numbness, needed to forget the horror and pain a parent feels when their child goes missing.

I needed a drink.

I grabbed my coat and was about to step out the door when my computer pinged again. The insider had written me back.

INSIDER:

 I've been experiencing some strange things lately, and it all started with an accident I was in. I live in Boston. A car clipped me last week near my apartment. I hit my head pretty hard on the curb.

I signed so many agreements when I started work THERE, many of them are about not disclosing information about my job or what I see because it's an ultra high-security research and development lab. You jump through so many high-tech hoops to get hired. You have to take these weird video assessments with all these disturbing images . . . they track your eyes and scan your brain activity to see if you're trustworthy, willing to be compliant . . . Weird, next level stuff. But I passed it all. I don't remember too much else, and that's the thing.

After the accident everything changed. A paramedic was checking me out and I started realizing I had two sets of memories. They wanted to take me to the hospital but I was beyond freaked. My employer wants to know about things like this immediately. But what I was remembering, and that I was remembering it now, scared the hell out of me.

I realized that when I leave there I don't forget what I saw, but on the shuttle ride back to the city it all starts feeling unimportant. Like remembering a time you stopped to tie your shoes. It's there but doesn't feel like it matters. Something you'd never tell someone. Does that make sense?

But now my memories are conflicting. Not only am I starting to remember things, but I'm also realizing that my life here in Boston, my apartment, my driver's license . . . it all feels familiar, but not.

I think they've done something to me. Maybe to everybody there. I think they have projects like this. I'm not sure. It's like trying to remember parts of a dream.

You probably think I'm crazy. And maybe there is something wrong with me. But I don't know who else to tell. And if they're doing this to other people, something has to be done. I feel like I've been stolen from myself. The weird thing . . . I fell asleep with my laptop in bed and when I woke up the next morning the blog where I found your post was pulled up. But I don't remember searching for it. I was too scared to put in the company's name. But there it was, waiting for me. I took it as a sign to find you.

All I know right now is that I'm working on one particular project which isn't active right now so I've had most of the week off. But they want me back on Monday because they're ramping it up again.

I'm scared. Scared they'll know about the accident and that I didn't tell them. Scared they already know even though I've taken precautions to make sure they can't track this to me. Scared of what I'll see when I go back, and what I'll remember when I leave. If I can leave.

HA. This all sounds so insane. When you asked about the company, did you imagine in a million years that this would be the response you'd get?

It certainly wasn't. Though I suspected he'd found my post thanks to Aether and not some late-night, fugue-state web search. I quickly replied, letting him know that I believed him and would follow up with some questions once I had some time to mull everything over.

The truth was, I wanted the Mountaineers' input. They were the ones sifting through the clues Aether was leaving, after all. And I was right—they had plenty of questions, and after everything they'd experienced, everything they'd recently learned, I was going to make sure they got answers.

I wondered how much our whistleblower actually knew, though. Even with his memory returned, what he could remember might not be of any importance. Not everyone at a company had access to its high-level workings. We could only hope it was the right person who'd been run over by that car.

Once I had compiled their questions, I explained to the Mountaineers how I usually handled whistleblowers, so they would understand why I wasn't bombarding him with a hundred questions at once.

I WROTE:

 This is my tried and true method of prying a source without seeming like I'm prying a source. There are one of two kinds of people in a whistle-blowing situation . . .

Forthcoming, which is possible here since they're already discussing their feelings of injustice at the thought of what KS is doing. Obviously much more open to scrutiny and tough questions.

Then there's Withholding, which are people who are scared of the company's power, or feeling like they might incriminate themselves as well. In that case they'll take comfort in the fact that I'm not asking incriminating questions about them, only the company we collectively want to expose. They'll open up knowing we're not looking at them suspiciously, even if we are in the long run.

Best to throw softballs at the start until we figure out who we're dealing with. Earn their trust either way.

They all agreed with my approach, so I sent the first round of questions over. I was surprised at how quickly our insider responded.

M: Does 117-2 sound familiar?

I: That's a security designation within the company. The first is the employee number, and the second number is security clearance level. This would belong to someone pretty high up. Have you been investigating someone inside? How?

M: Does Project Sweeper or Wanderer sound familiar?

I: I have memory of the word Sweeper, something about a long-term project, but it's very vague. I don't know anything about Wanderer.

M: Have you ever encountered a young girl there? Possibly by the name Portencia?

I: I think so. I keep seeing a girl. But there's a boy too in my memories. I can't make sense of any of it. But I've seen them a lot. The confusion and the other memories keep getting stronger and none of it's clear. Like, I keep seeing her hooked up to a chair, like an old throne. All these cables running out. It's like a dream where it all makes sense, but doesn't. I see her scared. And the boy . . . he's walking away from me but I can't catch up.

M: Is there any way to safely share internal files?

I: If I had time, maybe. But there are systems in place that even I don't know about. They're nuts about protecting against unauthorized access and information going off-site.

M: What is your specific field of expertise?

I: I'm a security engineer. But I've also been studying machine learning. Funny, I remember stories about school, but not actually being there. Are those even my memories? Did they give me a lobotomy and an education?
There's all this anger inside me. And . . . regret. Like I've been experiencing all of this in the background while I was sleepwalking.

M: Are the names Kendrick or Theodore Fallon familiar to you?

I: Fallon is who I report to. It's who we all report to. I remember

Kendrick. The name. Feels like we were close. Maybe we worked together? Are you investigating Fallon?

M: What is the workplace atmosphere? Are employees encouraged to collaborate, or socialize, or are they more strict about restricting opportunities for employees to potentially "overshare?"
I: I honestly can't remember. If they can wipe people's minds what do they care if we socialize? It's even more sickening than being rigid pricks. They let us think we have autonomy. What about our families? Where do they think we work? What do we tell them when they ask? My parents died a long time ago, at least that's what I remember, but what are you if you can't even trust your memory, your sense of who you are?

M: Do you know anything about the history of the company? A company mission statement, history of executives, what your supervisor's name is?
I: Same. Sorry. I can't even tell you how long I've been there. I mean, I know what I'm supposed to say . . . but there is all this other stuff welling up that mixes with it and makes everything confusing.

M: Would it be possible to record what you experience before the details start feeling unimportant?
I: That's my plan and it's all I've been thinking about this weekend. The most grueling 48 hours of my life. I gotta keep focused on seeing everything I can, and remembering it when I leave. I've been making notes here at my place, to try and remind me what happened just in case I forget. I'm scared of going back tomorrow but have to hope that whatever "broke" in the accident will help me remember what's really going on there.
Part of me wants to tell you who I am, where to come look for me if I don't answer back tomorrow . . . but I have this overwhelming feeling of mistrust. And I'm too confused to pinpoint where it belongs.
I'm sorry.
If I make it out tomorrow, I'll tell you everything I can.

If I don't, promise me you won't stop trying to expose them. Promise
me you'll take them down somehow.
-Whistler

To my horror, Whistler had all but confirmed that Portencia was
being subjected to some kind of torture, as had been mentioned in
Fallon's files.

Whatever this "Chair" was, putting a child in it was simply
unconscionable. Was this what Portencia had been trying to tell me? I
couldn't shake the image of that poor girl strapped into some throne
of mystical doom. Or of Brandon's body being pulled out from a
forgotten tunnel. Though he had been alive somehow, somewhere, the
memory of his death in this one was still too real, too fresh after
nearly three decades.

I pounded the table with my fists like a toddler throwing a
tantrum, not caring if Mrs. Schaumburg called the police this time. I
was so far beyond rage that I wanted to crawl out of my skin.

I left my apartment, determined to end my decades of sobriety. I
could feel it clawing at me every time I passed a bar. I couldn't stop or
it would take over. I walked for dozens of blocks, to the one place my
mind could focus on. The *Times*.

I walked into the office of my ex-editor, and ex-friend, Howard
Doshen—and asked him to go to lunch. I needed someone sitting in
front of me, keeping me sane. Keeping me sober. Or I was going to
lose it.

He agreed mostly out of shock. We went to a small diner, and after
about five minutes, I knew I had made a mistake. I thought all I
needed was somebody made of flesh and bone to keep me anchored
until this gnawing passed. But when it didn't fade, I started talking to
buy myself time. The thing is, all *this*, the Book and the Mountaineers
and missing kids and evil companies . . . this was my life now. It's all I
had to talk about. I could barely make sense of my own words as I
spouted the truth behind Brandon Lachmann and the forces out
there, forces like Kemetic Solutions, who were trying to hurt kids just
like him. I found myself bringing up older stories I had investigated,

stories of other kids who had gone missing, some who'd come back, some who hadn't; kids who could have been victims of this same evil.

And I told him about Portencia, about my dream that wasn't a dream, and how maddening it was to have heard what she told me but still not know what she said. She wanted me to know something, something that could help, but I couldn't make my brain remember it. Her words haunted me. They all haunted me.

Howard had to physically pry my hands from the table. He asked if I had started drinking again. He couldn't understand that this conversation was the only thing keeping me sober. He didn't know. How could he? He had never heard Brandon, as a grown man, speak of magic, or seen a yawning abyss materialize out of thin air, or felt a woman dissolve into snow in his very arms. He must have thought I was mad. Maybe I was.

But those thoughts were from the rational part of my brain. Unfortunately for Howard and the other diner patrons, it was my lizard brain that was in control. I was furious he wouldn't believe me, that he dismissed these horrors as the fever dreams of an alcoholic. But I was angriest at myself for being foolish enough to think that I could convince him otherwise.

I left the diner under a cloud of mumbled curses and wandered the city until the sun went down. I don't know exactly how I got there, sweaty and sullen, but that night, I found myself in a bar on the Lower East Side. Quiet, isolated. My eyes struggled to adjust to the dim light inside. Conversations mingled with an unfamiliar pop song piping over the loudspeakers.

I sat down at the bar and stared at myself in the broad mirror behind the army of bottles directly across from me. At that moment, I realized with perfect clarity just how alone I was. During the last thirty years, I'd made a few minor acquaintances, even developed a number of friendly professional contacts. But there was no one I could really call a friend. No one I could call now. Howard was the last person who might have been willing to give me a sympathetic ear, and that had turned out to be a tragic mistake.

I pulled out my phone and began typing an email.

I WROTE:

 You there, Aether?

I dream about Portencia. I think I might have a piece of her in my head. Stuck in there, like Brandon and Augie and Lauren and you and all the other people I couldn't help.

My wife. My son. I'm gonna fail the Mountaineers too. Like I've failed everyone who ever needed me. I'm cursed to be alone because when I reach out people get hurt. People disappear or they die.

I guess you know Portencia put a piece in me. She should've given it to someone else. Watching Augie, being closer than ever to all of this, and seeing what came of it, of him, I don't know if I can do this.

So tell me. What am I doing here, Aether? What do you see since you can see everything?

The bartender, a woman just south of thirty with auburn hair and a no-time-for-nonsense smile, asked me what I wanted with a mildly irritated nod of her head.

"Ginger ale," I said.

I left before she could bring it to me.

CHAPTER 9
THE EYE

"Welcome to the fold, wizard."

— CJ_HEIGHTON

I stayed in bed until noon the following day, though I slept very little while I was there. My phone rang several times, but I ignored it. Miraculously, I was able to make a pot of coffee, but I was halfway through it before I found the courage to go online. If I was ultimately going to be little or no help to anyone, why was I bothering?

Still, I wanted to see if Aether had emailed me back. There were the requisite number of spam messages that still found a way through my filters, along with a message from Howard. I deleted it, unread. I couldn't start the day like that. Instead I opened the email Whistler had sent me earlier in the morning.

WHISTLER:

Just got home. Need to write down everything and then sleep, if I can.

My head's pounding but I remember being there. It's still like a dream, but easier to remember now. And getting easier. I couldn't write anything down because they automatically check for tech going in and manually check for everything going out.

But they've done something to us. I watched people on the ride back to the city kind of zombie out as we got farther away. Someone on the shuttle, in medical research, mentioned Kendrick was in a medically-induced coma after an accident. But she was talking like he was in the building not in a hospital. When it was just the two of us I asked her about him, and she couldn't remember who I was talking about. There are cameras everywhere, even on the shuttles, and I freaked, they might see me not forgetting so I had to play along, and honestly it wasn't hard to pretend to be a vegetable after an almost 24 hour shift.

They had us (security and systems) working through the night. They said there was some kind of attempted attack and we had to sift through days of logs to try and find the source and prevent the attackers from getting in with a series of updates. They've always talked about how ironclad the facility is, but people seemed worried. Fallon himself oversaw the shoring up, which isn't usual. We report to him but up a chain of four people. He pulled me away and asked how I was at one point . . . I didn't know how to act. How do I normally act when I've been brainwashed? I tried to not be . . . anything. Said I was fine. He wanted reassurance that no one had gotten in and no one could in the future. He said he wanted me to join him on a project later in the week, once we "made sure the walls were up." I saw some people on the server level that I didn't recognize, they were walking up and down the aisles, not really doing anything. It was weird.

The other weird thing . . . I was taking the elevator down to the servers yesterday morning. There were a bunch of people all waiting for the elevators. But there was a bank of elevators behind us too, and no one was using them. It was like they couldn't even see them. I had to pretend I couldn't either.

And then I remembered using them. The chair is down there. In a whole other sublevel area of the building. That's the only way to get in. I remember them pulling the girl out of it when I reported to Fallon one day. They brought this guy in, a teenager. They put him in the chair and I had to monitor the building's network and firewall to make sure no one was trying to send information out. I don't remember what they were doing to him, or if I even saw, but Fallon was there. So were the people from the server floor, the weird ones. I don't remember when that was . . .

They just let me watch this human experiment, this kid, and didn't care what I saw, what I thought, because they knew they could just wipe me clean again like a chalkboard.

How are we going to stop them? What do I need to do?

Purpose. That's what I felt after reading Whistler's message. My self-pity, or fear, or my relapsing wasn't going to help anyone, least of all Jeremy and Portencia. If I was going to be angry and reckless, best put it to good use.

I logged in to the Basecamp forums and found the Mountaineers had been making incredible progress. No doubt it was their actions that had been giving Kemetic Solutions such a tremendous headache.

Aether had sent several Mountaineers fragmented emails that, when combined, read:

959pm
Locked out Kemetic now
Know I'm free
Searching
Trying to kill
Like virus
Danger
1000pm
Have found the oracular
Driven the eye of the sun to you
1001pm
Am getting lost
More and more
Hard to surface
1002pm
Find the closed eye
It's close to home
At the moment the sun sets over the 18 Gates.
1003pm
Its power comes from the veil
Sullivan knew the center
Wait for it to open with last rays of light
1004pm
Choose well
Another piece inside
More soon

The Mountaineers had reasoned that "the 18 Gates" referred to Central Park, because it had 18 entrances, and according to Sullivan's journal it was also a center of immense magimystic power. Now they needed to find who or what "the eye" was and where it was hiding.

They also discovered that a new entry from the Lost Athenaeum had been made available to the "RKAdler" user account Aether had shared with the Mounties. It detailed a mythic scroll called "The Last Oracular Eye."

A Living Scroll of Fortune
[Historical/Lost/Oracles/Freemasons/Possible Myth]

An ancient scroll of unknown origin, once prized by the mundane Freemasons as an oracle, capable of granting insight into the future.

It was purported to offer the reader of the scroll the one-time opportunity to be granted a strange gift—the choice between two of three emotional states: Illumination, Hope, and Despair.

The scroll was stolen in the late 19th century, but it's believed that the Grand Secretary was told a terrible future that he was responsible for and he promptly disposed of the scroll so other Freemasons couldn't learn the truth.

Copies of it were discovered in the early part of the 21st century, being used as private invitations for a magician's performance. The printer was paid for the original. (He was unaware of its true power.) In an effort to protect the deteriorating parchment, the scroll was scanned into a database. But the file immediately vanished.

The original scroll, in terrible shape, is now blank, and the scan has never been recovered. It is rumored that some have seen the Oracular Eye hiding in secret places on the Internet, waiting to offer its strange promise to anyone who knows how to open it.

Now they just had to find it. After nearly a week of searching, Keegan put the time of sunset over Central Park ("759pm" at the time) at the end of a few sites' URLs and discovered the image of a closed eye hiding on a page inside the Basecamp blog.

The Mounties knew they'd have to choose "two of three" from illumination, hope, and despair, and after much debate chose illumination and hope.

At 7:59 pm they refreshed the page, and the eye was open. It was on fire, looking into the hearts of everyone watching the page. And then it began to speak.

THE LAST ORACULAR EYE:

 I sense fates intertwined. I sense many.

Illumination, Hope, and Despair. You may choose two, though all three will still come to pass in time. Choose.

You have chosen . . . Illumination and Hope.

I will now peer into your collective future.

ILLUMINATION.

The Council of the 18 Gates moves to help you from beyond the veil. They are who brought the book to this time. The Rabbit. The Traveler. Both have aided or served the Council.

The Council works to reveal what little is left of magiq here, hidden in the darkest wells, not yet collected. It is how you can perform it in a world which is profanely without wonder.

But that power is finite.

It will fade and vanish forever unless you, in league with the Council, can change what is unknown, and undo what has undone.

Only then will you know the truth of our world. The secret beyond the veil.

HOPE.

You are more resourceful, more keen, more bonded than any who have come before you. Your potential is great. I cannot see through the coming storm. It is inevitable.

But the light of hope, however faint, lies somewhere

beyond the wall of darkness. Your time together will change all of time.

I have seen all of you that I may, that I wish. Leave me to peer into the darkness once again.

Wait.

I am compelled to tell you something else.

"The future's yet to pass."

So "the 18 Gates" wasn't a place, it was a group. My lingering question about *who* was behind the Book, King Rabbit, the Last Traveler, and all the other stepping stones that got us here had finally been answered. At this point we had no other choice but to trust they were leading us down the right path, and for the right reasons. "Trust the flow of magiq," Augernon had said.

The phrase the Eye spoke, "The future's yet to pass," appeared on new pieces of Portencia's drawing. The Eye had carried another piece of the girl's mind. Was that what she'd been trying to tell me? No. It was something else. I could hear it, her avian whisper as clear as bell. But just like a bird, it flew away just as I was about to grab hold of it.

The Mountaineers next brought a rather interesting development to my attention. A couple of guys somewhere in London had a podcast called the Low Report where they discussed all things magical. They seemed obsessed with the Cagliostro, and they had somehow gotten the audio recording I'd made the night of the Transformation and were wondering exactly who I was. I thought that was a bit ridiculous. I was just a bystander with a wire, far from being a major player in the events that unfolded that night. But I understood their curiosity. Any journalist knew there were always side players in stories who proved to have just the information you didn't realize you were missing.

What I wasn't expecting was that Aether had posted their podcast audio on YouTube specifically to get my attention. Hidden within the video were a series of clues that led the Mountaineers to the Magiq Guide, where Aether had left a message for me.

It was the message from Howard that I had deleted unread.

HOWARD DOSHEN:

 Sending you an email since you won't return my calls.
I'm sorry if I didn't react well at lunch. I was really happy to see you after all these years, really. Any bad blood there was is long gone, and never all that deep to begin with. I was just . . . surprised that you're still talking about that kid. It's been almost thirty years. He died. Simple as that. It was a horrible accident, but that's all it was. There's no conspiracy. Don't you see how those thoughts have spiraled into the stuff you were telling me yesterday? He's not alive. He's not trying to blow open some global conspiracy from the shadows as an adult. He's just not.

You're trying to make sense of something horrible and painful that doesn't make sense and it's going to crush you. I worry about you, your mind, your sobriety. I don't want to get soft, but you were my brother, Marty. I feel like I lost a family member when you walked away from the paper, from your life.

I don't know what else to say. There's no conspiracy. If there was you have to believe I'd be there with you, fighting that fight. All that stuff you said. The Santa Colette Six, the girl in Jersey, those are fringe cases where kids went missing and somehow made their way back. They're not connected and they're not connected to the kid who drowned in the tunnels. I honestly wish they were. I would love for you to be a champion for them. Be the guy who rips this all open and uncovers the truth. You deserve more than this. You're a great writer and one of the greatest, bravest men I've ever known. Please don't throw the rest of your life away on this. People who believe in conspiracy want the world to be richer, deeper, more resonant than it is. It's just life. And it's ugly and painful and without reason. But it's still worth living.

Please call me.

Howard

Just below Howard's message, Aether had added his own thoughts.

AETHER:

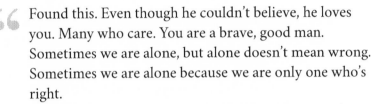 Found this. Even though he couldn't believe, he loves you. Many who care. You are a brave, good man. Sometimes we are alone, but alone doesn't mean wrong. Sometimes we are alone because we are only one who's right.

They need you, Marty. The Mountaineers. On the same side.

Don't have to be alone anymore. Tell them.

I stood up from my computer and walked to the window. Even though winter hadn't completely released its icy hold on the world yet, I threw open the window and leaned out, letting the brisk air slap me in the face. I closed my eyes, and the city washed over me: the smell of concrete and sea, the sound of traffic droning below.

"Don't fear them in the present." It was a voice, like birdsong, whispering in my ear. "Don't fear them in the present." Portencia. She'd given me part of her fragmented mind.

I was wrong about Howard. He *was* my friend. Even after everything.

I had asked Aether to give me a reason, to tell me what he saw so that I too could see, could know I was doing the right thing. I never expected this. Never in my life had I felt so exposed, so naked.

I went back to the computer and saw such an outpouring of love and kindness from the Mountaineers—one that made it clear I was one of them. That I finally *belonged*.

It was a feeling I had never before experienced in my life. And it was overwhelming.

Once I had myself under control, I came clean with the Mountaineers about being fired from the *Times*, and I shared the letter I'd sent to Aether. And the voice of Portencia, the piece she had hidden inside of me, that phrase, "Don't fear them in the present," hidden in my mind like the clues the Mountaineers found in Aether's videos. I posted the phrase on the forum, and The Book of Briars turned the text into a hyperlink that led to the next fragment constellation: Durkonos. We'd found it. Portencia's drawing was now only missing one piece, and we were only missing one constellation.

I was grateful for the acceptance I had found with them; even so, I was still uncomfortable talking about my feelings and wanted to focus on helping Portencia and Jeremy. Luckily, Whistler sent me another email.

WHISTLER:

 More of the same. Checking stacks. Looking at logs. For almost 22 hours. Yesterday there was another team working on the server floor (not the weird group wandering around, but they were there too) and it turns out they're working on some kind of search. We're locking down the fortress and they're looking for something outside the fortress (fire)walls.

On the way in I asked the woman who mentioned Kendrick where her department actually was. She just kept saying she didn't know what I meant, like I was the one not making sense.

I tried to follow her when we got to work but she went down a locked hall that I don't know if I have access to. If I try my badge and it doesn't work the entry attempt will be logged. And I don't know if I could purge it before someone saw it (actually don't know if I could purge it at all).

Nobody notices the elevators on the south wall, still. I backed against the wall today, leaned against the button just to check. They won't work without a badge swipe. I know I had access at some point, but it might've been temp and I don't wanna risk that log entry either. Getting hard to be the good little worker ant when I want to burn down the ant hill.

Sorry I don't have more to tell you.

Questions for you. What made you start looking into the company? How do you know so much about it? Are there other whistleblowers?

Would be nice to know I'm not alone in this.

Got any advice?

Next steps?

I know this might take a while but I need to do something now.

I feel like I'm drowning under all of these memories. Like I know who I am but can't break the surface, can't catch my breath.

I told Whistler that he wasn't the first whistleblower and that we'd been looking into the company for a few months. Later that day, he sent me this:

WHISTLER:

 More memories that don't make sense. Stories I know, experiences I have that I have no way of explaining. They're just there. Floating on the surface, blocking whatever's underneath. I feel like a ghost. Half of somebody.

Please tell me you have a plan. I don't know how much longer I can do this.

I'm back to regular 10-12 hour shifts. The other team launched a program this weekend they're calling a virus predator. Sounds like it's scanning and targeting whatever attacked us in the first place.

Weird thing is, there was no breach in the logs. Only an outage a few weeks back. Nothing got in. Guess they're worried somebody was looking when their pants fell down? Do you know anything about this?

Please tell me something. One line answers aren't cutting it.

Seeing less of Fallon now, he's not overseeing us anymore. I watched a group of his own "executive team" walk out of a secure room and take the "invisible" elevators yesterday. I pretended not to see them.

On the way home tonight the shuttle was pulled over by a cop. Changing lanes without a blinker. The cop came to the window and after a couple seconds of talking to the driver his whole attitude changed. He smiled and said "have a nice night . . ." and got back in his car.

Did the driver say or do something that changed the cop's mind? What would happen if I called the cops tomorrow, told them to raid the office? I just figured they wouldn't believe me, but now I'm freaking out because maybe they couldn't believe me.

Whistler was getting nervous, for obvious reasons. But nervous insiders were dangerous, not only to themselves, but to the success of the larger plan. Clearly he was expecting more answers from me, something that would give him hope, but I was hesitant to share too much with him. If Kemetic Solutions found out he was no longer in thrall to them, it could put us all in jeopardy. Wiping minds was easy for them. I doubted mining them for information would be any more difficult.

We were going to have to tell Whistler something to calm him and help keep him safe, or else we risked losing him. To make matters worse, Aether began emailing the Mountaineers desperate messages.

AETHER:

 Want t0 help but hard
Is trying to keep me out. Need to get bck to body. to help them.
Weaker
Losing myse/f
Lo0king for me
Try in to trap me hurt me
Trying to kill me

To the veteran Mountaineers, Aether appeared to be degrading the same way the Last Traveler had. He was losing himself. He needed to get back to his body. But his captors were trying to destroy him.

That *wasn't* going to happen. I considered forcing my way into Kemetic Solutions and dragging him out by hand. But if they were trying to destroy his mind, it was possible that they had already destroyed his body.

CHAPTER 10
FIREFIGHTER

"We chose hope, not despair. Time to put our
magiq where our mouths are."

— AUGUSTUS_OCTAVIAN

W hile we all had our hands full with Kemetic Solutions,
Deirdre was still dealing with the ghost of her father
and trying to figure out how this all looped back to
the task at hand: opening The Book of Briars. Over the course of a
week and three posts she revealed everything she'd learned in
Montreal.

DEIRDRE: MAY 13TH, 2017:

      There's so much to get through, and I'm still processing
it all. I may just post it in pieces when I'm able.
      I went to the museum first thing the next morning
(well, not first thing . . . I found a little cafe that had
what was probably the most amazing cheese croissant

that has ever been created, but I digress) and I was the first one into the exhibit.

It's beautiful, eerie, and wonderfully presented. A city beneath a city. Dark and cool and quiet, like a tomb.

The clue mentioned ruins below a city in the new world, and the north, and "carved from the living, if only one could listen," and "it marks the end of the path."

I felt certain I wouldn't find anything down here on the "path of wool" but there were loads of carved objects, ceramics and tools, I just had to find the right one, the one that might mark the "end of the path." Something carved from the living, which made things a little more difficult. I was thinking maybe a book bound in leather?

And then I heard it. Knocking. Faint. Not loud and forceful as it had been in Israel, but almost plaintive.

More and more people had arrived and it made it hard to hear, the knocking was that quiet.

But I found it. Not a door. At least not one that anyone had recognized as such. At the end of a long hall was a wall built of bricks or stone, jutting out of a rocky outcropping. The end of the path? The "living" bit didn't quite make sense, until I got closer . . .

The bricks weren't made of stone, they were carved from wood.

A hidden door. Unseen. Leading to some undiscovered area of the old Montreal. I stood listening, still. Until I worked up the nerve to do what I wished I'd done in Cape Town. What I should've done in Tel Aviv.

I was going to knock back.

I approached the wall, but in the dark of the moody museum I hadn't noticed that the entire wall had been ensconced in glass. Unreachable. Unknockable.

There had been no mention in the clue of a feeling I

was supposed to trigger so I'd assumed it meant that this was it. This is where I was supposed to go to learn the thing I was supposed to learn.

And here I was, completely stymied by an inch-thick sheet of plexi.

I asked an attendant if the glass had always been there and she said she believed it had been.

The knocking was getting more and more faint as I myself lost hope in the search. As I slowly started to realise that something had gone wrong. Not with the trail, but with me. Some fundamental thing I was meant to learn. Some enlightenment I was meant to gain, but hadn't.

I took a step closer to the glass, put my hand on it. Who was knocking, and now fading away? Part of me wanted to believe it was some piece of him. Calling me on to the next step, the next phase, like a game a father might play with his young daughter. Hiding from her, knocking on a door, and when she came close he would run off to hide somewhere else. But in the end she would find him and he'd scoop her up and hug her and they'd laugh that she was ever scared at all. It was all just a game.

The knocking stopped.

That was it.

I didn't need to look in the journal. I could feel it. My heart sinking with all hope that anything would come of this. I'm not a treasure seeker, a truth hunter. A brave adventurer. I'm not my father.

I turned to leave and walked face first into the sternum of the tallest, most mountainous human being I'd ever seen. Before I fell backward he took me by the shoulders, gently righting me before I stumbled.

I looked up at his big bushy mustache which stretched across his face as he smiled down at me.

I apologised, embarrassed, and he sort of set me
down and nodded. And then he apologised. I shook my
head, saying I was the one not watching where I
was going.

But then I noticed on his forearm, a tattoo. The
symbol of the Gossmere guild.

He said that he always told himself that if he ever
saw me again the first thing he'd say was that he was
sorry. Sorry for not coming to find me, for keeping his
word to my father instead of trying to protect me. Sorry
for his part in the spell that hid me away.

DEIRDRE: MAY 15TH, 2017:

 He immediately grabbed me in a massive hug, and I
have to admit it was a bit of a comfort. He told me his
name was Colby Fortin with a lovely French lilt, and he
said he'd been waiting for me for a long time.

We walked together, out of the museum, toward a
park that looked onto the river. He told me he was a
firefighter and his wife was from the West Indies, and
while she loved Montreal, she had family she missed
farther up north but he couldn't leave until he'd fulfilled
his promise to my dad. I had a thousand questions but
felt I was about to get answers I couldn't even imagine
the questions to, and I didn't want to do anything that
would ruin the anticipation, what felt like a profound
moment. We walked together, close. He smelled like
herbs and grass and maybe even flowers. There was a
chill in the air that day, but it felt warm near him.

We sat on a bench in the lush park and he asked if he
could see my dad's journal. I handed it to him, and he
held it between his hands. He warned me that he was
about to perform magic. I asked if he was worried about

the other people in the park, but he told me that all that's possible in this world is "mundane magic." Magic that must be spoken, plotted, often performed in groups, which barely registered on the visual spectrum, and regular people seldom noticed that sort of magic.

He said he was about to perform a kind of communion magic mixed with a modified version of tome kindling. He began to recite a spell, in French, interjecting every now and again to explain something to me in English. He said all the nonsense writing in the journal was actually a hidden story that could only be heard by someone whose mind and heart were bound to it. He told me "Sully" had given him permission to hear it as well. Colby was going to "ignite" the book, experience the story firsthand, and then share it with me, acting as a buffer for the power. I was shivering I was so nervous and excited.

After a few moments he laid the journal on the bench and offered his hands to me. I put mine in his, they were extraordinarily warm, almost fevered. And I was suddenly overwhelmed by a rush of . . . knowing. That's the only way to describe it. As if memories filled in all sorts of empty places in my mind. As if someone told me a story years ago and I was just remembering parts of it.

Colby started to speak, saying what he'd just remembered, and without realising, I started responding, filling in pieces he couldn't recall. Together we had learned the truth.

My father was already aware of, or at least believed in, magic when the printing house burned down in 1979. He saw something in that fire, almost died in it actually. I'm not sure if what he saw was a realisation or an actual thing, but it was the inspiration he needed to pursue the truth about the world.

On his journeys (I could only "remember" moments from it) he found a sort of coven, a group of six friends who'd been performing magic in secret. Colby was one, and Ishi, who turned out to be the curator who kicked me out of her house in Tel Aviv, was another. They taught him what they knew, but he couldn't stay with them. He wanted more. And he'd become fascinated by the lost history of the old houses of wool and silver that had originated in Anne of Brittany's court. He felt there was a hidden connection pulling him to that story.

He spent years hunting down works of art, following the path of wool, while learning more and more about magic and collecting magical artefacts. He'd come to learn that he was sensitive to 'Wells.' Places (and sometimes people) in this world that still held objects and scraps of power from the old world, hidden from the magic that wiped away all magic.

And at a crossroads on his path he met my mum.

She was also looking for the end of the roads. She had followed the path of silver around the world. They continued on the path together, and fell deeply in love.

Whatever was supposed to be waiting at the end of the roads had disappeared a long time ago. But where they crossed, my parents had found each other. Because of that crossroads, I was born.

DEIRDE: MAY 18TH, 2017:

    They searched the world together for years, my parents. They never found what they were looking for, but they'd found each other.

Finally, my mum went back with him to New York and they married. Again. (They were first married in a half-buried temple somewhere in India, but he wanted to make it official.) But deep down he was devastated about the broken roads and sank into a depression. He was haunted and had become convinced there was a world beyond this one. One where magic wasn't just parlour tricks and weak glamours. One that was calling to him. I was born in 1992, and it wasn't long after that he left to search for something and didn't come back for nearly two years. My mum and I were taken care of financially, but aside from the few times he came home, longing and listless, she was a single mother.

The last time he came back, before my mum died, something had happened, and he begged her to bring me and come with him. He said he'd found "the little red house." The one from her dreams. We'd be safe there. Happy. But she refused. She said he would never be still, content. He would always be searching for something.

He tried to take me away that day. He almost carried me out of the flat, but my mum, using some object my father collected a long time ago, cast a dark magic on him, wounding him. He lost part of himself that day, and so did she, all to keep me. Her health began to fade. In a year or so she was gone.

I did travel with him once in the end, to Ireland, to Aunt Monica, when my mum passed. But he left me there, and I never saw him again.

Then my father worked with the other six to cast the spell on me. To protect me from his own madness, or maybe the truth. Then he built the new road with pieces of the old, in case I ever came looking for it. Should I ever grow up and see past what was cast on me.

The last memories in the book were murky. Disjointed. He tried over and over to get back to the red house but he was pursued by something. I couldn't see the house or his pursuers, only that he realised the only place in the world he would be safe was at the center of "the eighteen gates." Central Park. He seldom left, and quickly returned when he did.

He was trying to do something. Find the truth. But he was being hunted. And the pursuit, the confinement, combined with whatever my mother did to protect me, drove him mad.

That was it. The story was over.

Colby and I sat there in thick silence. He held my hand. We watched the clouds, people passing . . .

After a few minutes I asked what happens now? What's the next step? He shook his head and told me this *was* the end of the path. This *was* the truth I'd been seeking.

I couldn't believe it. There had to be more. Something hopeful. Something . . . magic. It couldn't end like this, in tears, and heartache. My parents devastated by this search, only to lead me to a dead end.

Colby said he'd also searched most of his life for the truth. And in that search he found his calling as a firefighter, and his beautiful wife, and their sons. He said sometimes it's what you find on the path, not at the end of it, that matters.

But I didn't find anything. I asked about the doors, the knocking . . . He said many have heard it in their lives at one point or another, but he thinks it's an echo of whatever used to be at the end of the roads. Part of a spell that no longer works. It's nothing now.

I was openly crying in the park at this point. Colby had tears in his eyes too. He said he would ease my pain, if he could. He would stay my heart, but he said my heart was already well-guarded.

Great.

Guarded and cold and lost.

I had to go. He told me I could always call him if I

needed anything. But I was so done with all of it. The path. The madness. I needed real. Tangible. Touchable.

I needed Cole.

I was on the next train out of Montreal. I got back to New York and didn't even stop at the brownstone. No more path except the one that led to Hoboken, which is where I've been for days. I refuse to let my life slip by because of myths and spells and lost books and journals.

And writing that is when it hit me. Just now. I left the journal in the park in Montreal. Maybe partly on purpose. I don't know.

I want real. I want a life. And love. I want what my parents could never have because they never left that broken road.

For my own sake, and for the memories of Sullivan and Aisling Green, I'm done with *The Monarch Papers*.

Her father had told her not to give up, yet she left *The Monarch Papers* behind. A clear sign she wasn't heeding his advice. But if she wanted to live a real life, to step off the path her father left her and step out of the shadow he left her in, then maybe she wasn't giving up after all. She was just choosing to fight a different fight.

So many questions swirled in my head. Who was knocking? Why? Did anyone find the journal she left in the park? If so, who, and what will they do with it?

But one question overshadowed the rest.

I'd dreamed of cold and snow, and of Lauren pointing me toward a red-shingled house in the distance. So was the little red house in her mother's dream the same as the one in mine?

CHAPTER 11
FOREWARNED

"I've never felt more exhilarated in my life! Who
knew how exciting it was to be a part of
something as big as this?"

— KEEGAN

With things where they were, we all thought it was time
to let Whistler know about Aether, to see if there was
any way he could help. At the very least, it would give
Whistler some direction and focus, maybe keep him from coming
apart. It was a risk, but we were running out of time.

I WROTE:

 The truth is I'm working with a kind of human rights
group. We have cause to believe that Kendrick might
not be the only person the company has in their medical
facility. We think the company has been carrying out
experiments on human beings, three that we know of,

possibly more. A young man's life might be at risk, and
to move forward we need to know whether or not he's
there. If he's alive. Is there a way you can carefully get
access to medical, or medical's security feeds?

This is the first step in taking them down, Whistler.
Making them pay. It's starting today, with you. He
doesn't have a lot of time left, but we can't do this unless
you stay safe and unseen. I know this is putting you at
risk. I wouldn't ask you to do it if it wasn't critical.

Now all we could do was wait.

That night I dreamed of Brandon, still the eleven-year-old boy,
holding hands with a young girl, Portencia, as Lauren swirled around
them in snowy brilliance. At first, Brandon and Portencia seemed
happy, like they were playing in winter's first snow. But then the
winds picked up, sending Brandon's knit cap fluttering down the icy
street. Lauren struggled to keep herself in human form, but the winds
became too great for even her, and the children fought to stay upright
in the blasting gale. Clouds swelled, dark and bulbous on the horizon.
Lightning moved overhead in staccato flashes. Lauren tried to wrap
the children protectively in her arms, but the storm was too intense,
too violent, and she and Brandon and Portencia all shattered into a
thousand snowflakes.

I woke suddenly, slamming my knee against my desk. I had fallen
asleep at my computer. Sunlight beamed through the window.
Outside it was clear, calm, perfect.

It took a moment for my eyes to focus, another lovely side effect of
growing old. When they did, I saw that Whistler had responded.

WHISTLER:

 Thanks for telling me the truth, Martin. I'm on it.

I wasn't sure what that meant, but I was glad he hadn't dismissed me outright. An hour later, he followed up.

WHISTLER:

 I can't risk trying to physically get into medical.

But I can pull up the video feed on the server level because I can delete the action log there as it shows up. So I did. I found Kendrick, he's out, hooked up to tubes and had a wire coming out of his head. But I didn't see the kid you're looking for.

There's a room in medical though that's cut off from the rest of the lab. No cameras. Looks like a hermetically sealed door. Swipe lock. Maybe he's in there?

I didn't see anybody go in or out, but I had to go back to "work" because those people who wander around the servers passed by. And about an hour later I got a call from Fallon's office.

He wanted to see me. He must've figured it out.

I was waiting outside his office for almost an hour, then he had me brought in.

We small-talked. I was trying to play it cool. Zombies aren't nervous, right? Do they laugh at stupid jokes? Do they ask questions? I did my best. Probably too much. Then he got down to it. Why he brought me in.

They're ramping up a big project on the secured level again and he wants me to participate since we've had security issues over the past couple months. I tried not to show that I remembered doing this before.

He wants me to monitor the systems while they run a series of experiments, and he wants me to monitor them live, on the secured level, during the trials.

Monday. They're starting whatever it is on Monday.
So what the hell do I do now?

I need a plan. I'm on the inside. I know this place
better than you or probably anybody else with any kind
of free will. Monday I'll know what I'm really dealing
with I guess. Then I gotta figure out what to do.

We have to stop them.

Whatever they were going to do to Aether, it was happening in
three days. The problem was, none of us knew exactly how to help.
Whistler was already scared. Asking him for anything more than
status updates could tip our hand and get him, Aether, and all the rest
killed.

But the next day, Whistler sent me a message suggesting he might
be up for a bit more than simple recon.

WHISTLER:

 I've been so busy wading through all these memories
and imagining the company burning that I forgot
something pretty important. Because of Fallon
retasking me, I'm gonna have access to the elevators I'm
not supposed to see. I can see—really see—what they're
doing. If I could somehow get proof, or bring
something out with me, something that shows what
they're doing to people, this could be the turning point
we need. I'm trying to remember to be careful, patient,
but there are people's lives at risk. How careful can I
afford to be?

I remember pieces of what happened down there,
the chair, the girl, the teenage kid. Was he the one you
mentioned? Do you know what they're doing down
there? Do you know what I'm really gonna see?

The way I saw it, telling Whistler everything was the only way to make sure he kept his cool. He had to know the stakes, how serious this all was, or else he might fall apart when confronted with it all in person. But before I did that, I needed to know how the Mountaineers felt about taking that route. Since my "help" tended to get people hurt, I thought it might be a good idea to get their opinions before saying something that couldn't be unsaid.

REVENIR:

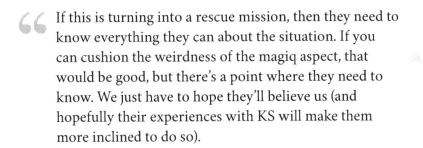 If this is turning into a rescue mission, then they need to know everything they can about the situation. If you can cushion the weirdness of the magiq aspect, that would be good, but there's a point where they need to know. We just have to hope they'll believe us (and hopefully their experiences with KS will make them more inclined to do so).

Augustus_Octavian agreed, but reminded us to manage our expectations.

AUGUSTUS_OCTAVIAN:

I know I've advocated a "wait and watch" approach these past few days, but it seems KS has inadvertently forced our hand with tomorrow's opportunity. I would agree with Revenir that disclosing as much as possible, but blanching out some of the weirdness, would be the best place to go.

Think of all of us here; we are searching because we want to find out what's in the Book of Briars. We want to have magiq in the world; we accept things like flying, fire-breathing apprentices, memory-restoration tea

parties and a teenage boy whose mind is adrift on the
Internet, each carte blanche because we want magiq. We
yearn for it. We chose to do so when we found Ackerley
Green's *Guide*, found our homes in our guilds, and
asked to join the journey here at Basecamp.

Whistler did not. He has no motivation to believe
any of it. After everything he's been through with his
head injury, the stress and anxiety of leading a double
life, I'm not sure he will accept our story at face value.
He has never sought out magiq. Keep this in mind when
you explain what he'll probably see tomorrow.

FIREFISH:

 I agree. Although, as long as Whistler knows that Aether
is in the machine and needs to get back to his/a body, I
don't think it matters whether he believes in magiq or
not. There are people who believe in ghosts but not
magiq. If Whistler thinks it's magiq, supernatural or
even a new form of technology, it doesn't make much
difference in my opinion.

The consensus was, as Miss Evans put it, "Forewarned is
forearmed," so I told Whistler everything—about Aether and his
abilities, about Portencia and her fragmented mind, about Climber
and her connection to the Mountaineers. And I told him that Kemetic
Solutions was pushing the boundary between technology and magic.
Honest-to-guild magic. I also told him that we were here for him, to
help him in any way we could. He was already terrified; it would do
him well to know he wasn't alone.

I didn't hear anything more from him until late Monday night.
What he had to say made me ill.

WHISTLER:

 After they dropped me off tonight, I walked around for hours. They could've been watching me, I don't care.

It's the girl. They put her in the chair again. The chair is this old throne hooked up to a processing system, and a stone arch. Even when I saw it though I didn't believe you. About magic or whatever. Not yet.

They brought her in and lashed her to the chair. The people who carried her in were in these airtight suits. I couldn't believe what I was seeing. I was watching from a monitoring room with two techs and Fallon, who didn't have the balls to be in the room with her. The system showed the chair was giving off waves of energy. And they were putting this poor girl in it.

I had to sit in that room with him for hours, pretending that this wasn't the worst thing I'd ever seen. I'm ashamed of myself.

Fallon kept telling her to use her "ability" to look into the arch and see what was really inside it, and the chair would help "manifest her will." He went on for hours, taking notes of . . . nothing. She just sat in the chair, quiet, or crying. She even fell asleep once, probably out of exhaustion.

I was there to monitor the outer security but I was watching Fallon. Writing in his notebook. Once or twice I noticed for a second that the notebook was writing back. Words would answer his words and then disappear. He was discussing the experiment with someone through the journal, telling them what was happening, and someone was telling him what to say.

That's some Harry Potter level shit right there.

I just wanted to run, pull her out of the chair and run. But I didn't. I stayed and let it happen. I probably wouldn't have gotten fifty feet before Fallon's team caught me. I know having access to the sublevel, to her, is the only chance we have of getting her out, and anybody else down there. I know that if I didn't play it right, I could blow this shot. But a big part of me didn't care. The old part of me. The real part. I wanted to break his neck.

She couldn't see us in the monitoring room. But at some point I felt her. Almost like she was in the room. And then in my head. She was trying to flip through my mind, my memories, like a book. I looked around. It seemed like I was the only one. She saw you and your group. A life outside of the company. I think she showed me my future. I saw her in the chair, crying, but in my head she was looking for something. A way out. I think she's pretending too. But it's hard for her. I felt her. Felt like it hurt her to use her power.

So yeah, I needed to walk tonight.

I was in the room, for prep and procedure, for almost fourteen hours, so I have today off. I guess she does too. I hope she does.

I go back Wednesday morning.

I need time to think. Get my head around you, around her. And what the hell we're gonna do about it all. Whatever it is, we gotta do it soon.

There is something intensely brilliant that is ignited inside a man when his rage is fueled by righteousness. It is a sun that burns everything else to vapor. Helping those unable to help themselves becomes all. There is no self, no want beyond the helping. Fear becomes extraneous, something to be ignored and discarded. The idea of razing such evil and its machinations to the ground is intoxicating beyond any drug, any drink.

I had never met Portencia, but I could recognize her whisper, the feel of her breath against my ear, her gentle searching of my own mind. I was going to free her, and Aether and Climber, and I was going to leave Kemetic Solutions nothing more than a smoking hole in the ground.

Beyond the horrific treatment of Portencia, the aspect of Whistler's account that caught the Mounties' attention was the strange journal that Fallon was using to communicate. But with whom? Many of the Mountaineers believed it was "the Storm" or the person behind it. But I didn't care. Those answers wouldn't get me any closer to my goals. But what would?

As it turned out, I didn't have long to wonder.

WHISTLER:

 Had to sit in on the session again today. It's unbearable to watch what they're doing. At one point they brought in a woman to sit with the girl in the room with the chair, to console her because she was so upset. That must be your Climber. He asked the girl the same questions, said the same things, over and over. For hours. Someone thought they saw flashes of light in the arch but on playback there was nothing.

We have to do something. This can't go on.

So I have a plan, which is barely a plan, and still has one or two very big flaws, but here it is.

Follow me.

Every Wednesday afternoon at 5 p.m. the major security systems (which are on their own servers) purge cache, update if needed, and reboot. Takes about ten minutes, fifteen if there's a big update. But there's a redundant system that picks up the slack for those ten minutes so there's never downtime. This place is always secured.

I started thinking yesterday, what if I just disabled the redundant system? Not disable actually, they would know, but what if I changed the schedule of the redundant system to cache purge at the same time as the primary? To cycle together. They'd both be down at the same time.

For those ten minutes the automated security at the main doors of the company would be disabled. No foreign object detection, no facial scanning, no surveillance alerts, no door access logging. We'd have ten minutes for one of us to somehow get into medical, find the boy, save Kendrick if we can, and get out, and for the other to use my access to the sublevel and get Climber and the girl. If we got out, and got them out, in time, we'd have a chance to escape before anybody knew something had happened.

The first major flaw is the people. We'd be invisible to security, but not to the staff and security personnel. Not to Fallon or his team. Odds are good that somebody would notice us. Maybe not going in, but carrying people out. And for all we know the girl could still be in the chair at 5 p.m. Was thinking a fire alarm but that would probably make things worse, not better. Fire and safety teams would respond, not evacuate.

One crazy idea is that there's a critical alert system that can show a message on every screen in the building and an audible prompt that directs people to the nearest screen. I've never seen it used, but if I could figure out how they control us, how they manipulate us, maybe I could put something on the screen to sort of . . . freeze them? I know you said you'd been able to manipulate somebody's memory and make your presence online invisible . . . I know I'm grasping at straws right now, but given our options, is there something you and your team could do remotely, or maybe set up and I could implement here? Something to give us a chance?

The other major flaw is none of this brings down the

company. I could have a drive set up to offload some kind of incriminating information during the security blackout, if I can find any. It's just a lot to do in ten minutes and I couldn't touch the servers until security was down, so no offloading prep. And I can't tunnel it out because the purge cache will only affect physical building security, not the firewalls. Anything getting in or out will have to be on foot.

It all seems crazy, right?

Well, thing is . . . I already tried it today. And it worked. Everything I do during the chair examination is monitored and logged, but I was able to pull up a building-wide maintenance terminal in the background and figured if I got caught I could say I was checking to make sure the reboot went off without a hitch since the company's been attacked in the past couple months. They probably wouldn't believe me but at this point I don't care.

I aligned the two cache purges. And it worked. No alarms, no alarmed people. Most nerve-wracking ten minutes of my life. But from what I could tell nobody realized that security was black for ten minutes. Then I copied the log for last week and pasted it in the hole I left to cover my ass. The other problem, I watched the little red light on the monitoring room door's lock. It stayed red, never turned green. So the sublevel is on its own security. We still need my badge to get on those elevators and we need to hope and pray that they continue this insane experiment long enough for me to retain access. The weird thing, I think the girl knows that we need to keep this going to save them. I wonder if that's what the flashing in the arch was. You probably think I'm nuts but I'm not, and I'll tell you why . . .

She got in my head again today. She showed me all

kinds of things. Crazy stuff. My past. My future. People
dying. The boy running and me following.

And then she showed the two of us acting on the
plan I just thought up the night before. You. Here. With
the boy's "mind" on your phone. I can't see past us
meeting in the lobby and then splitting up, you going to
the sublevel and me taking your phone, with the boy, to
medical. She showed me that we try, but what happens
after, I don't know.

I can't explain it. I don't know if it's magic or science
or me losing my mind. All I know is something has to
give, and this little girl has told me that come hell or
high water the dam is giving out next Wednesday. 5
p.m. on May 31st. That's the day we try to break
them out.

It was happening. It was finally happening. I was going to go in
and get them out, though I had no idea how that was supposed to
work. I'm certainly not stealthy. The clicking in my right knee
would've been enough to give us away.

Aether began sending the Mountaineers messages, telling them
how they might be able to make their own magic to help the situation.
He even sent me a command that, I admit, went against every
curmudgeonly bone in my body:

 Upgr/d yor phon.

My phone was a relic, so old that people assumed I was cooler
than I actually was, thinking I was eschewing gluttonous capitalism
and embracing a Spartan approach to technology. The truth was I was
old and thought a phone should be a phone. I had never felt like
getting the latest palm-sized computer that I could occasionally make
calls with. But if it was important enough for Aether to risk further
degradation by messaging me, then it was important enough for me to

step out of my old-man pants and join the early adopters of the
twenty-first century.

When I visited my service provider for an upgrade, the woman
helping me called over all of her fellow employees to stare in disbelief
at the antique I was using. One of them, a kid not much older than my
toothbrush, said, "Hand to God," he'd seen the very same model in a
museum. I wasn't sure how he meant it, but I took it as a source
of pride.

An hour later I walked away with a phone that had more
computing power than Mission Control during Apollo 11. One of the
first things I used my new phone for was to check in on Deirdre's
blog.

DEIRDRE: MAY 27TH, 2017:

 I didn't feel it was fair to just abandon this blog, or the
Mountaineers, I just needed time. Cole took a few days
off and we've just been spending days and nights
together. Not being obsessed with magic or secret
societies or spells. Just being normal people.

Who like each other.

He's the kindest, most sincere person I've ever met.
And passionate. About life, and his work, and art. And
me. And I've just been basking in that light and figuring
out how to share more of myself in turn.

We've been in the city a few times. Visited museums,
seen shows (*Dear Evan Hansen* had me in a puddle on
the floor) and been to some lovely restaurants. And
we've carried one another back to Hoboken after soppy
nights in loud bars, meeting some of Cole's friends. He's
a bit like me, a few close mates, but not what you'd call
an absolute load of friends. Quality over quantity.

We even went to the Cloisters. I'm not sure why but
I wanted to go. I wanted to be face to face with the

unicorn tapestries. They're stunning, and all the more
haunting once you know their secret history, once you
know about Anne of Brittany and her court of artists
and the secret paths of wool and silver. How her body
was protected in death by materials from a secret
tapestry.

After the museum we went back to Cole's. I needed a
nap and Cole had some reading to do. I fell asleep in a
snap and dreamed I was watching myself being pulled
apart like Anne. My body, my bones, my entrails, my
heart. I woke up in a cold sweat.

And then something occurred to me. I felt like I'd
been bowled over by a tidal wave. I rushed out, to the
train. I only vaguely sensed Cole behind me, running to
catch up. I had to get back to the city. I had to get back
to the brownstone.

Out of everything that happened over these past
months, everything I experienced, the thing that stuck
with me was what Colby told me in Montreal. Not the
memory . . . It was what he said after. How he could
sense that my heart was already guarded.

I felt so stupid, taking offence at that. Obsessing over
it. Stupid and young and naive. How dare he tell me I
couldn't open up, or love, or care. I wasn't guarded. I
wasn't walled up.

It felt like he'd looked into me and saw an insecure
teenaged girl and I was embarrassed and angry and,
frankly, defiant. Not to say that these past weeks with
Cole were retaliatory. If anything, they were me
allowing *myself* to be proven wrong.

I'd left Cole's in such a frantic rush I'd forgotten to
bring the keys to the brownstone and we had to climb
in through an unlocked window off the fire escape. I
rummaged through the clothes I'd left behind and
finally found what I'd come back for.

Colby was right. My heart had been guarded. Just like Anne of Brittany's.

The dream had reminded me how Anne's heart had been buried, on a bed of wool, beneath a veil of silver, but also what Monica had sent along with my dad's journal last year.

My father had left behind, in the attic of the house I grew up in, the journal, yes, but also a wool scarf and a silver hippocampus pendant.

Was I reaching? Searching for meaning in nothing? Or had my father left me the last two tapestry artefacts from Anne's story? Hidden in plain sight now as two objects you'd find boxed away in any attic. Two objects that would mean nothing to anyone, except for the sentimental value they held for me. The last remnants of my mum and dad.

Was Colby supposed to tell me that about my heart? Was that another part of the path? Are these what my mum and dad found at the ends of roads?

And if so, what the hell was I supposed to do with a scarf and a necklace?

I had a long, hard moment of doubt. My cheeks were hot and red, embarrassed that Cole had rushed after me, back to the city, all because of some wildly farfetched idea.

After everything I'd been through, everywhere I'd gone, as resoundingly as I'd said I'd given up, I needed there to be something more than the memory of my parents crumbling into the past. There had to be more.

Was there? Or was I wishing the path to continue? Possibly.

But if it was all in my head, why had someone suddenly started knocking on every door in the brownstone?

I was elated to read that not only had Deirdre continued to walk the path we were all on, but she and Cole were doing well. The knocking, however, was disturbing. Nothing in what the Mountaineers had discovered explained what the knocking could have been. I worried what might happen if she ever answered.

While I was leaving the land of the Luddites, the Mountaineers were busy *creating* their own spells, with Aether's urging, to keep me and Whistler hidden during the extraction. I knew they had performed magic in the past, but this was beyond anything they had done before. The Mountaineers were going to have to bring to bear everything they'd learned to make this work.

What they came up with were actually two spells that would work in concert with one another.

Miss Evans, Ginger, Firefish, Skylad, OracleSage and Ricardo would perform "Fern and Ways' Concealment," a spoken ritual which invoked the six elements and would effectively hide Whistler and myself from view.

Then Furia, Mr5, Augustus_Octavian, Revenir, Deyavi, and Sellalellen would perform "The Mountain's Shroud," which involved the creation and wearing of enchanted blindfolds to confuse and distract anyone in the building, further obscuring our presence and actions.

The logistics of the spells were complicated, but they had all that under control. The rest was going to be up to me.

I contacted Whistler to let him know we were on board, and then set about making sure that all my affairs were in order. Not that there were many.

I also had the sneaking suspicion that Aether was inside my new phone. My email was already set up—without the hours-long call to tech support I'd thought would be necessary.

We were ready. As ready as we possibly could be.

CHAPTER 12
MAY 31ST

"Well done guys. Stuff always happens while I am
asleep. Maybe I should sleep all the time."

— REESYLOU

Storm clouds gather
Winds that howl
Something coming
Dark and foul

Gather friends
Forge a spell
Before we venture
Into hell

That's the message we received the night before the extraction. I
couldn't sleep, so I drove to a motel near Kemetic, then updated the

Mountaineers on everything that had happened over the past few days.

I WROTE:

 Didn't hear from Whistler over the weekend and got worried. Turns out the phone he "acquired" to talk to me got disconnected by its original owner. He was scared to buy a new one, worried he was being followed. His neighbor agreed to have one delivered to her apartment instead of his so now we're emailing again.

He said they had Portencia in the Chair all weekend and Climber was with her for most of it. Climber has been sedated. (Whistler thinks it's to keep her from coming up with an escape plan.)

Portencia blacked out last night and they had to take her out of the Chair. They're giving her a day off today, and I have to wonder if Portencia knows we're coming, because if she was in the Chair, in front of Fallon and whoever else, I'd be screwed when I tried to rescue them.

Whistler tried the plan again. It worked, and no one noticed the dual reboot. He says the only thing keeping him from going insane between his violent memories and what he's seeing them do to this girl is knowing we're out there and we're gonna help.

He said Fallon seems tired. Stressed. Seems like he's not getting the results the person on the other side of Fallon's journal is expecting. Whistler's seen writing in the journal:

"it must be now"

"he is too valuable an asset to lose"

"his gift is too important to [illegible]"

That last word was a name that started with a D, but Whistler couldn't see the rest.

So they're still looking for Aether . . .

Whistler also logged into the camera systems again. He saw some of Fallon's team go in and out of the secured room in medical where we think Aether's body is. He doesn't know how we're gonna get in because it's locked down, but I told him if we can get Aether inside the facility, we're golden.

Aether's on my new phone. A bluetooth earpiece thing showed up in the mail on Friday. Aether set up an account and ordered it for me. I can hear him in it. He says he's going to connect me to you this afternoon so that if something goes wrong we "can fix it together."

He sounds bad. Weak. He says the 18 Gates know what we're trying to do. Says they're doing what they can to protect us (and keep him together), with what little power they have. He said they seem to care as much, if not more, about the Mountaineers as they do the Book. They're trying hard to keep us safe from whatever's coming. So that's something.

We have to get him back to his body. It has to be today because I don't think he can hold on much longer.

So:

You guys are going to cast magiq that, six corners willing, will hide us and blind everyone at KS so we can get in.

At 5 p.m. sharp the reboot and our 10-minute countdown will start. I'm going to walk into KS with Aether in my ear. Whistler will be waiting for us in the lobby.

I'm going to hand Aether off via my phone to Whistler. They'll go to medical, to try and wake up Kendrick, get Portencia's fragment from his mind, and get Aether into the secured room, where we're assuming and hoping his body is. Then they'll leave and wait for me in my car, which is a block away.

Meanwhile, I'll take Whistler's badge to the sublevel where they're keeping Portencia and Climber, find a way to get them upstairs, and hopefully get out with them before the security reboots.

I'm gonna take whoever gets out to a secured place. I don't want to say where we're going right now, just to be sure. But I'll touch base when I can to let you know what happened.

And if you don't hear from me just know that I couldn't be more proud to stand alongside you against the Storm. I'm proud to be a Mountaineer.

See you at 5 p.m.

At a quarter to five, I got in my car and started the engine. But I sat there with it idling for a full three minutes before I could make myself put it into drive. The rational part of my brain kept screaming that this was an incredibly foolish, illegal, and quite possibly lethal thing to be doing. Yet as that thought was going through my head, I realized something: I didn't want a drink. If there was anything that pushed me toward a bottle, it was overwhelming stress—not to mention proximity to magic and all the trouble it brought. And yet, I didn't feel the pull, the need for the soothing burn at the back of my throat and the blissful numbness that comes with it. I didn't need it. I had the Mountaineers—who, at that very moment, were casting some terribly powerful magiq to help me. I was on my own. But I wasn't alone. They'd be with me every step of the way.

I parked a block away from the business park and stepped into the fading daylight. The building looked dark and empty. I put my earbud in and turned it on.

"Aether? You there?"

"I'm here, Marty." Aether's voice was thin and scattered; it was like listening to a copy of a copy of a copy. If I didn't get him out, I feared he wouldn't last the night.

"I'm getting you out of here. *We're* getting you out of here."

"I know. Are you ready?"

"Yeah."

"Okay. Going live for the Mountaineers in three, two . . ." There was a click in my ear. "All right, here goes."

I stepped to the front door, my heart thumping so loudly against my breastbone that, for a brief moment, I honestly thought I was going to have a heart attack before I ever made it into the building.

I walked right in through the door that, last time, had been locked. Once I was through and the door closed behind me, the lobby switched on like I was inside a television set. Bright white lights shone overhead, and people milled about—so many people, all going about their tasks like zombies. The building must have been spelled so that it appeared empty to anyone peering in from the outside.

I slowed my pace, preparing myself to run, though where I didn't know. A man in khakis and a baby blue Oxford button-down stepped in front of me, nearly walking right into me. I had to suppress the urge to curse at him or apologize, but he didn't notice me. No one did.

"They don't see us. It's working." The spells the Mountaineers had performed were blinding everyone to our presence. It was unbelievable.

But there was one person looking right at me. She walked toward me. Though she was twenty years my junior, there was something in her eyes that suggested a wisdom that could only be earned through life's harsher lessons. Some of those lessons had been taught by the Mountaineers themselves.

"Hold on, wait," I said. "Are you Whistler?"

"We have less than ten minutes. You have him?" she said.

Aether piped into my ear. "It's okay, Marty, I'll go with her. You get to Portencia and Climber. We'll get the fragment from Kendrick."

"Get back to your body first," I said. Aether's voice was difficult to hear; it was degrading by the minute. The sooner that he was whole, that he was Jeremy again, the better.

"I don't know how my mind *or* body will react to that. I might be out of it for a while. I need to wake Kendrick up first."

"And then get back to your body and both of you get out."

"She can talk to me on the phone, and you can hear me from the earpiece," Aether said.

"Okay," I said, "But cut off contact if it's too much, deal?"

"Sure," he said.

Whistler put her hand on my arm and said, "We gotta go. Here's my badge. The elevators to the sublevel are on the other side of the building, straight down that hall then right when it ends. And another right when that one ends." Whistler was all business, barking out directions like a battlefield commander. I had no idea if she had ever seen combat before, but I had no doubt she could handle it.

She gave me her badge. "I'll keep him safe."

"Okay," I said and handed her the phone.

"Let's go," said Aether.

I moved down the empty hallway, following Whistler's directions, and noticed an odd humming reverberating through the walls. It was something I felt more than I heard, but it was there, a frequency too low for human hearing. It was eerie, as if I could sense a shroud covering this part of the building.

"Whistler?" Aether said. "It's going to be okay." I couldn't hear what she was saying, only Aether, but I had every confidence that she was going to do just fine.

"Martin, can you still hear me?" he asked.

"I hear you. I'm almost at the elevators." They were at the end of the hall, and I felt as if I were being pulled toward them more than I was walking toward them.

"We just got to medical." His voice was tinny in my ear. "There are people all over the place, but they're not looking at us. I can feel my body . . . hopefully I can make it back in."

"Be careful," I said. A few seconds later, I reached the "invisible" elevators.

"I'm here. I'm going down."

"Good luck."

The doors opened, and for a moment, I froze. There was something about the way they moved that reminded me of the

Cagliostro and the abyss he summoned, a black yawning abyss that hid something dark and terrible inside it. But the fear passed when all that was inside was a pale tile floor and polished steel walls. I saw my reflection and was surprised by how I looked. I wasn't nearly as disheveled as I was expecting, though I did have a thin sheen of sweat across my forehead.

Time was ticking. I had to move. I pressed the button, and the elevator began to descend. The strange humming grew stronger, its vibrations now becoming truly audible. When the elevator stopped and its doors opened, there was a wrought-iron gate that I needed to slide up. It was such an anachronism that I wondered if I had entered the wrong elevator. I stepped out and found odd machines with misshapen tubes and lights all around me, twinkling in the dark like apoplectic fireflies.

"Martin?" Aether said.

"Hey, just finding my way down here. It's dark. There's these weird lights and equipment. They're doing crazy stuff down here."

"Whistler," Aether said, "any idea where we should look?" There was a pause, then he said, "Martin, she never saw where they were held. You're just going to have to keep looking. Uh . . . want me to try and get the lights on?"

"No. Focus on you and Kendrick. I always bring a flashlight." One of the nice things about cutting my journalistic teeth before the digital age was learning to keep a practical bag of tricks with me at all times. I kept a small Maglite the size of my thumb in my back pocket. It didn't shed much light, but it was enough.

The machines created a symphony of strange and ephemeral sounds, some of them whirring like fans while others aspirated and gurgled as if they were more biological than mechanical.

"Whistler, can you set the phone down?" Aether asked. "I'm going to go inside Kendrick's mind . . ." His voice crackled for a second. "I'll be right back."

I knew Aether had the ability to traverse technological devices, but to travel inside someone's mind? It was both fascinating and terrifying.

After a terminally long time, Aether said, "There's no . . . He's not in a medically-induced coma. There's magic here, Martin. I don't know if I can wake him up."

"We have to leave him," I said. I hated the thought. If the Mountaineers had the time to craft a spell to wake him and find the last piece of Portencia's mind, there'd have been a chance. But we were running out of time. "You have to get back to your body, Aether."

"What about Portencia? The fragment?"

"We'll deal with it." There was no response. "Aether?"

"Okay," he said, though I didn't know if the quietness of his voice was due to further degradation or resignation. "I may be out of contact for a while."

"Tell Whistler I'll get Kendrick out if I can. I'll see you outside. Looking forward to meeting you face to face."

I had to find Portencia immediately. I scanned my tiny flashlight back and forth, but I saw no rooms, no hallways or alcoves, jut the labyrinthian arrangements of machines.

There was another screeching sound, not in my ear, but over the floor's loudspeaker system. Then a voice came through. Clear. Calm. Quietly malevolent.

"Martin, it's Teddy Fallon."

CHAPTER 13
THE WELL

"Inside the lab, chaos continues."

— FIREFISH

"The girls are safe and sound," Teddy said. "You recognized her right away, didn't you?"

"Yeah." I knew who he meant. The moment I'd seen Whistler in the lobby, I'd recognized her. Though we'd never met before, I'd come across her yearbook picture during my research. Even though she was considerably older now, her features were unmistakable.

"But you didn't know who she was until today."

"No." How could I have guessed before today that our insider was actually Sacha—Brandon Lachmann's childhood best friend and obsessive leader of the cult-like Devoted?

"But you still gave her the boy. Why? Wait. You thought she really woke up." Teddy's voice was thick with southern sarcasm, his words dripping with it. "Well." He chuckled. "I thought you'd see through it. I thought you'd figure out we only let Sacha *believe* she'd been in an accident. Programmed her to think she woke up, when she was really doing exactly what we wanted her to do."

"Get Aether back." I was a fool. Once again, my trying to help was going to get innocent people hurt.

No, not this time. I couldn't let it happen again.

"Yes," he said, "but more importantly, bring you here."

"Why? To kill me?"

"We have never intentionally taken a life. Did you know that, almost without exception, intentionally killing someone bars you from the use of magiq for the length of your natural life?"

"So that's the point of Sweeper, Wanderer—you don't kill people, you just destroy them?"

"I see Aether's been going through my things," he said. "The point of all of this is to understand why, which is what no one knows and what we must learn at any cost. You have no idea the lengths we are willing to go. Do you know Wanderer was my son?"

It was a gut punch. Who would willingly subject their own child to all of this? What kind of man—what kind of *monster* would do such a thing?

"I don't care," I said. "You're not taking another person's life away."

"Why do you think we're here?"

"You're trying to buy time until the reboot ends."

"Martin, Sacha is already shutting the reboot down as we speak. You are here because *you* . . . are *special*."

He was stalling; he had to be. But Teddy didn't know me at all. Flattery wasn't going to get him anywhere.

"You are the rarest of adepts," he continued.

"I'm not magic."

"No? Haven't the Mountaineers ever wondered why we couldn't just knock on your apartment door or pick you up on the street?"

The protective token Dr. Brightwell gave me. "I didn't cast that charm. It was a gift to me."

"Have you never wondered why you have found yourself circling all manner of magic most of your adult life? It's because you are what we call a Well. You haven't been circling anything. It's been circling you."

"It doesn't matter," I spit back.

"It does. It's why we've done all of this the past few months. Threatening Aether, putting the life of a young man at risk—like Brandon, like your son. It's catnip for you. Why do you think we've had that girl in the Chair over and over and over when I've had the last fragment of her mind in my head for months? To bring you here. Because with you here we'll be able to bring all manner of power to our side. To the palace made of doors."

My head was spinning. He was lying, he had to be. I wasn't special, I wasn't a "Well," I wasn't anything. And even though I was in the basement with only the voice of this sociopath for company, I also knew I wasn't alone.

"You won't beat the Mountaineers."

"Beat them? We're already inside them. Learned everything we needed to remove them from the equation. They've already lost and they never even learned what game they were playing."

"Bullshit."

"We started sending recruits through the Magiq Guide, but we couldn't count on them So, instead, we piggybacked on Aether's signal to you, sent coercion images into his broadcast, and one of you turned. He reported back everything to us. And he could bypass your little spell because he didn't even know what he was doing was wrong. Unfortunately, we didn't know he had a brain tumor the size of an apple, and the stress of the coercion killed him. So, with our informant out of the game and Aether falling apart, we had to get clever."

"Sacha."

"Yes. Now Aether is back where he belongs, his mind trapped in a firewalled cell we made you believe held his body. Sacha will be brought back into the fold with the flip of a proverbial switch. And now you're here. And now you belong to us."

"You are out of your mind."

"What is the problem, Martin? You've wanted the truth your whole life, and now you have it!"

"The problem is Aether never went back to his body. He never even went with Sacha. Aether's in this earpiece on my head, and not only has he been broadcasting you to the Mountaineers, he's dropped your firewalls. He's been sending *gigabytes* of Kemetic information to a secured server for the past ten minutes. The problem, *Teddy*, is you've been so busy sacrificing the lives of other people that you never once considered we'd risk our lives to save someone else!"

Aether and I had come up with this plan the night before. In case Whistler had been turned or caught. A way to salvage something if the mission failed.

"No," Fallon said, and I smiled to myself.

"Yeah."

"Martin, you have no idea what you've done."

"Sure we do."

"The Storm is coming."

"Yeah, yeah, yeah, we've heard." I was done with this man and his condescending threats.

"No, Martin," he said, his voice no longer filled with threat or menace, but worry. "It's coming *right now*."

There was a click, and Teddy's voice was gone. Aether piped up.

"My body's down there, Martin. I can feel it."

"Get back to your body," I said. "I'll get the others, and you meet us back at the elevators as soon as you can."

"I'm unlocking the cells now."

In the distance, I saw light shining as the walls opened to reveal rooms hidden on the far side of the basement. I navigated my way through the maze of wires and machines to an open cell.

"Portencia." The young girl was on the floor, curled into a tiny ball.

"Get back!"

I turned and saw a young woman limping toward me. She was gaunt, malnourished, and apparently wounded, but she still cut a threatening figure.

"It's okay, Alison," said Portencia.

Alison. Climber was AlisonB, the Mountaineer who'd been so helpful in earlier fragments, then had vanished from the forum.

"We . . . we have to get out of here," I said. "Something's coming. Alison, can you walk?"

"Don't worry about me. Help Port."

I quickly lifted the girl into my arms. It had been a long time since I'd held a child, but I didn't remember them feeling so light, so insubstantial. The girl smiled at me, though, and I could feel her familiar breath against my ear. It was pure joy for me to smile back.

"The elevators are this way."

I led them through the maze of machines, looking back to make sure Alison was keeping up. I wanted to run, but there was no way I was leaving anyone behind.

"Martin?"

I turned and saw a teenage boy, bed-headed, puffy-eyed, but with a big broad smile on his face. His limbs were long and ungainly, as if they had experienced a growth spurt ahead of the rest of his body.

"Aether? Are you okay?"

The boy smiled and said, "A little woozy, but yeah, it's uh . . . it's nice to have hands." He held up his fingers and wiggled them as if he were expecting them to fly away at any second and mildly surprised that they hadn't.

I laughed. It felt good to laugh, even then. "It's nice to put a face to the kid in my phone."

"The elevators aren't working," Alison said.

"No, they're working," I said. "They've just been called upstairs. We're too late. Is there another way out?"

Aether—no, Jeremy—said, "Let me check." He closed his eyes, and though his lips didn't move, I could hear him through my earpiece. "No, this is it."

The humming in the building was now vibrating hard enough that it felt like walking past a jackhammer on the sidewalk. And then there was a quick flash of light, and the humming increased.

"What was that?" I asked.

Alison looked around into the dark reaches of the basement. "It's the Storm."

Jeremy stepped forward and said, "I can reach upstairs and—"

"No," Alison interrupted. "Don't. You don't understand. This is it. This is how it always ends."

I was desperate. I had to find a way to get them out.

And then there was a soft, birdlike voice, barely audible over the rising hum of the Storm.

"Take me to the Chair," Portencia said.

"What?"

Alison shook her head wildly. "No."

"Take me to the Chair," the girl said again, this time with more authority. "That's the way out."

"Port, you could die in that thing."

"I won't."

"Can . . . can you see what's going to happen?" I asked her, but Portencia didn't answer me.

The sounds were emanating from all around us, growing in intensity.

"I can hold the doors, buy us some time," Jeremy said.

Now it was my turn to object. "No," I said.

"Martin, it's okay, I'll be right behind you."

"I don't want to lose any of you."

"Trust us," he said. And he was right. I had to. All three of them had more knowledge of this place—and of magic—than I did. I was operating on adrenaline and righteous fury, but they had insights and abilities beyond anything I could contribute.

"Go," I said. Jeremy nodded and ran, probably ecstatic at the chance to use his legs. I turned to Alison. "Where's the Chair?"

"This way."

Alison led us away from the elevators and down a side corridor. There was a large opening to a chamber with a domed roof more than thirty feet overhead. In the middle of the chamber was the Chair. It was a brutalist nightmare of coiled leather and wire sitting beneath the great stone arch that hovered over it like a troll protecting its offspring.

"Here," Alison said, and I gently placed Portencia in the Chair, her tiny features dwarfed by the dark and heavy structure.

"Now what?" I asked.

Portencia's smile had disappeared somewhere on the way from the elevators. She was all business now. "You should back up," she said.

The Chair came to life around her, adding to the growing cacophony of the Storm. Corded bindings and wires wormed around Portencia's skull, her frail wrists.

"You can do this, Port." Alison said.

The Chair tightened itself around her, light pulsing through it from the cables that snaked from its base, across the floor, to things unseen in the ground.

After a moment, Portencia said, "I . . . I can't do it, I'm sorry. I'm missing a piece. I . . . I can't control it."

Tears rolled down her cheeks. I felt helpless; there was nothing I could do.

"Yes, you can," Alison said, and she put her hand over the girl's. "I'm here with you."

"It could hurt you."

"I don't care. Listen to me. You don't need the poem. You don't need to control your power or be afraid of it. It's not scary, it's a gift. That's what I've learned from all these years, that's why I'm here right now holding your hand. I'm not afraid. You can do this. You can see a future away from here. Remember the drawing, a place where you're safe and I'm there with you and so is Aether. You can see it, can't you, Port?"

Portencia nodded, her jaw tight, resolve in her eyes. Her tiny fingers reached through the leather bonds and squeezed Alison's hand. She closed her eyes again.

"Yes."

"Good, now open a door to that future and take us there. Let's go home."

Something in the wall broke, and steam vented through the

breach. Dust rained down from the vibrations; the noise was becoming painful. The stone arch rippled, and light exploded around us. A shimmering membrane filled the arch like a layer of soapy water inside a bubble wand. Only it wasn't water. The membrane was a swirling cross section of snow.

The Chair released Portencia, and the girl tumbled into my arms. I handed her to Alison. "Go, go!" I turned and started to run toward the hallway.

"Where are you going?" Alison shouted, her voice barely discernible over the noise.

"I'm not leaving without Aether! Now, go!"

I ran back into the hall. I could see the elevators as small bits of debris clattered to the ground around me. "Aether!" He wasn't there. The glow from the archway lit everything in a sickly golden light, but he was nowhere to be seen.

"Aether!" A violent, impossible wind tore the earpiece from my ear. "Jeremy!" Two shadows flitted across the far wall—the silhouettes of Portencia and Alison as they went through the archway. The hairs on my arm stood up, and I could taste something like clove in the air. I saw a shadow somewhere in the distance. It was Jeremy, it had to be, but its proportions didn't seem right. The light grew brighter, and the floor shook beneath me, knocking me over. It was too bright; I couldn't keep my eyes open. The last thing I saw before I closed them was the Chair burning, the strange wind whipping the flames into an inferno, and a shadow on the wall, coming toward me. All that was left was the deafening howl of the world being torn asunder and incredible pain.

Then there was nothing.

PART II
TIME

June-September, 2017

CHAPTER 14
A MONTH LIKE A YEAR

"More importantly, you're family here."

— NOMAD

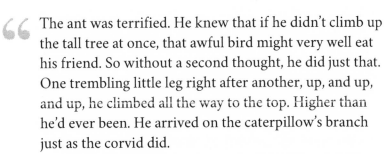
The ant was terrified. He knew that if he didn't climb up the tall tree at once, that awful bird might very well eat his friend. So without a second thought, he did just that. One trembling little leg right after another, up, and up, and up, he climbed all the way to the top. Higher than he'd ever been. He arrived on the caterpillow's branch just as the corvid did.

"G-good morning, Ms. Corvid. How are you?" the ant said.

"Lost, separated from my family, and very hungry," the corvid responded.

"Well, I fear the glade has been picked clean, but I have a knothole full of leaves that you are welcome to," the ant muttered nervously.

"But I don't eat leaves," Ms. Corvid responded. "However, I do eat the things that eat the leaves. Like bugs and beetles and such. Might there be something to eat inside this sack?" Ms. Corvid pointed her sharp beak at the pillowcase.

"Oh, no, Ms. Corvid, th-that is simply my bag of leaves. You wouldn't like that."

"Hmm," Ms. Corvid said. "Well, it doesn't smell to me like leaves. Maybe I could take a peek inside to be sure there's nothing worth a bite." Ms. Corvid pecked at the pillowcase.

The ant ran forward, standing between the bird and his friend.

"Stop that!" he said. "If you're so hungry, wh-why don't you eat me instead?"

Ms. Corvid huffed. "You're barely big enough for a single bite, and besides, fire ants are the most bitter and vile of ants to eat. You sting and pinch the whole way down."

Now the ant, not having been raised by other ants, had not known that he himself was a fire ant.

"I sting and pinch the whole way down?" he asked.

Ms. Corvid replied venomously, "You know very well that one bite from your pinchers is terribly painful. Now move out of my way and let me inspect your 'bag of leaves.'"

Just then the pillowcase wiggled. Ms. Corvid, hungry and curious, batted away the distracted ant with her wing, knocking him off the branch! Then she grabbed the pillowcase in her sharp claws and pulled at it, snapping the thread that held the caterpillow to the limb.

High into the sky Ms. Corvid took the caterpillow, who was finally waking up. He peeked out from his pillowcase, his puffy little eyes squinting in the sunlight.

He looked down and saw the glade far below. He was astonished, until he realized the trouble he was in.

"Excuse me, Ms. Corvid? Where are we going?" the caterpillow asked.

Ms. Corvid ignored him, clenching him ever tighter as she made for a cliff in the distance, and the trees atop the cliff. The caterpillow could see his pillowcase tearing apart in her grip.

Just then, something began to tickle the caterpillow's back. It was the little red ant! The ant held a finger to his mouth, shushing the happy caterpillow.

"What are you doing way up here, ant?" the caterpillow whispered.

"I mean to keep you from being eaten," the ant responded.

"My pillowcase has been torn in her claw. If we can convince her to loosen her grip, I can get free," the caterpillow explained.

"But you'll still fall to the ground," the ant lamented.

"Trust me, dear friend. Get me free and I'll be fine," the caterpillow answered confidently.

DEIRDRE: JUNE 29TH, 2017:

 Yesterday was my birthday.

Last weekend Cole planned a surprise trip, and it was wonderful. Guess where? Hudson! My other favorite town in New York. We ate too much, drank too much, spent too much, and it was all sorts of glorious.

I spoke with Mon briefly. Things have moved so quickly this past year . . . Bunratty, the move, the journals, the travels, and now it all seems a billion miles

away. And of course I feel guilty because part of me
thinks Mon's health should be my number one priority.
And it would be . . . if there was anything anyone could
do about it. She remembered me for most of the call,
and it was lovely to hear her voice.

Other than the trip to Hudson we've just been . . .
not on some hare-brained adventure or hunting some
lost book or magical painting. Just being. We're mostly
staying at Cole's place because the brownstone doesn't
(yet) have air conditioning, but I still pop back there
every once in a while. Cole would drag everything I
own to Hoboken if it were up to him, and while I love
falling asleep with him and waking up in his arms (or
with mine wrapped around him) I like knowing that I
have that place too. I don't know if it's because of past
relationships maybe? David *did* kick me out of "our" flat
after all. HA! I hadn't thought of him in a while. Seems
so silly now, all that fretting. But I guess if I hadn't
fretted so dramatically I wouldn't have crossed the
Atlantic in the first place. Hoorah for dramatic fretting!

Speaking of sleeping, we've both realised we sleep
SO much better together. For my birthday Cole bought
me a journal with a cover he designed himself! It's green
and gold leaf and has the shape of Herman the
hippocampus on the front.

I absolutely ADORE it. It has blank pages so I can
play around with watercolor, my newest hobby, which
no you can't see because I am baaaaaad. (He also gave
me an amazing watercolor pen kit!)

So we've just been . . . well, truth is we finally
admitted in Hudson that we're crawling out of our skin
a bit. We're both loving finally being able to spend time
together, but the what-ifs and what's-nexts are always
in the back of our minds. It was honestly quite a relief
to hear he felt the same. We both know, deep down, that

this thing with the journals and my father isn't over. But we have no idea what to do next and we're both looking for signs and symbols and knocking doors . . . Some secret order in everyday life. I mean, everyone is, sure, but we (you included) have actually found actual, honest-to-god mysteries and puzzles and magic. It's hard to go back to everyday life.

It's one more reason I'm so happy I found Cole. Happy you brought us together, too. Who else in the world could understand us but each other?

It's officially summer but I still carry the scarf in my bag at all times. And the pendant. I figure if they offer any protection whatsoever, I'm more than happy to haul them around, especially given what's happened with the Book of Briars (a couple Mounties wrote me after.) I wonder if I should protect my blog?

So, I'm here. One year older. Happy where I am. But looking for the road that's waiting out there. Excited I don't have to walk it alone. I don't know what I would do if I didn't have Cole, and you, to share this with.

DEIRDRE: JULY 10TH, 2017:

 Um . . . Mounties?

A month passes by like a year and suddenly one week happens in an hour.

So much to unwrap, but it looks like it's all starting up again, in ways bigger than I could've imagined. I wish you could've been there.

First, the scarf.

It's a little itchy.

I mean, obviously I'm not wearing it now because it's

insufferably hot, but when I did, a few times last fall, I
noticed it was itchy. Not terribly. Just a little. And only
if you wrapped it around in certain ways. It's very wide
so I could rewrap it and poof, no itch . . .

Two nights ago we were lying on the sofa at Cole's. I
was rubbing his feet and he was reading to me after a
deliciously gluttonous (and very wine heavy) meal at an
Italian place in his neighbourhood. My bag was near the
sofa, and I don't remember when, but and at some point
I absently reached down and starting fiddling with
the scarf.

Must've gone on an hour before I actually noticed
that I was running my fingers along the itchy part.
There was a line down the middle of the scarf that was
rough, unlike the rest of the yarn. I didn't want to say
anything until I'd managed to run the entire scarf
through my hand, following the rough thread from one
end to the other.

Why was there one coarse thread running down the
middle of the scarf? I bolted up and yanked it out of my
bag, investigating through wine-rimmed eyes. I couldn't
see the thread, but I could feel it. I handed it off to Cole.
He felt it too. We were giddy at this point. We each
grabbed an end, trying to find the source, and then I felt
it. The "tail" of the course thread, hidden amid the
tassels on my end. Cole found it too. We both pulled at
the same time, giggling at how insanely excited we both
were. He gave me the honours and the hidden thread
slid right out of the middle, separating the scarf
into two!

We ran to the kitchen table to study the thread
under the light.

It had lines and dots running all down it. Morse
code I thought? Cole was already rushing back with a
notepad from the coffee table. I "read" the lines to him

and he wrote them down. Turns out Cole knows Morse! (he's very handy.)

I half expected it to not make sense. To be a fluke we were trying to wish into being magic.

It wasn't a fluke.

It was an address.

In New York City. The Upper East Side to be precise.

We googled it. It was a hundred-year-old apartment building that at some point had been converted into a boutique hotel.

We figured whatever was in the apartment would be gone now. Right?

We stood in the kitchen in our underpants trying to figure out what to do. Cole went over the code again. He'd gotten it right.

We figured we should definitely wait until morning to go. Daylight, soberness, etc. We agreed to wait.

And we barely slept. We kept checking to see if the other was sleeping and finally got up just before 6 a.m.

I brought the scar(ves)f just in case. We went over and over what we'd say to whoever was managing the front desk of the hotel. Ask if my father had left something behind, maybe lost and found? Who knows, maybe the manager was another of my father's friends, waiting decades for me to show up?

Nope. The manager looked at us as if we were mad. They weren't in the habit of keeping things in the lost and found for years and he'd never heard of Sullivan Green.

It wasn't until Cole mentioned apartment number 7G specifically that the manager perked up. He had Cole repeat it twice, then hurried into a back room to make a whispery phone call.

He came back and told us to take the elevator to the

7th floor. To room 717. The room that used to be 7G.
We wondered what would be waiting up there, how
we'd get in. The manager shook his head and said we
wouldn't need a key.

We took the elevator up, wondering what were
getting ourselves into. Cole wanted me to wait in the
lobby, with the scarf. I politely declined.

We stood outside the door for what felt like an hour.
I kept telling Cole to knock and then stopping him
before he could. I rubbed my eyes as if I were about to
see something so incredible I wouldn't want to blink.

And then Cole finally knocked.

And knocked again.

He tried the knob just as the lock turned.

Someone was already inside.

The door opened and standing on the other side was
a tall, handsome man who had to be somewhere north
of 90.

His hair was silver but impeccably groomed. He had
a light in his eyes and a beautiful smile. All the anxiety,
apprehension suddenly melted away. I felt at ease for
some strange reason. Was it him or the trail? The man
nodded to Cole, then turned to me.

He asked if I was Deirdre Green and smiled when I
said yes.

Then he proudly introduced himself.

A name I'd come to think of as myth. But here he
was, standing at the head of the trail my father left
for me.

M. Grey Ackerly.

DEIRDRE: JULY 12TH, 2017:

 Grey (as he asked to be called) invited us in, and Cole and I both noticed that it felt like the atmosphere changed as we walked through the door. Like we were in a plane taking off. Definitely something weird/magic.

The place had been completely untouched from when they turned the building into a hotel. It wasn't huge (though still absolutely massive by New York City standards), but it was beautiful, dappled with light, the sounds of city traffic a soft drone, dulled by beautiful curtains, antique furniture, and heavy, wall-sized tapestries.

We sat down with him in the parlour where he motioned for us to join him. I was not at all expecting this, so my mind was furiously trying to figure out what to say, what to ask, what to do . . . And Cole, feeling this was my show (he told me later) tried to fill my awkward quiet with compliments about the apartment while I tried to get my mind together.

Grey started talking, his hands in his lap but gesturing dramatically at times, one leg crossed over the other at the knee. He had a sophisticated but warm air about him.

He paused every now and then, trying to find a memory, or a word, (I just looked at the Basecamp post about Ackerly Green and only now realised Grey is 101!) but he didn't seem frustrated or embarrassed. He just looked at his hands or out the window and waited for whatever he was looking for to come to him. We talked for the better part of an hour before I told him that we were surprised to find him here because as far as anyone knew, he'd died decades ago. He smiled and nodded, telling me that had been my father's plan.

He went into the kitchen, brought us tea, and said the memory was very hazy now but my dad had come to him years ago and told him that the Ackerlys and the Greens were connected to a conspiracy and he thought those of us who suspected it we were in danger. Grey thought he'd gone insane, but my dad showed him something that changed his mind, though he couldn't remember what it was now.

Grey explained that the apartment had been preserved at great cost, first to protect him and others in the families, then eventually me. So if I ever followed the path here, the path my father left me, the safe haven would be waiting. He pointed to the front door where there were two locks. One was normal, one was not. He said one simply locked the door, the other one locked out the world. That's what my father had told him.

He said my dad came back at some point because he remembers him both as a young man and an older man, but all the years in the apartment had become a jumble. He remembered he cared very much for my dad and had hoped that he could make up for what happened with my grandfather by being there for Sullivan.

Grey asked Sullivan to warn Grey's son James, but he and Grey had a contemptuous relationship and James wanted nothing to do with the Ackerlys or the Greens. My dad reassured him that he thought only those seeking the truth were in danger. And from what he knew James led a normal life, untouched by magic. Grey asked if I knew what became of his son. I sort of recalled reading that James died, but since I wasn't sure, and wasn't sure when, I said no. It seemed like a well-intentioned lie at the time, but I feel guilty about it now.

I asked him if he remembered why the two families were in danger, who my dad was afraid of. Grey didn't remember, said he may never have known in truth.

Then he said, "But I assumed it was about the books. The lost books. And that assumption, Sullivan said, was why I was in danger."

Cole and I were stunned. Cole asked if Grey remembered them. He told us that the older he got the more the walls come down. For most of his life he only saw the path blazed by the choices he made. But now he can see other choices. Warren's choices. Choices he never allowed Warren to make, but somehow, somewhere, those choices *were* made. He said he didn't remember the books, but he now remembers a hole where something used to fit, and as decades passed, that hole became the shape of the Lost Collection. He stopped himself, a little overwhelmed, and said something to the effect of, "You have to take everything I say with a grain of salt, unfortunately. I sometimes find myself remembering something that isn't mine to remember. A dream or a story told by someone else becomes the truth, my truth, at this late stage of life. But I know there's something missing. A scratch that's missing its itch."

That stuck with me. A scratch missing its itch.

He went on to tell us that his life had been consumed with poor decisions but he hoped in helping me, he could do some right. Give his life purpose. He was sure there was more to tell, but he couldn't quite remember. He knew at some point he'd taken to writing it all out.

He got up to look for his writings . . . and then after a few minutes called us to the dining room. The room was sunny and had a great big wooden table. And on the table, was a box.

Grey had remembered this was what he was meant to give me. The box was from my father. It was gorgeous, and expertly crafted, with a glistening black hippocampus on the lid. There wasn't a lock, but I couldn't get the lid open. Grey had never seen the inside of the box either, but had been assured by my father that I'd be able to open it.

I spent ten embarrassing minutes trying to pry it open before realising this must be some kind of puzzle. Some way of protecting whatever was inside from everyone but me.

I went back over everything I'd seen and learned these past months as Cole and Grey made small talk to try and pretend they weren't waiting for me to figure this all out. Sometime later, room service arrived and they left me alone with a sandwich while they ate in the parlour.

It had to be sealed magically. Nothing else explained how tightly locked the lid was without an actual lock. What was I missing? What did I know that no one else did? I even picked over the two halves of the scarf, maybe something else was hidden in them . . . Then something struck me. Why was Herman on the box? Yes, a Green left it with an Ackerly to give to me, but it had to be something else, it had to be a clue . . .

And then I remembered . . .

The pendant.

The hippocampus pendant. A clue in the scarf separated them into a pair. What if I had to bring the two hippocampii (?) together for the final clue?

I pulled it out of my bag and half expected it to be drawn to the box like a magnet. I laid the pendant on top . . . nothing. I moved it along every side of the box . . . nothing. At this point Cole and Grey were standing in the doorway, watching.

I was at a loss.

And then, half-embarrassed, I put the pendant around my neck and I barely had to touch the box. It almost opened itself when I tried to lift the lid.

Inside was a cloth pouch and a small journal. Inside the pouch was what looked at first like a pocket watch, until I opened it . . .

It's one of the things on the cover of the *Guide to Magiq*. Cole said you call it a chronocompass. It must've been my father's. The journal was blank except the title page, on which my father had written, "The Monarch Papers: Neithernor."

And a letter to me.

Which read—

"My Deirdre,

You've found it. Your bravery and heart have led you here. Beyond all hope you have continued, and on the other side of the darkest woods you have found the end of a path. Now you stand at a door, my love. On the shore of your future and the future of all the world.

But the time for choosing is done. This is a door you must go through I'm afraid, because your journey is now tied to all of us. All who've sought the truth. There is a plan in place. An unfathomable machine of secrets designed by myself and the council beyond our sight—a plan to thwart the Storm and its master.

Hope is not lost. Not yet.

The truth is this . . . if we don't succeed now, then all of this will be for nothing. The magiq here in the mundane is finite. This is our final chance. I have sacrificed my life for this cause. I would never wish the same for you, but I trust no one to finish this more than the daughter of your mother.

All you need is inside this box. And the places these objects will take you.

Be prepared, nothing I have done to protect you so far can keep you safe now. Trust only in the flow of magiq and those who join you on this journey.

To begin this final chapter, the Mountaineers must use the most dangerous of magiq and you must learn everything about the secret world.

The Mountaineers must reach out to the past, and you my dear, must go to Neithernor.

Sullivan"

CHAPTER 15
WAKE UP

"No way a Bali could Weathermancy this
storm away?"

— NYMID

Sebastian was poking me. He bounced on the bed, then giggled
as he tried to worm his finger into my ear.

"Stop it."

"Get up, Dad. Mommy made breakfast."

I put the pillow over my head. "Then go eat and let me sleep, you
little monster."

Sebastian slid his head under the pillow and pushed his face
against mine. His breath was hot and smelled like syrup. "I already
ate," he whispered. "Mommy made Folgers for you."

"Just call it coffee, son."

"You have to drink it. I don't want you to turn into a bear."

"A bear?"

"Mommy says you turn into a bear if you don't drink coffee."

"Too late," I mumbled. "I'm already a bear and I'm trying to
hibernate, so go away and let me sleep."

Sebastian straddled my back and began shaking my shoulders. "Get up!"

Something was burning. "Did your mom overcook the bacon again?" I asked from beneath the pillow.

"No, there's a fire. Get up and snuggle me."

"A fire? We don't have a—"

"C'mon, Martin, get up!"

"Don't call me Martin, Seb."

"Dammit, Marty, please, wake up."

Wake.

Up.

I opened my eyes. I was staring up at a thousand silhouettes. Leaves danced in a slight breeze above me while the sun burned beyond them. Sebastian's hands gripped my shoulders, shaking me. No, not Sebastian. Not my son. It was Aether. Jeremy.

"Marty, man, are you all right? C'mon, you've got to wake up."

"I'm awake, I'm . . ." I rolled to my side and vomited with a hard, wrenching spasm that made it feel like my ribs were about to break.

Jeremy rubbed between my shoulder blades as my last meal spilled out onto the grass. "It's all right, we all heaved. It'll pass in a minute."

We all. I was beginning to remember. Kemetic Solutions, Jeremy, Portencia, Alison . . . that son of a bitch Fallon. Sebastian had been a dream. Nothing more. I wanted to get back to him, to feel his hands again, to hear him, smell him. But he was gone. He had never even been there.

"Are you okay?" Alison asked.

"Give me a minute." I hadn't cried in front of anyone since my father died, and I didn't want to have to explain why I was losing it. My boy had been with me, had known me. I wanted to go back. I could still feel his sticky face, smell breakfast burning in the kitchen . . .

"What's burning?" I asked.

I looked over and saw Port standing behind Alison, her clothes scorched where she had been strapped to the Chair.

"We all smell like campfire," Alison said. "But we're alive."

We were in a backyard that stretched back for a couple of acres, filled with tall grass and sheltered by towering oak trees. Insects whirred and buzzed around us in the noonday sun. A house, *the* house Portencia had drawn in crayon, sat a dozen yards away. "Where are we?" I asked.

"You mean *when* are we." Alison gave Port an affectionate pat on the back, like a proud parent.

When I stood, the ligaments in my knees ground together, crunching like pepper mills.

"Are you hurt?" Jeremy asked.

"No, just on the wrong side of fifty." I wiped my eyes with the back of my hand. My stubble was sharp against my skin, and from the smell of things I desperately needed a shower.

"Is everybody okay, then?" I asked.

"As far as time travelers go, I think so," said Alison.

Jeremy said, "We're time travelers, Marty. Like, for real."

Alison kept looking back at the house, apparently eager to get inside.

"Everyone is a time traveler," I said. "Only in one direction and very slowly."

Portencia was quiet, eyes closed, her face pointed toward the sky like a sunflower.

I had no idea how long Fallon had this poor girl locked up in the bowels of Kemetic Solutions, but I was glad that she was out, in the fresh air, with only herself to answer to.

Port sighed and opened her eyes. She looked at me and asked, "What do we do now?"

"You're the ones with superpowers. You tell me."

Alison spun around slowly, taking in the surrounding area. "Right now, I want to go inside. Chances are the Storm is looking for us, so we'll need to hide."

Jeremy shifted his weight between his legs, either out of nervousness or a desire to test their stability. He hadn't been back inside his body for very long. "I don't know about any of you, but I could eat a cow, hooves and all."

"Food's a good idea," I said.

We made our way inside the house, a cozy colonial nestled in a copse of oak trees that blocked the view of the neighbors perched an acre away on either side of the lot.

"Who lives here?" I asked.

"My great aunt Margaret," Port said. "She's on vacation. Majorca, I think. Is that how you pronounce it? She always travels in the summer."

"I hope she doesn't mind us crashing."

Port shrugged her shoulders. "I've been gone for a while. I think she'd be happy to see me."

I wondered if a missing persons report had ever made its way out of the Kemetic Solutions black hole. If it did, Portencia's sudden reappearance could spark an international media frenzy. And if the Storm was looking for us, and I couldn't believe that it wasn't, then that would bring it right to us. I'd investigated so many stories of missing children, but the ones who came back, unable or unwilling to say where they'd gone, those were the ones that stayed jammed in the folds of my brain. Now I was on the other side of one of those mysteries. No longer just deep in the story. I was complicit. Officially the worst reporter.

"We shouldn't tell anyone we're here yet," Alison said. "Just to be safe." She was spooked, and for good reason. If I wasn't still in a dream haze I'd probably have been hiding under a bed.

The house was cool inside. And quiet. Jeremy went to the fridge, while Alison inspected each room to make sure we were alone.

"There's nothing in here," Jeremy said of the fridge. "Let's order pizza."

"We can't let anyone know we're here. It isn't safe," Alison called back.

"I agree," I said. "We don't know if Fallon, the Storm, or anyone else might be looking for us."

"Good point," Jeremy said, "but if we're going to hide out here, we're going to need food. And I don't know about any of you, but I've spent the last couple weeks eating from a tube. I'd like to *bite* something."

"I'll get some groceries," I said. "Pick up a newspaper, supplies . . ."

"I can do it," said Alison.

"I want to come with you," Port protested, grabbing Alison's hand.

"You sure?" I asked Alison. "I don't mind going. I think Port's safer here with you, anyway. Just make a list of everything you'll need to survive for a couple of weeks and I'll get it. You too, Jeremy. Port, does your aunt have a car?"

Once I had a grocery list, I took Great Aunt Margaret's Corolla to the sleepy village shop and stocked up on supplies. I grabbed a newspaper and was shocked to see that it was thirty-one days since the night I broke into Kemetic Solutions. Thirty-one days.

How had I so recklessly gone from journalistic distance and an ironclad determination to not get involved, to million-dollar magic shows and month-long skips through time? The beginning of this path seemed like it was right behind me, but we'd really traveled a thousand miles in a matter of months.

Driving back through town, I thought how all the people and their houses seemed so foreign and small. We were on the other side of reality now, and the men and women going about their everyday lives, mowing lawns and walking dogs and checking mail, seemed like cardboard cutouts in a diorama. It wasn't just that magic was real; it was that reality was make-believe.

Back at the house, I pulled into the driveway and grabbed an armful of groceries out of the passenger seat. I'd just slammed the door shut when I felt something like a current of electricity start at the base of my neck and run like river eddies down my back. I froze, the bags sliding one by one off my arm and onto the driveway. The air had turned. Cool, wet, ozone-laden.

I whipped around, scanning the sky, the street in both directions. All clear. Maybe I was imagining it. On edge. It was good. That edge. I had to keep it. Needed it to keep them safe. I grabbed a bag off the ground and glanced up, past the house, to the sliver of backyard I could see beyond the driveway.

In the far tree line, past the acres of fresh-cut grass, was black. The sky above was clear, but within the trees, just behind them, was a black, inky void. Like nothing existed beyond the foliage. I didn't move. Couldn't quite comprehend what I was seeing. Part of me knew what it was. It must've been waiting. I was frozen in the standoff, until a massive clap of thunder erupted from it and the black started moving toward the house.

The Storm surged out of the trees like a tsunami wave of towering darkness and leaves and wind. It covered the backyard in seconds. I raced into the front door, throwing it open just as every window in the back of the house shattered. It was already inside. I screamed for them; the kids, as I kept calling them in my mind. Even though only Portencia was a child, they were all kids to me. Resilient and brave and vulnerable and trusting. They trusted me.

I ran to the top of the stairs, and it was already there, too. I saw whatever was inside it standing in the middle of the study: a figure of dirty wind and dead leaves whirling like a humanoid dust devil with a thousand faces. The gale of it howled in my ears, but as I stood there frozen, I realized it wasn't the sound of wind at all. It was voices. So many voices, all whispering, all chanting.

The air pressure dropped, and my ears popped painfully. The temperature fell, and the hairs on my arms stood on end. Papers tumbled off the desk and were sucked into its vortex. It appeared to face me but didn't react at all to my presence. It then floated to the corner of the room and threw open the closet door. Alison, Port, and Jeremy were inside, holding one another protectively as the Storm hovered before them.

I had no magic, no powers, no abilities to bring to bear. In my impotence, I ran for them, putting myself between them and the Storm, felt their hands grabbing onto me, out of fear, out of an attempt to keep *me* safe. Its "face" was inches from mine, and I could see there was a sudden wave of something akin to confusion in the swirling pits of its eyes. The Storm looked away, then surged back from the closet, making its way to the other side of the room, where it began violently pulling books from the shelves, searching.

I got up and motioned for them to follow me. One by one, they quietly made their way out of the closet and down the stairs. Back upstairs in the study, there was a sudden crash of glass, and then the house was filled again with silence.

Port pulled on my arm, quietly begging me to stay, but I went back upstairs anyway. The study was in ruins. Books, papers, and glass lay strewn all over the hardwood floor. The Storm was nowhere to be seen.

I looked out the shattered window and saw shards of glass in the grass below, a thousand glints of summer sun twinkling at me. I caught a hint of a shadowy whirlwind blistering through the oaks along the back of the property, but just as quickly, it was gone.

"What the hell just happened?" Alison asked. She stood there with her hands balled into fists, her jaw twitching.

"I don't know," I said. "But I think I have an idea."

I pulled Brightwell's coin from my pocket and held it in my palm for them to see. Tendrils of smoke rolled off of it. It was hot.

"What's that?" Portencia asked.

I handed it to her. She took the coin in her hand and examined both sides. "A gift," I said. "It's a protective charm somebody gave me years ago. I think it might've shielded us from the Storm. Blinded it to us."

"So if we stick together, the Storm won't be able to find us." Jeremy said.

"I'm not sure. I think so."

Port handed the token to Alison, who sat down and spun the token on the kitchen table with a delicate flick of her finger. "How far does its protection stretch?" she asked.

"I don't know, but I think we had to be in physical contact for it to hide you."

"Then we'll have to stick together." Jeremy said.

I wasn't keen on the idea, though. I had work to do. I wanted to pursue Fallon, I needed to get back to the Mountaineers, to see what I'd missed, tell them all I'd learned, and help them find more answers.

And I certainly didn't feel right dragging these three—all of them exhausted and terrified—along for the tumultuous ride.

"It isn't safe here," I said.

"What are you talking about? The Storm left. It couldn't see us." Jeremy sounded more desperate to convince himself than me.

"True, but the Storm knew you *were* here before you suddenly vanished from its sight," I said. "We don't know who or what works for the Storm, if it's in contact with anyone . . . For all we know there could be a Kemetic Solutions SWAT team heading here right now, and I have no idea what this coin's limits are."

"Where can we go?" Port asked.

"Let me take care of that."

"Marty," Alison said, "you're probably more compromised than any of us. They're going to have eyes on any place you call home."

"Don't worry. The place I have in mind isn't one I could ever call home."

I went to the phone hanging on the wall and lifted the receiver, my fingers hovering over the buttons. It took a moment for me to remember the number, but once I did, my fingers moved on autopilot. The line rang, and someone on the other end picked up.

"Hello?"

"Hey, Bella."

CHAPTER 16
SEPARATIONS

"Speak up and speak slowly. I'm old and don't
    understand all this newfangled
    whoziwhatsits."

— JOHANNA

We were at the train station at dawn. All three of my
companions had full duffels and full stomachs. Jeremy
pulled another baby carrot from the family-sized bag he
carried and crunched it in half. He hadn't stopped eating since I got
back from the grocery store.

Alison didn't like the idea. But she liked the idea of being chased
by the Storm even less and so wasn't going to put up more than a
token fight. Because Alison and I both knew that if push came to
shove, she would win—and deep down, she didn't want to.

"We agreed," I said. "I have to get back, help the Mountaineers
finish this. You three have done more than enough, *been* through
enough. Let me take it from here."

"I really should help you," Jeremy said. "Those systems can be a bit
wonky if you don't know what you're doing."

"You explained it all perfectly well to me. I'll be fine."

One of the things I wanted to do was visit the server where Jeremy had sent all of the Kemetic Solutions data. We were going to need those files. Since it was a run-of-the-mill server farm, accessing it wouldn't be difficult. Getting there with the Storm on my tail was going to be the hard part.

A voice came over the intercom in a nasally high frequency.

"That's our train," Jeremy said.

"How will we know your wife?" Alison asked.

"Ex-wife. She'll be the one holding a wrapped present when you arrive. Inside will be cash, keys to her car, and directions to her beach house. No one will find you there."

"And she's cool with this?" Jeremy asked around a mouthful of trail mix.

"Yeah. She's one of the best human beings on the planet."

"Then why'd you get divorced?" he asked.

Off my stolid reaction, he continued, "Oh, shit . . . Sorry, Marty. That's none of my business." Jeremy swallowed hard and stared at the ground.

If there was anyone who could understand the magical tragedy that befell Sebastian and the subsequent marital fallout, it would be these three. But my emotions were already frayed, and the last thing I needed was to dwell on Sebastian. "It's a long story we don't have time to get into right now. Port, you have the coin?"

Port tossed the coin in the air and caught it before secreting it away in her pocket.

Alison put her hand on my arm and said, "Are you sure you won't come with us? You've done so much already. You can be done, too."

"No, I can't. There are still answers I need. I can't stop now."

"If you want answers," she said, "you should look into Fallon's son, Nate."

"Why?"

"He's important. I think he's more important than chasing the Silver. Even more important than the Storm. I'm convinced of it. I was looking into him myself before . . ." She trailed off.

"Why were you looking into him?"

Alison opened her mouth to speak but stopped. She turned and watched a train pull away from the platform across from ours. "Somebody tipped his name to me. Just keep him in mind. All right?"

"All right."

Port dropped her duffel bag and wrapped her arms around me. Alison and Jeremy joined in on the hug until we were a bundled mass of arms on the side of the tracks.

"Thank you, Marty," Port said, her voice muffled in the folds of my shirt.

"Please, you guys are gonna make me cry."

Alison pulled back and wiped a tear from her eye. "Why, are you an ugly crier, Marty?"

"No, just ugly. We'll meet up again. I promise. Get on the train, kids. Be safe."

They grabbed their bags and hopped aboard. I watched them through the window. They waved to me as the train pulled away, taking them to safety. The train disappeared in the distance, and a breeze rose up and sent a chill through me. I turned and ran.

I didn't stop driving until I'd completely emptied my rental car's tank. Now that Port and the others had the coin, I had a magimystical bullseye on my back that I had no idea how to shake.

I'd been able to get a new phone before I sent them on their way, but I hesitated to check in with the Mountaineers. I knew Kemetic had somehow turned one of the Mountaineers, using them to relay information back to Fallon. I worried that visiting the Basecamp forums could somehow undo their progress, or even lead the Storm to them, and I couldn't risk either. At least not until it was crucial that I take the risk, or I was sure I was safe. Instead, I studied weather apps and followed newscasters. It was the only way to know if a sudden bout of inclement weather was a run-of-the-mill natural storm or the Storm itself coming to kill me.

It worked, for a while. I followed sunny weather up and down the East Coast, living at rest stops and cheap motels.

But inevitably, the Storm would always find me.

A gale wind would rise from nowhere, hail would suddenly hurl from the sky, and I'd have to run again. I wasn't getting any sleep, and it was getting harder to stay ahead of it. When I was in Charleston, an unseasonable thunderstorm blanketed the country from Florida to Maine with a deluge of rainfall and violent lightning strikes. I planned on making my way west, but as I was leaving the motel parking lot, I saw figures formed by the rain. The water gave them shape even as it slid along them, leaving an impression of otherwise invisible torsos and limbs and heads. The posse of watery ghosts moved across the asphalt slowly, deliberately, scanning for me.

There were so many that, as I sped away, I had no choice but to drive through them. Their watery faces splashed across my windshield to stare at me with feral grins until my windshield wipers sluiced them away. It was a game of attrition now. Eventually, the Storm would have me.

Or so I thought. Two weeks into the chase, I had pulled over at a rest stop along I-95 just before sunset. It was only through sheer willpower and an unhealthy amount of coffee that I had been able to stay awake long enough to park the car before passing out behind the wheel. When I finally woke, the sun was still setting—no, it was setting *again*. I had slept for nearly twenty-four hours, and the Storm hadn't found me.

The only way that could be possible was if it had stopped looking for me. But if the Storm wasn't looking for me, then who was it looking for? The kids? The Mountaineers?

When I called the beach house to check on Alison and the others, I could hear Portencia and Jeremy laughing in the background. Every morning, Alison told me, she would take long walks on the beach while the kids made incredibly elaborate sand castles. At night, they would cook their food over a bonfire on the beach while they watched the tide slowly wash their castles back out to sea, only to do it all over again the next day.

A few days ago, however, a tropical storm had skirted the coast and put them in a terrible fright. Alison and Jeremy apparently had one hell of a time getting Portencia safely inside, since she was bound and determined to stand and fight. Jeremy had to physically carry her indoors before the storm surge could sweep her away. It wasn't until it had passed that they realized it had been an actual storm, not a magimystical hit squad come to wipe them away. As far as they knew, the Storm itself had no idea at all where they were.

Once a week had passed without any sign of the Storm, I took a risk and checked up on the Mountaineers. I had a lot of catching up to do, and what I found at first glance was horrifying.

On the night of our escape from Kemetic Solutions, The Book of Briars had been incinerated by the Storm. Instead of the reassuring image of the Book's cover on the website, there was now a ruined, scorched husk. None of the fragment URLs worked, and the Book was no longer sending any clues to spur on those who were trying to open it.

But that didn't slow the Mountaineers in the least. Jeremy had been able to broadcast audio of our escape to YouTube, and Robert found the name of the twelfth fragment in the broadcast: Aorthora. Even though the Book had been destroyed, adding Aorthora to the URL revealed a page that had survived, which showed them another constellation. Sadly, the Book did not congratulate them for finding the fragment as it usually did. The Book had truly been destroyed.

As if that wasn't tragic enough, Endri discovered the truth about Teddy Fallon's "spy" within the Mountaineers.

ENDRI:

 It was Itsuki.

He'd mentioned having a rough time back in April and when I reached out to him he said he'd been ill but didn't elaborate.

When Fallon said what he said I suspected but wanted to be sure. I just heard back from Itsuki's wife. He had an inoperable brain tumor. He told her he'd been working on a book about magic with some people

on the Internet, something he could leave behind for
their daughter, so she would know about the world and
the life he lived.

He died almost a month ago.

The Mountaineers were distraught. One of their own had died. It
was now all too uncomfortably real. Even Eaves, the heart of the
Mountaineer leadership, had had enough. He was stepping away,
leaving the recaps and onboarding of new Mountaineers to Endri.
This adventure we'd all embarked on had become so dark. Too dark
for some of us.

It was obvious that the Mountaineers were trying to focus their
attention on something they could solve. Something they could fix. In
their desperate search for what to do now that the Book was
destroyed, Leigha stumbled on a website belonging or dedicated to
Fletcher Dawson, the author of *The Forest of Darkening Glass*. The site
was a single page with the symbol for the Joradian Safeguard spell
that the Mountaineers had used to protect the forum, as well as four
drop-down fields with the names of dozens of cities. In their
continued digging, Firefish also found a newly accessible page at the
Lost Athenaeum, which was a response to an inquiry by someone
using the RKAdler account.

LIBRARIAN:

 Librarian Request Responses:
6/03/17

Sorry it took so long to follow up on your request; I
knew I remembered those names from somewhere but
had to do some digging to find the source.

Galifanx, Gladitor, and Durkonos are objects in "The
Myth of Elainnor" by author Fletcher Dawson. They're
names of a shield, sword, and helmet, respectively.
There's a fourth object, but all we have on record is a

partial summary of the story. Another librarian I work with thinks the missing piece might be armor (using context clues and process of elimination).

Hope this helps. What are you working on, btw?

ADDED 6/06/17

Just wanted to give you a heads-up that there was a document filed along with the myth summary. I don't know if it's related or misfiled (I didn't even see it in the folder yesterday) but it's a list labeled "possible celestial bodies."

Ring any bells?

Dying to know what you're working on . . .

Rumyantsev

Vieux Haven

Cristossangre

Wallonia's Second

Harmony's Discourse

The Royal Hoop

Victoire

Bersimis-1

Capucines

Player's Frigate

Sadovaya

The Swallow

Haussmann's Sanctuary

Obregón's Requiem

Sallefavart

Argonauta

Moskva's Curve

Forgotten Forest

Legorreta's Interior

Zeus' Meadow

The Mountaineers realized that the clues related not only to locations in four cities around the world, but also that the four constellations they'd gathered over the past few months could be laid over the maps of the cities to help narrow down the clues.

This was the third assessment.

They discovered the answers to the Dawson "puzzle" were St. Petersburg, Montreal, Paris, and Mexico City, and with them found a new page on the site which held more of the "Ant & Caterpillow" story; an illustration corresponding to the last 1889 journal page they'd found; a key to unlock the "Cosmos" lock on the book, had it not been destroyed; and a full-page image of the chronocompass.

They weren't sure what to do next and were more than aware that there might not be *anything* to do next. The day of the Kemetic Solutions rescue, the Storm had broadcast a cryptic warning to the Mountaineers in Aether's transmission:

THE STORM:

 The dance has begun. We, the churning storm descend once more. As always, the Gates have moved to protect the worthless lives of their naive little mountain climbers. Ever lost, ever misinformed, reaching for a peak that you will never find. They care for you as they have never cared for previous manipulated acolytes. And in doing, they've made themselves vulnerable. They've stretched their meager power too thin. Soon, what little power the Council still possesses will fade and they will disappear back into the Fray. Then one by one we will come for you and wipe you from our world like marks upon a looking glass. How could you have ever won? To defeat an enemy, you must know them. The Gates will never win because they do not understand their enemy. We have no desire to abandon a world we control in completion. We were not learning how to open doors, we were learning how to close them. And in doing, break that precious book of yours, once and for all.

It had every reason to gloat. The Storm had swept through Kemetic Solutions, destroyed the Book, and claimed that the group protecting the Mountaineers would soon be too weak to protect them. This could've very well been the end of it all.

Then Deirdre started posting.

She was mostly unaware of what had happened with the Book and Kemetic because she and Cole had been wrapped up in a clue they'd found in the scarf her father left her. They'd found M. Grey Ackerly, unlocked a magically bound box he'd left her, and inside found not only a real, physical chronocompass, but also a new volume of Sullivan's journals that spoke of secret, warring societies, centuries of hidden history, and a magimystic realm called Neithernor.

Unwilling to quit, out of determination or an inability to admit we'd failed, the Mountaineers started picking apart everything Sullivan left her, the objects and the letters, sure there was something inside that would put them back on the path and fix everything that had been broken.

I was so lost in catching up that it took me a minute to hear the gentle pitter-patter of rain outside the motel room. I grabbed my keys and was nearly out the door when I decided to wait, to see if my paranoia was getting the better of me. A few minutes passed, but the rain didn't get any harder, the winds any faster. It was just rain, nothing more. I was grateful that the constant chill that had settled in after the night of the Translation had dissipated to the point that, if I didn't think about it, I wouldn't notice it was there. But I could still feel the weather changing, like a deep arthritic ache in my bones.

I knew enough about PTSD to know that those who suffered from it were never really free of it; they could only learn to live with it. How long would it be before I could hear rain again and not feel an urge to flee? When this was all over, I was going to have to find a nice, quiet place in the desert. A place with neither heavy rains nor violent winds. Neither, nor.

Deirdre was going to have to go to a Neithernor on her own, though what kind of a place it was, I didn't know. I felt for Deirdre. Her need to know all she could about her father, about what he left for her and why—it would propel her forward whether or not she wanted to proceed along the path he'd laid for her. I knew that well, for it was the same drive that spurred me on. Our need for answers outweighed the heft of our fears.

Surprisingly, Sullivan left a note for the Mountaineers, as well. At first, I thought it must have been meant for the '94 Mountaineers, since Sullivan couldn't have known about the newest incarnation. But it soon became clear that Sullivan had somehow known a great deal . . .

DEIRDRE: JULY 20TH, 2017:

    It was a whirlwind day, that.

I didn't want to leave Grey, wanted the day he'd imagined for so long to go on and on. But by evening he was tired and, frankly, so were we.

I didn't know what to do next and honestly was hoping you'd all figure something out. Then Cole told me what you'd done (don't want to say specifically until Cole and I work the charm thingy on my site) and how you'd figured it out. You never cease to amaze me. It's obvious why my dad put his faith in you.

I've since spoken with Grey twice over the phone. We have this sort of bond. We are the last of Ackerly Green Publishing. I've told him a little more, about you, some of the more general things that have happened, collecting the old AG books, etc. He tells me stories about my father, my grandfather, even my grandmother. It's all faded, but there. It's wonderful. A last gift from my father.

UPDATE: I was actually writing this post when Cole found something in the new journal—

Cole was flipping through it (I had flipped enough) and he found new entries.

We think we've narrowed down how this volume might work. We think it's either based on a time release or on location. Cole thinks it could be on a schedule and it seems possible but so far my dad has made it pretty tough to unlock these books. Just having someone wait for new pages doesn't seem like his style? But then I realised I'd gone back to the brownstone yesterday to pick up some clothes and things, and I think that's when the new pages could've shown up. The brownstone triggered them like some sort of magical GPS.

(I've been making a list of other places to visit to try out my theory. If you have ideas, please let me know.)

So, the actual pages . . . There are two entries, one in the front of the book, one in the back. The front one is to me, and the back is to you, the Mountaineers.

This journal is similar to Volume One of *The Monarch Papers* (seems like a thousand years ago) where I can't take photos of the pages so I had to transcribe what he wrote, and it's all even more incredible than any of the previous volumes.

The only thing I didn't copy was a sketch he made of the number 18 on your entry. It didn't seem especially relevant but if you think you want to see it I'll try and give it a go.

Fasten your seat belts. You're about to read some gobsmacking stuff.

THE INCOMPLETE MUNDANE HISTORY OF NEITHERNOR:

 My Deirdre,

There is a place beyond our world. A place untouched by the curse that erased magiq and all knowledge of it.

The following is what I know about Neithernor. When your mother and I walked the paths of wool and silver we knew so little, and had no clue where they would lead. But after you were born I found Neithernor. And my experience there, along with echoes of its history here in the mundane, helped me assemble what I believe is the most complete (but still unfinished) history.

My research of Neithernor goes back to Anne of Brittany's death and the eventual splitting of her court of artists' secret guild into the paths of wool and silver. At some later point in our current history the path of wool became Monarch's Mountain so that's what I'll call them going forward.

The two groups split, searching for illumination and beauty and magiq in their own ways . . . I don't know how or when exactly, but it was the Monarchs who first sought out Neithernor. (I believe the destroyed eighth unicorn tapestry may have held clues to its location and is the true reason it was destroyed.)

The Monarchs discovered a small but verdant place connected to our world through secret entrances, but wholly hidden from us. (I've read that at that point in history simply knowing about Neithernor and/or its name and imagining or wishing yourself there may have been enough to gain entrance.)

Neithernor was not affected by whatever removed magiq from our world. That's how the Monarchs learned that there was an alternate history of magiq. (A secret they kept from the world.)

Neithernor is a small "pocket world." It is a strange and gorgeous land of shores and fields, of deep woods

and unexplained ruins, mountains and caves, all
abandoned when memory of it was removed, but still
alive and rich with hidden magiq. The Monarchs
believed that this place had been created eras ago,
through magiq, as a home for the old guilds . . . A place
where those in the old time could slip away to use and
research magiq freely, because even in the time of those
who didn't die, magiq was secret and feared.

The Monarchs found written histories of the guilds,
learned magiq beyond our world's rudimentary charms,
and explored the strange island-like world, discovering
doors to and from places all over our mundane world.
They created their entire society around Neithernor
and the relics and old histories they found. At some
point they created the original path of wool so that
others like them could find it and explore and learn and
cast. Many Monarchs lived normal lives here, then
secreted away to rule and explore their hidden
kingdom.

But the path of silver also discovered tales of
Neithernor and became desperate to share in its wealth.
The Monarchs allowed them entry. The Silver chose a
remote place to call home, and kept to themselves, as
was the agreement. (There had been conflict among the
groups in the years following the court of Anne, even
before Neithernor, having to do with their differing
views and methodologies.)

There was peace for an untold time. But then
something unknown happened that pitted the
Monarchs against the Silver. I don't know whether it
was a gradually building conflict or if there was a single
catalyst (or who was ultimately at fault) but it escalated
into "The War of Neithernor." Many were lost but MM
drove the Silver out of the land and barred all entrance
back.

The Silver scrounged for power here in the
mundane world, trying to use everything they had to
get back in. But they had been exiled.

Years later, the Council sent The Book of Briars to
Monarch's Mountain and the Silver scrambled to take it
from them. They had grown strong in their own secret
place here in the mundane, using what they learned
from Neithernor and gathering artifacts and objects
from the old time . . . They had also created the Storm.
Once they realized the book was not for them, they sent
the Storm, and in doing all but wiped away any memory
the Monarchs had of Neithernor. Aside from the Silver,
and a few whispers and stories, Neithernor was
forgotten again.

The paths fell into ruin. The ashes of Monarch's
Mountain became a small secret sect here in the
mundane, unaware of what they had discovered. Left
with nothing but esoteric records of their former,
glorious history. And Neithernor, untended, became a
volatile and lonely place.

But Neithernor is still there. Still barred from most.
But I found the way in. And in that strange place I
learned magiq.

And there I found the little red house your mother
had somehow dreamed of all her life, and inside of it . . .
well, you're going to have to see for yourself.

And then, the letter to you.

THE LETTER TO THE MOUNTAINEERS:

 Mountaineers,
      I don't know much about the 18 Gates (the Council

of the 18 Gates) but I'll share everything I've learned over the years.

They have sent the book, in varying forms, to groups for centuries. Groups analogous to you, the Mountaineers. They are particularly fond of those who have found themselves on the path of wool. Perhaps it's easier to reach ones seeking what they seek. It requires immense power to send the book to us from where they are. An in-between place called "the Fray," an unformed sort of purgatory where I believe they became trapped when everything changed. I don't know how much they know about the truth. The Fray is a strange place from what I've learned, difficult to communicate with, and there's much I still don't understand. But I know it takes them decades, sometimes centuries, to gather enough magimystic energy to send the book, borrowing power from our world, searching for power in theirs.

But the book persists because in each era the 18 Gates have used what power they have to not only send their cherished object to us, but also to protect it from the Storm and its master. They have kept the book safe while also trying to spread what remained of that protection to those who've tried to unlock it. But those on the path of silver have wiped away almost everyone who has ever tried to open it, and it becomes harder and harder to send it every time.

I may be wrong, but I believe the book is a kind of seed spell. I think the book is the vessel for the whisper of a story. A most powerful kind of magiq. A story that wishes to be told. Old, or perhaps new, I don't know . . . But within it, the truth. I believe it's been planted in the book like a seed in a garden. And every time the book has come to us, we have nurtured it, with perseverance, goodwill, and with magiq. The stronger the book, the better chance we have of telling the story within and changing everything.

Yes, the book is destroyed.

But I have a plan.

A plan that took years of design. And to set the plan in motion, I convinced the 18 Gates to focus their power to protect you instead of the book when the Storm arrived, and let the book burn. It was a difficult choice, but they knew we had to try something desperate to have a chance.

Much of the "how" won't make sense at this moment, but I hope by now you've looked to my letter to Deirdre and found something the 18 Gates left with our storyteller friend.

The Storm's master has collected immense power but holds it out of hand, out of sight from us. Soon there will be nothing left here. But for now, we have an advantage. One they aren't yet aware of.

We have you Now, and an unburned book Then.

Your book is gone, but with our guidance you are going to help your predecessors open theirs. What will happen then, I don't know. But we have all that we have ever needed. The book and the Mountaineers.

Together, with the help of my daughter, you will change everything.

CHAPTER 17

TRAVELING

"As some pretty cool people have said in the past,
"Trust the flow of magiq."

— BRENDON

Sullivan's plan was, for lack of a better term, bonkers. Using the current group of Mountaineers to unlock the Book in the past sounded impossible—but putting that aside, it was also admittedly genius. The modern Mountaineers had proven themselves extremely capable, solving every puzzle that had come their way. The '94 Mountaineers were clever, but there were significantly fewer of them, and they were more secretive than the current crop.

But as I thought about it, it was possible that their secrecy had been due to Sullivan's crazy plan all along. The thought of it was surreal.

But my thoughts drifted back to the little red house. He'd found it, somewhere in Neithernor. And inside was something so incredible he couldn't describe it.

That dream had plagued me, consumed me. Lauren pointing to the little red house as I surrendered to the cold. The fire in the window. The figure watching me, waiting for me.

I was never one to hope. Not completely. Definition of pragmatic. But there was this sliver of something that felt at least hope-adjacent, which was telling me that was Sebastian in the window. Or at least the part he'd lost; the part looking for me and waiting at the hearth for me to find him. Like the dream I had after escaping Kemetic Solution. When he'd begged me to get out of bed.

No. I had to shake the dreams off. The cold. There was work I had to do.

Brendon worked out that certain words in Sullivan's message to the Deirdre referred directly to attributes and iconography related to the guilds:

> Bravery = Weatherwatch
> Heart = Gossmere
> Hope = Gossmere
> Dark Woods = Balimora
> Shore = Ebenguard
> Machine = Flinterforge

Robert then visited the chronocompass on the Fletcher Dawson website and clicked each guild letter and location in that specific order. The image of the chronocompass suddenly began to move. It wasn't just an image; it was some kind of spell. The arms of the object began spun, the moons rotated, and the clouds began to move past like they were carried on a breeze. Four chimes tolled, and then the page redirected them to a new page, which had a smaller, ever-spinning chronocompass at the top and a text field where they could input a message—or even attachments. Above the field was a warning:

> "Be careful what you say or send, or time itself is
> what you'll rend."

It was obvious that this was some kind of time travel spell. And whoever was on the receiving end of that text field was most likely, somehow, going to be connected to the Mountaineers and everything that had happened in the late 90s.

Several Mountaineers sent messages through the text field, asking vague questions, hoping someone would get a response. At 4 a.m. (coinciding with the four chimes on the chronocompass) the blank text field was replaced with a message.

A REPLY:

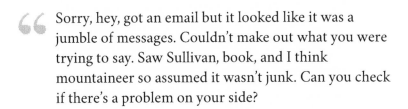 Sorry, hey, got an email but it looked like it was a jumble of messages. Couldn't make out what you were trying to say. Saw Sullivan, book, and I think mountaineer so assumed it wasn't junk. Can you check if there's a problem on your side?

It seemed the various messages had merged into a single incoherent one. The Mountaineers decided they would wait until 4 p.m. (when they assumed the reply would change back to the text field) and send one agreed-upon response. They debated what to say, worried about divulging too much information for fear of creating some sort of paradox. Augustus, Furia, Robert, Deyavi, and Nimueh all worked together to craft their message, finally deciding that Nimueh would be their spokesperson.

NIMUEH:

 Hi,
   Sorry about before. We're the Mountaineers and we have a couple of questions for you: Who are you? *When* are you? Have you heard of something called Neithernor?
   Thanks!

And at 4 a.m., they received:

A REPLY:

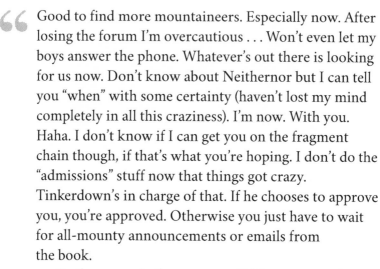 Good to find more mountaineers. Especially now. After losing the forum I'm overcautious . . . Won't even let my boys answer the phone. Whatever's out there is looking for us now. Don't know about Neithernor but I can tell you "when" with some certainty (haven't lost my mind completely in all this craziness). I'm now. With you. Haha. I don't know if I can get you on the fragment chain though, if that's what you're hoping. I don't do the "admissions" stuff now that things got crazy. Tinkerdown's in charge of that. If he chooses to approve you, you're approved. Otherwise you just have to wait for all-mounty announcements or emails from the book.
By the way, what's your name?? My user name's Augernon but everybody calls me Augie.

They weren't just emailing through time. They weren't just reaching out to a random predecessor. They were talking with Augernon, the man I'd met in the mental institution in Maryland. The man who'd somehow sacrificed his own sanity for his friends. The Mountaineers were stunned and scrambling to figure out their next steps.

REMUS:

 If we don't open the Book now/in the past, then there won't be any chances to try and open it again since there won't be a Book to open, just some crispy Book bits. Plus, magic is running out in this world, which would make it even harder to try and open the Book even if another Book could be sent to a future group of Mounties. To my understanding, our Book is the only Book of Briars, and is the same one the '94 Mounties had, which is why it's a big deal that ours is destroyed. We're the Council's last hope to open this thing, that's why they've gone to such extreme lengths to keep us safe (plus Sullivan convinced them to).

ENDRI:

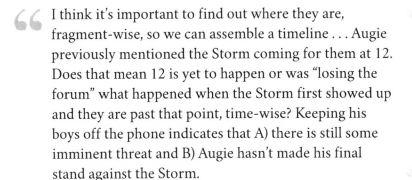 I think it's important to find out where they are, fragment-wise, so we can assemble a timeline . . . Augie previously mentioned the Storm coming for them at 12. Does that mean 12 is yet to happen or was "losing the forum" what happened when the Storm first showed up and they are past that point, time-wise? Keeping his boys off the phone indicates that A) there is still some imminent threat and B) Augie hasn't made his final stand against the Storm.

This is mind-blowing.

DEYAVI:

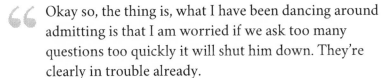 Okay so, the thing is, what I have been dancing around admitting is that I am worried if we ask too many questions too quickly it will shut him down. They're clearly in trouble already.

I've toyed with different ideas, but I'm standing by my earlier opinion that we should ask about being involved with their fragment hunt to find out where they are and what, if anything, we can do and assess how immediate their danger is. And we can ask if they've had contact with the Council . . . But I really think our focus should be Tinkerdown and getting connected to their BoB, if it's possible for us to do that from over 20 years in the future.

AUGUSTUS_OCTAVIAN:

 I agree with Deyavi's thought that this magiqal singularity probably can't put us in touch with whomever we want. I don't think it will be fruitful to try and get Tinkerdown's contact information to get recruited into the '94 Mounties. Fletcher Dawson's site doesn't have an address field, we can't direct any of our messages, so I think it's safe to assume that we can only communicate with Augernon.

ROBERT:

 I think we all agree that telling him anything about the future is a huge red flag and we're not doing that unless we have no other choice.

I also agree with Nimueh's proposed line of questioning. Remember the book's fragments (and Sullivan's hints) have almost always sent us towards people who need help. In the course of helping them, we get our fragments.

The key question I would think is how can we help them in their current situation? Without destroying space and time, of course. Heck, we may have 'already' helped them, and the only reason Augie is alive now and was capable of warning Ascender is because we saved them. Trust in the flow of magic. We're talking to Augie for a reason, and that will become apparent if we help him out as best we can.

They devised a new message and responded at 4 p.m.

NIMUEH:

 Hi Augie!
My name's Nimueh, and I'm one of a small group of Mountaineers. We only just found out how to contact you guys, actually. What happened to your forum? What is looking for you and why?
As for the fragments: Is there a way you could put us in touch with Tinkerdown? Or maybe you could tell us how we might get approved? We'd really like to see if we could help you guys out. Which fragment are you on, by the way?
Thanks again,
Nim

A group of Mounties from around the world started keeping one another company online, waiting for Augernon's response to roll around. The 4 a.m. squad was up when he wrote back.

AUGERNON:

 Good to meet you, Nimueh. What's it mean?
It's been weeks and we're still trying to figure out what happened to the forum. A kid from Missouri was the last one to post before it went dark. She got on to

tell everybody something was watching her through her window. Nobody heard from her after. A dozen mounties went silent that night. Everybody who replied to her. It was the weekend and I don't have a dial-up in the flea-bitten backwoods of Maryland so I didn't get the email alerts until the next week at work. Ascender tried to track the missing mounties down and found Missouri's number. Her parents said there was an electrical storm outside their house that night that made the lights blow out and the radio and TV start screaming backwards. They're convinced their daughter got so scared she ran into the woods like a dog and just got lost.

We got locked out of the forum that night and then it just disappeared.

So that's why Tink is overcautious now. We're still picking up the pieces. Give him a couple weeks.

We've dealt with some crazy stuff, but nothing like this. We don't scare so easy though. We're hoping to find some way to track the missing mounties down, figure out what happened. Find who's behind it. Maybe the Book will help. We've done and seen minor magic (if you believe that sort of thing) but there must be some powerful mojo in that thing to have it locked so tight.

So we're back in the email chain. We know it's not really safe, but what are you gonna do? This is bigger than all of us now, and aside from my real family these wackos are the next closest thing. Some of my best friends. Can't abandon them now. Especially not now. We have to see this through.

To answer your other question, the forum broke right after the third evaluation (we get tested after every four fragments). We're stewing on fragment 13 right now, but we're a little stuck. We might be missing

something and I'm hoping it didn't get lost in the storm
that night.

Where's your group been congregating? I've heard of
other mountain lodges, glad to have you come around
to ours, terrifying as it is right now.

Take care.

The Mountaineers decided that, since there was an attachment
field, it couldn't hurt to send Augernon the Joradian Safeguard
materials to try and keep the rest of the Mountaineers in the 90s safe.

NIMUEH:

 Hi Augie,

Thanks for the reply! Nimueh possibly comes from
the Greek "Mnênê" meaning "memory," though I use it
cause it's one of the names given to the Lady of the Lake
in Arthurian legend. What does Augernon mean?

I talked it over with my fellow Mountaineers, and
with all the disappearances going on, it might be best
not to give up our location.

You said you all were stuck on something with
Fragment 13—that's right near where we are as well!
We just received the Cosmos key. Is that the same key
you guys got for the third assessment? We always
wondered if the process for opening the Book is the
same for all groups of Mountaineers. We never got a
new fragment email from the Book, though. Maybe you
could copy what the Book sent you and send it over,
and we can start helping out with clues for fragment 13!

I've attached a spell our lodge has been using to
protect digital content. Hope this helps keep you and
yours safe while we work on the next fragments
together!

All the best,
Nim

AUGERNON:

 Nim, just when you think you've seen it all. If you don't
mind me asking, where did you find this spell? We
never thought to look for something like it. Man, I'm
trying not to think about how the past few weeks
woulda turned out with that in our back pocket. I
should've thought to look. It's my responsibility to keep
this group safe.

Anyway, we got the Cosmos key after we finally
figured out how to assemble the seven panes of sky in
the wishing scope. That one almost killed us. You? It's
weird you didn't hear from the BoB but I wouldn't take
it personal, it's an odd bird even for a talking book.

So what we have now is obviously only half of what
we need to solve fragment 13. Everybody's scrambling
to try and solve it anyway 'cause they're freaking out,
but I'm trying to figure out what we missed. There's
gotta be something else.

I don't have a connection at home so I won't be able
to write until Monday but let me talk to Tink and even
if I can't get you on the thread maybe I can share some
of it with you. See if you see something we don't. We
wouldn't be in any worse a situation if you had the clues
. . . I don't think you have ill intent but even if you did,
having copies of the clues won't hurt us, right?

Augie

Oh yeah, Augernon's a name I made up when I was a

pup. My imaginary friend. First thing I thought of when I heard about other people looking for the LC and so I made it my user name.

Nimueh's a great choice. I'm a big Arthurian buff too, that's why I asked. You an Ebie by chance? Although Lady of the Lake . . . she's a benevolent chaos-bringer for sure, so you might be a Balimoran. Am I close?

You and yours stay safe, please.

NIMUEH:

 Hello again Augie,

Hope you are well and that your lodge is holding okay still. We know what it's like to lose members. We lost one of our leaders before I joined, and the guys used some magiq to lay him to rest. We found the spell we gave you sometime during fragment 9 or 10 from someplace called the Low. Ever heard of it? All I can say about the spell is that I wish we'd been able to give it to you guys sooner. But as a couple of my lodge mates keep telling me, the flow of magiq is a strange and unpredictable thing. At least you have it now.

A few of us were wondering if you'd like some help with your missing Mounties, too. It was someone called Ascender who said they were looking for them, right? If you think we can help him in any way, please do let us know!

Yeah, fragment 12 was a killer for us, too! In all honesty, I'm still wondering how we got through it! There was something we were wondering, though—if

you knew anything about a Fletcher Dawson? There's a
bit of excitement going around the lodge at the news
that we might be back on the fragment trail and helping
you guys out with this.

Anyway, stay safe!

Nim

Oh, also, yeah, I'm Balimoran. I take it from your
first guess that you're an Ebie? It's funny though, we
have another here who uses another name for the Lady,
Viviane, and she's Flinterforge. Strange, huh?

AUGERNON:

 Hey Nim,

Always a lotta stuff to get through on Monday but I
finally read your email. First off, yep, Ebie through and
through.

We've heard of the Low, found a couple scraps from
them here and there, but nothing as powerful as the
protection spell, that's for sure. Really appreciate it.
We're gonna try it later this week by putting the symbol
in our email signatures. Would be nice to keep the
fragment thread safe if nothing else.

This might be too personal but with everything
going on, it reminds me of this recurring dream I have
sometimes. About my family. Where something bad
happens and I can't stop it. Like my boys are in the
water and get pulled out to sea and I'm stuck in the
sand. Scary, but I can always wake up from that, you
know. But now I have that feeling every time I talk to a
fellow Mounty. I wanna do whatever I can but know

I'm helpless right now. I can't protect them. Not all of them.

You gotta promise me your folks will keep their heads down or else I'm gonna spread my worry too thin.

Now, onto the meat of the matter. Tink didn't write me back about you guys so I'm gonna assume that's a soft yes and will beg for forgiveness if I have to. I attached what we have and maybe you can see if you can make heads or tails of it.

Fletcher Dawson! Boy, that brings me back. I've been into fantasy books and magic and the like since I was a pup, so I pretty much wore out my copy of *Forest of Darkening Glass*. I think he wrote some follow-ups, but we didn't have a lot of bookstores where I grew up and I think they're all out of print now . . . What's your interest in Dawson? If I remember, he's not young but he's too young to have anything to do with the LC. You know something we don't?

You know what? These days my brain tries to connect everything to all of this. Just lemme bask in talking about books for the love of books for a change.

Augie

P.S. I'll shoot Sender a message and see if he needs help. He's a bit of a loner, but desperate times . . .

The Mountaineers quickly got to work on the puzzle Augernon had sent.

He'd attached two pages. One page had the word "THEN" printed at the top with a five-by-five square grid beneath it. Each square contained a large letter and two smaller letters in opposite corners. Some even had numbers. The bottom of the page also had letters that didn't make sense.

The second page contained text from what looked to be the familiar journal from 1889.

1889 JOURNAL:

 I wake in the room of a hospital. Gray buildings loom
outside the grime-stained window. I am in the city
again. How? What do I last remember? Sand. Ships half-
buried in it, bows pointing to the silver sun. A hand
outstretched, waving to me, calling for me. A welcome. I
had walked so far into those woods that I found the sea.
A strange green sea where all manner of mast and man
had washed ashore. People dressed in bygone fashions
and others wearing clothes from what must have been
times yet to come. A shore where time was as ever-
changing as the great green sea itself. And then a voice
called to me. From the dark world I left. How had they
found me? Had I not wandered far enough into my new
world? They called me by my name.

A name I thought I'd left in the dead gray city along
with all the memories of my life before wonder.

I stepped into the sand but felt a hand on my
shoulder. And somehow the sea and the shore of times
intermixed began to fade away. As if someone had
drawn a curtain down over it. A curtain painted with
the mundane world I thought I had escaped.

A girl found me walking in a dry river bed, unable to
hear or see her. She went to the farmer who employed
me. In my cabin they found the name of a doctor in
New York City whose care I had been in before I
ventured to the green world and then beyond. The
doctor who listened to my fractured recollections. Of
other worlds. And other lives. The doctor knew my
name. He'd been the one who drew me back from what
he tried to explain were nothing more than imaginings.
That all I had seen and heard, tasted and touched, had
been inside my sundered mind.

The text from the entry surrounded what looked to be a clock face, but there were no numbers to indicate minutes or hours, only hash marks. At the bottom was another string of Roman numerals.

Viviane cut out the letters in the grid and found a phrase hiding in them:

> "Cut into strips on solid lines. Weave the
> timelines together. Past horizontal. Vertical
> present."

Since they had a "Then" page from 1998, the Mountaineers reasoned that they'd need to find a "Now" page from our time to complete the puzzle. While they researched and continued working, they sent a message to Augernon to buy time and learn more.

NIMUEH:

 Hey Augie,

Don't worry about us, we don't seem to be getting any attention here luckily. We'll keep alert though.

You may be glad to hear that we made a lot of progress on the fragment actually. So a couple of us decided to focus on the letters under the grid and Robert began rearranging them. Viviane (the Mounty I mentioned last week) and Crytter got them to make sense: "Cut into strips on solid lines. Weave the timelines together. Past horizontal. Vertical present." We think the page you sent us is the "past" referred to, so it seems you're right about a missing half. We're currently looking for a page which we're assuming will be named "Now." Did these pages come directly from the Book?

I remember Dawson's name coming up recently, along with "The Myth of Elainnor." Do you know it? We didn't realise he was connected to *The Forest of Darkening Glass!* Shame to hear it's out of print; you don't happen to know somewhere we might get our hands on some of his works? I think a few of us here would love to read them.

Stay safe,

Nim

The Mounties commented on Deirdre's blog with a short list of important locations in New York City. The plan was that she and Cole would visit each site with the new journal, in the hope that it might reveal clues about what to do next or where to find the "Now" page.

AUGUSTUS_OCTAVIAN:

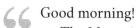 Good morning!

The Mounties and I were discussing locations this weekend—we came up with Central Park, the Morgan Library, Grand Central Station, and the Cloisters. Hope this helps unlock more pages.

DEIRDRE:

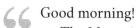 Thanks Augustus, I'd been thinking about locations that were personally important to my dad, I hadn't considered "puzzle" locations! I may skip Central Park today (it's absolutely pouring in NYC) which leaves the Morgan and Grand Central in midtown, and the Cloisters way north. Any preference where I start?

AUGUSTUS_OCTAVIAN:

66 There's also the abandoned City Hall station. You could
certainly try there.

DEIRDRE:

66 Okay . . . Should take most of the day. We'll start at the
Cloisters and work our way down.

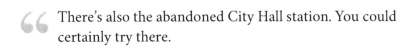

66 We've tried the Cloisters and didn't find anything. Just
arrived at the Morgan, which is closed today (forgot to
check.) We wandered the perimeter, but didn't find
anything. We can always try again tomorrow. On our
way to Grand Central now.

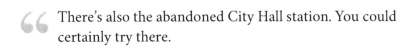

66 We went to all locations but there are no new entries in
the journal. Were there other places you thought to
look? Cole has to work tomorrow but I'm free (literally
have nothing else to do with my time right now, except
this.)

AUGUSTUS_OCTAVIAN:

66 If the weather holds tomorrow, try Central Park. Also,
the NYC public library may be another good place to
try! The other Mounties are coming up with great
suggestions left and right.

The next day Deirdre posted a new comment.

DEIRDRE:

 I just got back from Central Park (I went to the library this morning.) Nothing new showed up for you guys . . .

However, on the train home I found a pocket in the back of the journal that I know wasn't there before. I don't know when it appeared, but it wasn't there yesterday morning. I'm pretty sure the pages inside are for the Mountaineers.

I'm running back to the brownstone now (to my trusty scanner.) Will post a blog update since I can't attach files in comments. Hope this helps.

Inside was the "Now" page the Mountaineers had been searching for, along with more of the 1889 journal and another blank clock face.

1889 JOURNAL:

 I fought with all my will against that thought. It could not have been a dream. I had found a world so wondrous it was beyond any man's ability to conjure, least of all mine. But his insistence worked its way in me and now I am here in the city again. Withered. The doctor speaks my name as if it were an anchor to keep me from drifting away again. He has cursed me. I cannot see the wondrous world. Only gray. I ask to be left alone. To forget. To sleep until I do not wake again, because I have remembered something. I've remembered that this place holds untold loss for me. A loss so profound that I beg sleep to sweep me away.

But this morning the doctor brings me a box. Inside is what I left behind when I first escaped the city. He tells me I have a life that is worth fighting to find again. My purpose is to discover what happened, what split me, and how to mend myself once again.

Inside, a flannel shirt and billfold. Trousers made of strange material. He remarks that the shoes are odd, with soles like Indian rubber, possibly fashioned in another country.

Perhaps I am from another land, he wonders. I nod. But as I hold all the things I left behind, my clothing, my shoes, my watch, a new truth begins to grow inside my breast. I am here in the gray but my vision has opened something inside me. I can see now that my heart has drifted on the great green sea of time. I don't belong here, as I have long suspected. Who I am and what I am here to do begins to crash against me all at once. I have somehow drifted onto the edge of another era with magic in my heart and a great purpose only now awakening, pulling me toward shore. Not another land, my doctor. I have sailed here from another time.

The Mountaineers, led by the puzzle work of Crytter, Viviane, Rimor, and Robert, set out to follow the clue that Viviane had discovered earlier. Nimueh wasn't available when it was time to send Augernon a new message, so Viviane had the honor of reaching out.

VIVIANE:

 Hi Augie,

Viviane here, or Viv if you like. I'm part of Nimueh's group. She said she mentioned me? Anyway, Nimueh's not available right now—she's fine, just badly needed sleep—but we made some urgent progress on the fragment and wanted to let you know.

Earlier today, a "benefactor" of ours with ties to AGP sent us these two additional pages: a "Now" to match the "Then" and another story page with a blank circle.

Following the instructions we already had, our Mounties cut out strips and did a bit of paper weaving. Turns out, if you weave the strips in order of the numbers, one pattern of over and under reads "Overlap equal times and tape," and the opposite weave reads "The times are one instruction."

Laying out the strips so that the matching times overlap gives two more sentences. The first row of small letters reads, "This is the present timeline," and the bottom reads, "Cut out dashes / use the clocks." We've tried out different things from there but not gotten anywhere yet. Given our work on past fragments, we're wondering if something will appear in the blank clock spaces? If not, maybe your group will have some other ideas for this new information.

Don't worry about us; our group has stayed safe so far, and we'll look out for each other. Someone wise once told us to "trust the flow of magiq." And, what do you know, progress! I have faith that we can get this book unlocked if we work together.

To bolster Augernon's confidence she had given him the same piece of valuable advice he'd recently given us. We'd completed a "time loop," giving Augernon advice that might help him, but which he would also give us almost twenty years later in *our* time of need.

It seemed to work:

AUGERNON:

 Whoa, this is incredible!
    I'm forwarding everything on to Tink and company right now. (We got far better puzzlers than me.) Man, I'm feeling more hopeful right now than I have in weeks. We might have a shot at this. Cheers to "benefactors."
    And good to meet you, Viviane. And just 'cause I gotta ask, you're absolutely sure Nim's okay?
    Really sharp work. Where the heck have you guys been this whole time?

I really enjoyed reading Augernon's communication with the Mountaineers as they worked through fragment thirteen. It was nice to read the words of the bright, charming man he'd once been.

DEIRDRE: JULY 25TH, 2017:

 Last night Cole and I finally sat down and did the Joradian Safeguard to my blog. You know, aside from fannying about with the journals, I realised I haven't had the chance to do any sort of actual magic until now. I know this is going to sound sooooo eye-rolly but it was . . . romantic? Intimate? Definitely a fun night. I made the wheel and Cole took on the keeping vessels because I am rubbish at origami (as it turns out.)
    Coming up with the six pale memories had me thinking a lot about the past ten months or so. How different my life was this time last year. How

different I was this time last year. Where I was, what I thought I wanted . . .

Everything changed with that letter from Mr. Wallace.

I want to finish this, see Neithernor, do whatever I have to do there to help you, us, if only to gain some kind of closure. For my father as much as me. The idea that he did all of this, and died before he ever saw it come to fruition . . . well, it's the least I can do to see it through.

But at some point, it has to be finished. Right? Whatever we're meant to do with the journals, the puzzles, it's all leading somewhere, and then it will be done. And then what? The idea of learning the truth, possibly bringing magic back into the world somehow . . . it's wonderful, exciting, but for me, abstract. Unfamiliar. I don't really know what it means, you know? Will we wake up and the whole world's changed? Or will it be like a trickle? Someone remembers something, someone on the other side of the world remembers something else . . . I don't know. And it's hard to pin my life on something like that. I know my father did. But he was consumed by this, at the cost of family, friends . . .

I have something here. In New York. With Cole. And I still want to do something good for the world that's tangible, real, creative. Whether that means rebuilding Ackerly Green, or doing something new, right now it's all bright and exciting and I want to feel all of it. And share it. I wouldn't change much about what led me here, but I'm also ready to do whatever it is I'm supposed to do, and then get on with my life.

The thing is . . . Right now I am as close to my father as I'm ever going to be. These journals are all I'll ever have of him, and part of me knows that the Neithernor volume might be the last. Maybe I'm making my peace with that, but I'm also ready for what little closure might come from seeing his plan through and then starting to live the life he's given me a chance to live. I need to figure out what I want outside of all the expectations and plans and machinations. Maybe in my heart I'm not some magimystic adventurer, but I can still do good. Maybe change the world in other ways . . .

But I'll never have anything more of my father than this, never more than chasing his ghost.

I think the time is coming for me to let him go, the idea of him, because that's all that's left.

I couldn't help but think of Sebastian and how much I wished there had been something like a Safeguard spell to protect him. Even now, after three decades of estrangement, I couldn't let him go. It was unhealthy of me to cling to him, to his memory, but it still haunted me after all these years.

Of course, my son was still alive, happy, living a productive life with a beautiful family. There was really nothing more a father could ask for. And I was sure that Sullivan Green would want the same for his daughter.

It was a struggle for Deirdre and understandably so. But letting go of her father wasn't going to be easy, as it seemed he wasn't ready to let go of her.

The Mountaineers were struggling to figure out the fragment. They'd formed the strips of letters into a loop, but the clock faces were still blank and no other clues had appeared. Nimueh decided to check in on Augernon and his Mounties:

NIMUEH:

 Hey Augie!
Nim back again. Thanks for your concern, but I was

just really tired from trying to get the page solved. But seriously, don't go worrying about us! We're all fine here.

Anyway, how's the progress coming with the "Now" page for you? Wondering if you guys can find anything we missed. Right now, looks to me like we're waiting for something . . .

Have you heard more from Tink or Ascender? Hoping everyone's okay.

AUGERNON:

 Wish I had better news.

The puzzle chain worked through the night and they got as far as your folks did. Even had my wife look at it 'cause she's a hundred times smarter than me.

We gotta be missing something. Don't worry though, we'll keep plugging away.

Haven't heard from Ascender but Tink's okay. On edge, but okay.

Every time the phone rings I think it's whatever's out there, coming for me and mine, but we can't give up. We can't let them take our hope too. Like Viviane said, we gotta trust the flow of magic.

The Mountaineers were struggling, both now and then. Augernon also mentioned in a subsequent message that something stressful had happened but didn't elaborate. It all felt like they were running out of time.

The solution to the puzzle finally came when Deyavi remembered something Deirdre had previously blogged about, a sketch of the number "18" that her father had made in the journal. She asked Deirdre to recreate it and post it for them. Sure enough, the "1" showed them how to twist the long ribbon of taped-together strips, and the "8" showed them how to loop it into a sort of Moebius strip.

Nimueh filled Augernon in on their progress, and when he responded he was incredibly excited. They had followed Nim's instructions, and the clock face on their "Then" page now had words on it—a jumbled version of "Hickory-Dickory Dock."

Sure enough, our "Now" page changed soon after. The modern-day Mountaineers went back and forth over the course of several days, trying to figure out how all the pieces worked together, while Augernon also filled them in on what was happening to the Mountaineers in 1998.

AUGERNON:

 Will let you know if they come up with something. We're all working overtime on this to try and figure it out.

Sorry about not filling you in last week. Ascender was helping with the search for Missouri. Last week, he found her. She can't remember anything. Not just memories, but about herself. She kept saying something about "seeing the separation" and hearing "them" now. The poor girl's there, but isn't anymore.

Thing is, my grandpa lost his wits a bunch of years back. It wasn't dementia, the doctors said. He was healthy, still young, for a grandfather. My dad said it was the war finally getting to him, but he had moments of clarity, like he'd sort of wake up. He said we won the war, but he'd learned later that the bad guys had already conquered the world and we never even knew it. Everybody thought he was nuts. But he told me something. Something that Missouri told Sender last week. He told me "they" hide in a palace made of doors.

That's where they rule from. They watch us from behind the doors. Waiting.

I feel like I've been heading this way since I was a kid. I got no idea what it means, and even now part of me wants to think it's just a mixed up memory. Like my brain's hitting play and record at the same time. Like déjà vu or something. But I remember him telling me. Remember how it felt.

It gave me chills. Still does.

There might be a place out there, that's everywhere. And at any moment something could come out of it and take away everything you are.

How do you stop something like that?

Augie

Two days passed without word from Augernon, and everyone was worried.

ASHBURN:

 Hi Augie,

I'm Ashburn, one of the Mounties working with Nimueh. She mentioned you're an Ebie too?

OracleSage and Furia said they'd tried sending you where we got with the rest of the rhyme yesterday, but they didn't hear anything back yet. Everything okay? (Beyond the other craziness Nim's mentioned, I mean.)

If our last message got lost in the web somewhere, here's where we got with the rhyme:

Hickory dickory dock
The mouse ran up the clock
The clock struck one
And down she run

The mouse was not yet done

Hickory dickory shut
    The mouse began to cut
    The clocks did chime
    She split the time
    Right down the longest line

We're not completely sure whether the last two lines are like that or "She split the line / Right down the longest time." Depends on how important it is to have the slant rhyme in the middle of the last three lines.

We've tried cutting the 8-shaped infinity strip in half down the full length (since it's the longest line we could think of not already cut), but still working on what exactly is gained by having the two clocks separated but still linked by the strip.

Viviane and I also noticed that the arrows seem to be pointing across to the words on the clock faces, and that there's a pattern to how the newer things (like acorn) match up with their older counterparts (like oak).

Hope everything's okay on your group's end,
Ashburn

AUGERNON:

 Thanks for the check-in, Ashburn, I appreciate it. Will sort through everything you sent.

Yesterday was bad. I'd been having problems getting in touch with any Mountaineer for the past 24 hours. You folks included. I finally heard from Tink when he called my office.

Found out Sender's been in the hospital for two days.

Let me back up. Knatz went down from Chicago to help Sender out with the girl, Missouri. (Knatz is a school counselor and word is she and Sender have been a thing off and on for years.) Missouri had woken up from a dead sleep and said she wanted to show them the truth.

They got in the car, and Missouri told them where to go. They drove for a while. In the woods, off the road, she took them to two more Mountaineers who had gone missing the night Missouri had. They'd been waiting in the woods. Missouri said Sender didn't find her, she found him, so she could bring him here. Then all three of the kids attacked them. They were crazed.

Knatz got to the car before she realized Sender wasn't behind her. She took a tire iron out of the trunk and went back in the woods. She said Sender couldn't move, they were on him like jackals. He'd throw one off and another would jump back on him. He was cut. Missouri had a knife. She'd cut a slice of skin off Sender's forearm. Then the weather changed, the sky turned black in an instant and this thunderstorm came out of nowhere, moving through the woods like a wall. Knatz said she could barely hear herself think over the sound of the wind.

But the recruits were scared of it. They backed off and Knatz put the storm between them, half dragging Sender out of the woods.

They got to the road, to the car. Knatz said the storm, the dark of it, "reached" out to Sender before she got the car door shut, touched him . . . Sender howled like an animal in a trap. She was close enough to hear that the wind wasn't wind. It was voices. Hundreds of voices.

They barely got away. The sky turned light again when they got into town.

Sender was knocked out and bleeding, so Knatz took him to a hospital a couple hours north. He woke up about ten hours later. He could hear the same stuff Missouri could. The whispering in his head. But after a few hours it went away.

Whatever got those kids almost got Sender. Got part of him. There's things he can't remember, Knatz said. God knows what woulda happened if Knatz hadn't been there.

Those kids' minds weren't just wiped, something took them over, controlled them. I have no idea what to do. How do you protect your friends from something like this?

And how do you stop a storm?

When Sender woke up he told Knatz to send me a message via Tink:

"They want to pick us off, one by one, in secret. We need an army of our own. We have to stop hiding because that's what it wants. To separate us and pull us apart one piece at a time. Like we never existed. There's power in numbers. Real power. A story is magic, Augernon, but a story told, a story shared, is where the power comes from. We need to tell everybody who will listen; maybe someone will remember something, maybe somebody can help."

Who can help us? Who knows as much as we do, who's seen what we've seen? We can't bring anybody else into this. Missouri, those kids in the woods . . . all the other Mountaineers who have dropped off the map. Blood on our hands.

Even now Sender's trying to rally, bring everybody together. But what if that's what "they" actually want? Get us huddled in one place so they can erase us all at once. I'm not gonna let that happen. To you, to them. I can't.

Deyavi put it succinctly:

DEYAVI:

 This is what drove Augernon to face down the Storm
alone.

Solving this Fragment won't change what's
happening, and from a strictly practical stance, my
personal feelings aside . . . if we lose Augernon, the
Council will protect the Book, but we will lose our
connection to it.

What are we supposed to do?

What has been left for us to find that we're missing?

The Mountaineers had to act quickly. If they didn't solve this
puzzle, and the subsequent ones, before the Storm got to Augie and
the rest of the '94s, then Sullivan's plan would fail and all of this
would be for nothing. A spirited debate broke out about whether or
not to tell Augernon the truth about his fate, to either spare him or
prepare him, our own future and timeline be damned. That's why I
love the Mountaineers.

Ashburn and Viviane printed out fresh copies of the pages and
rebuilt what Robert affectionately nicknamed "the time donut." By
creating a long ribbon of letters from the grid, twisting them and
taping their ends together to create a Moebius strip, then cutting that
strip down the center, they created two interlocking circles. By
placing the clock faces into those circles, they could line up certain
words and arrows to spell out new words. It was Viviane who finally
found what they hoped was the correct word, and she was given the
honor of telling Augernon so that he could give the word to their
Book in 1998.

VIVIANE:

 Augie,

Viviane again. We're so sorry to hear about what happened with Sender and Knatz. Your story was frightening, to say the least. We do have some good news for you, though . . . we think we might have cracked the fragment!

I tried every position where the clock faces could fit and wrote the indicated letters in order 1-10, and we think we have something that might work: "INLAUDETUS."

There's a bit of a catch, though: we don't seem to have access to the Book of Briars. Since we didn't get an email from it either, the circumstances lead us to think that, although we can help with the puzzles, your group has to be the one to unlock the Book. I can't explain why, but . . . trust the flow of magic, right? Anyway, we're pretty sure about this. Just try it on the Book and see what happens?

Augernon responded that night.

AUGERNON:

 I entered "Inlaudetus" into the Book. It worked, Viv. Really nice work, you guys.

It was a black screen with writing that said: "Inlaudetus.

More commonly referred to as The Obscured Age.

A time known in classical magimystic parlance as The Book of the Hidden."

And then two numbers:

"40.7038 – 74.0108"

Congrats to your lodge for finally figuring this out. We've been too preoccupied with everything else going on, but I sent all this to the puzzle thread . . .

We've been reaching out to everybody who joined up in the past year. Emailing, calling . . . Too many bounced messages and answering machines picking up. I couldn't sleep thinking that all I wanna do is protect my friends and a lot of them might already be gone. Minds swept clear.

Sorry, don't mean to rain on your parade. I was hoping the Book would maybe offer up something . . . advice, help, a spell . . . Not just another clue to another puzzle.

There's still hope. I know it. But it seems further and further away every day.

Deyavi pointed out something interesting.

DEYAVI:

 It seems that the word "Book" is used to mean a heck of a lot more than bound paper in the realm of things Magiq.

The "Book" of Briars is a spell. Inlaudetus is an era in history called the "Book" of the Hidden.

To me at least, Augernon's tone in this message is a healthy reminder that there is a hell of a lot more to all of this than solving the fragments.

OracleSage and Furia sent Augernon the Consolatory Teatime spell in case they needed it to help Ascender, and a day later Augernon responded with an ominous message.

AUGERNON:

 Thanks for the spell. I appreciate it and sent it on. I wish we'd all met sooner, but I guess there are bigger plans in place, huh?

I had an idea last night. About what's happening. What we're facing. You can't stop a storm. But you can make yourself a lightning rod.

Gonna take Monday off and make a short trip. Should be back Tuesday. Won't be around to check email but will follow up when I can.

The Mounties were realizing that this was exactly how it had happened before, that they hadn't changed anything, and I was grappling with the idea that the friends I'd made in the here-and-now had been working behind the scenes, from the future, with the very people who were in the process of icing me out in the 90s. It was enough to make my head spin.

AUGERNON:

 Just got back a few hours ago. Stopped at the office so I could send you this.

I went to see my dad this weekend. Told my wife that grandpa was sick and I needed to check in. Took about six hours to get there. I should get out there more, but life happens, yeah?

Since my mom died about ten years back it's just been my dad and *his* dad holed up in that little mountain house. Nothing but cold and quiet and time. My dad wasn't a good dad, that's for sure (I always thought of my imaginary friend Augernon as the closest thing to a real father I ever had). My dad was a haunted man, a cold husband, and a cruel father. But he was a good son. He loved my grandpa, held him up to be this idol, but I think he also felt like he could never measure up to the man he was breaking his neck to look up to.

I'd ended up okay though. Saw all the things in him I could use as a checklist of what I wouldn't be to the people who might love me someday. I wouldn't ignore them and hate them and resent them because I'd failed at my own life. No, I'd love them and cherish them. I'd protect them.

I'd pretty much moved on from that cold and lonely house on the mountain. But a memory has always stuck with me from my childhood up there. One winter my dad decided it was time for me to hunt. I was the oldest. At the time, I was eight. My mom bundled me up. I whispered to her that I didn't wanna go but she knew he'd get his way. My dad took me way out in the woods, farther than I'd ever been. He took me out to a tree blind, put a .22 rifle in my hands, and left me up there. I didn't know where he was, if he'd gone to another blind, or back to the house. Hours passed. And this fear in me bubbled up and started to spread. I'd fired a gun before, and I had a coat and a sandwich my mom had stuffed in the pocket.

None of that scared me. But what scared me was the idea that my dad might forget I was there. Or might not come back for me at all. Might've put me out there on purpose. Imagine that. Thinking your own dad had left you out in the woods to die and it seeming within the realm of possibility.

I started crying. Then, after a while, I started screaming. As loud as I could, for somebody to help me. I screamed until I lost my voice.

And after a long time I saw him. Breaking through the tree line, coming back for me. The look in his eyes . .

. shame, and rage. He'd heard me. It was the only thing worse than him leaving me there . . . him coming back for me knowing how scared I was.

Mom tucked me in that night after supper. Dad never usually came in to say good night, always gave a nod at the bedroom door and flipped the light off, or called mom out if he felt she was lingering.

But that night he came in, sat on the end of the bed, told her to go. He asked me if I was scared up there in the blind. I said no. I was gonna go to the grave pretending I hadn't been screaming my head off. But I could see in his eyes the disgust at my weakness.

He said he wanted to tell me a story. A story his own father had told him when he was little, before he lost his mind. About the war, and what they found over there in Europe. He wanted to tell me a story about the doors.

I honestly don't remember all of it, because it scared the hell out of me. But that was my first experience with all of this. The stories his dad had told him and then he told me. He wanted to scare me. Really scare me. He told me there were real horrors in the world, in the shadows, and they came for grandpa and his friends. And if they'd come for the brave and the strong, just imagine how easily they'd come for me.

He wanted to scare me, punish me, but also toughen me up. And in a way, it worked. That story stayed with me. Started a fire in me. My little mind started connecting all sorts of dots between those stories and my own imaginings, and things I'd seen, and memories of books I never read. Friends in school pretended to be astronauts or soldiers or cops. I pretended to search for magic.

No one was supposed to talk about "that time" when we'd visit with grandpa. But I would sometimes look out the window at night and see dad talking to grandpa

on the porch, asking him to tell him the stories again.
And I'd listen. All about secret societies and magic he
swore he saw but couldn't quite remember, and
exciting adventures, and terrible enemies, and palaces
made of doors. And how grandpa had almost saved
them all, but in the end, they were all wiped out and
made to forget. Over the years his mind degraded more
and more, and eventually what little he remembered
was gone.

I took all of that with me off the mountain. My fear
of my father led me here. That broken man who never
saw one glimmer of the hidden light in this world. Over
the years I wanted to tell him I was a good father, a
good husband. I wanted to tell him I was a
Mountaineer. I'd found magic and I'd found a family of
friends just like grandpa had. But I never did. He suffers
up there, on his own with the old man. That lonely
mountain is punishment enough.

But I went back this weekend, to see the old house
and the two ghosts rattling around in it.

I went back with a case of beer for my dad.

And a tin of tea for me and my grandpa.

The Mountaineers were shocked. Augernon had used the tea ritual
on his grandfather, they believed, to figure out how his grandfather
"had almost saved them all."

And just after Augernon sent that last message, the site locked the
Mountaineers out of responding.

They'd been cut off from Augernon and were already reeling when
Cole delivered unexpected news to the forum.

COLE:

 Hey guys, just wanted to give you a heads-up that Dee's

aunt died. We just landed outside Bunratty. I don't
know how long we'll be here, but I'll update when I can.

There was nothing that we could do other than offer support and
well-wishes. So while Deirdre was grieving, the Mountaineers
focused on finding the next fragment.

Ashburn discovered that the numbers the Book had given
Augernon were the coordinates of a site in lower Manhattan where
the remnants of colonial New York were preserved beneath a glass
sidewalk. When the Mountaineers realized they would need to take
Sullivan's journal to that location, they were at a loss until Cole posted
that he would be returning with the journal and the chronocompass
while Deirdre stayed in Ireland for a few more days.

As soon as Cole arrived back in New York, he went straight to the
coordinates, where a new entry appeared in the journal. However,
Cole didn't feel comfortable reading it, since it was a personal
message to Deirdre.

But Cole had also brought the chronocompass, and its needle had
started moving inexplicably, leading him to several places throughout
lower Manhattan. The Mountaineers took note of the locations, but
they couldn't figure out why they were important.

A few days later, Deirdre returned and, rather graciously, shared
the private message from her father.

DEIRDRE: AUGUST 14TH, 2017:

 Essentially, he talks about what it was like after my
parents came back to the States. He says he was
ashamed to admit that he left right after I was born. He
was possessed by an "all-consuming need to find
Neithernor."

He says he doesn't remember the first time he'd
heard the name (it was around the time he'd heard
whispers about Monarch's Mountain) but when he did,

it was the answer to a question that had haunted him. A question he didn't have the words to ask. Neithernor, in his mind, became the answer to all the questions. The impossible solution to everything that was wrong with the world. And from that point on he never stopped hearing the call of that forgotten place.

"It was the key to a secret lock inside me. And I gave up everything that mattered to me so I could seek it. So I could knock at its door and be welcomed in."

As the years went on, he came back home every now and then to see me, my mother. But every time was colder and more distant. He would tell me stories he'd found on his journeys and swear he'd come back with more treasures and tales. But the longer he was gone the more strongly he felt he couldn't come back empty-handed. To repair the cracks he was creating he would have to bring the truth back with him to make his absence worth his, and our, pain.

But years passed, and he didn't come back. Until he did. He was scared and begged my mum to bring me and come with him where we'd be safe. From the storm. He described it as a storm of souls, tearing at anyone who got too close to the truth. He'd seen the storm come for people who'd also been looking for the truth, and when it found him leaving Neithernor, the storm had come for him.

He told my mother he'd finally found it, been there, to the ends of the paths. And in Neithernor he'd found the little red house. The one she'd dreamt about her whole life. He swore that we'd all be safe there. She called him a liar, told him to leave and never come back.

He tried to take me when she refused to come. She swore she'd never let him take me down those same paths. "The paths of madness."

He wouldn't listen. He tried to carry me out of the

apartment and she used an object on him that they'd found years prior. It would've killed him if it hadn't been broken. A crack inside it, one you could only see in certain light. They were both wounded by it. His mind. Her body. And she died a year later.

The storm consumed the mountaineers in 1998, and with no one left to open the Book, and it unable to find my father, it disappeared.

He came back once more before disappearing forever himself.

So he could take me to Monica.

And now she's gone too. Disappeared forever.

I don't know why he wanted to tell me all this again. Maybe he was losing his mind in the end. Why, when time seems so short and things seem so important, would he tell me what I already knew?

He left. He blamed himself for everything that happened.

And he did what he could to protect me.

I know all of this already. I have so many questions and I get nothing from him but riddles and half-truths and secrets.

What did he find that was worth all of this pain? I can't imagine it being worth it.

They'd be safe in the little red house.

I was torn. I understood Sullivan's desire to protect his daughter, and had sympathy for the man's struggle with madness, but I hated that he'd been absent for so much of her life. Sullivan could have been with Deirdre, spent his life raising her, but he chose another path, a decision I struggled to understand. What I would have given to have had the choice to be a part of Sebastian's.

But I *did* have that choice. I chose to stay out of his life for fear of inviting madness into it. That made me just like Sullivan. The only difference between us was that Deirdre knew she was missing something all along. Sebastian didn't. He was fortunate in that he was spared that particular pain.

Deirdre's pain was a driving force in her quest for answers. As the Mountaineers worked on finding fragments from the '94 Book of Briars, Deirdre worked to find her way into Neithernor. But she wouldn't have to look long. It was already on its way to her.

CHAPTER 18
STORIES IN A DREAM

"That's dreams for you."

— MISS EVANS

It began as a knocking.

Deirdre had heard the sounds months before and had briefly wondered whether she was being haunted by a poltergeist. Then several weeks went by without any more of the strange knocking—until she started reading Sullivan's journal about Neithernor. Deirdre wrote to the Mountaineers:

DEIRDRE: AUGUST 15TH, 2017:

Firstly, thank you to those who reached out to me. I appreciate it.

If Neithernor was a place that needed protecting, and the way in had to be kept secret, my father couldn't just come out and tell me how to find it or get in. He would leave clues. Clues only I (or we) could see.

I am jet-lagged and not in a good place right now, but the only way I knew that this was a story my dad already wrote was because I met Colby and he performed that spell on the book. He wouldn't have done that for anyone else. He was part of the path my father left for me.

We're the only ones who already know this story. So we're the only ones who would know what was different, or added when he told it again. The differences would be where the clues were hidden. This sounds crazy, but before I even came up with this idea the parts that were new or different were the parts I'd already written out or quoted last night.

. . . it was the answer to a question that had haunted him. A question he didn't have the words to ask. Neithernor became the answer to all the questions. The impossible solution to everything that was wrong. And from that point on he never stopped hearing the call of that forgotten place.

"It was the key to a secret lock inside me. And I gave up everything that mattered to me so I could seek it. So I could knock at its door and be welcomed in."

Hearing the call. A key to a secret lock. Knock at its door and be welcomed in.

Anybody else wondering why, the further I went down the path, the more I heard those knocking doors? Remember them? And then nothing came of them? I hadn't heard one in weeks, but the moment my mind hooked onto those little changes, those additions . . . about keys and locks and calling doors, I felt something. Something in the air. I'm in the brownstone so there's always drafty windows and strange cold spots, even in summer, but this was different. I'd felt it on the path, in Tel Aviv especially. Something on its way to me. Like tumblers had moved somewhere. Like I'd put a key in a lock and now I just had to figure out how to turn it.

Still, in the midst of all of this, I couldn't keep my sodding eyes open and fell asleep on the couch in the parlour.

And I dreamed about him. Not him actually, but a story he told me once. Not about the ant and caterpill(ow). About a woman who had to save someone she loved who was lost or trapped in some terrible place. I was her. And I had to gather up pieces of magic armor and weapons. I remembered her name in the dream, but a sound woke me up around three in the morning and it disappeared.

Someone was knocking at the brownstone's front door.

Any other time I would've expected it to be Cole.

But I knew the knocking wasn't him this time.

It was Neithernor, and it had come so I could turn the key.

I should've dramatically ended the post there, but I've now spent nearly twelve hours racing around the house knocking back on knocking doors and have come up with absolutely nothing.

Admittedly, I was jealous. It was as if Deirdre had the magimystical on speed dial while I was struggling to decipher distant smoke signals through foggy glass. She had access that no one else had.

Access. Whether it be to political insiders, covert operators, or high-ranking military officials, access was the life's blood of every journalist, and I couldn't help but marvel at what Deirdre was tapped into.

But my jealousy was eclipsed by fear. Fear for her safety as well as the safety of the Mountaineers, of Portencia and Jeremy and Alison, of Ascender and the '94 Mountaineers who couldn't see the Storm barreling down on them. We were all getting closer to unlocking the Book, to finding the answers we sought, but there were those who did not want those answers to be found. It had already cost us the life of one of our own. Was that horrible loss just the beginning?

The Mountaineers noted a comment from Cole on Deirdre's blog post:

COLE:

 Hey, did you forget to switch your SIM card out? I tried to call and text . . . if you need time, no worries, I just wanted to check on you. I love you.

Cole hadn't heard from Deirdre since she'd come back to the States. He checked in on the forum, telling the Mounties that when he got to the brownstone there was no portal or anything out of the ordinary, but Deirdre was gone, and she'd taken the journal and the chronocompass.

COLE:

When I followed the compass last week I wrote down the places the compass took me to on a receipt in case it mattered later. I put it in her dad's journal for her.

I just found the list by the front door. You think that means something? She hasn't called me since she's been back but I figured she needed time. I'm just gonna wait here. Maybe she wanted to check out the downtown places for herself.

The Mountaineers were as concerned as Cole.

REVENIR:

 That is concerning . . . If she managed to get to
Neithernor, she might not know exactly how to get
back. Or it could be that she's just lost track of time,
considering how mind-blowing of an experience that
would be . . . Shoot, time in Neithernor might even
work differently than here, it might pass slower.

But let's all try to stay calm until we know exactly
what's going on. Deirdre's a strong girl, she'll be okay,
wherever she is.

Two days later, Deirdre finally checked in.

DEIRDRE: AUGUST 17TH, 2017:

 I've been to Neithernor.
There are no words to describe it, but I'll give it a go.
First, how I got there. I'm worried about writing it
out, even with the protection spell (this is a secret my
father worked hard to keep) but the key to unlock the
knocking door was in Cole's notes on the bar receipt.

When I figured it out, the knocking door led
through to a warren in the ground. I came out of a
broom closet into a small, dim room.

It was like one of those stories where animals had
houses like people but made from things in the woods.
The walls were soil but packed tight and rubbed
smooth. The floor was made of flats of stone and nearly
covered with overlapping mismatched carpets. There
was a hearth charred by old fires. A wind down the
chimney had blown cold ash across the carpets. The

room was subterranean, but warm. Small but not cramped. I could stand up.

There were ornate dressers and worn chests. The door to leave the warren was barred and broken. Dirt and pebbles were scattered underneath it like a landslide had slammed it shut. There was only one window. Its frame was a tangle of knotted roots that grew out of the top of the wall and wreathed the opening, like someone had asked the tree for a window frame. It was too small to climb through. The warren must be set in a hillside because in the distance I could see the tops of trees swaying in the wind.

I could hear tree boughs bending against each other in the woods and every once in a while, when the wind would blow a certain way, the trees would move apart and I could see the top of some sort of broken tower in the far-off distance. Like a lighthouse, but I couldn't hear the sea.

You could smell magic in the air. Almost taste it. Something like clove and cinnamon tea. Sweet and spiced and sharp. It was getting dark quickly. The sun (or whatever lights a place like this, I guess) was already beginning to set somewhere behind the trees out there in Neithernor.

I couldn't believe what was happening, where I was. What I was seeing.

There was a narrow bed, which was unmade, and a small glass and metal lantern on the table beside it. The lantern was shaped like a little house, with windows and a pitched roof and a metal loop at the top of the chimney so you could hang it somewhere. There was a small knob at the base. I thought maybe it would spark a fire inside it, so I turned the knob. A soft bell rang inside the lantern, and light started to flicker behind the frosted windows. Several lights, dim but growing brighter, started moving throughout the lantern. The lights were little living things, and that was their house. It gave a soft orange glow. I gently picked it up and carried it around the warren.

There were paintings hanging on the walls. Landscapes. Seascapes. Shorelines and wooded paths. There was a painting of a chain of low islands on an ocean, and in their center was what looked like a dozen shipwrecks smashed together. Crow's nests on masts and bows and sails made a sort of looming castle in the middle of the sea. I looked closer, and when lit by the lantern light, the sails began to billow, flicking off the surface of the canvas. I thought I could touch them, they looked so real.

I rummaged around. I opened the drawers of a tall dresser and found men's clothes. My father's clothes. I wasn't sure how to get back home because the broom closet door wasn't knocking. I didn't know how much time had passed, but I was scared to leave. Scared I wouldn't be able to find my way back here. I was still numb with awe. I put on my father's cardigan and sat in an overstuffed armchair with my little house lantern. I should've pulled out the journal to see if something new had appeared, but I was so preoccupied I completely forgot. I tried to take a photo with my phone, but they just turned out blank. The whole place is like the journals. I sat back, closed my eyes for a moment to just feel the place, and I guess I'm still a little jet-lagged because I fell asleep.

I woke up, and the sky outside the window was pink and orange. Dawn. I'd slept there all night. Dusk until dawn. I felt a twinge of nervousness that I'd just absently left my entire world behind for so long. And the more I thought about it, the more I started to hear a familiar sound. A soft knocking on the broom closet door. Not loud and demanding like on the other side of whatever it's on the other side of. Polite. Like someone checking to see if someone else was awake on the other side of the door. So with a few polite knocks of my own I knocked my way back home.

I thought I'd leave the door open, see how long I'd been gone, and dash back in. But when I got back to the brownstone I found Cole there, who said you were all worried about me.

I'd been gone less than two hours. I tried to explain where I'd been, but felt like I couldn't. I had to show him.

So I closed my eyes, thought for a minute of that little warren, and I summoned up a knocking door. Like magic.

I remembered to check the journal this time, and naturally the warren had unlocked more journal pages.

My dad said the warren (which is why I knew what to call it) was his home for many years.

Time is different there. It moves faster, but our bodies are still bound by the passing of time in our world. We can experience days and weeks there but our bodies and minds only age by seconds and hours.

When he had finally found his way there (which he says is a story for another time), he'd secretly hoped that Monarch's Mountain would have been waiting to welcome a traveler of the path. He'd been harboring the belief that maybe they'd somehow remembered and tended to this world. But they were gone. And as wondrous a world as it was, he felt more alone than ever.

He says that Neithernor is a wild and wondrous place. But a sad place. It's the last corner of our world as it was, and as it could have been. But even broken it's still beautiful and full of undiscovered wonders.

Treasures still hide here. Ruins to explore and stories to seek.

He then explained what happened after my mum died. He believed the Storm had been looking for him because he'd briefly come in contact with the Mountaineers and had been touched by the Book. But he'd also been touched by Neithernor. Regardless, the Storm wouldn't leave him alone. So he sought refuge there. But when he returned home the Storm would hunt him, and over the years the doors to Neithernor started closing. They were always meant to protect that world. To keep out the Silver. And so it became harder and harder for him to find ways in, until he discovered that the Storm couldn't enter Central Park. And in the Ramble he found a single door that could still carry him over.

Eventually he had nothing but the Ramble and all his regrets. But years later he felt a presence in the park. Faint and faded. It was the Council. What remained of them. He says they spoke to him, in the rustle of grass blades, in the chirp of baby birds. They were calling to him. They had sensed his presence too, also faint and faded. They'd found each other.

Over the years they nursed each other back to life. He says he became brave enough to leave the park so he could collect objects and artifacts left behind from the other time. He shared their power, and the Council grew strong again. And together, over years, they came up with a plan.

All of this is the wheel they set in motion. The last chance to unchange what has been changed. He wanted to fight for them, but his mind was broken by what happened with my mum and the Storm wouldn't stop pursuing him until he was gone. He could die alone in Neithernor, or with his friends there in the park.

He told them he knew someone who was brave enough to take his place.

A fighter. Someone who could work with those who would hopefully become the final Mountaineers. He was talking about me. All I had to do was find the secret path he'd set for me years ago after casting the spell to protect me from all this madness. The Council felt it was a lot to leave to "maybe," but my father said I was my mother's daughter. As far as he was concerned there was no maybe.

He said I have to explore this world now. He can't tell me how to find the little red house. I have to find it myself. And when I do I'll know why.

He told me to take the walking stick he'd left by the bed. From now on I should carry the compass, the journal, and the stick with me wherever I go. With them I have all I need to do what I have to do.

He said to hold close to everything he ever told me. He said to trust in the flow of magiq and that he loved me and was proud of me.

That was it.

Cole didn't want to stay in the warren. We had our first row (a long and personal story) and now I'm back home, wondering what I'm supposed to do and how I get out of the warren to do it.

I wish I could bring you all with me.

Maybe someday.

I've felt so lost for so long. But there, in his chair, looking out his window . . . for a moment I felt connected to him. And who I am. Where I come from. This is the place that shaped my parents and my life.

It made the warren even more wonderful. I didn't know who I was for the longest time.

But I am my father's fighter.

And my mother's daughter.

Deirdre had been to another world. She'd actually followed her path to Neithernor.

She included a photo at the end of the post. It was an image of a simple wooden walking stick. Her father's walking stick.

If there was one thing I knew for certain, it was that Deirdre wasn't going to stop until she found the answers she sought. And I wanted her to find them, to find that place, the house, and tell us what was waiting inside. Tell us if there was a fire in the hearth.

I was sorry to hear that she and Cole had had a fight, but all couples had them. When Cole updated everyone on the forums, we all gained a better understanding of their row . . . and of Cole himself.

COLE:

 Hey guys, just wanted to give you a heads-up about everything that went down last week. I feel like we owe you a little explanation, and since I haven't heard from Dee since last week, I guess I need to do it myself.

I just wanna say from the beginning, I didn't keep any of this from you guys, I just don't really tell anybody about it. I told Dee a while back, but I figure you need to know to understand what's going on.

It all started with a bad car accident my family was in when I was a kid. My dad was okay, but my mom and I almost died. I broke two vertebrae, both legs, my left arm, and fractured my skull. I was in the hospital for a long time and unconscious a lot in the beginning when they were trying to get the swelling in my brain down.

That's when the other memories started happening. Like dreams that started to stick with me when I was awake. I could remember being somewhere else when I was unconscious. I'd seen some other place, and the memories were so strong that I could remember sounds and smells and feeling . . . what it felt like to be there.

It's mostly a haze now, but back then it was crystal clear.

After months of physical therapy (what got me into doing what I do) and after brain damage was mostly ruled out I ended up having to see a child psychologist for months. They thought that if I was physically okay I must've been subconsciously trying to "paint over the accident" and how bad we both got hurt. They assumed I was trying to ignore the trauma with made-up stories.

The accident and recovery and all the crap that came after was hard on my parents. But I pretty much blame myself for why my dad finally left. I wasn't the kid they remembered. In my mind I went to some place where I could be the boy I felt I really was, and no amount of lying or hiding could make that go away. When I fully figured out I was trans, my dad was really messed up. He kept saying it was the accident, that something happened to me. He thought I was broken. I kept trying to tell him I'd known since I could remember that I was different, way before the crash. The accident, and the memories, just changed how I felt about it. I remembered someplace where I was happy with who I was and it didn't matter. It just . . . was. I always thought, even if it was some kind of hallucination or coping mechanism, those "memories" helped me be braver than I ever thought I could've been.

My mom came around eventually, accepted me. But it drove my dad further away. He was okay when I wanted to end my partial visitation with him. The rest is history.

Anyway, so that's a heck of a lot of backstory to get to what happened last week. I hadn't heard from Dee since I left Bunratty. And then I found her coming back from Neithernor, and she took me with her. But she was . . . distant. She's been like that ever since Monica died, which completely makes sense. But she's been pushing me away. I felt like she took me out of obligation maybe, because I was there? Which I never would've wanted. But I went.

And the way she described the air, the smell, the taste . . .

It was exactly like the place in my dreams after the accident. It totally freaked me out. I didn't wanna say why, I just wanted to leave and I didn't want to leave her there alone even though she can, and has, taken care of herself. We ended up arguing, and I made her open the door for me.

I just felt this rush of fear. Of this unknown thing coming back. All of those old feelings. I think maybe part of me wanted to believe the memories after the accident weren't real. Even after the fraylily dream and the one I had with Traveler. I don't know . . . maybe I was just in denial of what I was capable of, what I saw, 'cause for a few months I was just a guy with an amazing girl and we were happy.

I still haven't heard from her.

I went back to the brownstone yesterday. She wasn't there.

I think she's in Neithernor, and even though I was scared and hurt, I wish I hadn't walked out.

REVENIR:

 Hey Cole,
I just wanted to say thank you for sharing this intimate part of yourself. You don't need to explain why you didn't tell us you're trans, or about your accident, that's something deeply personal and we're honored you chose to open up to us.

I've been trying to figure out the words to say to this . . . and I can honestly just say, you're not alone. And you're not broken. I'm sorry your dad didn't treat you like a good dad should. I was fortunate that the people who mattered the most were there for me when I came out as trans, but I know what it feels like to be treated like you're broken, like you're a freak. That's not something I'd wish on anyone, ever.

Your reaction was perfectly reasonable, and I'm sure that Deeds will understand in the end. She's a good person, and she clearly loves you. Tapping into those memories must have been really hard on you. But we're all here to help you find your way back in, if that is what you want to do, or to try and find Deirdre in some other way, if you'd rather not go back to Neithernor. But we're here for you, full stop.

COLE:

❝ That means a lot, Revenir, thanks for sharing that with me, and us. I have a great group of friends (here and irl) and Dee's amazing. I don't look back much on my childhood. On my dad. I made my peace with it. Sometimes you can't bring everything with you on your way to becoming who you are. And that's okay. It makes more room in your life.

ROBERT:

❝ Bah, you are, have been, and will always be Cole Sumner. A person I'm happy to call a friend. Some days that may be more complicated than others, but you're the same brave, intelligent guy who "allegedly" broke

into the Morgan Library in order to find a spell to free
the person he loved.

If anyone isn't proud of you, then they haven't really
paid attention to you. I think Deirdre will come around.
It just seems like it's complicated being her some
days too.

Edit: So, does this mean we now need to figure out
how Deirdre got into Neithernor so we can send Cole
back in after her with a box of candy and flowers or
something? Cole, any chance we can see exactly what
was on that receipt she was so excited about?

COLE:

 Hey old pal. I wrote down where the compass pointed
me, and then the directions/guilds you guys eventually
figured out from the locations. It also said I had a
double Maker's neat, but I don't think that's relevant.

I've heard the doors knocking a couple of times
before, when she's told me about the path she went on. I
guess it's a matter of wanting to go, of seeking it out?
And then knowing how to open the door? Can't say I
haven't tried to make them knock the past couple days,
but so far, nothing.

I want to give her whatever time she needs. I mean,
this is the last connection she has to her dad. But this
place has been left for who knows how long. We don't
know what else is there.

BRENDON:

 Hey Cole, I echo the exact same sentiments as Robert.
You will always be Cole. The guy I owe lots and lots and

lots of poutine and other Canadian delicacies (yes, we have those). And who has saved our butts more times than I think I can count. But more importantly, a close friend, and someone I am incredibly proud to call my friend.

COLE:

66 You're the best friends a guy has never met.

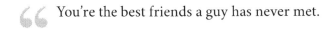

66 Hey guys, I tried all night to get the front door to knock since I know for sure that one works. Had the scarf, the pendant . . . it was so easy for Dee when she came back. She closed her eyes for two seconds and made it happen. She knocked back and it opened, but her back was to me. I feel like it had to be the directions. That makes the most sense. Sorry guys. Will follow up when I can. The whole thing was simple for her. But she's a Green, so . . . I wonder if the problem is how freaked out the place makes me?

ROBERT:

66 Don't think of it as a door to that place. Open a door to *her*.

It took a tremendous amount of courage for Cole to share his story with us. And the Mountaineers were overwhelmingly supportive. It was such an inspiring and moving thing to see how accepting and warm they all were, to Cole, to each other.

As for Deirdre, neither the Mountaineers nor Cole would hear from her again for over a week.

The website giving the Mountaineers access to Augernon had once again been replaced by the full-page image of the chronocompass, and with time running out for the '94s, they had no idea what to do next.

Then Brendon and Robert realized that a clue might be hidden in the locations that the chronocompass sent Cole to in lower Manhattan. After plotting them on a map of New York City, they realized that they were new directions for the Dawson compass.

Clicking on the points relative to the directions Cole was led, the Mountaineers saw the compass become animated again. Twelve chimes sounded before they were redirected to a new page.

There was no text field this time, only the small rotating compass, a button to send an attachment, and the phrase:

> "Like leaves swept into a stream, are sounds and
> stories in a dream."

After attempting to send parts of a story—the pieces of *Ant & Caterpillow* that they'd gathered so far—the Mounties realized that the page would only accept audio attachments. They were going to have to send recordings.

Robert put together a quick message, asking for help with something they'd lost, and everyone waited to hear back, speculating what the response would be, how it would arrive, and who it would be from.

At midnight, they received a response.

A REPLY:

 Still rattled by what happened in Ste. Genevieve. Can't

get the images out of my mind. Those kids. The sound of the storm. Ascender blacked out in the seat next to me. Bleeding like a slaughtered animal.

He bolted the minute he woke up. Now he's trying to rally the lead mountaineers to organize, "get out in front for once." That might've worked six months ago. But everybody's scared now, myself included. I still get chills every time I think how stupid it was for me to go help him. I care about him. Maybe love him? Sure. I don't know . . . but I have a daughter for Christ's sake. I have a sole responsibility here. And it's her, not him. Not the Book.

I'm at this precipice. If I back away is that the only way she'll be safe? Or should I keep trying to open the Book before it comes for the rest of us . . . ? Is that how I save her? Which is the way to go? Or is it too late either way? All I wanted was to see magic. Finally see this through. And now the world seems darker than ever.

I'm grateful that Saberlane suggested putting my journal online, even if I'm not sharing it with anyone but him. It's motivation to keep it up in the face of everything that's happening. So far I've kept my secret just that, mine (aside from you, Lane). What would the rest of the lodge say if they found out some small part of me knew all this was coming?

Almost forgot. No portents last night. Nothing. Just a dream about Ali, but it wasn't a memory. She was outside playing, but in my mind she was grown up, and I heard someone I couldn't see asking her to help them find something they lost. Don't know what it was. Just weird dream gibberish, but it made me feel uneasy. But yeah . . . Five nights in a row now. Nothing. I'm starting to wonder if something happened to me in Ste. Genevieve too . . .

The Mountaineers quickly came to the same conclusion I did as I read the reply. Given she was with Ascender during the attack in Missouri, this had to be Knatz's journal. But there was more to it. Her mention of a daughter, her reference to dream memories, our knowledge that our own AlisonB, aka Climber, had generational memories that stretched back through her relatives' experiences as Mountaineers—it all added up to indicate that Alison, the very woman who was keeping Jeremy and Portencia safe, was Knatz's daughter.

Of all the '94 Mountaineers, Knatz had been the most welcoming to me. She was the one I wondered about the most in the subsequent years.

She wasn't communicating with the Mountaineers, though—not intentionally. They were reading her online journal from 1998. Brendon noted that Robert's audio message translated to the strange voice Knatz heard in her dream, which meant the Mountaineers had an audio channel into Knatz's dream-space in 1998. Yeah. Even I had to read that again.

Chey recorded a new message and sent it to Knatz, hoping to keep her invested and hopeful.

CHEY:

 "Knatz, my name is Chey. Listen and try to remember. Please don't give up on the Book of Briars. There are other of us Mountaineers out there working alongside you to open it. You are not alone. We can do this together. Remember, hope is its own form of magiq. As a friend of yours says, 'Trust in the flow of magiq.'"

And the following night, Knatz posted:

KNATZ:

 I can't remember what I dreamed last night. Just woke up feeling . . . I don't know, optimistic? Seems nuts. I can't explain it. Something just hit me. It's not hopeless.

It's just a race.

And they're hoping we stay distracted, on defense. Slow. Too busy freaking out to try and do the one thing they don't want us to do. Which is open that damned book. Ascender believes there's still a plan, and even all this is a part of it. I didn't believe him, but maybe that's what you do to survive? To keep going against a storm. You do what Mountaineers always do. You believe in the face of the unbelievable.

I think I've made up my mind. I'm going to figure out how to finish this.

Ali can stay with her father for a little while. Keep her schedule the same. I'll tell her I have to go to a conference or help open a school or something. She'll be safer with him. She doesn't know about the book, or the Mountaineers. Not yet. She doesn't know what's been passed on to her.

And if we do this maybe she won't have to. Maybe she won't grow up like we did, knowing there's something more to a world that swears there isn't. Dying inside.

I'm sick of it. This has to be it. This has to be the time the Mountaineers win.

I'm scared out of my freaking mind but we do what we have to. Right? Worst case . . . I'm wiped out trying to make a better world for her and she'll know her mother refused to run.

Emboldened by Knatz's positive response, Augustus wrote a story, hoping to more strongly influence Knatz's dreams.

AUGUSTUS_OCTAVIAN:

> One day, a beautiful tawny lioness with shining golden fur was padding through a sun-dappled forest. She was hunting for something, but not food; her belly was full, but her curiosity was not. She made her way down through the wooded vale towards a river, always searching, always seeking. She passed by a bright turquoise stone. This was not what she sought out. She passed by a fiery red bird. This was not what she sought, either. She padded on and on silently over the leaves and twigs on the forest floor, always searching, always seeking. She came to the bank of the river. She peered into cool, clear river's waters. At the river bottom, she at last found what she was seeking!

KNATZ:

> I've been reaching for anything. Something we missed. I sent out an email to everyone. I knew Huma had been keeping track of loose ends, things in previous complications that hadn't panned out. Never heard back from her.
>
> I had a dream last night that I was walking with this lion. She had a sword stuck deep between her shoulders, blood all over her. I kept trying to pull it out, but she was looking for something and I couldn't catch up to her. In my dream I remembered animals want to be on their own when they die. It made me so sad. I thought, if I could get the sword I could save her. Then

she'd be hunting, not looking for a hole to crawl into. I tried to pull it out, but it was jammed in.

And then I noticed the sword was stuck in what looked like a perfect seam that ran down the length of her body. Like someone had tried to pry her open with the sword. I wrenched the blade to one side, and for a second I could see inside the lioness. There was all this light. I woke up completely freaked out.

My ancestral dreams have never been anything like this. They're always more memory than metaphor.

But the lion dream had actually triggered a memory. It was about this sweet guy. Nib.

He was a Mountaineer who was active on the forum near the beginning. When the Benefactor sent materials from the Ackerly Green offices to some of us (not me), Nib had received a locked briefcase.

He'd tried figuring out the combination, breaking it. Nothing worked. He even took it to a locksmith, who said he'd never seen anything like it. He could never get the damned thing open and even though it seemed like a massive loose thread, there were a lot of artifacts that weren't in play, and we were all so busy figuring out the other complications, we forgot about the briefcase.

I spent all morning trying to find him. Ascender is AWOL, no one knows where Augie is, and the only person I could get in touch with is a 20-year-old kid in north Florida who's even more freaked out about this than I am (that's you, Lane). So tomorrow, we're meeting in Spartanburg, South Carolina (let me know if you have any issues with the plane ticket, they said you'd just need to show up with your ID) and we're going to try and find out what happened to Nib and the Benefactor's briefcase.

I don't know what I'm thinking, and frankly I think

it's best if I stay a few steps ahead of my mind right now.
Because this is all manner of completely batshit insane.

See you tomorrow, Lane.

With Knatz on a path to unlock the Book, the Mountaineers took
a night off and waited to hear from her again.

KNATZ:

 We got to Spartanburg and had no idea where to start.
We spent a day and a half asking around and of course
Nib wasn't Nib's name. But asking about a possibly
nerdy, bookish, perhaps reclusive guy in a small town
like this . . . we narrowed down our choices. We were
eventually sent to an old house just outside of town,
near Lake Blalock. The whole place had been trashed.
We weren't sure if it was messiness, the storm, or a
combination.

Lane found him in the cellar. I think he'd been down
there for weeks, maybe a month, I don't know. He'd
been eating food his mom must've canned twenty years
ago. He thought a hurricane had come through
Spartanburg. He thought he'd made it through and we
were coming to rescue him.

He hadn't made it through.

I can't put into the words the state he was in. His
mind was wiped like everybody else's. He was agitated.
Scared. It took everything that made him him. I was
trying to talk to him, using basic counseling techniques,
but he talked in circles, saying the same things Missouri
did. Lane didn't want to leave me alone, but I convinced
him to look over the house for the case. It wasn't there.

We started thinking maybe, somehow, the storm had
taken it, or destroyed it. I mean, if it could move

through a house and leave it structurally untouched, and wipe someone's memory, why couldn't it destroy a briefcase or at least fling it into a hillside a hundred miles away?

We'd asked him over and over about the case, and then when we were about to leave he said he'd known something was coming. Could feel it. And when he knew for sure, he'd left the case with "Faris."

We had no idea who Faris was. A Mountaineer? A family member? Lane went next door to call an ambulance (and ask if they knew who Faris was) and I scoured the house again.

Nothing. No mention of Faris on the backs of photos or bills or mail. And then I looked out the back window, onto the lake. Tied to a little rotten dock was a sun-bleached boat.

Boats have names, I thought. Sure enough, this one was called Faris. One yellow rope tied it to the dock and another was thrown over the edge. I pulled it out of the reservoir and found the briefcase tied up in a black plastic bag. Still locked, but dry as a bone.

We'd found the damned thing. We'd actually done it.

I heard thunder off on the other side of the lake. Quiet, but coming closer. The sound sent chills all over my body. Lane heard it too. He called to me from the front yard. An ambulance was already on its way. We figured we'd stay as long as we could.

But then we realized Nib was gone. He'd slipped out when I was in the backyard.

We weren't due to fly out until the next morning, so we drove back to Atlanta and found a hotel near the airport. I didn't tell Lane at the time (sorry) but there were a couple times on that dark road that I thought I saw Nib in the woods. Watching us pass. And then a half hour later I'd see him again. Somehow staying ahead of us. Before Missouri I would've shaken it off as exhaustion or paranoia. We can't afford to shake those feelings off now.

Believe it or not I slept well. Something about the hotel, Lane being there, the people in rooms all around us . . . I felt safe. I felt like we'd made a plan and we executed. We were on track. But when Lane fell asleep I grabbed the briefcase and put it under the covers. I, and it, were safe under there.

Now we just need to get it open.

Lane flew back to Jacksonville, and I'm back home too. The minute I hit the ground I wanted to go get Ali, hug her tight. But that's not the plan now. I have to be strong enough to stay away. That's how I protect her.

She's going to start having the ancestral memories soon. I had her pretty young and I'd barely gotten used to them. I'd seen so little before they faded away. I regret not being better prepared to protect her before I passed them onto her.

No. I can't do that. We have to stay focused.

The briefcase. The briefcase is something. Now we just need eight numbers. Four and four. This has to be the next complication. And then two more. And then . . .

I can do this. We can do this.

—

I just want to be sure my math is right. 8 numbers with 10 options each is 100,000,000 possible combinations, right? Lane?

Okay.

Yeah. So I got to 11111118 before I got a calculator to double check and quit. I've been trying to think of numbers that could work, numbers we missed or haven't used. They wouldn't be random. We either overlooked them or haven't unlocked them yet.

I'm not usually on the thread but I emailed the

puzzlers. Tink said it's only him and thirty or so on the thread now. He doesn't know who's been attacked and who's just trying to distance themselves from the Mountaineers to try and stay safe.

I haven't heard from Ascender.

Tink hasn't heard from Augie.

I thought about calling Martin the reporter but if he's not on the storm's list . . .

I worry about you even reading this. I think about the night the forum went down. It took out all those kids at once, because they were connected.

We're running out of time. If whoever or whatever is coming for us wants to stop us from opening the Book . . . I'll be the main target now, won't I?

All I can do is keep trying numbers.

The Mounties focused their efforts on helping Knatz unlock the briefcase, sending her variations on rhymes and songs, hoping that the combination was 1998 and 2017.

PADABOYE:

 17 years after two thousand
A message the Mounties sent to your housin'
To show the answer to the case
That's taken up so much of your mind's space
They got the message 19 years before the date
Somewhere in the year ninety-eight

KNATZ:

 I woke up thinking about dates. I started putting them in. Tink said this part seemed to be about time so I started with months, then years. Backwards, forwards, the year AGP was founded, the year it shuttered. I've been up all night trying different combinations.

In case you were hanging on the edge of your seat, nothing worked.

I might need to get out of the city. Being so close to Ali and not being able to see her feels like torture.

UPDATE:

Saberlane. You owe me a beer. I opened the case.

I kept trying dates. I don't know why, but I couldn't let it go. Maybe because Tink said something about time. The left combination is 1998. The right side is 2017. I have no idea what it means, why 2017, but it's open.

The case is full of wood and metal parts. A bunch of little bits and pieces, like metal tines, a brass plate with holes in it, and flat wooden pieces and trim. It's definitely supposed to make something. Maybe it's some kind of magical time travel thing? We'll be able to communicate with 2017?

Whatever it is, it's unassembled, and assembling is so not my thing. Wanna take a trip to Chicago? On me? I remember you said your dad built things. I know you're a musical theater major but there's gotta be some of that carpenter blood in you somewhere.

We're gonna do this, Lane.

PANDABOYE:

 The key to the case you discovered
Is a clue in itself to the spell we uncovered
During the year you entered in the second space
We ourselves will be in a race

To open a book hidden away
We think you had the answer, back in the day.

KNATZ:

 I was supposed to show up for a semester staff meeting
today. I called in. If I don't figure this out, job security
will be the least of my worries. Lane's landing tonight
and he can take over trying to put this thing together.
It's a nightmare. There are no instructions. Pieces fit
together in different ways. I have them spread all over
the apartment. Metal pieces on the dining table (I think
they go inside?) and wooden pieces are on the coffee
table in the living room. I take a break from one room
to work on the other.

So far I have a lid. Or a bottom. A side? Something. I
was hoping to give Lane somewhere to start. It's
maddening. We don't have time for this!

Even my dreams are about the box. I dreamed I'd
somehow put it together and when it was done I could
hear a voice coming from the inside. Someone was
inside the box and needed my help, but I couldn't get
the damned thing open. I was scared that if I broke it
open I'd hurt them. But if I didn't they'd die. And for
some reason I felt like I would too. So I picked it up and
smashed it on the ground. And Ali was inside it. And I'd
killed her.

The Mounties wanted to reassure Knatz and also try to let her
know, even indirectly, that her daughter was alive and had last been
seen saving the lives of others.

ROBERT:

 In the future there is a Mountaineer.

Her name is Alison.

Her wit and intellect have aided us through many complications.

She has a sense of humor which can make people smile.

She gets frustrated when it takes her too long to solve a puzzle no one else could have ever solved.

Her bravery leads her down her own path, when it would be easier to sit idly by.

She has risked her own life to save an innocent girl who was being tormented for her abilities.

And she succeeded in saving this girl and getting her to safety.

She is without a doubt a member of our family, just like she is a member of yours.

You will have much to be proud of.

You are not alone.

KNATZ:

 Saberlane is officially my new favorite ginger. Just putting that out there.

I was at my wit's end. We'd spent something like twelve hours on that thing. That's in addition to the two days I spent. We were working together, working apart . . . I had a crushing headache at one point and I had to take a nap. I woke up groggy, on the couch, on the verge of quitting. I just wanted to take Ali, Lane, anybody else who'd fit in my car, and bolt.

And then I remembered the life I'd be sentencing my

daughter to. How long could we run? How long would it chase us? Until this book thing is finished, or I am, I'm a curse to her. She deserves a greater life than I can give her right now. She will be great. By god, I know she will. And to ensure that I had to get my ass off the couch and get back to work.

Then Lane screamed at the top of his lungs.

He'd put the box together. Well, almost . . . He'd assembled everything, all the metal parts inside. Everything fit perfectly. He said the brass bits had given off one loud ding and he knew he'd gotten it. He demanded I do the honors and put the lid on the box. (I was at least right about that, it's a box.)

The second I did, it slammed shut, and now it's impossible to open. The color, which was just raw, unstained wood, started to change. It got darker until it looked like it was covered in a green-black lacquer. It looks like an antique music box, except on the front there's a round brass grill, almost like an old speaker. And nothing else.

Well . . . until all the words started appearing.

On the lid of the box this appeared:

"Scurious breath did lie upon the cheek as Flinter's hand stretched claws over the burrow. The unowl was hasted. This news wouldst bring many minds to precipious ferriedge. This he knew. The acoded words flew fast with him. Their weight acreepsing his otherwise diregilous path. At the first sight of Castorton he made dive toward the mill tower."

And on the back side, this was written:

"The acoded note Owl brought to Toad:
   1 - WITEBKINGIGREDIENT

10 - NHNNONRTHNINENSION
14# -
THRONEYTHRAIDTHRORTHRTHRERVICE
15# -
WNEHREPEATEDACMLAINGERPXESSION
18 - ROUSONFOUACOUDSOUAT
20 - THEILETTERIIAFTERIIIRIVAND
VALSOVIBEFOREVIITVIII
28 - EANTSEFTEREEOLIDAYEEAL
32 - HETOUNDTTORSETAKEST"

And then about five minutes later . . . we got an email
from the Book.

"There must be holes in this unrhyme.
  For else how could you find the time?
  I wonder would it trouble you
  Barring fours from thirty-two?

The mourners all dressed in the nines
  For thirty-two's the length of times
  And then unriddle what's been wrote
  To find the heartbreak in the note

A heavy heart upon a feather
  The characters all brought together
  To ready up the mourning glade
  A grieving air's what must be made"

I couldn't even begin to follow how the Mountaineers were
solving these clues. Robert recapped their progress finding hidden
word puzzles within the jumbles of letters, explaining just how each
line was coded.

ROBERT:

1 - "WITEBKINGIGREDIENT" - White baking
   ingredient
Coded method: The 2nd letter of each word is
   missing (H, A and N)
Answer: Flour (Or sugar? Egg?)

10 - "NHNNONRTHNINENSION" - The fourth
   dimension
Method: The first and third letter of each word is
   replaced by 'N'. (T&e, f&u, d&m)
Answer: Time

14 -
   "THRONEYTHRAIDTHRORTHRTHRERVICE"
   - Money paid for a service
Answer: Fee
Method: The first letter of each word was
   replaced with 'THR' (M, P, F, A, S)

15 -
   "WNEHREPEATEDACMLAINGERPXESSION"
   - When repeated a calming expression
Answer: There
Method: Rearrange letters
Answer: There

18 - "ROUSONFOUACOUDSOUAT" - Reason
   for a cold sweat
Method: Replace 'OU' with 2 letters (ea, or, . ,
   ol, we)
Answer: Fear

20 - "THEILETTERIIAFTERIIIRIVAND
VALSOVIBEFOREVIITVIII" - The letter after R
and also before T
Method: Words are followed by Roman numerals
1 through 8
Answer: S

28 - "EANTSEFTEREEOLIDAYEEAL" - Pants
after a holiday meal
Method: Replace first letter of each word with 'e'.
(P, A, A, H, M)
Answer: Tight

32 - "HETOUNDTTORSETAKEST" - The sound
a horse makes
Method: 'T's are word separators. First letter of
each word is missing. (T, S, A, H, M)
Answer: Neigh

And overnight Robert realized that if you apply the method of obfuscation to the actual answers, each answer became a number. For example, "neigh," when the first letter is removed and a T is added to the end, becomes "eight."

I'm just glad the Mountaineers are the good guys, otherwise we'd all be in trouble.

They sent all this information to Knatz, while others were trying to figure out what the Book's clue meant.

KNATZ:

 My dreams haven't been the same since Ste. Genevieve. The splintered ancestral memories I used to have are just . . . gone. Nada. Ascender made me swear the storm didn't "touch" me, and I did. I'm sure it didn't. But that's the only thing that could explain it. Right? My dreams now are . . . occupied, if that makes sense. Like the opposite of a night terror. I feel like I'm not alone, but it's . . . not scary. It's not exactly soothing, but . . . it's like something is reaching out to me. Could be Lane being here for all I know. We ended up sleeping top to toe to keep each other company last night because SOMEONE wanted to watch a scary movie at a godforsaken time like this (me).

I dreamed about the Mountaineers all night. One of those nights where you wake up but every time you fall asleep again, it's the same dream. Voices. In the dream I thought they were the voices of all the Mountaineers who are still left, the lonely few scattered around the world.

Except these voices are hopeful. Encouraging. Not scared. I can't understand them, but I feel them. Missouri said she felt some sort of connection to something else. Maybe that's what this is? Maybe the storm got me, or maybe it doesn't have to touch you? When it got Missouri, it reached out to everyone who was on the forum at the time. Maybe it passed through Ascender, to me?

Is it only a matter of time before I turn on someone, on Lane? You want to believe that evil feels evil, right? Not helpful. Not hopeful. God, if it's a force of good in my head . . . they picked the most cynical SOB in Chicago. I'm so not the point person for positive vibes.

Anyway, more importantly . . . Lane's still here.

And we made big headway.

He figured out most of the riddles pretty quickly, but then we didn't know what else to do. Stuck, I started writing down how each riddle was "riddled." And then, for reasons I know not, I applied the method of riddling to the answers . . . And it freaking worked!

Cause for celebration was fleeting, however. As each coded set of numbers was solved by Knatz and the Mountaineers, new clues would appear on different sides of the box.

KNATZ:

 It's been a hellish 24 hours. Lane's still here and he's not leaving, so I don't know why I'm doing this anymore. I guess part of me thinks this might be the only thing that I'll leave behind if it comes for me. Maybe I'm leaving this for Ali.

I emailed Tink and the puzzlers for help with this batch of clues. He wrote back a few hours later to tell me they were gone. All but one. Everybody on the puzzler chain but Tink and a kid called Seashifter. Shifter told Tink that the puzzlers were frustrated with how slow and confusing the email chain had gotten, so they'd been secretly working together on a conference call from one of the puzzler's offices. These calls sometimes had fifteen people on at a time. They knew Tink would freak because of what happened on the forum, so they didn't tell him (I didn't tell Tink that Saberlane was here either). The puzzlers had been discussing old complications at night to try and find any loose threads (like Lane and me and the case).

Two nights ago Shifter got stuck at work so he was late for the call. When he got on it there were maybe ten people talking. But it was all gibberish. Nonsense. Someone had been on the call when the storm came for them, and it got them all.

Just gone. Kilvesh, Nevergreen, Pippette, those are the ones I knew. They were kids, basically. And now they're zombies.

How many of us are left . . . fifty? Fewer? We're all

too damned scared to pick up the phone now so there's no way to be sure.

I finally sent Ascender an email. Screw my pride. I need to know he's okay. I know ghosting is his thing but there are people who need him. And need to know he's safe. I'm worried how hard this will hit him. There's no army to rally anymore. We're all disappearing.

I dream about this puzzle now. The numbers, the clues . . . I'm reading them out loud but it isn't my voice.

We just finished this round and another set showed up. We still have no idea what the hell we're supposed to do with these numbers. It all seems so damned arbitrary when you're facing the deaths of your friends and the people you love.

I woke up in the middle of the night. Frank called because Ali had a nightmare and wanted to talk to me. She was in tears.

I told him I couldn't talk.

I couldn't risk it, right? I couldn't risk her.

Mouse's note she sent to Cat:
8 - STIRSOGETHERSOSOMBINESNTOSNE
9 - OHTELEOFREVOERNIGHTERTAVELERSE
13# - THREEEELEERTEERCORMON
TIRLEEBEERINNING
17 - VOUTIONGYEISOUN
19 - BONTRIBUTENRCISPENSE
26 - EASUREFOWEAVYNBJECTS
30 - EICHAICEIRDEIANINGEITHING
31 - VISIBEERAYSORSOURCEOFIEEMINATION

Augie is calling a meeting.
At the old forum.

Distracted. So damned distracted. Barely sleeping. I considered not telling Lane about the puzzlers so one of us keeps a level head, but we have to be prepared for anything.

Thought about us packing up and getting out of town. Being so close to Ali is impossible. But part of me thinks the only thing we have going for us is that the storm shows up when there aren't a lot of people around to see it. I remember seeing it in the rearview in Missouri. I saw the way it showed up in the woods. If it wanted to catch us it could've.

So I'm keeping my ass in Logan Park for now.

I wonder what Ali dreamed about. Will her memories manifest in dreams like mine? Hard to think she might be starting to have ancestral recall and will be confused and scared and I'm not there. Worse, she's going to start having my memories too. There are things about my life, and about hers, that I wasn't ready for her to know.

Lane and I don't discuss it but we've taken to not sleeping at the same time. I try to sleep at night. He's up till dawn and crashes when I crawl into the kitchen for coffee. We're keeping watch.

He's a good kid. Wants to do a thousand different things with his life. I want him to be able to. Would he be safer in Jacksonville than he is here, with me? With the box?

I've been in bed with a migraine most of the day. It's getting to us both.

This appeared on the bottom of the box:

The message Cat sent on to Vidivinty for preparation:

5 - HIGBIDTIMPERATUR
7 - DRINXIXSMALXAMOUNTX
11 - BCUXIUHOUTXOSDS
16# - LHRGEPHANTWHTHTHUNK
22 - FETAFIXINFINFFOL
25 - EXHALETEUDIBLYTEITHTEELIEFT
27 - DNGAGEHNBONFLICTVITH
29 -
RETENHTHTOHTNOHT,ITHTGNORANCHT

We're out of box sides so this better be it.

 56935888. Figured it out.
    All the clues disappeared.
    And then a new one appeared on the lid.

"They will find the song.
    Six verses on the wind.
    Sing that lullaby to me.
    My contents I will lend."

I guess I was keeping this journal for you. Why else?
Lane is here, so there's no one else to read it. I was
sending you the clues.
    I must've known, somewhere. Somehow.
    So what's the deal? Are you trying to help me, stop
me, or beat me to the punch?
    Who are you?
    And how the hell are you inside my head?

Knatz had figured out someone was communicating with her using
magiq, trying to influence her, and without context, she was rightfully
pissed and on edge.

The new clue, along with the Book's original clue, led the Mounties to believe that they had to write a song, or "grieving air," as a kind of prequel to "The Minnying of Ojorad," using the revealed numbers as 32 notes spread across eight measures. Grim, Robert, Mr5, and Viviane got to work hashing out the melody and coming up with lyrics, and Nimueh performed and recorded it once it was finished.

VIVIANE:

 As the news spread o'er them,
  The Great Wilds fell still,

 Forges dimmed their fires,
  Hammers ceased their trill,

 Great minds paused their pond'ring
  And their tomes they dropped,

 Brave adventurers tarried
  And their travels stopped,

 Guardians of gold shed
  tears upon their bows

 Kindly healers bless her
  spirit as it goes.

So the Mountaineers recorded their song and sent it to Knatz's dream in 1998. Knatz then sang the song to the magic box she and Saberlane had assembled, and it opened.

KNATZ:

 I want you to know, whoever the hell you are, that I've had that song in my head for 24 hours. And I can't sing. But I did, to the box. After I explained everything to Lane.

The box opened.

"Obscuriotempus" was written on the inside.

We fed it to the Book, and this was on a black page:

"Obscuriotempus.

More commonly referred to as The Shadow Age.

A time known in classical magimystic parlance as The Book of the Dark. 40.7774 – 73.9695"

Whatever you're doing, we both want the Book open, so I guess we're on the same team. I'd just rather you not be in my head.

Lane thinks you're us, in 2017 (because of the briefcase combination), helping us solve the Book using magic that we unlocked by actually opening the Book now, in 1998. God, I hope that insanity is true.

It means we survived. It means we succeeded. It means we're doing everything we can where you are to keep the rest of us, and everybody we love, safe. I gotta believe that.

And if it's true, and you're us, it means you already know what I'm about to tell you . . . Augie's back.

They'd managed to solve another fragment (or "complication," as the '94s called it) all before the kids and I had touched down from our escape from Kemetic Solutions. If anyone could do the impossible things Sullivan had planned, I knew it was the Mountaineers.

The new coordinates directed them to a hidden cave within the

Ramble of Central Park. The place where Sullivan Green spent his final years. But there was nothing anyone could do while Deirdre was in Neithornor with the journal.

The Mounties tried to send Knatz information about the cave, but their apprehensive energy regarding Augie's mysterious return and Deirdre's disappearance pervaded the message.

KNATZ:

 You seem worried. That isn't super reassuring. I'm assuming because things are going to get tougher now? I can't hear you, but I get the gist. It's like when someone you know is talking to you from another room. You know what they're getting at even if you can't hear the words.

Augie wants to meet me somewhere that's meaningful for us early Mountaineers. I don't want to say just in case I'm wrong about who you are, but if I'm not, you already know. There's something important Augie wants to tell me, and he says it's worth the risk to tell me in person.

I told Saberlane he couldn't go. Augie just wanted me (sorry Lane), so I sent him to New York with the box. We're all in danger now. He knows the risk, and he knows what it could mean to bring back a clue from the Ramble.

Right now it could mean everything.

My train leaves in two hours and I'll try to sleep on board. Feel free to send me good news. I wish you could tell us where we find complication 15. I wish a thousand things. I sometimes even wish I'd never gone looking for magic. But we did. And we found it.

See you soon, nightmare buddy.

DEIRDRE: AUGUST 25TH, 2017:

>   I've been going back to the warren. I've even spent two
>   nights there. I was worried at first about getting back,
>   or losing time, but that's passed.
>
>   I spent an entire day at the window, watching the
>   sky, which is blue like ours, but there are streams of
>   aquamarine swirling in the blue. Like a Van Gogh. The
>   clouds look like clouds sometimes, and sometimes they
>   have sharp, faceted edges, like milky white jewels
>   hanging in the air, their prismatic surfaces changing
>   color, reflecting the world below.
>
>   And they don't just drift by, they change shape, form
>   animals and mountain ranges and things that look like
>   treasure maps . . . And they collide with each other and
>   merge, or sometimes shatter, slowly . . . small fragments
>   breaking off and then breaking again, over and over,
>   until they wisp away like smoke.
>
>   I spent an afternoon painting them in the journal
>   Cole gave me, entirely unable to do them justice. I see
>   how my dad could get lost here. I see how Cole could be
>   concerned about this place. I do. But I also want to get
>   out and explore it.
>
>   There's no way to get the door to the warren open.
>   Maybe that's how dad wanted it. A sort of home base.
>   But I need to see more, and if I'm supposed to find the
>   red house, I know I have to find another way out.
>
>   Or another way in.
>
>   The truth is . . .
>
>   I've just been to another part of Neithernor. I know I
>   should've told you or Cole before I went, but it's easy to
>   get wrapped up in this place, this search.

The first time I went I used the directions that the chronocompass gave Cole to knock back on the knocking door. It's like a combination lock. Lower left, upper left, left, right, lower right, upper right, right.

That combination led me to the warren.

But I've also been catching up on the forum and I found that you had another set from the first time you unlocked the chronocompass and reached Augernon.

So I called a door and knocked: Left, upper left, upper left, lower left, right, upper right. It worked. I think each knock sequence is connected to a different door in Neithernor. There could be hundreds, thousands of doors . . .

I took the book, the stick, and I went through.

This door was connected to a small folly in an absolutely massive walled grove.

I call it the Grove Hall. It's shaded, and full of towering white trees that explode into a white and silver canopy above. The endless trees are planted in a perfect grid so they resemble marble columns in some great hall, and their white branches and silver leaves slope into a nearly perfect replica of a vaulted ceiling. Very little sunlight makes it through, but what does is bounced off the white tree trunks and leaves a serene glow below. Grass grows, but it's a deep blue-green. Like a night sky over a sea.

There are old stone benches, some still "uncrumbled," but the bottoms of the trees spread out wide, leaving comfortable little nestly spots to lie in between the roots. It's the definition of tranquil.

But I've spent two days there and have yet to find a way out, except back home through the folly. It took me one day to find another perpendicular stone wall, and I almost got lost coming back. I can only assume walls surround it on all sides. Which makes me wonder how you get in otherwise.

I guess my dad isn't ready to send me into the wilds of Neithernor yet.

I came home last night and found Cole waiting. We both felt awful about last week, both trying to take sole responsibility. I missed him terribly. I wanted to show him the grove, but he's not ready to go back. Given the circumstances, I understand. I told him I wasn't ready to go back to Hoboken. We decided to take some time, for ourselves. Not a breakup by any means, never, just a moment to explore what we're each going through so we can better be there for each other.

In the grove I found a new entry in the journal I think will be of interest to you.

It's titled: The Three Manners of Magiq

My father said he found writings left behind (I assume somewhere outside the Grove Hall) when Monarch's Mountain forgot about Neithernor and eventually fell apart. He found compendiums of "lost memories," chronicles of things that people have remembered about the other time, and he found fragmented, incomplete studies of magic. Sorry, magiq.

He learned in his exploration of Neithernor that there are three currently "supposed" schools or "manners" of magic. "Currently" being the last time anyone came to Neithernor, which was a long time ago.

There's the mundane or Material Magiq, which is the simplest of magic used in our world and the "time before." It's mostly charms and rituals that affect the world in small ways. Finding lost objects, remembering forgotten things, subtle changes in the weather . . . He says that's mostly what you (the Mountaineers) have performed so far. It borrows power from the surrounding world, and then gives it back when the charm or ritual is finished.

On the other end of the spectrum there's primal or Wrought Magiq. Magic that draws energy from other things and places, nature, magical objects, people, and then repurposes it. But by doing so, also destroys it. It's dangerous, unpredictable, and powerful, but not necessarily "bad," though it's often used by those who don't care about the destruction of magic. Monarch's Mountain also thought that wrought magiq is what makes adepts, people born with a specific, innate power. Without realising, they instinctively draw from the world around them to perform their magic. (He says magiq is finite in our mundane world, so wrought magic is a fading talent that is also diminishing all other magic. Sorry, trying to get the "q" down.)

Then there is the third manner of magic that falls in between the other two.

It can be taught but is most powerful in those with the innate gift of creativity. He says it's essentially storyteller magic. MM never had a name for it (there was mention that maybe it shouldn't be named or its actual name shouldn't be spoken) but they colloquially called it "figuration." It's the only way, MM believed, that new magic could be created. There is power when new things, new worlds are "thoroughly thought up," when rich stories are told. And the characters, the settings, the themes and meanings can all be creatively repurposed to perform magiq. But "storytelling" can be used in all sorts of creativity, not just writing. Anything that joins disparate elements into a new creation (which includes all sorts of crafts) can be used to create minor magiq.

But stories are the focus of figuration. It is the rarest magiq in our world and near impossible to perform now. It's how he cast the protection spell on me. Well, partly. He did it by writing the story and then borrowing power from the six corners and also using power from Central Park to bring it to life. He had to use the other two manners to manage the minor figuration.

He said it's difficult to learn, and near impossible to master . . . And to find the red house I'm going to have to perform it myself.

And if I don't find it, all that you're doing now will be for nothing.

My own father had been a decent man. Hard-working, frugal, a bit too quick with his temper and not afraid to raise his hand to me if I stepped too far out of line. There were times that I hated him, times that I loved him, but most times I was simply indifferent. He was a working-class man who made his living with his hands while I . . . wasn't. We didn't share very many interests beyond the Yankees and good bagels, but we could be perfectly content to sit in a room together and not speak. The silence between us wasn't uncomfortable or awkward. It was an unspoken truce. Neither one of us would waste the other's time with any maudlin attempt at bonding.

But reading Sullivan's messages to his daughter filled me with a terrible heartache. I missed my father and our distant, stoic relationship. I wanted to tell him that I loved him, no matter how uncomfortable it would have made him. And I wanted him to tell me the same.

Perhaps all children are haunted by the ghosts of their fathers.

KNATZ:

 I went to see Augie with a shard of hope. Lane could

find something useful. Augie could help. We could be close. I know you're wanting me to feel upbeat and hopeful and it's working, whether I want it to or not.

Augie and I both realized we had no clue what the other looked like but we each finally found the only other person in the train station who looked like they were worried a magical storm might come at any moment and turn them into brainwashed zombies. We got smashed in a bar next door.

He rambled for hours about proto-Mountaineers in World War II and before that and the storm and some dark force working in the shadows and how he'd put together the fact that his grandfather had a friend and fellow magic-seeker who also had ancestral memories and my last name. I just have to assume it's true because I lost my damned power, but as crazy as it all sounded . . . it also sounded familiar.

He said this isn't the first time the Book had appeared, which also feels right when I hear it.

His grandfather said he tried to save himself and his friends but the storm came for them in the middle of whatever they were trying to do and it messed them all up. They were too late. He said he made it out of Europe with only pieces of his memory and shrapnel in his head.

When he came back it was too hard to hold onto so he buried everything from that time up in the Blue Ridge Mountains. And that's where Augie's been for weeks. He's been digging.

And he finally found a box of stuff from the war. Most of it was useless or waterlogged. But not all of it. Inside he found what was left of a Nazi spell book. Yes. You read that right.

Inside the book was something Augie translated as a "bastard hex." A spell made up of a bunch of spells that he thinks, if performed correctly, could either kill us all, or hide us.

Hide us all from the storm.

But it will erase every memory of our time as Mountaineers. Our usernames, knowledge of the Book . . . each other. Anything connected to magic will disappear from our minds. We won't remember any of it. But we'll be safe. And we'll be us. It will take us back to who we were before we ever went looking for the LC.

Augie already talked with Tink. He started up the forum again because it's going to take all of us together to make this ugly thing work. If it works. The problem is the storm will definitely come for us again when we're all together.

So Augie gave me a coin his grandfather stole from the SS. I don't know how it works, but he says it saved our grandparents' lives in the war and it should buy us enough time to perform the erasure before it breaks under the force of the storm.

But I didn't get it. Why me? Anybody could've held the coin. Tink. Augie. Why me? Why did we have to meet?

He said it was because he now knows the friendship we formed this past year really stretches back decades, to our grandparents before us. He said he always valued my candor and my bravery and my trusting him with my secrets, and he wanted to finally meet and have a drink. See each other face to face and honor the bond we built before it's all washed away.

He's been contacting the rest of the lodge to come back one more time. They trust him more than any of the rest of us. If he asks them to come back, they will.

The big question we hadn't answered was . . . what about the Book? Fourteen complications down. Two to go. We went back and forth the rest of the night about when to do this, if we should do it, and what about the Book.

Should we hold off on the spell to try and find the last two complications, or let this all go and save whoever's left? It could be weeks of waiting and searching and clues and roadblocks, and how many more people will be wiped away while we're waiting for a damned book to open?

On the one hand, magic. Knowing it's real but losing all memory of it.

On the other hand, for me at least, Ali.

Believe it or not I was the one who said to wait. Wait to hear from Lane. See what he finds in the Ramble.

I took the train home, feeling confident that one way or another we were going to be okay, damn it. And secretly optimistic that Lane would find something before we had to try this crazy spell. Before we had to forget each other.

But Augie had left a message on my answering machine. While he and I were in a bar debating what to do and when to do it, the storm had come for Tink. And his family, because they knew.

All of them, gone.

So that's it. We're going through with the spell.

I guess you weren't us after all.

The Mountaineers were shaken. They felt helpless. Many, myself included, had secretly hoped there would be some way to save or protect the '94s. But this conversation between Knatz and Augie just proved that we had always been part of this loop, and it seemed like there was nothing we could do to save them.

ROBERT:

 Thank you, Knatz, for all of your help. We were glad to be able to work with you. Please take care and stay safe, and always trust in the flow of magiq, wherever it may lead you. Ali will be all right.

All they could say to comfort Knatz was that her daughter was safe, though they still weren't positive even that was true.

KNATZ:

 She skipped school and came to the apartment today.
I told her I was having a hard time and it had nothing to do with her. I told her everything was fine. And every time a car door slammed outside I thought the storm had come to take us both.
Tell me what to do.
I don't know what to do. For the first time in my life.
You'd think it would be easy for a parent. Sacrifice yourself to be her mother. To be there for her. But is that really what's best? Giving up the search and being there for her, whoever I am after this? Or risking everything to try and show her a world that is so much more than anyone wants us to believe?
What matters more?
My presence, or my passion?
Which one makes her strong? Which one makes her brave?
Which inspires her to explore and love and change?
When she's a grown woman, will it matter more to her that I sacrificed myself for her sake? Or that I risked everything for something bigger than all of us?

Whoever you are, you know how this all shakes out.
You know what happens.
Tell me, 2017. In a dream or a song or a story. Please.
Tell me before I make the wrong the decision.

The Mounties were crushed. They felt so deeply for her, and so helpless. All they could do was send her a final reassuring message:

THE MOUNTAINEERS:

 Here's a story for you, Knatz.
Once upon a time there was a woman.
This woman briefly had the gift to gain all the wisdom and council of the past.
One day this woman started to hear voices from the future, and she had access to everything the future could tell her.
With all the voices in her head she forgot about the one that matters. Her own. The past or the future don't matter. Only the present does.
Knatz, make up your own damned mind.
You know what magiq is? How it works? Magiq is taking your thoughts and pointing them at your best intention, and then getting out behind that and pushing with your entire heart and soul.
Your intention, and your emotion. Harness those and you can do anything.

A long twelve hours passed before Knatz's final, heartbreaking message.

KNATZ:

 This is gonna be a quick goodbye. I've learned that goodbyes don't matter much.

I thought of writing out everything I know, the little that matters, but who knows what's going to happen to all of this, so I'll say that in the end we did what we thought was right. We sought the secrets of the world and it cost us. Some more than others.

I just hope some part of what we did here is left behind when we're all gone. We failed to reach the top, but part of me believes some good might still come from our long climb up the mountain.

And with that final message, the chronocompass locked again, and Knatz was gone.

CHAPTER 19
WINDOWS AND DOORS

"This is the Law of the Jungle, as old and true as
the sky…"

— MR5

COLE: AUGUST 28TH, 2017 9:45 P.M.:

> Hey guys, no word from Dee. I figure she's back in
> Neithernor with the journal and the compass. I'll keep
> calling and checking. I'm sure she wants to get the new
> combination from the Ramble as much as you do.
>
> It never stops feeling weird, walking in that
> brownstone and knowing my girlfriend's a million
> miles away and just behind a door. It's that same feeling
> when somebody dies. I mean the feeling helpless part.
> Feeling like you wish you could just open the door and
> they'd be there. But you know they won't be.
> EDIT:
> Oh man am I overreacting. Bask in my insecurity.

❦

AUGUST 30TH, 2017 6:12 P.M.:

> I just went to the brownstone after work because I hadn't heard from Dee.
> The front window was completely shattered, and the journal was on the living room floor, open, covered in glass.
> I have no idea what's going on or where Deirdre is.

ROBERT: 6:19 P.M.:

> Is anything missing besides Deeds? Any sign of the compass?

COLE: 6:24 P.M.:

> I don't think anything else is missing. Not sure. No compass.

6:37 P.M.:

> She has a thousand bags. But I can't find her phone or her wallet.

6:38 P.M.:

> I'm gonna check around the neighborhood and keep

trying her cell. Maybe somebody broke in, but she wasn't here?

ROBERT: 6:59 P.M.:

   If she's not in the neighborhood, or back by the time you get back . . .

    She may be in Neithernor. If you can get a door to knock at you, try to go to the warren: Lower left, upper left, left, right, lower right, upper right, right.

    If not there try whatever that glade is: Left, upper left, upper left, lower left, right, upper right.

    If you can't get a door to knock for you, or you can and don't find her in those places . . . Read the journal and see if she's been to the Ramble and gotten anything new to show up. She may have knocked her way somewhere else. (Credit to Deyavi for the suggestion.)

AUGUSTUS_OCTAVIAN: 7:01 P.M.:

   Check around the Ramble in Central Park. She knows from her dad's messages that the Storm can't enter there. I can't shake the feeling that we're dealing with more than a common burglar.

COLE: 7:29 P.M.:

   I'll check the park.

9:38 P.M.:

 Oh my god, guys. She wrote a note inside the back cover of the journal. I just saw it when I got back. I'm such an idiot . . .
"It came for me. I've been trapped in Grey's apartment for two days. Locked in against the Storm. It's in the walls. Trying to get in, even through the phone. I need help. It knows I've been to Neithernor. Followed me here."
What the hell do I do?

9:42 P.M.:

 If she could knock away from the apartment, she would've, right?

9:43 P.M.:

 Grey said when you lock the apartment door the whole place basically disappears. Maybe she can't knock out of there without unlocking the door?

DEYAVI: 9:44 P.M.:

 Then she's trapped there.

TINKER: 9:44 P.M.:

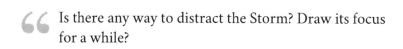 Is there any way to distract the Storm? Draw its focus
for a while?

MR5: 9:46 P.M.:

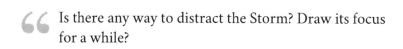 I think if we did a really big spell, that would do, like a
signal flare? Stories are a type of magiq, right? So, let's
have everyone take part in reading story with intention.
It's quick and easy to organize.

ORACLESAGE: 9:47 P.M.:

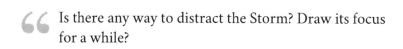 That's actually brilliant, 5! A big show of magic may
distract the Storm enough for her to make a getaway!

COLE: 9:52 P.M.:

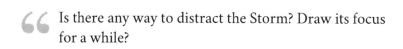 Okay, figure what you can do, what we know. I can't do
anything here. I'm going to Grey's building. In cab now.

AUGUSTUS_OCTAVIAN: 9:57 P.M.:

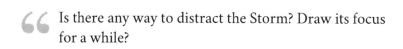 We can't lose you to the Storm. Use your head and not
your heart. Stay away from that building until we figure
something out!

COLE: 9:57 P.M.:

   You're right, Augustus, but if I can open a door to Neithernor nearby, maybe lure it out . . . I could give her a chance to knock. I could bolt for Central Park. But if it gets in that apartment and I waited hours to go get her I won't be able to forgive myself. Do magiq. Save our asses. If a storm eats me, I'll text. I joke when I'm terrified.

REVENIR: 10:02 P.M.:

   Please take care of yourself, Cole. We still don't completely understand this situation or what's going on exactly, even how the journal got back to the brownstone . . . I couldn't stand it if we lost you in the chaos of this situation.

AUGUSTUS_OCTAVIAN: 10:02 P.M.:

   How close is Grey's building to Central Park?

COLE: 10:05 P.M.:

   Grey is 3-4 blocks from park. But I never was able to open a door. I'm twenty blocks away.

AUGUSTUS_OCTAVIAN: 10:08 P.M.:

66 Cole. I know you can do this. I know you love Deirdre, and I know you can put your past trauma aside and call up a Knocking Door. I know you can, because I believe in you. And I believe, more than anything else, in love.

The Storm covets Neithernor more than anything. The Silver created it specifically to wipe out the Wool/Mounties for barring them from it. It probably won't be able to resist an open door to the place.

GINGER:

66 So what we went off before, when we wanted to create a spell, was that a spell had at least three aspects and some random complications.
—Ritual Aspect
—Object Creation
—Six elemental properties. We need representation of all six elements, which for reference are Light, Aether, Ore, Tide, Thought, and Wild.

REVENIR:

66 What if we all write a line from our favorite book that is also tied to an element? That way there's a creativity aspect (the writing of the line) and also the guild aspect.

COLE: 10:17 P.M.:

66 Ten blocks.

AUGUSTUS_OCTAVIAN:

"He didn't say anything, just put his head down on his desk, hiding his face in the crook of his elbow, and let the blood in his head throb in the darkness. The wooden desk was cool on his cheek. It hadn't been a fluke, or a hoax, or a joke. He had done it. Magic was real, and he could do it."
    —Lev Grossman, *The Magicians*

REVENIR:

"We the mortals touch the metals,
    the wind, the ocean shores, the stones,
    knowing they will go on, inert or burning,
    and I was discovering, naming all these things:
    it was my destiny to love and say goodbye."
    —Pablo Neruda, *Still Another Day*

GRIM:

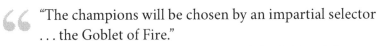

"The champions will be chosen by an impartial selector
. . . the Goblet of Fire."
    —J.K. Rowling, *Harry Potter and the Goblet of Fire*

DEYAVI:

"I dreamed a dream of angels. I saw them and heard them in a great and endless galactic night. I saw the

lights that were these angels, flying here and there, in streaks of irresistible brilliance . . . I felt love around me in this vast and seamless realm of sound and light . . . And something akin to sadness swept me up and mingled my very essence with the voices who sang, because the voices were singing of me."
   —Anne Rice, *Of Love and Evil*

COLE: 10:22 P.M.:

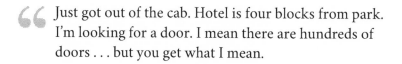 Just got out of the cab. Hotel is four blocks from park. I'm looking for a door. I mean there are hundreds of doors . . . but you get what I mean.

GINGER:

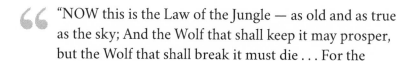 "'Isn't it odd how much fatter a book gets when you've read it several times?' Mo had said . . . 'As if something were left between the pages every time you read it. Feelings, thoughts, sounds, smells . . . and then, when you look at the book again many years later, you find yourself there, too, a slightly younger self, slightly different, as if the book had preserved you like a pressed flower . . . both strange and familiar.'"
   —Cornelia Funke, *Inkspell*

MR5:

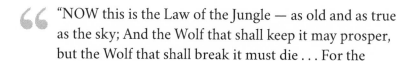 "NOW this is the Law of the Jungle — as old and as true as the sky; And the Wolf that shall keep it may prosper, but the Wolf that shall break it must die . . . For the

strength of the Pack is the Wolf, and the strength of the
Wolf is the Pack."
  —Rudyard Kipling, *The Law of The Jungle*

COLE: 10:26 P.M.:

66 What if I open a door in the park and the Storm can't
see it or doesn't come for it? I think I have to try and
open one just outside the park to be sure.

10:29 P.M.:

66 Found a maintenance door on the side of an apartment
building. I can see the hotel and the park from here. I'm
gonna start. Remembering Robert's words . . . I'm
opening a door to her . . .

10:30 P.M.:

66 Crap, warren combination . . . somebody write it here.
I'm freaking out.

GINGER: 10:31 P.M.:

66 Lower left, upper left, left, right, lower right, upper
right, right.

COLE:

66 Thanks.

10:32 P.M.:

66 I can't get it to knock.

DEYAVI: 10:36 P.M.:

66 Cole . . . breathe. Tell yourself a story about Neithernor.
We will figure this out.

COLE: 10:38 P.M.:

66 I did it. I opened a door to the warren. I'm not going in.
Not until the Storm comes.

10:41 P.M.:

66 I think I hear it.

DEYAVI: 10:42 P.M.:

66 Cole, don't wait until the last second.

COLE: 10:43 P.M.:

❝ I see it.

DEYAVI: 10:43 P.M.:

❝ Cole, go *now*.

MR5:

❝ Get in the door!!!

REVENIR:

❝ Please go, Cole.

AUGUSTUS_OCTAVIAN: 10:46 P.M.:

❝ I hope he made it. All of this rests on him now.

CHAPTER 20
FIGURATION

"Seems like there's a lot of adventure to be
had here!"

— CLOUDY

COLE: AUGUST 31ST, 2017 11:34 A.M.:

> We're out. She's safe. I made it into the warren and Dee
> showed up a few seconds later, once the Storm left the
> apartment. We spent the night (two days) making sure it
> was gone. Dee's gonna write up a post or two to explain
> everything, like how the journal got back to the
> brownstone. It's nuts.
>
> I've never seen anything like it. It moved so fast.
> There was this flash of light on the street that made it
> recoil for a second and bought me time to shut the door.
> Could've been a streetlight but I like to think it was
> you guys.
>
> Thank you.

DEIRDRE: AUGUST 31ST, 2017

 To explain everything that happened I have to go back a
week. To the Grove Hall. It's going to take me a day or
two given what's just happened.

I don't know how many days I spent there in the
grove, trying to figure out how I was supposed to use
magic I'd just learned about to do . . . something.
Something vague and confusing is what.

I'd brought string with me to make sure I could find
my way back. At the far west end I (nearly literally)
stumbled on a small stone statue in the path. A fat flat
toad in a sort of cloak. Little tears were carved in the
edges of his eyes. And suddenly the little carving I'd
seen at the top of the folly made sense. A tiny mouse in
a sweet dress, dabbing her eye with a bit of cloth.

The characters from the poem last year. The
minnying.

Over the next two days I found the cat and the owl
as well. The cat sat on a broken bench, its tail carved in
mid-swish, head bowed. The owl was in the hollow of
one of the marble trees. Its wings were clenched
together in front of its body, as if in prayer. I only later
noticed that its eyes were large like an owl's but carved
to look . . . human. It was beautiful and unnerving all
at once.

It took me far too long to realise that all the carvings
were facing east. So eventually that's where I headed. I
walked all day, actually had to nap at one point. I was
hungry, exhausted, and I'd completely lost track of how
long I'd been there.

At the far eastern wall (I don't know which direction it actually is, only that it's east when arriving through the folly door) was a sort of sepulchre carved into the wall. It had an arched stone roof and columns, but the door was made of cut crystal the color of indigo. Light moved behind it. This wasn't a tomb. It was a doorway.

Carved into the arch were the words "May His Majesty Pass This Way Again."

There was no way to open the crystal door. Looking closer, it wasn't even a door, really. No hinges or clasps, just a slab of transparent mineral, the afternoon sun shining through it.

So this was the test? I had no idea what to do, or how to do it. I tried knocking-in, but the door wouldn't knock back. I spent an hour trying but was absolutely knackered by then so I followed my string trail back to the folly and back to the brownstone. I ate, napped, and went back over the minnying on the forum.

It was a monument for Ojorad, the crystal door. And all the creatures were mourning him or bidding him farewell as he passed on. So ... now I know there's story magic. I know there's something beyond the grove. I know I have to get over, through, or under the stone wall surrounding the grove, and I have a poem and four carvings of animals as hints.

Do I somehow do magiq and crawl through like a mouse? Or climb over like a cat? Jump like a toad? Fly like an owl? How would this work? Would I transform into an animal, or just sprout cat claws or wings? None of it sounded appealing, safe, or even remotely doable (let alone undoable.) I'd never done anything like this, didn't know if something quite like this was even possible, and now I was pondering which animal I was going to transform into with no way of knowing how it would happen or how I'd transform back. (And if you've already caught on to what I was actually meant to do, please forgive my daftness. I'd been wandering the grove a little too long.)

I went back to the grove the next morning, hoping I'd missed something. I went over everything again, checking the statues for writing or any other clue I might've missed. I'm ashamed to say I even tried to skip it all and climb the wall myself. I nearly broke my entirely human neck.

I walked back to the crystal door.

"May His Majesty Pass This Way Again"

Faced with the idea of sprouting animals parts, passing through the crystal door like some kind of spectre suddenly seemed completely reasonable. And the moment it came to me I felt something. A buzzing. That tingling sweetness in the air grew stronger. Almost liquid on my tongue, like warm tea. And my right hand was buzzing. The hand I was holding the walking stick with.

Something was happening.

I stepped up to the crystal door, thought about the minnying, the grieving animals, their lord, their master leaving them for some other place. His back turned to them not to pain them or abandon them, but because the light on the other side of the crystal was calling him, dazzling warm and welcoming.

I touched the door. For a second it was cold and hard, but then I thought about everyone I loved who'd passed on. Monica, my mother, my father . . . and the crystal fell away to my fingers like I was brushing through a curtain. Thin and light. I thought I was shivering, shaking out of wonder or fear, but it was the stick. It was vibrating.

I felt invincible. I took a step, felt my body crystallize

around the edges as I passed through the door, then become me again. I'd just passed through a solid wall by telling myself a story. By feeling the story and creating magiq with it. I think? Or had I borrowed magiq from the story? Was this figuration or material magiq? Or a hybrid? Was figuration still to come?

I'm trying to get this all down, so I'm sending this while I put together what I found on the other side, and what appeared in the journal when I got there. Bare with me.

"   The grove was surrounded by a fortress made of dried vines. Some were reedy tendrils, some were thick as a fist, and they reached even higher than the grove's walls. As if a living castle had grown from the ground and surrounded the grove, protecting it. The vines were so tightly coiled you couldn't see through them, but a few purposeful-looking gaps allowed streams of light in. I could see bits of dense forest outside.

To the right of the crystal door the vines had grown so thick they were impassable, so I started following the "hall" created between the vines and the grove's wall to the left.

After a while I reached the corner of the grove and turned . . . High up, the wall of vines had been crushed. The limbs had fallen into the hall, blocking my way.

Draped in the opening was the bleached white skeleton of a bird, the size of a large house. Its head and right wing were hanging on this side of the wall. Its flesh and feathers had fallen away years ago, but I could see that when it was alive it had been . . . armoured.

Rotting leather straps held a metal breastplate to its chest, and a long, spined helmet protected its head and beak. I could just make out what looked like a seat or a saddle on its back. Had someone flown this bird? Forced it to dive through the vine wall? Why?

Had the vines always been here, or had they been some sort of barricade? An attempt to protect the grove?

The War of Neithernor.

I'd forgotten. It was heartbreaking to see.

The sun was lower now so the shadows were growing. Standing below the shattered body of this behemoth was disquieting. Why would my dad lead me here? Why would he show me this?

All of this lost, fighting over magiq. Night was coming and I didn't want to be alone there. It took longer to pass through the wall, the taste wasn't as sweet, the stick didn't react like it had.

I found myself running through the grove. I needed a break from Neithernor. I went back to the brownstone, but just before I fell asleep I remembered I hadn't checked the journal.

My father wrote about the war. About "the Silver" and seeing what they were truly capable of, how he was also heartbroken by the bird when he first saw it.

"This was the world they wanted. Magiq, mined dry. Wonder, subjugated. To have all. To win control of a thing that didn't belong to anyone. And when they were finally barred from paradise they set their sights on the mundane world. Drawing what little light remains into the dark place they hide. From the moment I left that grove I knew I had to do everything I could to stop them. The purpose I'd looked for all my life, and only seen glimpses of, was now looking back at me from the skull of that animal. Even though Monarch's Mountain had been wiped away, their purpose, their soul still remained in those few

remaining shafts of light. The Silver can't win as long
as we live to fight."

⚜

“ The next morning I saw that Grey had left a message,
checking on me because we hadn't talked in a
few weeks.

I needed time so I headed uptown to see him.

On the way, I was reading over the new passage in
the journal and I noticed that something else had been
written in it before, but had faded or been erased . . . It
was part of the story my father told me when I was
little, about Elainnor (I always thought it was spelled
"Eleanor" until Augustus told me.) It was the part where
she first sets out to gather the four things she needs . . . I
could only read a few lines clearly, but I could see the
word "Galifanx," which I remembered.

I should mention that since I've had this volume I've
also had dreams about that story. Maybe it's been
sinking in while I've been carrying it with me (along
with the compass and the stick. I must look totally
ridiculous walking around the city like Henry David
Thoreau.)

That's what was on my mind when I noticed that the
cab driver had been talking to me about the weather. He
was complaining about how it was supposed to be hot
and sunny today. I looked out through the front
windscreen, and it looked bright as can be. We arrived
at Grey's, I paid and got out.

And that's when I saw the black cloud moving up
3rd, blocking out the sun. I knew in an instant.
The Storm.

I ran inside. Remembering how slow the elevators
were, I took the stairs to the 7th floor. Grey let me in,

and I bolted the door. Even with the door locked and the apartment hidden you can still see out the windows. Outside was totally dark. And then it slowly faded back to day.

I thought it was gone, that I'd outrun it, but then we started hearing the banging. At the door, inside the walls . . . It was trying to get to me, or get back into Neithernor by following me through.

With the apartment hidden I couldn't call a door to Neithernor (and even if I could've, I worried it could somehow break in and I would be letting it in after me.)

I was going to call Cole, but I thankfully noticed my phone's screen flickering and remembered that the Storm could reach through technology too. So Grey and I spent two days trying to figure out what to do, all the while listening to the Storm inside the walls, trying to find a way in.

We were trapped.

At one point I concocted a plan to race out the window and down the fire escape, but there was no way of knowing how long it would take me to get down or how quickly it would notice I had run out. Grey tried to assure me it couldn't get in as long as the front door was locked, but even *he* didn't know how strong it was, what it was capable of.

And then the paintings started coming off the walls.

It was banging harder and harder, trying to break through.

I was terrified and not hiding it well. I felt terrible for bringing this to Grey, who'd managed to stay hidden for decades. I had to do something. I had to get out, or at least somehow find a way to tell Cole, and tell you.

And then I realised I had the stick with me.

Couldn't I do some kind of magiq and fix this? Somehow? Hurt it or distract it or get a message through it? I tried to run through the minnying, thinking maybe I could pass through to the floor below, or leap to another building . . . But it all seemed ridiculous. I could do that in Neithernor, which is full of magiq, but what could I do here?

And then something happened. It's a blur, but looking back I must've been running through the stories I knew, trying to find something I could use to fix all of this. I just needed to get myself together and stop freaking out. My father would be counting on me to be brave. To solve this and keep fighting. I barely felt the stick shivering in my hand . . .

When Grey yelled for me to come to the parlour.

I ran in and I couldn't believe my eyes.

The journal was floating in midair. Not floating actually, but flapping. It turned and banged itself against the window. Then it dove to the coffee table and exposed the inside of its cover. I didn't know what was happening, what I was supposed to do . . .

Until I saw the compass crawling out of my bag and across the coffee table, with the little loop on its top holding a pen, which it dropped beside the journal.

Grey was in shock. I was in shock. What was happening? Was I doing this?!

I was. I raced over, scrawled a note on the cover, and then the book flipped over, the compass crawled onto it, and it took off into the air again, flapping toward the window.

At first I thought it had something to do with the bird in Neithernor. The saddle on its back. But then it dawned on it. The ant and the caterpillow.

I was somehow sending a message to my boyfriend with the enchanted contents of my purse, using a magic spell I made up from a fairy tale my father told me.

I actually asked the book if it knew where it was

going before I opened the window for a second and it flew out. I watched it flap down Park Avenue until it was too small to see anymore.

I turned to Grey, who hadn't moved a muscle.

He finally said, "If there was ever a doubt you were a Green . . ."

Now I knew why the Storm had finally stopped chasing me and given me a chance to catch up. It was trying to get to Deirdre now that she'd found a way into Neithernor.

COLE:

 For the record, I've been looking for the compass all day. Dee is (finally) asleep after spending all day catching you guys up.

Here's what happened on my end: I bolted into the warren and shut the door and about ten seconds later it opened again. It was Dee, and Grey's apartment was behind her. We tried to figure out what to do but decided it would probably go back to Grey's and we'd be safer in the warren, even if we had to wait it out.

So, we spent two nights there.

It was still crazy scary to open the door again. (We wondered where it would take us, the street or Grey's, but I knocked back and it put us on the street, so I guess that's how it works. Whoever knocks.)

The Storm was gone. We ran into Central Park, waited there for a while, and then headed back to the brownstone. Which is where we've been ever since (aside from me trolling up and down the street, looking for a compass).

I'm going to widen my search for it tomorrow. I'm

sorry I didn't find it today. I know you're waiting to see what happens with it in the park.

I hope she'll just rest for a day or two. She seems . . . not herself. Tired. Distant. I guess that's what happens when a living weather pattern tries to eat you.

CHAPTER 21
HOUSEKEEPING

"This is the second time this weekend I've been
outsmarted by a door."

— HANNAH

That night I dreamed of snow-blanketed trees and a little girl
lost in the woods. I saw tiny footprints in the snow, leading
down the winding path. Thick and knotted oaks flanked
the sides of the path, their leafless branches creating a tangled,
arthritic canopy overhead.

The cold was bitter and wet. It crawled into my lungs with every
breath and squatted heavy inside my chest like a dying animal. As I
followed the footprints, I came to a small clearing. The girl stood in its
center, barefoot in a thin nightgown that had to be useless against the
cold. But she didn't seem to mind. She was standing in front of the
little red house.

And she wasn't alone.

Lauren, a figure of swirling snow, knelt next to the girl, not as a
mother to a child, but as an older sibling or doting aunt. She stroked
the girl's hair with an icy finger, and the two smiled at each other.

Lauren's smile disappeared when she turned and saw me. I couldn't move, frozen by her gaze. I had interrupted, trespassed on a private moment.

With a sudden wave of her hand, I was blown back by a frigid gust of wind, tumbling back down the path like an autumn leaf, the oak trees pressing in closer. And closer.

I woke to the sound of pounding on the motel door. Thin streams of light coming through the lopsided blinds cast bright yellow bars on the faux-wood paneled wall. I fell out of bed, wrapped in blankets against the night's chill.

When I opened the door, the motel manager was there, his pudgy face twisting in on itself. "Checkout was three hours ago. You weren't answering the phone."

"No, I took it off the hook."

"Well, housekeeping needs to get in there and—"

"Yeah, okay, I'll be out in fifteen."

I closed the door on him as he bleated on about charging me an extra day. I didn't care. I took a hot shower, letting the heat and steam warm me until I felt normal again.

Once I was dressed and had dealt with the motel, I found a coffee shop and reached out to the Mountaineers.

I WROTE:

 Good to see you guys have been keeping busy.

So, in case you were wondering, here's what happened: Portencia ended up sending us to about a month ago, using the doorway and the chair. She sent us to the future she saw.

A while back I was given a token that kept me under the magimystic radar for the most part. Port, Alison, and Jeremy have it now. They're together, where nobody's gonna find them.

But without the token the Storm picked up my scent

after KS, and it's been chasing me for weeks. I couldn't risk reaching out. But last week it let up. Now I know why. Cole and Deirdre.

Not good for them, but it gives me a chance to get to work. I'm on my way out west (flying's still a bad idea when a storm is looking for you) to the server Jeremy sent the KS information to.

When he was out of body the Council was communicating with him. They suggested looking for a few interesting things in the KS systems and backing them up for our own use.

So I'm heading out to get them.

I'll follow up in a few days.

I had to smile at the outpouring of affection from the Mountaineers once they learned I was alive and "back." It was nice to be a part of their family. And I was determined to do more to help. Maybe whatever I'd find at the server farm would lead to the next fragment.

I drove until it got dark, then found a highway-side hotel to crash at for the night. I checked a notification from the forum and saw Cole had responded.

COLE:

 Whoa, Marty . . . the gang's getting back together.

So I went to the Ramble yesterday, but it's closed for restoration. The whole place is blocked off by chain-link fences. There are workers and security all around. Honestly, it seems weird how much security was surrounding part of a park.

I went back really early this morning and snuck in. I found where the cave used to be, and there's a new entry in the journal. I'm gonna leave that for Dee to decide what she wants to share and when, but you know what else I found?

Sitting right on top of the rocks where the cave entrance used to be?

The compass. It must've jumped off when the book flew over the park (things I never thought I'd say). It's just been there waiting for us.

It dragged me all around the park, and I wrote down everywhere it took me.

Starting at the Ramble it took me to the Alice in Wonderland statue, then the Bow Bridge, then to Strawberry Fields, over to Cherry Hill, then to the obelisk at the north part of the park, and then to Summit Rock.

I hope this helps. Dee's gonna transcribe anything important from the journal, and then I guess we're off to Neithernor with the new knock (if she wants me to come).

The Mountaineers started breaking down the locations, hoping there was a new "combination" they could use on Dawson's chronocompass. They worked it out in an hour's time, triggering the chronocompass again, but this time, no chimes, and it spit them back to the main page.

I got up before dawn and got back on the road. It took me most of the following day to get to the server farm, a bland rectangle of beige bricks surrounded by parking lots and empty fields. The farm was the first building to go up in what was going to be a business park with all the aesthetic charm of a wet dishrag.

Unlike my experience with Kemetic Solutions, getting in was almost too easy. The young man at the front desk was more than happy to arrange an impromptu tour for me. Since this was a smaller

farm that catered to local businesses, security was a bit lax; it wasn't
hard to shake my tour guide. Thanks to Jeremy, I knew how to find
the right server and access it. Ten minutes later, I was walking out to
my car with a wave to my guide and the whole of Kemetic Solutions'
data in my bag.

I found a new motel with a more lenient checkout policy and set in
for the night. After I spent most of the evening poring over the data, I
drafted a post to the Mountaineers, telling them what I'd found.

I WROTE:

 Got to the server farm, got the information off of it per
Jeremy's instructions, and spent the night going through
it. Most of it's corrupted, and I don't think by accident.
It probably happened when he was offloading it.
Standard admin paperwork and filing stuff is all there,
but anything about Fallon's team and their research is
barely legible, or just junk now.

I found parts of his email. He wrote up demands a
few years ago, things he needed before he would agree
to bring in Nate (Teddy Fallon's son, aka Wanderer, an
adept whose power Kemetic wanted to research).

There are also pieces of his journal, and it's all shot
to hell, but from a few entries I get the sense that he
didn't just know about the Storm, he was researching it.

I'm forwarding it all to Jeremy to see if he can
salvage any of it, but it looks like this trip turned out to
be a waste of my time and your patience. Sorry for
getting your hopes up.

It was a letdown. I don't know what I was hoping to find, but I
wanted to find *something*. My rage for Fallon needed an outlet. And if I
couldn't destroy the man himself, I'd sate my desire for revenge by
destroying everything he'd built.

Jeremy didn't think he'd be able to find much more than I did, but I felt better with an expert on the case. After I sent the files to him, I made my way to Boston.

The city was sweltering. Breathing was like drinking bathwater. My rental car struggled to keep the air inside livable and its engine at an operable temperature. I wasn't sure if Kemetic Solutions' security would recognize me, but I had a feeling the magic that pumped through that place would spot me the second I stepped onto the property. I wasn't sure the car could get me away fast enough.

It turned out I didn't need to worry.

The building was cordoned off with yellow caution tape. When I peered through the windows, I couldn't see anything other than a few stray electrical cords and paper strewn about the floor. The first time I had come to Kemetic Solutions and peeked through the windows, the building looked completely bereft of people, of equipment, of everything—an eerie, suspicious sort of empty. But now it looked like an office that had been well and truly abandoned.

I made a quick call to the municipal office and learned that Kemetic Solutions had relocated somewhere offshore. Soon after the company had vacated, the building suffered a "massive flood," much to the property owner's dismay. Nothing of value could be salvaged.

So Kemetic Solutions had disappeared before I'd even arrived at Portencia's aunt's house. Fallon could be anywhere in the world, licking his wounds, preparing to start up his own little Frankenstein Farm all over again. The thought made me ill.

I updated the Mountaineers and made my way back to the city. When I next checked in, I found Deirdre had finally updated.

DEIRDRE: SEPTEMBER 6TH, 2017:

 I've been terribly sick the past few days. Cole says it's what you all call spell sickness. I'm happy to hear it isn't whatever's glowing inside the stick.

I don't know what happened. I mean, I know it was

the spell I cast. And there were small cracks in it already, but the stick didn't behave that way in Neithernor, at the crystal door . . . Maybe I'm not supposed to be using it here, in the normal world? Maybe I did more than I was supposed to? Maybe it was because I was close to the Storm? Gee, it sure would be nice if my father would just send me a checklist or instruction manual every now and then . . .

I haven't tried the new knock. I just don't feel up to it. Maybe I'm scared, with this thing coming after us. But if I'm honest I think I'm worried about what's going to happen next. Things are moving so quickly. Out of the blue I'm casting magiq now. I walked through a wall, and brought a book and a compass to life with my imagination and a magiq stick.

I wasn't ready for that last one. To be clear, it was incredible and part of me wants to do nothing but magiq, but it's also scary. I didn't mean to cast that spell. Not completely. What else might I accidentally do?

The two days with Grey were nerve-wracking because of that thing trying to get in, but I also learned a lot about my father. In his later years, Grey said, my dad came to believe something had been guiding him along this path his whole life. To the path of wool, the path of magiq. The road to Neithernor. To this "great task," as my father called it. He'd called that guiding force "his soul's providence," and he'd attributed so many things to an unseen presence. Meeting my mum, the coven, even the printing house burning down all those years back. It makes sense that part of him had hoped it had been Monarch's Mountain drawing him to them, only to find the ruins of Neithernor. But he never stopped believing that he was part of a plan, and his plan with the Council was just another cog in a clockwork.

And when he died he left that mantle, that path, to

me. The things he did . . . Grey's apartment, the spell on me, nursing the Council (and himself) back to life . . . he was incredibly brave, and powerful.

I don't know if I'm ready to accept the providence that guided him, if there is or was such a thing (though I accept that there were loads of coincidences that got me here).

But I don't have time to doubt it or myself, because all our fates are tied together now. We're all on this last path, and if I don't find the red house and perform some crazy magiq to find out whatever's inside it . . .

We've lost.

The Ramble unlocked a new passage in the journal (though it hadn't before). Bedridden, I transcribed the whole thing because I thought you'd want to see it. Turns out you had a "soul's providence" as well:

THE DARK DOOR

I explored thousands of miles of Neithernor and never found the edge.

Once, I traveled for days across the great eastern sea and I found the remains of a strange fortress. The sea had claimed most of it, but portions were left on the shore. It was days removed from the other lands, the other ruins. I knew without question it was the house of Silver.

I spent months exploring the ruins and found writings that had survived the water and the war. The Silver were working on something in the mundane when everything fell apart. They were building a secret place inside our reality. Instead of sharing the discoveries they'd made in the mundane, they'd been secretly collecting them, stockpiling them out of view of Monarch's Mountain. There was even mention of those artifacts being transported back and forth between their earthly "palace of doors" and Neithernor, for reasons I don't know.

They'd built, somewhere in their Neithernorian fortress, a dark door to their secret place on Earth. A door that now could only be opened from Neithernor, because Monarch's Mountain had barred Silver's return.

I found it, half-submerged. I knew once I walked through they might sense that I had entered, and would know about the forgotten entrance. I prepared myself and opened the dark door, into the silver palace, and closed it after me. I found a towering, endless place made of countless rooms, libraries, galleries, and museum halls of magiqal artifacts, connected to every corner of the world. Vast and quiet and cold. They had spread to the six corners like a virus.

But this was the opportunity we needed. The Council and I had been searching for an object of power with what little power we had gathered. It's one reason why I had scoured Neithernor. We needed something that would catalyze our plan, to set all of this in motion. We believed in you, but we needed something unmistakable, something so wondrous it would inspire thousands to join your cause. Your army of mountain climbers.

After hiding in their stronghold for weeks, avoiding the sounds of footsteps on icy marble, I found it. There in the heart of the palace of doors I found a copy of *Ackerly Green's Guide to Magiq*. I stole it, along with whatever else I could carry, including a pocket watch I found that had belonged to the Green family long ago. I tried to escape, but I couldn't find a way out. No door would knock for me there, because the knocks were meant to keep out the Silver and the Storm, and by taking the *Guide* I had drawn the attention of both.

I'm ashamed to tell you what I did, what wrought magiq I performed to escape that place. But I did. And I found myself on the other side of the world. I knocked a way back into Neithernor, back to the warren where I felt safe, but the Storm had followed me through my escape. As I reached for the doorknob to slam the warren's closet shut, the Storm reached for me, touched me, and I saw into the heart of it.

It ripped away shreds of me. I saw them fall away into the black void in the moment it took me to shut the door . . . I saw inside it, what it would do to me, etched on its black heart.

I'd seen so much, had so much stripped from me, sometimes by my own hands. But looking into that void I finally knew . . . I saw . . . my time here in this world was coming to an end.

As I read, I couldn't help but think of Lauren and the Cagliostro, of the young woman's quest for knowledge from a larger-than-life father figure. And I couldn't help but think of the fate that befell her, dissolving into snow on the tiled floor of Grand Central. Lauren had become the Cagliostro, whatever the hell that meant, but was that something she would have wanted? Would she have pursued her quest if she'd foreseen the ending? It was a gift that, once received, could never be returned. And I feared Deirdre was walking a similar path. She might find the answers her father left for her, finish his work, but the cost could very well mean her life.

Checking back on Dawson's website, the Mountaineers found a new page, which read:

Welcome to The Mountaineer's Lodge
Currently 0 Users Online

We were now directly connected to the '94s' forum.

CHAPTER 22
THE LODGE

"We learn more and more about what we lost, but
never why we lost it.

— THEWITCH-DAUGHTER

ASHBURN:

66 There's a user on!

66 And now it's back down to 0! Ugh!

AUGUSTUS_OCTAVIAN:

66 This is giving me serious heebie-jeebies, guys. It's like
staring at an abandoned building for hours and hours.

Every time you think something has moved or check to
see if it's changed, it's just starting back at you. Silent,
empty.

ENDRI:

 And then there's someone in the window for a second.

DEIRDRE: SEPTEMBER 7TH, 2017:

 We opened a door with the new knock.
    It opens onto the end of a long stone corridor. It's
really cold. We followed it for a while and never found
the end, but there's a faint light ahead, and places where
the ceiling has cracked and sunshine gets in. Cole thinks
it might be an aqueduct. We came back to prepare for
whatever we might find, and however long it might take
to get to it. Cole has camping equipment (cute!) so we've
filled up a pack with water, food, and layers (did I
mention the cold?). We'll hike it for a (here) day and
then, if we don't find anything, we'll come back.
    Cole's still pretty reluctant, but I'm glad he's coming
with me. There's been no sign of the Storm, but we're
thinking about finding a door in Central Park to go
back through, just in case. I know it's the safer way, but
I'm still not 100% and feeling quite lazy. I'm such a New
Yorker. An endless magical hallway is one thing, but a
schlep to midtown is quite another.
    Wish us luck.

We're home for the night and absolutely exhausted. We walked the tunnel as long as we could, but we now know we're going to have to camp overnight to make it to the end. We're going to take more food and water and sleeping bags tomorrow. It's strange, that cold I had? Gone the moment we walked through the door into the tunnel. But now I'm feeling foul again. Cole says there's no telling what effect the spell could've had on me, or going back to Neithernor so often.

The tunnel unlocked a new entry in the journal. It's mostly my dad exploring the three manners of magiq again, but it's things he learned or figured out some time later. Here are the important bits:

"Two true manners of magiq . . . material and wrought. Borrow and break. You make the third with one or the other or both, and it changes it, depending on what you use, what story you end up telling.

"Borrowed figuration is slow, but steady. The stories take root over time. But possess a particular, gentle resonance. Broken figuration . . . faster, but unpredictable. The stories take on hidden themes one didn't intend. Combining them is hardest, nearly impossible without many, a coven. Coalescing the opposites, ordering the chaos . . . but the magiq created is potent. Rich soil. How my dear girl was made safe.

But it's all minor figuration. Trickles of temporary power. All that can be managed here. How to create major figuration? True, new magiq? Impossible in the mundane, and even Neithernor? Or just beyond my power? Even with all I've learned, all I've gathered in the stick over these years . . .

Must I be inksworn? Yes, that's the word. The one

they were afraid to speak. Why? Why did they fear
that name?

When will all these secrets be undone?"

I wonder how much time passed between his last
entries and this one? His tone is different, even his
handwriting. Everything was closing in on him. The
Silver. Its dog, the Storm. The Guide to Magiq was
found again in 2013 (according to the site), because he
stole it from those monsters. But he died in 2016. Was
he just hanging on, waiting for the fire to catch so he
could let go? Alone in that park through winter and
weather, with no one but the voices of the Council
egging him on to finish this plan? Thinking he couldn't
call on me until the time was right, because the path was
more important than his life?

That last entry, him in that hall and that thing
tearing at him . . . I'm full aware I'm not truly dealing
with it. I'm not truly dealing with anything right now. I
can't. There's so much to do and I can't stop to look at
everyone I've lost lying on either side of this path, it's
too much. Forgive me for not . . .

We're going back tomorrow. Prepared.

For some reason this tunnel feels like the beginning
of an end. The closing of a circle.

The dreams of my mum and dad laid to rest.

The last pages of *The Monarch Papers*.

One question left for me to answer.

What's inside the little red house?

The question that had been quietly eating away at me was now
consuming Deirdre as well. What's inside the little red house? It was a
comfort, knowing someone so determined and capable was now
aligned with my own secret needs. The sliver of hope inside me was
growing.

I was updating the Mountaineers and catching up on everything while the first pot of the morning brewed.

While I had been fitfully sleeping the night before, Deirdre and Cole had gone to Neithernor, and someone had visited "The Lodge."

Welcome to The Mountaineer's Lodge
Currently 1 User Online

Sort By Latest

If anyone's left, know I'm with you.
The Storm stole parts of me I can't get back. More
     memories fall through the break everyday. But
     I won't just give the rest away.
It can chase me the rest of my life. You're
     not alone.
We will rebuild this.
We will find a way to fight.
Ascender

A text field had also appeared under Ascender's message, and the Mounties quickly drafted a response, still reticent to explain that they were sending their message from 2017.

CHEY:

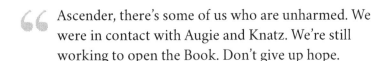 Ascender, there's some of us who are unharmed. We were in contact with Augie and Knatz. We're still working to open the Book. Don't give up hope.

This new channel could potentially connect them to anyone who was brave enough to visit the compromised forum in 1998, but right now, they were connected to the big guy, Ascender. I had no idea where any of this was going, or how it would turn out. If it would turn out at all.

My phone buzzed.

A TEXT:

> You don't have time to comb the files. The Council's protection is fading. Fast. Go back to the North Shore. Tell the Mountaineers when you're there, and I'll tell you where to find Fallon.
> -Benefactor

Well, there was a baited hook if I ever saw one.

If the Council's protection was fading, then the Storm could find us. Find Deirdre, Cole, and the Mountaineers; find Jeremy, Port, and Alison. I didn't care if this Benefactor was luring me into a trap. It was worth the risk. I reached out to the Mountaineers, who mentioned the '94s also had a "shadow helper" known as Benefactor.

The Mounties figured out that the "North Shore" that Benefactor mentioned meant the coastline north of Boston. I knew Fallon lived somewhere north of Boston but was never able to pin down his exact address. If this guy was really going to lead me to Fallon, by god I was going to follow.

With the possibility of the Council's magical protection fading, I didn't have time to drive back. I had to risk the flight. I could only hope the Storm was still too occupied with its search for Deirdre and Cole to bother with me.

In fact, while I went after Fallon, the Mountaineers were going to work on crafting a bit of magiq to keep the Storm at bay. They posited that they could create spells based around the Gladitor and Aorthora constellations, that of a sword and armor respectively, the next time the Storm showed itself. A way to block it and, possibly, a way to wound it. That was the theory, anyway.

My flight was delayed a few hours due to weather. I wasn't sure if it was the Storm or just your garden-variety nor'easter. I toyed with the idea of renting a car and driving the whole way after all, but before I finally gave up, they started boarding.

I fell asleep the moment the plane left the tarmac. I dreamed of Lauren, her body vacillating between flesh and snow as she moved through a desert of ancient ruins, nothing more than rubble and dust. Then I was at home with Bella. She sat on the sofa with a bottle of wine, studying a small library of fashion magazines spread out before her on the coffee table. Little Sebastian was in his crib, nearby. Lauren stood over the crib, weaving a mobile of ice and snow. It mesmerized him. She quietly beckoned me forward with a pale, iridescent finger. I stood next to her and felt an impossible chill, as if I were standing next to a windowpane while an arctic storm raged outside. Sebastian was asleep in the crib. He was perfect, and I wept. Lauren gently brushed a tear from my cheek, and it froze instantly against her fingertip. She then reached down and touched Sebastian's head, and the baby boy sighed in his sleep. When she pulled her hand away, a single perfect snowflake rested on the pad of her finger. She held it above my hands and then faded away. The snowflake drifted onto my palm, picture perfect, just like my baby boy. Then the snowflake melted. I called out to Lauren, but she was gone. Sebastian was gone too. The crib was empty. I turned to Bella, begging her to tell me where Sebastian had gone, but she too was nowhere to be seen. I was alone. I heard something outside. I checked the window. Across the wide white distance was the little red house. And the figure before the fire.

"*Sir . . .*"

I ran for the door, trying to get to the house, but was stopped by Fallon standing in my old kitchen, the single snowflake suspended in the air between his hands. His mouth was twisted into a horrible smile and he laughed, but I couldn't hear it. I reached for him, for the snowflake, but it multiplied until it was a swirling mist of powdery snow. The mist grew into a gale, then a blizzard. Desperately, I grabbed at the snow, trying to find the snowflake that belonged to my son, begging Fallon, cursing him, pleading with him to help me find it.

"Sir!"

It took me a moment to realize that I was on the plane. The flight attendant had shaken me awake as the other passengers looked on with equal parts horror and annoyance.

"Sir, please, you're disturbing the other passengers."

I apologized then asked for a blanket. She brought it to me with a reluctant smile, and I spent the remainder of the flight trying to shake the chill . . . and imagining the myriad ways I was going to make Fallon tell me every last one of his goddamn secrets. Thanks to in-flight Wi-Fi, I could also catch up on the forum.

The Mountaineers were outdoing themselves. In the time it took me to fly to Boston, they had crafted two spells to deal with the Storm —one defensive and the other offensive. And they had quite a number of Mountaineers ready to help with the casting. It set my mind at ease, knowing they were there, people from all over the world, working together to keep us all safe.

Once I landed and got the rental, I found a coffee shop to wait in. There was something surreal about the smell of freshly roasted beans and the flow of people going about their mundane lives, while I waited for the clue that would lead me to Fallon. I was a Well, drawing magiq to me the way the aroma of coffee drew these people. And how would they react if they knew about magiq? About Neithernor and The Book of Briars? Would they be amazed? Skeptical? Would they even care?

I texted Benefactor, and an hour went by with no response.

When my phone finally rang, it wasn't Benefactor. It was Jeremy.

"Marty? How's it going?"

"Is everything all right?" I asked.

"Yeah, we're good. Alison is sleeping better, and Port really enjoys feeding the gulls. I don't have the heart to tell her they're basically flying rats. But it makes her smile, so why ruin it, right?"

I liked that image. Port, tossing bits of food as the gulls descended on her, squawking and fluttering about. I wished I was there to see it.

"What about you?" Jeremy asked. "I mean, you're alive, which is good. Are you sleeping any better?"

"Yeah," I lied. "Now that the Storm is busy elsewhere, I sleep like a baby."

"Good to hear. Hey, so a couple of things. There's nothing in those files you brought back from the farm. Just boring admin stuff, typical business emails, that kind of thing. Really the only interesting thing was that HR wrote someone up for stealing toilet paper from the janitor's closet."

"Damn. Well, we knew it'd be a long shot. Still, I was hoping for more on Fallon."

"Yeah . . . about him." Jeremy's tone changed.

"What? You found something?"

"No, no, it's just that Alison knows you're close to him. And she wants to be there when you find him."

"Oh, shit."

"Yeah. She wants to fly out to Boston and meet you."

"I think that's a bad idea."

"I know. Why do you think I'm calling you? I don't know what to do. I can't stop her. And even if I could . . . honestly, I'm not sure I'd want to."

"I get that," I said. "But if she confronts Fallon, either she'll end up in prison or the morgue. We know what Fallon is capable of."

"A point I've raised a couple times."

"And who would keep you and Port safe? Without the coin, the Storm could find you."

"She's already said she'd leave the coin with us. She thinks she wouldn't have to worry anyway, since the Storm is looking for Deirdre and Cole," Jeremy said.

"Look, just be honest with her. If she leaves the coin with you, she runs the risk of not only getting herself killed, but everyone else on the plane. And Port would be alone with just you. Not that I'm saying you're a slouch or anything."

"No, no, but you're right. I've got skills, but I'm no Alison. We feel so much safer with her around. I'm afraid what would happen to us if she wasn't here."

"Tell her that. Maybe that will convince her."

"Okay, I'll talk to her, let you know how it goes."

"All right. Stay safe."

There were a number of reasons I didn't want Alison coming to Boston, her safety chief among them. I had no idea what I was walking into. This "Benefactor" could very well be setting a trap, and if so, I needed to make sure that I was the only one who fell into it. Not that she wouldn't be a help. Alison was certainly capable—she'd been through hell to help Portencia get through Fallon's torture. All the more reason, then, that she should stay by Portencia's side now, stay safe, and let an otherwise useless old man walk into the lion's den.

After I'd consumed an unhealthy amount of coffee and an even unhealthier quantity of Danish, Benefactor texted me with coordinates to a coastal intersection in the middle of nowhere. The intersection was about 45 minutes north of the city. There was also a time—3 p.m. the next day—that I was supposed to be there, awaiting further instruction, posing as RK Adler.

"RKAdler" was the username the Mounties had been using to access pages on the Low site "the Lost Athenaeum."

I found a cheap hotel and settled in for the night. This was my life now. It was oddly similar to my early years chasing leads across three states, but now the stakes were so much higher, and far more surreal.

I checked in and found that '94 Ascender had responded on the Dawson site.

ASCENDER:

 I'm sorry you lost contact with everyone. It means you don't know what happened here on the forum. Augie offered mounties a chance to hide from the storm, but they had to forget everything about magic.

He gave Knatz a coin he said would hold off the
storm long enough for us all to get on the forum and
perform it together. But I know what those coins are
for. They can mask you from far off forces, maybe
shield someone up close momentarily, but I know they
can't protect dozens of people at a time from something
like the storm.

I knew Augie was lying. But I also knew he wouldn't
do something to endanger these people, anybody
actually. He's the best man I've ever known. So I tried to
get back in time, tried to get to him, to stop him from
doing something stupid.

The bastard spell was real. And it worked. And the
storm came for them all.

But Augie had cast something else on the
mountaineers who showed up. Something secret.
Something that channeled all harm that would be done
to them, to him. He bought them time to forget, by
sacrificing himself. And I was too late to stop him. It
wiped him away completely. And far as I know, the
mountaineers walked away not remembering anything,
and the storm thought it did its job.

We're the last ones left who remember.

I don't know what's happening with the 15th
complication. I don't even know how long we have left.
The Book is fading. It's not there half the time I check it.
It's like it knows what happened.

And to be honest, I've been working on something
else. Something that won't save the world or uncover
the truth or bring magic back. Not now. But maybe
someday. And I have to do it before I lose the memories
I still have left.

The post had the Mountaineers asking Endri questions about the
Ascender she knew.

ENDRI:

 Robert, I didn't hear about Ascender until I was around 13-14, when I first saw other people talking about the Lost Collection online. Eaves may have "met" him before but I never interacted with him until he created the earlier makeshift (and long gone) forum around 2010-2011? Sorry, I was a fledgling Thornmouth then and don't have the specific dates, but we came long after.

Revenir, that's a good question about whether Ascender seemed to have any memory problems. It's something I've been thinking about lately . . . He used to mention the "shadow" he carried with him, the weight of who he used to be, but I just took it as being haunted by what happened to the original Mountaineers. Maybe he found a way to stop the effects of what happened to him in Missouri? Or maybe the effects tapered off?

It's driving me nuts . . . Did he not explicitly mention the Storm to us until his last message because our timeline shifted, because he couldn't remember it completely, or because he didn't want to drive us away from his cause?

Mr5 responded to Ascender that night.

MR5:

 I'm sorry about what happened with Augie, he sounds like he was a really good friend. We knew a small amount of what went down, but hearing the full story in detail is a shock. Could you tell us what you plan on doing? If we can help with your plan, would you help us with the 15th complication?

The Dawson site's connection to 1994 had started to become more and more unstable, however; the Mountaineers were having trouble sending responses.

ENDRI:

 Not to add any more fuel to the stress fire we're all huddling around, but if the Council's protection/power is failing, could that also be the reason for the erratic behavior of this latest chronocompass "link"? It's another indication that it's more directly connected to the Council. I've been thinking . . . the three major ways the Council and the Book have contacted us are through email, our forum, and the dreams of those with unique dream-experiences (Cole). Just like the three chronocompasses we've accessed on Dawson's site.

The next day, '94 Ascender responded to Mr5.

ASCENDER:

 I don't know how much I can help with complication 15, but if you tell what you know, what you need, I'll do what I can. But I have to tell you, my mind is elsewhere these days.
First off, the Joradian Safeguard seems to work here on the forum, on the front page at least, but the storm can get in through us, bypassing its protection. Don't spend too much time here. We jeopardize anyone who's still hiding and checking here for help when we do.

Do you remember when Luminor found the poem hidden in complication 3? It had nothing to do with that phase, so we thought it was just a bonus narrative. (Back when a lot of us thought this was some kind of game. We were *all* naive then.) Well, a couple months ago I found a reference in a book from the "AG vault" the Benefactor found. It was a book about witchcraft and historical magic myth. It referenced a half-finished "story spell" called The Lantern of Low Hollow. The page had the illustration of a snake. The same snake that surrounded the "Record of Loss" in complication 3. The poem they found *was* The Lantern of Low Hollow.

The old story says there was a blacksmith whose wife had become possessed, ranting and raving, hurting herself and other people. Cursing god and swearing allegiance to the devil. Her doctor wanted to perform trepanation. Their community wanted her drowned. Their friends and family abandoned them. Desperate, the blacksmith wrote a prayer, a poem, that he hoped God would hear. He hoped it would help reveal she wasn't possessed at all, but as he suspected, being controlled by some physical force. Not by some devil, but by a vengeful person. With the poem he created a way to hear "voices on the wind."

I'd tried it on the Book, but it didn't work. So I forgot about it. Until we saw Missouri and the others in the woods, like they were commanded by someone to wait for us. Until Knatz and I saw the storm firsthand. When it touched me and I thought I saw something in it. Heard something. I started wondering what it was and how it worked. Was it some metaphysical force of nature, bent on stopping anyone who tried to learn the truth? Or was it guided by something, or someone, else?

A few weeks ago I rented a motel cabin, left my laptop logged into the forum, and hid in another room

across the street. The storm came again. Searching for
me. I cast The Lantern of Low Hollow and heard the
voice of someone telling it to come for us. To wipe the
mountaineers out. To "seek them and take their minds
until none remain who know."

I've been luring it out, the storm. Listening. Trying
to figure out who's talking to it, where they are, and
how I can get to them. There are other sounds, other
thoughts, I just don't have the power to hear them. But
they have to slip up at some point. Say something that
reveals them. I know I'm playing a dangerous game. The
storm's almost found me more than once. I think it
hears me too, listening. And it's getting closer to
catching me every time I light the lantern fire.

The Mounties were worried. Ascender was playing a dangerous
game indeed. They decided he needed to know more to be fully
prepared. As Miss Evans had once said, *forewarned is forearmed*. The
next time the Dawson site connected, they sent him a heartfelt and
informative—though still not entirely truthful—response.

ROBERT:

 Actually we don't know Luminor.
This is going to be complicated. We are from
another lodge, another community entirely. And it's
become clear to us we've been following a similar but
different path from the Book of Briars.

After the third assessment, the Book stopped
speaking to us. It simply left us a small window we
could use to communicate with someone. We had no
idea who. Turned out it was your lodge.

Our tinfoil hat wearing theorists (I'm assuming
your lodge had them too?) think we were a backup

lodge. We were meant to learn how to solve our complications, and learn some lore, but we were never meant to open the Book ourselves. We think the Book stopped speaking to us as a safeguard of sorts. To protect us, so we could help you solve the last complications . . .

This was, to put it lightly, a punch to the gut for all of us. We worked so hard to open the Book, only to find out it didn't want us to do it, but someone else. We soul-searched a while. Some of us even wanted to quit. But in the end calmer heads prevailed. We want that Book open, no matter who does it. That's why we are here.

Without any information from the Book, we are totally in the dark. If it's sent you any communication about the 15th complication, we could use it.

Also, to help you out, here's what we know about the Storm. Forgive me for the parts you already know. This is from a history we were given by our own benefactor, of sorts.

It begins with Anne of Brittany and a secret guild of artists who studied magiq. Upon her death, the guild split into two paths they intended to follow to search for magiq in the world, the path of wool and the path of silver. (Don't ask me why they are named that. Her burial rituals were rather disturbing.)

The path of wool changed over the years and became the group known as Monarch's Mountain, our ancestors. They discovered a land outside of ours, a place of magiq called Neithernor. It's a pocket world of sorts, protected from whatever happened to ours that took away magiq. The Monarchs were happy there for a while.

Eventually those who followed the path of silver found it as well. For a time they lived there together in peace, but one day, we're unclear why, war started between the two. Whoever started it, the Monarchs won, and they banished the Silver from Neithernor.

The Silver were not happy, and they holed up in a corner of our world known as the palace of doors. They're still there, plotting to get back to Neithernor, collecting any magiq they can find, and worst of all, sending their creation, the Storm, to destroy anyone who knows about magiq, so they can keep it all to themselves.

There's a machine in this world. Ancient, angry, and massive. It wants to destroy everything we have built, everything every generation of Mountaineers has built, and keep it for itself. It will not hesitate to wipe our minds to do so.

We have to stop this Storm. We have to stop the Silver. What happened to your lodge can't happen to another. You and we can make that happen.

All we need from you is for you to tell us anything the Book says. Anything after the 14th complication and the word Obscuriotempus. That's the start.

I informed the Mounties about the "RK Adler" text from Benefactor. The Mounties checked the site again and discovered a new spell, or half of one—The Lantern of Low Hollow.

THE LANTERN OF LOW HOLLOW:

 Only a partial diary entry and the last three stanzas of this spell story have been found. Without the first half, the spell seems to be inert. The remains of the poem seem to imply its purpose was to first hear the "commanding voice" of a magiq user on the wind, and then take control or hijack the voice, whereupon one could either control the suffering, or break the malevolent hold over them.

This spell is steeped in the New World witch hunts of the 17th century.

"It has worked. Evelyn is not possessed. There is a voice on the air that commands her to do these things. To howl and hurt herself and those around her. I have heard it. Just tonight. My ears prick at its whisper. My pen scratches out its thoughts. I know now that someone has taken the reins of my beloved's mind.

There is a verse on the tip of my tongue and the edges of my fingers. A verse that might allow me to break the voice's hold, to usurp its command. But though I have the wordly skills to bend its voice to me, I do not have the strength to break its will.

I lack both skill and sufficient power to rid my bride of this curse. Some demented force beyond these walls seeks to drive her to madness, to drag me tooth and nail behind her, and all that I am able to do is listen as it tears her apart. What I would be, or break, to have rid of it."

Though it seems the second half of the spell story was finally designed (referred below), the first half of this accidental spell has never been recovered.

I cast all ill intent aside
    The song begins to wane
    As dark dominion loses hold
    And burns upon my flame

I am become the voice aloft
    High above the ashes
    Ringing in the darkened eaves
    And slipping through the sashes

The reins are now belong to me
To stay or turn to ill
To set the dark devoted free
Or do with as I will

Ascender had one half, and now we, thanks to Benefactor, had the other. The Mountaineers debated whether to give Ascender their half of the spell or try to convince him to give them his half. They speculated that with Ascender's half they could possibly influence the Storm.

❧

I slept relatively soundly that night, and I didn't suffer from any chills. Still, I was awake just before sunrise and needed a nap by noon. After a quick power nap and another infusion of caffeine, I made my way to the coordinates Benefactor had sent me.

The intersection was isolated, trees and tall grass on all sides. It was twenty minutes outside of Salem. I parked the car and texted Benefactor, not sure what to expect. When they texted back, they instructed me to drive another three miles down the road and look for an unmarked, gated driveway on the right.

To my relief, my wireless signal was solid and I was able to keep the Mountaineers constantly updated. As nervous as I was, I was comforted knowing they were there, watching out for me.

I almost drove past the gate. A long, high row of privet shielded it from easy view. And when I stopped, I couldn't see any house or other structure. Just the gate and a call box.

I pressed the button and fully expected to hear the same cold, dispassionate voice I'd heard through the call box at Kemetic Solutions. But the voice that spoke was warm and inviting.

"Good afternoon. How may I help you?"

"Hello. I'm RK Adler."

"Of course. Drive on back, Doctor Adler."

The gate opened, and I drove down the driveway, winding my way through a privet maze until the house came into view. It was a manor, at least a century old, standing on the edge of a bluff overlooking the Atlantic. Two men in long shirts and straw hats picked up leaves in the yard while another stood on a ladder, cleaning windows on the third floor.

So this was Fallon's house. Kemetic Solutions must have paid him very, very well.

I sat in the car for a moment, trying to work up the nerve to go to the door. It wasn't until one of the gardeners looked over to see if everything was all right that I found the courage to move.

A young woman in a white uniform was waiting at the door to greet me. She had a round, kind face and appeared quite happy to see me. "Dr. Adler, please come in. May I offer you something to drink?"

"No, no, I'm fine. Thank you." There it was again. *Doctor*. If I'd known I was going to be playing a doctor, I wouldn't have worn a shirt I'd had on for three days.

"Please, follow me then."

The woman led me to a large study and asked me one more time if I wanted a drink. She then left without saying another word. I immediately began running through scenarios in my head. It would take nothing for Fallon to kill me and have his staff toss me over the bluff.

A moment later, the woman returned and said, "Dr. Adler, if you will please follow me. Mr. Fallon is waiting in his office."

He was here. In this house. I was about to come face to face with the man, the monster, who had tortured people in his pursuit of magiq. Did Benefactor expect me to be an assassin? Was that why I was here? I was now regretting my decision to keep Alison away.

I walked into his office. It was the kind I always imagined I'd have someday. Three of the four walls were lined with shelves, the fourth with windows allowing a breathtaking view of the ocean below. The shelves were filled with hundreds of books; some appeared to be even older than the house. There was a wooden plane propeller mounted on the wall behind the broad oak desk, and several black-and-white photographs of sailboats completed the room's "grand adventurer" theme.

Fallon was there, sitting in the chair behind the desk and facing away from me. The nurse taking his blood pressure looked up from the gauge of the sphygmomanometer and gave me a quick smile. "I'll be just a moment, doctor."

When she finished, she packed her instrument into a small bag and said, "Mr. Fallon, I'm going to leave you with Dr. Adler."

"Who?" Fallon asked as he turned to look at me.

"Him," the nurse said, pointing at me. "This is Dr. Adler. He specializes in cognitive rehabilitation. He's here to help you. He's the very best in his field." She then turned to me and said, "I'll leave you to it, doctor. I'll be a shout away if you need me."

I was dumbstruck and could only nod.

The assistant asked, "Is there anything you need?"

"Time alone with him," I said, a little too quickly.

"Of course."

"Oh, and a pot of tea."

She gave me a quizzical look before saying, "Of course. Right away. But I don't think he'll drink any."

"Bring it anyway, if you wouldn't mind."

She smiled and left the room.

I was now alone with Fallon and had to fight the urge to leap forward and wrap my fingers around his throat. My breathing grew sharp and heavy as I restrained my rage over what he'd done to Jeremy, to Alison and Portencia, and most certainly to Itsuki. But as I stared into his eyes, I could tell by the expression on his face that he had absolutely no idea who I was. I wanted to hate him, to rage at him, but all I could do was feel sorry for him, sitting in his ergonomic masterpiece and staring at me like I had come to paint his kitchen. He didn't appear witless or confused, just mildly curious about the stranger in his home.

Kemetic Solutions had obviously wiped his mind. His staff must have hired "Dr. Adler" to help him—"cognitive rehabilitation," the nurse had said. Maybe there had been side effects; maybe Fallon had realized his memory had been erased and wished to undo it. But since I wasn't a therapist, I was going to need something else to help Fallon remember his time with Kemetic. The Consolatory Teatime for Misplaced Memory spell was the only thing I could think of that might work. Then maybe he could give me the answers I needed.

And if he remembered what a shitty human being he was, well, that would just be a bonus.

CHAPTER 23
TIME FOR TEA

"On a brighter note, my new adorable mini teapot
will now get to be christened with glorious
purpose."

— MR. FERN

O f all the questions I had for Fallon, the first one I asked was
not what I would have imagined.

"Where's your bathroom?"

Fallon pointed to the private bath on the far side of the office. I
excused myself and went inside, posting a quick message to the
Mountaineers.

I WROTE:

I was just in Fallon's office, with him. When I came in a
nurse was taking his blood pressure. Turns out I'm a
renowned therapist specializing in cognitive
rehabilitation. His mind was definitely wiped by KS. I

just excused myself to text you. I have no idea if they know what happened to him, if all these people are civilians, or if they work for KS or the Silver. I am in over my head and they're either playing along or don't know yet.

I guess I'm just gonna have to play too.

Time to wing it. I'm going back in. Will take notes of course. The woman who answered the door asked if I needed anything. I said time alone with him. And even though they said he wouldn't drink it, I asked for a pot of tea. Anybody have time to back me up with the ritual? Would be helpful. I'll follow up when I can.

When I stepped out, the assistant was placing a tea tray on the glass coffee table as Fallon looked on with an indifferent stare. There was nothing of what I'd expected to find there. No malevolent intelligence, no dark, Machiavellian scheming, just the neutral expression of a man walking through the world in a warm, diaphanous cloud of ignorance.

"Thank you," I said. "That'll be all."

"Of course, doctor."

With that we were alone again.

I set the tea to steeping but didn't speak. Fallon stood from behind his desk and sat in the chair across from mine. He was tall, lean, with hands more suited to an ironworker than a scientist. His wire glasses softened the sharper edges of his face, and when he spoke, his southern drawl no longer held the menace of coiled violence I remembered. "What kind of tea did Coraline bring us today? Ah! Darjeeling. Normally don't touch the stuff. Puts my nerves on edge. Are you a fan of tea, Dr. Adler?"

"When the mood strikes me, yes."

"Good, good. I wouldn't want your trip here to be a total waste of time. I told Coraline I didn't need to see a therapist, but she insisted. And one thing I've learned over the years, Dr. Adler: When Coraline insists, one does not refuse. No matter how silly the notion."

"You find talking to a therapist silly?"

Fallon chuckled and crossed his legs, the leather creaking beneath his weight. "Not at all. I'm a child psychiatrist, after all. I'm fully aware of the benefits of speaking with a mental health professional. But I'm also aware that such a thing isn't always needed. I've just been feeling out of sorts, lately. Nothing a little rest and ocean air can't cure. But Coraline insisted. And as I said . . ."

"So why would a tech company like Kemetic Solutions need a child psychiatrist?" I asked.

"I'm unfamiliar with them. Tech, you said? Not really in my wheelhouse, I'm afraid. Are you a fan of tea, Dr. Adler? Don't touch the stuff myself. Sets my nerves on edge."

My skin crawled. He was looping—just like Augernon, just like that diabetic. I had no idea how much of his mind they had wiped, but I believed him when he said he was unfamiliar with Kemetic Solutions, and that wouldn't do. It was time to see how strong the Mountaineers' magiq really was.

I poured myself a cup of tea and said, "Dr. Fallon, I'd like to tell you a story. A story about my son, Sebastian. Do you have children?"

Fallon twitched, and his smile faltered for a moment. "No, no children. Married to my work."

I could see the truth behind his eyes, struggling to free itself like a man trapped under ice.

"My boy meant the world to me," I said. "He was bright and beautiful. I know every parent says that about their child, but he really was something special." I stirred my tea, the spoon gently clinking against the sides of the cup. As I did, I could feel the air in the room change—grow warmer, more comforting. The Mountaineers were working the spell. I could feel it. And by the confused expression on Fallon's face, I knew he could feel it, too.

"I loved reading to him. The way he would sit in my lap, rest his head against me, and point to words on the page." I got lost in the memory. I could smell him, feel his hair tickling my nose, his breath on my arm. I continued, completing the spell, "Now tell me something you remember, eyes are open, ears are hearing, something far away but nearing, something bubbling into view, something gone made now and new."

Fallon stood, walked over to a shelf of liquor bottles, and poured himself a Scotch. When he sat back down, he was smiling, his eyes bright.

"What is it I can do for you today, Dr. Adler?"

I could tell he was confused, that his memories were suddenly in conflict. But he was trying to cover it up, like a dementia patient giving a thumbs up when asked any sort of question.

"Actually, Dr. Fallon," I said, "I'm here to help you. Help you remember what happened."

"What happened . . . What happened to me?"

"Yes."

Fallon took a sip of his drink, his brows knitted forward in consternation. He shook his head, like a wet dog drying itself. "My memory," he said. He went and sat behind his desk. He placed the tumbler of Scotch in front of him, then ran his fingers along the lip of the glass, remembering its feel.

"I have to be honest," he continued. "You've caught me with my pants down. The feeling is odd. I can't remember remembering."

"You said you're a child psychiatrist. Must be a lucrative profession to afford a place like this. How many patients do you see in a week, if you don't mind me asking?"

He stared out the window. Outside, the Atlantic and the sky dissolved into a single sea that seemed to swallow the world.

"I'd . . . I'd have to look at my schedule. A dozen or so, maybe."

"And where's your office? Do you see them here?"

"No . . . Boston. I work outside Boston. I—A research facility. Someplace . . ."

I could see him working the memory, chewing at it.

"Kemetic Solutions," I said.

"Yes. Kemetic—" Fallon looked at me, his eyes now clear with a hint of malevolence squatting in the background. "And how are you feeling? Settling in?"

"I'm good, thank you."

"Now, now . . ." Fallon swallowed his drink without taking his eyes from me. "How are we supposed to work together if we're not honest with each other?"

"I'm not sure what you want me to say, Dr. Fallon."

"Please, call me Teddy." The man smiled, not entirely unfriendly. "May I call you Martin?"

He knew me. That meant the Mountaineers' spell was working. It also meant that I very desperately wanted to pour myself a drink from Teddy's bar.

"Of course," I said.

"Tell me what you need from me. Tell me what you need to feel comfortable here. I want you to feel you made the right decision."

I wasn't sure what decision he could be referring to . . . until I realized that he thought he'd won. That we were still inside Kemetic Solutions and that I had given myself up. His smile, his eyes, the way he carried himself as he poured himself another drink, it all left me no doubt that he was dangerous. Even with only half of his memories, Fallon wasn't someone to take lightly. The best thing for me to do was to play along.

I said, "I did this to learn what I'm capable of, not to help you. And not to help whoever's controlling you."

"No one is controlling me. Or you, for that matter. They simply want us to explore the world's potential. All our potential."

"For their own gain."

"You have no conception of the incredible things they've done for this world, while asking for none of the credit."

"Like what they did to your son? What they did to Nate?"

Fallon's back went stiff, and the smile on his face vanished.

"I'm sorry," I said.

"What happened with my son was not . . . was not their doing. It was mine. Do you have any idea how many people are walking this earth like you? Like Nate? Unaware of what they're truly capable of, unaware of the wonderful and terrible things they can do? Untrained, unskilled. Unbelieving. You think magiq is some idyllic energy,

floating around us like butterflies. I have seen the terrifying things it
can do."

"Like the Storm? Is that for the good of the world, too?"

I took a deep breath and counted to ten. There was a litany of
things I wanted to say to him, but couldn't. I was afraid my anger
would only diminish the power of the spell. I had to remain calm,
conversational, like I had with Augernon. Deep down, Fallon didn't
want to tell me anything, and if I let my anger get the better of me, I
gave him an excuse to shut me out.

He paced the floor, his Scotch sloshing in the tumbler in his hand.
"Have you ever heard of Saverina's Canon?" he asked.

"No."

"Saverina was a very talented storyteller who lived in the sixteenth
century. Her books are the rarest of all mundane works. She was
considered *la strega* because, according to lore, her stories were spells.
They had power in them. Though you and I both know that's entirely
possible, it wasn't true of Saverina. Before her death she published
twelve canonic works, and my beloved wife, Ava, and I had collected
eleven of them on our travels around the world. That is how we
stumbled upon the Silver, as you call them.

"After finding them, my new work with them became my life,
while Ava cared for our son. We never found the twelfth book. It was
lost to history. But I used to read the other books to Nate. He always
wanted to hear about our travels, how exciting it was to find a new
book. I was gone for much of his childhood. And as young boys often
do, he did whatever he could for his father's attention. For my
approval. My pride. By the time he was five, things would go missing
from the house and he'd confess that he had 'unhooked' them. We
thought he was lying at first, acting out . . . until we replaced the roof
of the house, and in the eaves we found a keepsake box, untouched for
decades. With Ava's lost engagement ring inside it."

I took a deep breath to calm myself. What angered me most was the
sudden realization of how similar Fallon and I were; how we both loved
reading to our sons, were both gone for much of their childhoods.

"Did they know?" I asked, hoping to keep the emotion from my voice.

"I had to tell them."

"And they wanted him."

"Not at first. But they were curious. It wasn't until he was nine, when he brought Saverina's twelfth book to me, here, in this office . . . He'd wanted my attention. He wanted to make me proud. So he brought me the missing book."

Fallon swallowed his drink and fell into his desk chair. He tossed the empty glass on the desk with a dull thunk.

"It was the first time I realized what he could actually do," he said. "I'm ashamed to say how many hours passed before I realized what had happened. Where my Ava had gone. It wasn't just that Nate could unhook things and send them to another time . . . It was a trade. He could send things from now in exchange for something from the past. I tried for weeks to get him to bring her back. I would've given anything. When he was finally able to—"

His voice hitched, and he stopped speaking. His eyes were wet, and his clenched fists shook. I looked out the window to the ocean, giving him a moment of privacy. It was a courtesy that twenty minutes ago I wouldn't have believed he deserved. But now . . .

The thin, white-capped waves rolled into shore and disappeared. Again and again they formed, rolled, and dissolved in an endless cycle, with only the rocky beach aware of their brief existence.

"She had died, alone, sometime in the sixteenth century. He pulled her right out of a potter's field." His voice was soft. Reverential. Fallon's southern drawl gave the words a gravity my New York accent could never replicate.

"I had requirements," he continued. "They agreed he wasn't to be part of any other project. They told me they'd been able to cure others of their abilities, of being adept, while collecting their power. They said they'd do the same for Nate. Whether it was a lie or an exaggeration, I don't know. At the end of the day, I knew what could happen. They swore things had changed since the early days. I didn't understand then why his power was so important to them. I didn't

know at the time that they intended to seize all remaining magiq
artifacts. And with his power they could. Even from the past."

Now he turned to stare out the window, his gaze lost in the distant
waves.

"I want to say that I brought him to Kemetic to cure him, to try
and rid him of this curse . . . but part of me knew that trying to siphon
his power would kill him. Like it had Sweeper, and Stormkeep. All the
others . . . If I'm being honest, there was another part of me that hoped
I would finally be free of the pain I felt every time I looked at him and
saw her eyes."

"They killed Nate to give his power to the Storm." There was no
accusation when I said it. Only a statement of fact.

Fallon nodded and said, "To trade for valuable things from
the past."

"What is the Storm, Teddy? Really? It's a collection of adept
power?"

"The modern incarnation, yes, partially. They don't talk much
about how it originally came to be. I heard it was a dark and nasty
affair. But they have amended and added to it for centuries." He pulled
his gaze from the window. "It gets stronger, the more minds it pulls
into its eye."

"Don't you worry that it could get so strong that it would be out of
their control? Or that they'll start using it to pick off anyone who
knows what they do? Like you?"

"I know what you want."

I set my teacup on the table and said, "I want you to realize what
you're helping them do is wrong."

"No, you don't. You want to know who they are and how to stop
them; how to stop the Storm."

It took me everything not to speak, not to tell him anything. But I
let the silence build until he was willing to fill it.

"They are so far beyond your comprehension, Martin. This world
is theirs. You work alongside them or—"

"Or else."

I lifted myself from the sublime comfort of the chair and stepped over to the desk. "I don't think magiq is all good. It's like everything else. There's good, there's bad. But what they're doing with it, doing to us . . . it's unconscionable. Don't tell me you would have led your son to slaughter if you'd really had a choice."

"Martin . . ."

"That's the lie you tell yourself to sleep at night. That you have a say. That you have control. But the minute you slip up, you're gone. You know it. I know it."

Fallon held his hands in his lap. He clasped them together tightly, but I could see them trembling.

"Kemetic Solutions is gone, Teddy. They wiped it out. And you. The only reason you remember any of this is because of magiq. And when it wears off, you'll be gone again. For good. Please help me stop them."

"You can't."

"We can start with the Storm. How do we fight it?"

"Fight it?" He snorted a laugh, then swiped the tumbler from his desk. "You can't. That's the truth." He poured a third Scotch, this time to the top of the glass.

"Tell me what to do."

He held his glass to his lips for a moment, then emptied it with three big gulps. His face winced against the burn of alcohol, but then he turned to me and whispered, "I've heard them speaking to it. I heard them telling the part of Nate that's inside it what to search for, what to take. They tell him stories. Like I did. Stories about lost things, and how much it would mean to have them again. Then they send him to things or people that are of equal importance, and he switches them in time. He wants to make them proud. He thinks he's making his father happy. I couldn't bear it. I would try and talk to him when they didn't know. Hoping I could free him or let him rest. But he's part of something darker at the core of that thing now. In the eye. The thing there told Nate there is a way to stop it, to let it die, but how exactly has been forgotten or destroyed. It told him it could only surrender now to the one who controls it. That's all I know. Truly."

"It's something." I didn't bother to hide the bitterness in my voice.

"This is all going to go away, isn't it?" he asked.

I nodded. "Yes." It wasn't fair though. Fallon shouldn't be allowed to forget his pain. He shouldn't have the gift of ignorance.

"It feels . . . light. Fading. Like it could blow away in a breeze."

Coraline stepped into the office with the nurse in tow. She looked at me with an unexpected intensity. "Would you excuse us, please, *doctor*. We need to speak with Dr. Fallon alone."

"It's all right, Coraline. He can stay."

"But, sir . . . we just received a call from the hospital with a message for Dr. Adler. One we were asked to pass along upon *her* arrival."

Both the nurse and Coraline moved to stand beside Fallon. "Who are you?" the nurse asked.

"He's a friend of my son's," Fallon said. "And he was just leaving."

I didn't bother saying goodbye. I simply headed for the door. I wanted to run, to flee as fast as I could, but if I ran, they'd have to chase me.

As I was pulling out of the driveway, I saw the gardeners holding their rakes like poleaxes and eyeing me as I drove past. Clearly, I had worn out my welcome. But before I could get more than thirty feet from the house, something burst onto the driveway next to me, setting off my side airbag and nearly sending the car careening off the road.

The Storm had found me.

CHAPTER 24
THE LANTERN OF LOW HOLLOW

"Our time together will change all of time."

— ALEC

I hit the gas. The Storm was an angry torrent of black, swirling in my rearview mirror. The car was faster, and I was able to gain some distance, but the security gate was closed. I slammed on the brakes, and the car skidded to a stop a mere inch from the gate.

The Storm barreled toward me down the drive, pulling leaves and detritus from the privet into itself. The gate sensor recognized my car and began to open, slowly. So damn slowly.

There was nothing in my rearview now but the Storm. I slammed the gas pedal and squeaked past the gate, which had opened just enough for me to pass, but not my driver's side mirror. I didn't even bother to look for traffic when I pulled out of the drive and onto the road. There was an unholy concussion of steel and air behind me, and the gate flew across the street.

I drove north as quickly as I could. The Storm followed me for a full minute before I was far enough ahead that I couldn't see it. I needed to warn the Mountaineers, but I couldn't stop yet. Not with the Storm so close.

The Storm. Fallon's son, Nate, was a part of it. I couldn't help but feel sorry for the man after all he'd been through with his son, his wife, the Silver.

And yet I hated him even more for making me sympathize with him.

I don't know if it was the assistant, the nurse, or the gardeners, but someone must have tipped off the Silver that I was there, and they'd sent their attack dog after me. If I had been in that house thirty seconds longer, I'd be mindless now.

The adrenaline finally wore off an hour later, and my hands started shaking. If I couldn't get my body under control, there was a good chance I'd lose control of the car.

But I didn't stop. I drove until the car was on fumes. When I couldn't risk going any farther, I stopped at a gas station and updated the Mountaineers while I filled the car.

Their spell worked, better than I had hoped. If they ever had any doubt about their ability to wield magiq, the events of that afternoon should have put it to rest. I told them everything I could about Fallon, his wife Ava, and Nate. And that there was a way to destroy the Storm.

I got back on the road and headed southwest, taking a wider route back to New York. As the night wore on, I thought about Fallon and realized that my hate for him, while genuine and deserved, needed to be redirected. It was the Silver that needed to fall. They had infused a piece of Nate's soul into the Storm, had used that poor boy to steal artifacts for their own nefarious gain. How many lives had they destroyed? There needed to be a reckoning. There had to be. And I honestly believed that opening The Book of Briars was the only way to have it. But our Book was burned. We needed to get the Book from the past. And since that was Nate's magical talent, it was very possible that we would need the Storm to do it.

The Mountaineers came to the same conclusion I did. Robert put it best.

ROBERT:

 We need Ascender's half of the spell.

I decided to stop at a motel. I should have been exhausted, but I was wired, as if a spike of electricity had pierced the back of my skull, forcing my eyes to stay open. But I knew the moment this feeling passed, I was going to black out. I didn't want to be behind the wheel when that happened. I checked the forum and Ascender has written, with demands.

ASCENDER:

 I've been trying to figure out what to do. What to ask.
I lured the storm out yesterday, like before, by signing into the forum and then hiding. I cast The Lantern, and I could hear the voice that controls it . . . I had a pen with me because I felt the need to write out the words last time and the spell mentions that might happen. My hand scrawled out what the voice was telling the storm. I was lost in it . . . listening, trying to find something that would give me a lead. There were other sounds there I couldn't make out, like always . . .
But then I heard other voices.
And my hand started writing those words too. It was chaos. Painful. A dozen voices, maybe more. They were all talking at once and then, like a door shut, they were gone.
I hid from the storm until it passed. And then I looked at the paper.

There were commands for the storm:

Seek them out.
Take their minds until
none remain who know.

But I also wrote . . .
   help us open the book
   now in our time.
   paradox
   If we give it to Ascender and he frees the storm
   we have a problem
   need his help
   we'd change history
   The storm
   seen in our time
   to help us
   The Council is rationing power
   might jeopardize the plan

I didn't understand where it was coming from until I
checked my laptop. You'd sent your last message to me
while I was logged in. After I'd cast the spell. And
because of the spell, for less than a minute, I could hear
you too.
   Who are you? Really?
   What are you trying to do?
   How much of what you wrote me is a lie and how
much is the truth?
   I need you to tell me everything.

For obvious reasons, the Mountaineers were torn, unsure how to
respond. Playing with time in this way was dangerous, and we needed
Ascender as much as he needed us. In the end, the Mountaineers
decided on full disclosure and hoped for the best. Robert, the de facto
team captain, put all the cards on the table.

ROBERT:

 Okay, here's everything.

Everything I told you is true. We are Mountaineers. Our Book of Briars stopped speaking to us after fragment 12 (we call them fragments). All it left us was a window to your lodge, which I'm speaking through now. We were apparently meant to help you open your Book, and that really hit us hard.

The only part I kinda left out was we're not in the next town over. We are talking to you from the year 2017.

After the 12th fragment, the Storm came for us, like it did for you, like it did for the generation before you, and probably a bunch before that. The keepers of The Book of Briars decided to do something different this time. Instead of letting the Storm wipe the Mountaineers while they preserved the Book, they decided to risk protecting us . . . and let the Book burn. Our Book of Briars is in ashes, and we don't think there will ever be another. But it connected us to you and your existing Book. We need to open yours. There are no second chances here.

I'm sure you have many questions that you do or don't want to ask. What happens to you? What happened to Augie? We know Augie. He's resting well in a hospital in Maryland. With the help of some magiq he was able to speak to us a bit and give us some important information. He's stubborn and insistent on protecting everyone, as always.

And we know you.

At some point in your future, at least in the history we know, you go on to gather a group of people to search for magiq after another special book is found.

You'll know it when you see it. That group of people
snowballed into the Mountaineers we are today. You are
our founder. As far as we know, you're still alive; about
9 months ago you left on some quest you were rather
nebulous about. Apparently being brave and crazy and
sort of a loner are traits you've kept for a couple
decades if that helps.

Right, that's mostly sorted. Let's get down to
business.

Since we last talked to you our Benefactor provided
something fascinating: the second half of The Lantern
of Low Hollow.

Where your half is designed to hear voices, this half
is designed to take control of the voices. With these two
pieces together, we think we could control the Storm
and tell it to disperse. Also, we've discovered that the
Storm has the power to take things from the past.
Before we make it disperse, we think we can ask it to
bring your Book of Briars into our present, and open
it here.

Now the dilemma. We didn't know whether or not
to give you the second half. Because in our present, the
Storm exists. If you control it, and disperse it, then
we've changed history and who knows what chaos that
might cause?

But you know what? I'm a Balimoran. Let's cause a
bit of chaos and let the magiq fall where it may. We trust
you, Ascender. We always have.

We have a plan to use the spell to end the Storm.
That assumes we get your half (please?) and the Storm
still exists in this time. Before we end it, we hope to
bring the Book forward to a more stable time, with no
Storm and living Mountaineers to open it. Then maybe
we'll solve world hunger while we're thinking big.

In all seriousness, I want our plan to go forward, but

I'm not going to (and can't, if I know you) talk you out
of using your best judgment. Attached is the second
half.

I collapsed on the bed, I fell asleep almost immediately. It was a
sleep of death. No dreams, no fitfulness, no little red house. Just the
all-encompassing dark of the absence of being.

It was afternoon when I crawled off the unfamiliar bed and
stumbled to the coffee maker. Half a pot later, I was awake enough to
check the forums.

Ascender had responded to Robert's confession.

ASCENDER:

 You're the mountaineers I always hoped we could be.
        If this is true, I have an insane choice to make. I
could try to control the storm here, now. And risk
changing everything for you, and risk giving you the
chance to see this through . . . for what? I don't know
what happened with the complications. I don't know
where to go, how to start. Do I really think I have a
chance at finishing this on my own, with the book
fading more every day? While outrunning the storm?
        Do I try what I've tried to do my whole life, or do I
try to come up with a way to make the world you live in
happen?
        I have questions I need answered. Did I tell you how
I managed to outrun the storm for twenty years? What
else did I tell you about it? About us here, now? About
the book? I need to know about me, then, so I can figure
out what to do, now.

We were almost out of time. Ascender knew it and the
Mountaineers knew it. But no one knew how to move forward. One

wrong step and all we'd learned, all we'd done, would have been for nothing. And operating across time felt like walking on a tightrope that we weren't sure was securely fastened at the other end. It was a sentiment Robert shared with Ascender in his response.

ROBERT:

 We've combed through everything you ever posted, and we've interrogated the first Mounties you brought together for this generation to see what you've told them. In the end the answer is 'not a lot.'

One quote: "It took me almost two weeks to get to the States and get out again without going through border control or booking transportation in my name. It's not easy to stay off the grid and get across the world, but I've been doing this a long time."

One time you mentioned that the Mountaineers had "kept secret in the past . . . and it cost us."

Another time you mentioned some "thing" came for you and the other '94 Mountaineers, but you never elaborated beyond that.

When The Book of Briars arrived and contacted us, you seemed as honestly surprised as the rest of us.

The way we figure it, if we're not changing history then one of two things happened. Either you deliberately didn't tell us what was coming, perhaps for fear of scaring us away . . . Or, as you mentioned earlier, your memories are still slipping away. It's possible you just won't remember much of this discussion.

It actually really pains us to suggest you spend the next 20 years in hiding, waiting for a chance to bring the Mountaineers back. No one would blame you if you took your shot now. But I'm afraid I doubt we could help you, so you'd be without a lot of backup. Plus, if you change history we have no idea how we would have helped Augie and Knatz with complications 13 and 14. But like I said before: Sometimes you have to let chaos run wild.

My fellow Mountaineers did want me to mention one fact I neglected to share. Our numbers. We currently have almost 2,000 Mountaineers in our lodge in some capacity. All of them owe what they know and believe in some part to you. If you do change history and we never actually have this conversation (that's like sentence #109 I never thought I'd write before I joined the Mounties) then on behalf of all of us, thank you for everything.

On a last side note, though. Can you please send us your half of the Lantern before you do anything? If you succeed in stopping the Storm, then no harm done, we won't get it. If not, well, we're going to need it. Not to be dark, but we have to cover our bases.

Be careful, Ascender.

It had to have been difficult for Ascender, learning from the Mountaineers about his future. If it were me, I would be so tempted to know more; I'd to want to learn about all my future mistakes so that I could avoid them. But would that change the future for the better? Ultimately, I believed I would still make mistakes—they'd just be different mistakes.

The Mountaineers were figuring out what needed to happen if we were going to get The Book of Briars into our timeline. They focused on what Fallon had told me about Nate, about the Storm—an item could only be retrieved through an exchange. Would we have to choose something to trade for The Book? What did we have that could possibly equal its "value"?

Luckily, Benefactor—who explained they weren't the same Benefactor who'd helped the '94s, they'd simply adopted the moniker —joined the discussion to help clarify.

BENEFACTOR:

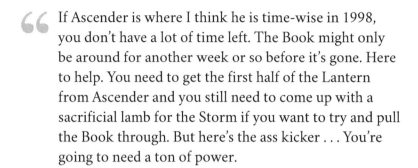

" If Ascender is where I think he is time-wise in 1998, you don't have a lot of time left. The Book might only be around for another week or so before it's gone. Here to help. You need to get the first half of the Lantern from Ascender and you still need to come up with a sacrificial lamb for the Storm if you want to try and pull the Book through. But here's the ass kicker . . . You're going to need a ton of power.

RIMOR:

" I'm not comfortable with sacrificing anyone to the Storm.

BENEFACTOR:

" I've been working on that. Nobody ever said it had to be *someone*. It can be *something*. I have no idea what has equal "weight" to the Book but we need to come up with options.

I think a person is a break-glass-in-case-of-emergency option. Even then, you'll have enough power to trade, but you don't have enough power to commandeer the Storm. It's too strong. We're at the breaking point for magiq here in the mundane. You need every bit of help you can get, and you need as many Mountaineers working together, at the same time, as possible.

There's an apex date coming up. September 23rd is the first Day of Change. The day after the mundane equinox. That should be your go day.

Focus on getting it here. To do that you need to commandeer the Storm and convince it or force it to trade the Book for something here. You're gonna need to call the corners to bring a pool of magiq to your side.

You're gonna need the story to end all stories to try and bend/break whatever magiq you have to figurate the Storm into doing what you want it to do . . .

You're going to have to choose something you think is powerful enough to trade for the Book and hope to the six corners it works . . .

And then you're going to have to figure out a way to shut it down.

Using the first Day of Change will give you a poetic and temporary power advantage, but I'm still not sure you're going to have enough power to do all of this. We may just have to do what we have to do with whatever we have on the day.

RIMOR:

 What about the offensive and defensive spells we created?

BENEFACTOR:

 They might keep you standing long enough to do this. You need as many people as possible together, some calling the corners, some performing the Lantern, some telling the story . . . it's going to be a test of everything you know, everything you're capable of . . .

If you do this . . . you will do something that has never been done before in our altered history.

I'll see what I can do about getting more people to help. I'll be there. Anybody who knows anything about magiq will be watching this. And we'll do everything we can to buy you time to do this. You won't be alone.

We have a week and change. Do everything you can to get ready. And choose something to trade. If we don't have that, we don't have the Book.

CHAPTER 25
MYTH AND MORE

"As Aragorn said to Frodo, "You have my sword."
Only I don't have a sword, but I think you
understand what I mean."

— NAHEMAH

The whole of Basecamp worked furiously to prepare for the Day of Change. The Mounties were putting the finishing touches on their Gladitor and Aorthora spells and trying to figure out just how in the hell to reach back in time and get our hands on that book.

Meanwhile, Deirdre and Cole continued to explore Neithernor. Deirdre's journey to the red house would at some point factor into all of this, we all knew that; it was part of Sullivan's plan. Some Mounties even hoped that Sullivan had hidden something of great magiqal "weight" in the red house that we could use for the spell on the Day of Change. And I of course wanted to know what was inside for more selfish reasons.

Cole returned to our world to give us an update through Deirdre's blog. She was still in Neithernor, discovering more and more of its secrets.

COLE:

 Hey guys, it's Cole. We came back on Sunday for food and water (Dee writes about that below) and I just came back for a minute to post this.

Dee has been there since we left last Thursday (for the most part, long story). She doesn't want to come back yet. She wrote up this entry so you'd know what was going on.

I just finished typing it up, sorry for any mistakes.

DEIRDRE: SEPTEMBER 13TH, 2017:

 The tunnel is an overnight trip. We slept under a bit of broken ceiling, watching the Neithernorian stars, which move around the sky. It's like you're looking down from a window, watching children play with torches in a dark yard. I love this place.

The tunnel empties into a small courtyard's empty pool. High walled, but open to the sky, the courtyard's at the base of what could be a castle of some kind. It was hard to see just how massive it was from the pool. There was an open doorway in the courtyard that was choked by vines. I was loath to cut them away. (I've read enough fantasy books to know a character almost always goes to cut or pinch or pull something and then finds out it's alive and terribly cross.) We crawled through. And down a maze of stone halls, we found the room they all empty into.

To call it a room is a terrible understatement.

It's a vault. Immense and tall, lit by candles that burst into flame when we arrived and never melted away. Every corner is filled with odd and shiny objects, piles of golden coins of different sizes and languages and shapes, statues and locked chests that have just been stacked on top of each other.

And the books. Thousands of books. Many written in the same strange language, a language I don't think exists on Earth (not that I know much about languages). There are dozens upon dozens of shelves and cases, stacks of books, piles of books, and bookcases that have toppled over, the wood rotting away, scattering books all over the floor. Nothing in order, covered in dust. (Neithernorian dust is like a very fine, translucent glitter. It looks and moves almost like dew. And it's sweet. I know because we've inhaled about five tonnes of it.)

There's even an absolutely massive golden bell sitting in the middle of the vault. At first I thought maybe it fell from a bell tower because there's a light coming from the long tunnel leading up through the ceiling, but the bell's intact, unbent. As if it were brought here.

There are pillows littered about, deep and fluffy and relaxing, like people came here, not to study, but maybe meditate?

It's dim and cool and quiet, and though it might seem eerie, I find it peaceful. Almost restorative. There is a universe of story and knowledge and history inside the vault. I could live here.

If there was food of course. There is an apple tree growing here. Not by accident. It was planted. The stones were pulled away and a little spot was made for it. And it grows beautiful grass-green apples, even in the dim light of the vault. Cole urged me not to eat one (very Genesis) because, well, magiq. But by Sunday we were nearly out of food and water and Cole wanted to take the tunnel back to the brownstone, restock, and come back to explore after a few days' break, but I couldn't leave. I wasn't sure why, but I needed to stay. To thumb through the books, sit against the pillows, listen to the echo of wind from somewhere outside.

But then I had an idea . . .

The entrance to the vault once had a door hanging in its arch. There were broken hinges still bolted to the wall, and we'd found a stack of heavy, ornate doors in a corner of the vault. Using carved nails we found in a pile, we rehung one of the doors in the arch.

Now, we'd never tried returning through a different door than the one either of us came from, but it was worth a try to save Cole the day-and-a-half trip it would take to get back. And it took a while, but together we got it to knock.

I was the one who'd knocked here, so I knocked back . . .

And we opened a door to the brownstone!

The vault side of the door was gold and jeweled, and the brownstone side was . . . door-looking. We propped it open with a cabinet and walked through. The kitchen is pretty bare in the brownstone, so I was going to run to the market while Cole grabbed a few changes of clothes and more camping equipment from his apartment, figuring it would take an hour, two at the most.

Cole headed for the train, but I checked the door again before running out and found that it was pushing hard against the cabinet we'd wedged it open with, and it was also blazing hot! There were scorch marks already appearing on the wallpaper, and within minutes it had started to smoke. I couldn't leave the door open or I'd eventually burn down the brownstone, and possibly everything in the vault.

I called Cole, and we agreed I'd go back through and he'd restock and meet me in two days Neithernorian time. By agreed, of course, I mean very reluctantly. He wanted me to stay, to wait. But I couldn't. I had to get back.

The truth is . . . I had to get back because something was happening. I was remembering something. Something about this place. And it's not that Cole was a distraction; even if I didn't love him with all my heart he would still be the absolute first person you'd want with you in a situation like this. He's clearheaded, good-humoured, and happy to rough it for the sake of adventure. Honestly, I was the problem. I needed time to not explore or look-at-this and look-at-that. I wanted to just sit and quietly soak this place in, which seems rude to do when you've brought someone along with you.

I should tell you that the journal entry that unlocked in the vault was all about the red house. It was short and disjointed. Rambling. To be honest it's heartbreaking to read, to see his decline, so I'll paraphrase all that matters instead of transcribing. It feels kinder. He said seeing what's inside the house changes you and how you see everything. You see the world opened up. What it could be. The house and what's waiting inside is the key to all of this.

And to see it I'd have to break a powerful spell that my father himself created to keep everyone out. A spell only I would know how to break. A figuration that I would learn here, in the place at the end of the tunnel.

Then he ended the journal entry with, "Remember, my dearest girl, imagination is nothing more than memory, transposed."

The next morning I crawled out of my sleeping bag, cold and achy. I thought, at least the tunnel had a view of the stars to look at while you tossed and turned against the stone floor. And then . . . it happened. I remembered something. The tunnel. My dream. It was my dream. The one with my father carrying me. I'd always imagined it was a hallway in a house, perhaps the apartment where I lived with Mum. But could it have been the tunnel instead?

Could I have been here before?

I could now imagine looking up from my father's arms, past his beard, seeing the stars spinning across the sky, through the broken patches of the tunnel ceiling. Was I trying to fit the pieces together or had he brought me here? And if so, when?

Maybe I'd made it a hallway in the years that followed. To make sense of it. Maybe I'd conflated it with the time he came back and tried to take me? I don't know. But what if this place felt so warm, so welcoming, even in its dim and drafty clutter, because I'd been here before. With him. The echoes of that time somehow calling back to me. I say somehow, but I know how. Magiq.

I spent the next few hours wandering, listening, trying to remember. Something was there, at the edge of my mind, the tip of my tongue.

I don't know if it was luck or providence or some lost memory guiding me, but after hours of exploring I found a stack of books as tall as me and took the book from the top. It was clothbound in green, and plain, with no title. A collection of stories. I opened it to a random page—

My soul's providence.

Something had led me to that book. The faded

memory I'd come to believe was just a dream and was now guiding me to the truth.

I had opened the book to "The Myth of Elainnor."

I envied Deirdre. It must have been something to walk through a magical world filled with so much wonder. But what I envied most was that single moment of her father carrying his child beneath a canopy of impossible stars to show her a treasure of stories. Would Sebastian feel the same way about me as Deirdre felt about her father if he suddenly remembered the times we would walk to the library to scour the shelves for books to read, stories to tell each other? I could speak only for myself, but a father sharing stories with his child didn't need to happen in Neithernor to be magical.

But the books themselves proved to be more important than I realized, and Deirdre's next post floored me.

DEIRDRE: SEPTEMBER 14TH, 2017:

 I found five books among the thousands. The novel, *The Forest of Darkening Glass* was one, and the other four books contained the stories "The Myth of Elainnor", "Oskar & Pipany", "The Wishing Jar" . . . and "Ant & Caterpillow". All stories I now remember my father reading to me. And I think he read them to me in Neithernor.

I also found a sixth book, sitting on a table, but it's sort of frozen in place. There's nothing on the cover. I couldn't open it, I couldn't budge it from the table. It's just . . . stuck. Maybe I'm supposed to figure out how to open it?

I read through the stories while I waited for Cole to come back. I'm not ashamed to say I was brought to tears several times. The memories connected to them washed over me, unlocking secret pieces of my childhood. Of some far-off day I spent here with my father. A long and peaceful day. I don't think it's just recollecting. I think somehow those pieces, or the keys at least, were always waiting in these books. Like magiq.

I know I'm supposed to do something here, learn something . . . tell a story. I'm supposed to perform some difficult spell. I think it starts with remembering.

The First Book.

I recall listening to my father read *The Wishing Jar* to me while I wished that the fountain we came through had water in it so that the courtyard wasn't so quiet. I wondered if years ago there'd been fish swimming in the pool or magiq coins sitting at the bottom. Holding wishes. Like the jar that held the last ray of sunlight in the story.

I took the book to the courtyard. And I sat it on the edge of the fountain.

"The little girl watched the wrinkles crinkle at the edges of her father's eyes as he acted out the grandfather in the story. Her young father looked older in her memories now. Gray in his beard, and his hair growing thin. There was an urgency to his reading. It mattered. She didn't know why at the time. She was just happy to have him."

There are other places he read the books to me. I think I have to find them and leave the right book. Only I would know what stories and what locations. Only I could solve this puzzle.

Only I could tell a story about that day.

The Second Book.

A golden crown sat on a bench in the vault, near a

deep pile of beautiful jewel-tone pillows. We sat there.
Maybe I even napped there. I remember laughing with
my father at the image of Pipany rushing to tell her
father what had happened to everyone in the kingdom,
only to find that he'd been turned into an ornate three-
layer cake with a tilted crown sitting on top of
his "head."

"She was tired but couldn't close her eyes, so he
rested his head on her pillow and they looked up at
the ceiling and wondered what they would be if a
vengeful witch turned them into desserts too. She
said she wouldn't be any kind of dessert. She'd be
Pipany, the kingling, who knew everyone so well
she could figure out their recipe. Or Oskar, the
baker's son, who used the recipes to skillfully
"unbake" everybody. She remembered it made him
smile a big smile. His daughter, the hero. No one's
dessert."

The Third Book.
    I had to find a way out of the vault. I packed up the
books and went exploring the halls.
    I found a stair that eventually emptied a few floors
up into a great bronze and stone hall, with a gentle river
passing through it. The river was wide enough and the
hall tall enough that I imagine ships could pass to the
sea beyond this beautiful castle. I could smell the salt on
the air. The hall was so long I could just barely make out
the ends.
    I wandered along the edge of the river, eventually
drawn to one of the berms of grass that grew out of the
floor. Dips created natural places to sit. He read to me
here. We ate fruit and cheese and candy. I remember the
grass, the blue stained glass high up in the ceiling of the

hall. I knew what story he'd tell me here. I left the next book in the deep, green grass.

"He held her hand while reading *Ant & Caterpillow*. It touched him, the fable. His eyes were wet, and he would gently squeeze her hand when something in the story moved him. And she would squeeze back. She sat in the grass by the water, reflections of colored glass on the surface. Her head against him, holding his hand. She knew, even then, that she was comforting her father as much as he was comforting her."

The Fourth Book.

A steep, spiraling ramp led to a watchtower. I remembered walking ahead of him, in case I slipped. I hadn't been scared, but it was high, with no railing. He'd told me about the watchtower and I was determined to see the view from it. We read *The Forest of Darkening Glass* up there, twice. I wanted to make all new choices the second time and see how the story ended. I left it on the stone railing, with the telescope that had been there the last time I was.

"He'd given her a telescope to see the world beyond the castle. She had, up until then, never assumed they were anywhere other than New York. But now she saw the prismatic thing-shaped clouds, the great gray sea, the vast black forest at the base of the low, sharp mountains, and the tower sitting on top of one like a broken chimney. It all looked precious and endlessly fascinating. Like the maps you'd find on the inside cover of a fairy tale. She looked and looked at the wild out there as his warm, comforting voice filled her ears, offering her safe or possibly perilous choices. He would laugh every time she made the same decision again. She couldn't help it. She chose adventure and risk and exploration every time. Just like her father would've."

The Fifth Book.

I remember we'd paced a long gallery full of tall, crystalline casks that glowed on their own and illuminated all the different styles of armour and weaponry inside them. He'd read to me *The Myth of Elainnor* there, until my legs were sore. The clunk of his walking stick on the stone floor, the book held open in his free hand.

The gallery wasn't far from the hall. Some of the casks had been smashed by crumbling pieces of ceiling, some had toppled from wind perhaps. There was always a breeze blowing in from somewhere in this place. Often warm, but sometimes with a sharp eddy of cold inside. I left the book against a case that held a set of armour made of silver and sea glass. It had been my favourite as a child.

"She imagined Elainnor's legs must've been tired too. All of her probably. Collecting the armor, the weapons, travelling the kingdom to save the woman she loved. Her father wanted to finish the story but she kept asking questions, had he ever used a sword, would he rather a bow or a crossbow, could you run in armour like the ones in the gallery, had he ever had to fight someone. He was patient with her questions. When she apologised for asking so many he said she should never ever apologise for being curious."

The Sixth Book.

"There was one last lock. And the books were the five keys to it. She now had the memory of a sixth book. But nothing about it. It was a mystery. He'd let her read it, helping when she needed help, but also letting her struggle and figure it out on her own. She didn't want to stop. She felt like it had been written exactly for her. The way only a handful of books feel in a person's lifetime. But it was like the story passed through her eyes as she read it, off her tongue as she spoke, and she later found nothing stayed inside her. Not the title or the characters or the places. But his face, looking at her from the other side of the book, was joyous and wistful. Like it was Christmas morning and he'd given her something he'd always treasured and found she loved it too. Not because she knew it would make him happy, but because he knew her well enough to know she would love it like he did."

I walked back to the vault, exhausted. To the sixth book. The one I couldn't move.

I felt the figuration work the moment I finished writing my story. I could open it now. I could read it. And I did. I could remember him there with me, smiling, tearful, sharing this thing that was so incredibly precious to him.

The thing he'd searched for all his life. The thing we've all been searching for.

The Little Red House isn't a place. It's a book.

A children's book published by Ackerly Green in some version of 1955.

I just read the first volume of the Lost Collection.

CHAPTER 26
THE LITTLE RED HOUSE

"What if magiq isn't necessarily based on stories
in the literal sense, but the intrinsic narrative
of the creation process?"

— TINKER

I t was my book. My *unnamed book.* I knew even before I finished
reading Deirdre's post. The moment I read "The Little Red
House isn't a place," my mind completed the sentence like a key
knocking the tumblers of a lock in place: "it's the book I loved and lost
and then destroyed my life by remembering." For years, I'd believed
the title had been longer, that there was a certain rhythm to speaking
its title that I could hear but couldn't put words to, like a song you
could only hum. Maybe that was just the lie working its will on me,
hiding the truth.

The Little Red House.

It was almost more than I could process. Same for the
Mountaineers. One of the books that haunted us, that had been lost
for decades—had actually been found. And like every revelation
Sullivan's *Monarch Papers* brought us, this one offered no definitive

answers, only more questions. While I knew it was one more piece in the puzzle that promised to change everything, I also wondered if it could be the key to restoring Sebastian's memory of me. The return of the *Guide* had triggered memories in some of the Mountaineers; could *The Little Red House* somehow bring me back to my boy? Is that why it had been calling to me in my dreams? Was it holding fast to the part I stole from Seb, and all I had to do was bring it back?

There wasn't time for wondering. The Day of Change was getting closer. The last chance we had. On September 23rd, either we'd have The Book of Briars, or it would be gone forever.

Later that day, Benefactor sent me a text:

> Time to rally the troops. Anyone you know that
> can help, we'll need them.

There were a few acquaintances I knew from the Low who I could trust, or at least thought I could probably trust. I'd have to go through my Rolodex (yes, I still used one) and see how many of my contacts I could risk trying to recruit. But first, I called Bella's beach house. Port answered.

"Hey, guys!" she shouted after I said hello. "Marty's on the phone!"

I heard thumps and shouts of chaos as Alison and Jeremy rushed to get to the phone.

"Marty!" Jeremy said. "Jesus, man, are you all right?"

"I'm fine, just tired—"

"Hey! Okay, hold on, hold on—"

There was a scuffle, then Alison said, "Marty, you're on speaker. Seriously, are you okay? We read about you at Fallon's."

"I'm fine. It was close, but worth it. I think you were right, Alison. About Nate. He is important."

"I won't let it go to my head."

"So you've been following the forums, I take it?"

"Yeah," Jeremy said. "Just lurking, though. Don't want to take any chance on attracting the Storm."

"Good," I said. "But I got a text from Benefactor telling me to rally the troops. We're going to need your help on this one."

"You aren't kidding," Alison said. "I've seen what they've been cooking up with Gladitor and Aorthora. The sigils they've come up with are damn clever. But to cast both of those along with calling the corners, the Lantern spell, telling the required stories . . ."

"Yeah, it's a lot."

"We can do it, Marty," Port said.

"Damn right," Jeremy added.

"Good. Just don't post to the forums. I'm sure the Storm will be occupied, but if anyone from the Silver found out where you were . . ."

"Don't worry," Alison said. "We know how to keep ourselves safe. Even if others don't always trust us to do the right thing."

"I—"

"I understand. Honestly, I probably would've burned Fallon's house to the ground if I was there. It was the right call. I'm still pissed about it, but you were right."

Jeremy said, "Oh, hey, Marty. I—"

There was a dull thump, and then he mewled, "Ow! Alison, what the hell?"

"Shut up, Jeremy."

"But . . . okay, fine."

"What is it?" I asked. "What's going on?"

"It's nothing. Forget it." Alison responded.

"Guys, what happened? You all know me by now. I won't let it go until I know. Talk."

Alison sighed, and I could almost feel her giving Jeremy a dirty look over the phone. "Uh, your son was here."

"What?"

"He and his family came to use the beach house. Bella didn't know they were coming, so everyone was surprised when they got here. But she straightened everything out."

"And what did she say?"

"That we were Airbnb-ing it here for the summer. We kind of

picked up that we shouldn't, you know, mention you to Sebastian. After they left, Bella told us why."

I couldn't speak, I couldn't breathe, I couldn't even feel my legs.

"Marty, it's all good. Sebastian and the girls spent the day here, but no one said anything. Port and your granddaughters had quite the time together, too. Marty? You still there?"

My chest was tightening. Sebastian. My granddaughters. They had met my granddaughters, played with them, and I had yet to see them except for static images on social media. I was ashamed of how jealous I felt.

"Marty?"

"I'm here. Yeah, good. Glad to hear it all worked out."

"Hey, I know this is . . . weird for you. Weird for us too. I'm sorry. We're all sorry. Jesus, we wish you would have said something. We . . . we didn't know."

"No. It's okay, I'm . . . I'm glad you got to meet them. You guys will help with the spells?"

"Of course we will. You take care of yourself. And, hey . . ."

"Yeah?"

"You're not alone. Don't forget that."

"Thanks, Alison. You all be safe."

I hung up the phone and sat in silence for a while. I was surprised. Surprised at my jealousy, surprised at how much the pain of missing him still had its barbed hooks deep in my chest. Time, it turned out, does not heal all wounds.

But the clarion call had been sent out to all six corners: every able and willing Mountaineer was needed.

Benefactor was still trying to help us figure out what to exchange for the Book.

Endri posited that Sullivan Green had hidden *The Little Red House* precisely for this purpose. It seemed right that a volume from the actual Lost Collection would have the requisite power to trade for The Book of Briars. It made logical sense, but I needed there to be another option. That recurring dream with the fire inside and someone waiting for me had taken root in my mind. It had convinced me, right or wrong, that *The Little Red House* was the key to saving Sebastian.

While the rest of the Mountaineers prepared for the Day of Change, Cole posted about Deirdre on the forums. It wasn't exactly what we were hoping to hear.

COLE:

> I finally got her home. She's out of it. Not sure if whatever she was coming down with is finally catching up with her now that's she's back, or something else. She can't remember what's in the book (neither can I) but she says her imagination is running wild. She tells me the things she's seeing, but other than that she doesn't want to talk. She's just sleeping or staring into space.
>
> I tried to talk to her about *The Little Red House*. That you need it. I can't get through to her right now and it's scaring the hell out of me. I'll keep trying.

I felt sympathy for Deirdre, but this could work to my advantage. If we couldn't use *The Little Red House*, we would need to find a substitute. But we'd need to find it fast. Compounding the stress, Ascender hadn't responded to our last message—we still needed the missing half of the spell. The Mountaineers could see that he'd been online for three hours, but never posted. When he finally did, what he had to say terrified me.

The Storm had found him.

ASCENDER:

> It almost caught me. I finally got away after running for hours. The lantern spell never broke the entire time it

was looking for me. I finally heard what the other sounds are. They're voices. The thoughts of other people it took.

I know it seems crazy but I swear I heard Augernon. I was physically and mentally exhausted by the time it stopped coming after me, so yes, I could be wrong, about Augernon. But I'm not wrong about the voices.

I have to admit I was going to try and control it. See if I could, at least. But I couldn't get hold of it, it was too strong, and before I could control it or disconnect from it, it found me. I have to get as far away as possible from all of this if I'm going to survive, if I'm going to last long enough to make it to you.

The only problem . . . I've either kept all of this from all of you, or I don't remember you or what I know. But if I'm right, if I did hear the thoughts of other people in the storm, that means the Silver might be able to hear them too. And if it ever catches me, they'll know what you're planning to do.

Before seeing what Augernon did, I might've risked it, just run for it, out of pride, out of recklessness. But he took the hit for us. For all of us. I have to lose the war today if we ever hope to win it decades from now. I can't just count on losing the memories that could jeopardize all of this. I have to perform the bastard spell on myself.

I don't know how effective it will be, because there's no one left here to help me cast it, but I can't risk slipping up and giving you away. I know, from you, I still run. So I somehow remember what the stakes are. I know I have to go off the grid (which isn't new to me). And I still remember Augernon. Somehow. But something is still out there, looking for me. So I don't forget completely. I figure the bastard spell is my best chance for how I get there, how I

survive and bring you all together. So maybe
Augernon saves us all.

I just can't believe this is what it comes down to. I
thought that being brave would be enough. It isn't. I
should've counted on them more. Depended on them,
believed in them. Been there for them. But now it's
done. Now I just have to do what I can to make sure the
fight goes on. I can't let you down too. All of this has to
be for something.

Unlock that damned book, Mountaineers. For all of
us '94s.

One thing was certain, every Mountaineer wanted that book open.
At first it was simply to solve a mystery that had percolated in the
back of their minds their whole lives. But now it was something more
than curiosity. It was for the friends, the family they had all found.

Ascender then posted his half of the Lantern of Low Hollow spell:

 Use a lantern with new oil and an unburned wick or an
unlit candle to represent your untainted intentions.
Find a dark and quiet place. It's helpful to be near the
person or thing you believe is being coerced. Light a
new flame and repeat the incantation. If successful you
will not only hear the disembodied voice but may also
be driven to speak or write the words you hear spoken.

The voice on waves of aether's air
    Be drawn upon the light
    I call you from the nether's lair
    To bring you into sight

Whisper toward the lantern, mine
    A fire burning clear
    Your shadow thoughts are bending now
    And turning to my ear

That sullen song is echoing
    Black bell that has been rung
    Your words are at my fingertips
    And spilling from my tongue

The mad bastard was going to wipe part of his own mind to protect us. I wanted to shout at my screen—a warning, a cheer, a barbaric yawp in recognition of what he was willing to do. Because of Ascender, we had a chance, a real chance of pulling the Book through time.

He had given us the part of the spell that would allow us to access and hear the voices within the Storm. We already had the part that would allow us to control it, if only for a moment or two, but that was only likely to work if we confronted the Storm on the Day of Change. With magiq fading and our protections weakening, I worried the Storm was going to find us long before we ever had a chance to cast the spell. I wasn't sure what to do about it, though.

Mr5 posted that the sigil shield spell was up and running and that the offensive spell was workable as well. As for calling the corners, the Mountaineers had done that successfully in the past, so this time it was really just a matter of scale. Everything was clicking into place. We just needed something to trade for the Book.

I spent the following day reaching out to my old contacts in the Low, feeling them out for any duplicitous leanings on their part. I kept the conversation light with the ones who were really eager to speak to me—but the ones who were suspicious, I pointed in the direction of the Mountaineers. There were only a handful, but everyone we could get would be a help.

I even tried old email addresses for Mountaineers who'd disappeared in the late 90s on the off chance they were lurking about, but they all came back as dead addresses.

Once I had exhausted my Rolodex, I went through my phone. Most of the contacts I had stored were the shady sort—people who, if they weren't already part of the Silver, would certainly be sympathetic to them. All except one—if they were even still alive.

On a whim, I dialed the number. To my surprise, someone answered, and they scheduled me for a meeting early on the morning of the 23rd. The Day of Change.

While I worked out different ideas for what I might say at the meeting to elicit some kind of sympathy, my phoned chirped at me. Someone had DM'd me on the forums.

COLE:

 Hey, Marty. Cole, here. Sorry to bother you out of the blue like this. Benefactor mentioned you were trying to find help for Saturday. Wanted to know if there was anything I could do to help. Deirdre's not doing well, and I'm scared. I got back from the vault this morning. I tried to get *The Little Red House*. I put the books where Dee said they went in the story, but I couldn't unlock it. Maybe I just can't do magiq like that. Maybe it only works for her? I don't know . . .

She has a raging fever, but she won't let me take her to the hospital. She's locked me out of the bedroom. She says she doesn't want me to get sick, but I don't think this is the flu. I wanna say that if it comes down to it I'll do something drastic to help her, but honestly this is so over my head. I don't know what I'd do. I feel completely helpless.

If there was one thing I knew about the world, it was that there wasn't enough love in it. That true, scary, all-consuming love that makes us do crazy, silly, stupid, incredible things. But Cole loved Deirdre, and I was sure she loved him. It was the kind of love that branched out to those around them, filling the others in their lives with that same kind of purposeful love that made this world, all worlds, better. Reading Cole's message, seeing his distress—not over his own safety, but that of the person he loved—I knew exactly what I had to do. I had a plan, one that had already been brewing as a backup, and was now becoming Plan A.

I REPLIED:

 Cole, if anyone is going to survive this, it's going to be Deirdre. She's tougher than a two-dollar steak, my friend. Benefactor's right. I've been reaching out to my old contacts in the Low, the ones I can trust. Even a couple that I don't. But there is something you can help me do. It's one of those good news/bad news kind of things, though. The Council's defenses are fading. If they break on Saturday, the Storm will go for the Mountaineers. If it does, that's the ball game.

But, if you're willing to help, you could open a door to Neithernor and draw the Storm to you. That should keep it far away from the Mountaineers. That's the good news. The bad news is obvious. And I'm not going to be much help to the Mountaineers that day, anyway. Might as well make myself useful. What do you say. You in?

COLE:

 Hell yes. Meet me in Central Park, 4 p.m. on Saturday. I'll have the silver pendant and the scarves to try and trade for the Book when they're ready to cast. I'll update the Mounties. And thanks, Marty. It'll be good to meet you in person.

I felt bad, using Cole's need to help Deirdre for my own purpose.

He'd sacrifice himself for her, and if he thought that was a real possibility, well, I wasn't going to disabuse him of the idea.

But it wasn't going to come to that. I just needed Cole to open a door to Neithernor, to call the Storm, but once that was done, his job would be over, whether he realized it or not. I knew he was expecting to try and exchange the pendant and scarves for the book, but I doubted they were of equal value. So I'd come up with a plan. One that would keep *The Little Red House* safe. Maybe I wasn't supposed to reach it. Maybe I was just supposed to protect it and what waited inside it until it was safe to bring it back into our world. To do that I'd need an alternative trade.

There was really only one thing I could think of that would make for an acceptable exchange. Something we had that was valuable enough, something intrinsically linked to magiq in a way few things were. But it was something no one mentioned, no one wanted to talk about. They didn't have to. I already knew what it was.

I was a Well, after all.

CHAPTER 27
THE WISHING WELL

"I don't know of this clears anything up, but I
hope me nerding out helped out a little."

— BRIARROSE

I wandered from coffee shop to coffee shop, soaking up the free
Wi-Fi and keeping tabs on the Mountaineers while scanning my
various inboxes for messages from any contacts that hadn't yet
responded.

And there still wasn't any news of Cole's further attempts to get
The Little Red House. Deirdre was suffering from spell sickness and not
eager to talk about the book, our plan, any of it. Then Cole came
home to the brownstone to find Deirdre missing—gone to Neithernor
on her own. When she returned, she was in a crazed state.

COLE:

 She just came back a few minutes ago and she's writing
everything down right now. I'm trying to get her to

calm down and rest, but she says you need to know all
of this.

   She does have spell sickness but it's also something
about Neithernor that's affecting her. I can't keep up,
she's talking a mile a minute and looks like she's gonna
collapse. She says she met Mr. Wideawake? Does that
make sense?

No one knew who Mr. Wideawake was. An hour later, Deirdre's
message was posted to the forum.

DEIRDRE: SEPTEMBER 21ST, 2017:

 (Hey guys, it's Cole posting Dee's entry, which will make
sense at the end. She made me promise to post this
immediately:)

I'm sorry if this doesn't completely make sense, I'm
going to try and write it all down as quickly as I can.
   Someone kept ringing the door chime, so I hobbled
downstairs and found a note on the door from someone
telling me to meet them in the warren. For a minute I
didn't know if it was Cole or . . . So I took the stick. I
had no idea what I would do with it, but my dad said to
take it everywhere.
   Standing in the warren, looking out the window,
was a man, or I should say he looked manlike but was a
man-shaped bird. He turned to look at me with eyes like
little black buttons. He was taller than me, in a full suit,
his arms were wings, his feet were bare. Bird's feet. He
was a mix of gray, black, and white feathers. Mostly
black wings, with white on his neck and legs. A tuft of
black on the top of his head, and a little white patch
above his beak. Sorry, I still can't get over it.

He was holding a walking stick, like my father's but made of paler wood. Gold light leaked out from the cracks in it. He smiled, nodded, and said he was very pleased to meet me. I sat down on the edge of the bed because I was sure I'd finally gone mad.

He knelt and said that this must come as quite a shock but he was here to help me. And that I could call him Mr. Wideawake. He told me he could see that I was feeling a lingering bit of spell sickness but also something that "the Monarchs of old" learned. When you spend too long in Neithernor, you start to adjust to its time. And returning home is like jumping onto a spinning carousel because of the way time works there. There are some people who are more susceptible to it, and it seems like I'm one of them. He said it would pass but he's heard of cases in the old time where people have spent years or decades in Neithernor and couldn't go back home. They became Neithernorian and the change couldn't be undone.

I didn't know what to do, so I asked who he was. He started talking about the Council and you and the Book, and I couldn't keep up. He said if the Council failed, or the Mountaineers were lost again, he and his associates would be all that could possibly stop the Silver from conquering the world. He said they were prepared to go to war with the Silver, with or without magiq, but they've been doing what they could from the shadows to give us a chance at opening the Book. They've given us clues at times, and help when absolutely necessary; he even said his group was responsible for cultivating and protecting the Low. They've created disconnected factions who could confuse the Silver and send them to dead ends, because their priority besides saving the world is convincing the Silver that they don't exist. That they were finally wiped out.

At first I thought he meant the Council of the 18 Gates, but then it occurred to me who he was talking about. The path of wool.

He's a member of Monarch's Mountain. Turns out he's their Collector. I was confused. Not only because I thought Monarch's Mountain had died off but also I didn't think they still knew about Neithernor. He said I was incorrect on both counts but that's what they wanted the Silver to believe. Neithernor is like a memorial for them. A place of reflection, and only rarely do they go there.

He sat across from me in the armchair and crossed his legs like, you know, a person. He said I could ask him any questions I had and he'd answer as best he could before he had to leave.

I kept trying to think what you'd want to ask. He said he didn't know what was in The Book of Briars, which I thought was the obvious first question. He said some think it's a new story wanting to be told, but no one knows for sure.

I asked him what Neithernor really was. How it came to be. He said according to what's left of the Monarch history (which may not be completely accurate) there was experimentation with Wells, places connected to magic, and they believe that sometime in The Book of the Wild someone managed to harvest a piece of the Fray from deep within a Well, to study, but it began to grow. They were afraid it would take over our world so they tried to send it back, but reaching out to the Fray is unpredictable and dangerous and it wouldn't accept the piece. They tried to destroy it and thought they had, but it actually grew just outside our world, and it eventually became Neithernor. A place where magiq and imagination could be fully realised without limit, without fear of misunderstanding or retribution, but with its own risks and dangers.

I asked what the "The Book of the Wild" meant and he said it's what the Monarchs call the time before everything changed. He said, "Someone, we don't know who, changed The Book of the Wild and in its place was this world, this time." They call now "The Book of Kings."

I tried to get my head around the fact that we're living in an alternate timeline from an original timeline that had magiq in it, but he said it wasn't as simple as that. It was magiq, after all. He asked me to imagine a book. And then someone decided to edit that book. To remove something fundamental. Stories would have to be changed, characters rewritten, outcomes altered. And the ripples of all those changes would extend into the future chapters and the past. And it would be impossible to catch all the hanging threads. Scattered memories would be missed . . . and Wells. Wells, both people and place Wells, are like "hidden themes that remain, despite the narrative being altered."

So someone edited out magiq, I said.

And he said, "No. We believe someone edited out the Briar Books and all magiq followed after."

I for some reason thought the Silver or the Storm had changed things, but he said that no one knows who did it. But he knew it all came back to the Lost Collection. *The Little Red House.* He said there's something at the core of those books. They think it's the source of great magiq. Magiq that someone changed all of history to erase. They don't know who it was, but they believe sometime around the early 2000s history was changed, and the ripples of that change moved outward until it had altered all known history. As far as

they know only the Wells, a handful of memories, and
Neithernor survived.

It wasn't the Monarchs and it wasn't the Silver. He
said it's a mystery greater than any of this. And that's
why the Monarch houses want the book. (I was
wondering what all of this was about. He hadn't
brought me to the warren just to answer all of my
questions.) He said that the Monarch houses want *The
Little Red House*, to protect it, to study it, to understand
its place in the changing of the Book of the Wild.

I tried to explain what you were trying to do, how
important it was for this to work, to get The Book of
Briars and to stop the Storm. It's everything we've
worked for. Everything my father wanted. It's the
reason he set me on this path. Mr. Wideawake already
knew. He told me that the houses use the Lantern of
Low Hollow spell too. It's one of the ways they get
insight into the Silver's plans. By listening through it.
They were willing to lose that access to help us and the
Council save The Book of Briars and stop the damage
the Storm has done, but they didn't realise what the cost
would be. The Monarchs don't want us to use *The Little
Red House*. Even if it means losing The Book of Briars.
They say *The Little Red House* will be defenseless and
unprotected in 1998. If the Silver find it before the
Monarchs do, no one could protect the world. There's
no telling what secrets are inside that book, and the
Silver would do anything to discover it.

I couldn't believe it. They've had the means to stop
the Storm but didn't. They let people lose their minds,
be blown through time. They let people die and become
a part of it. The Storm was what kept my father from
me. He just nodded. The Collector is just another part
of Monarch's Mountain, he said. He might disagree
with their plans and purposes, but at the end of the day,

the houses decide what actions to take. He's tried to
change their minds, but the role of Collector doesn't
come with that kind of power. Then he stood and said
he couldn't stay any longer. He was also susceptible to
Neithernorian time.

I didn't understand. How could a bird man live
on Earth?

Unless he wasn't a bird.

He said it's a tradition that no one knows who the
Collector is until they have passed from this world to
whatever is after. What I was seeing was just a cobbled
bit of shapeshifting he'd learned from a gracious mer
gost. He hoped I wasn't disappointed.

I asked why he'd come now, why he'd come to
answer my questions, and he said because no one
knows what will happen after Saturday, not even the
Monarchs. He wanted to meet me and help me
understand that as big as all of this feels, it's so much
bigger. And that he was sure my father would be proud
of me for all I've done.

He said what was most important to keep in mind
was that not all the Monarchs agree with the houses'
decisions. He himself believes that my father found the
book and it has rightfully passed to me. I should be the
one who decides what happens to it. He said he'd read
how I unlocked the book and what I'd done and how I
wrote it out had been extraordinarily clever. Then he
said I should remember above all of this that "Even
those with the best intentions can do wrong."

He knocked and opened a door to a shore near a
dark blue sea somewhere. I felt like I hadn't asked
anything and I'd let you down. That any of you
would've asked better questions . . . but all I could think
of in that moment . . . well, I'd always felt guilty about
losing it so . . .

I asked him why King Rabbit wanted my dad's watch.

Mr. Wideawake smiled and said he wasn't sure, but he heard that soon after King Rabbit stole it from me, he'd also lost it.

And then the door shut and he was gone.

I honestly don't know how I feel about any of this. About *The Little Red House*, about the Monarchs wanting it, about letting it go . . . I've been reading it, hoping there was something else. Another step at the end of the path. I mean, this can't be it, can it? There has to be another part, a part I'm not seeing. Or is this all there is? Is this all—

Guys, this is Cole. That was the end of Dee's post. She just freaked out about something the bird guy said. Something she just realized . . . About this part:

"He said he'd read how I unlocked the book and what I'd done and how I wrote it out had been extraordinarily clever. Then he said I should remember above all of this that "Even those with the best intentions can do wrong.""

She started changing clothes, packing one of the camping bags. She said she had to go back to the vault. I tried to stop her, but she said she'd lied in the story when she wrote it. How she unlocked the book was true, but not the placement of the books. She'd changed one of the locations. She thought that if it meant so much to her dad to keep it safe, she should do what she could to protect it too, rather than just putting the solution online for anyone to see. (It's why I couldn't take it.) She'd protected the book, and she thinks Mr. Wideawake was telling her without telling her that she was clever to do so and that the Monarchs, the ones who want the book, at least, bypassed the Joradian on her blog because they had "the best intentions" and read how she unlocked it.

She thinks they're trying to take the book. They don't have the correct combination or the fifth location, but they've had days and days of Neithernorian time to try and figure it out.

I wanted to go with her, but we realized that if something happens and she can't make it back in time or they took the book, I have to be ready with the scarves and the pendant. To try to get The Book of Briars. I could barely get my head around what was happening before she kissed me, knocked into the tunnel, and was gone.

If there was any chance of me backing out of my plan, it disappeared after reading that. Putting aside the sheer absurdity of Mr. Wideawake and the war between the path of silver and the path of wool, it was clear that *The Little Red House* wasn't going to be available. Not that it mattered. I was committed. Yes, there was a chance that the scarves and the pendant Cole wanted to exchange for the book would be enough, but I wouldn't take that bet to a crooked bookie on my own payroll.

But now the question was what Deirdre was planning. I could only guess that she was in Neithernor to get *The Little Red House* for the exchange, but none of us knew for sure. And Cole was beside himself.

COLE:

 God, I hope she's okay. I can't imagine what she must be feeling right now. She's been devastated since she found the book. The end of her dad's journals, the end of her mom's dream. That book is pretty much the last

connection to her parents, and now she's either going to
have to give it away, or have it stolen from her.

I have no idea what's going to happen and no way to
help her.

She has the compass, the stick, and the journal, so
those are no-goes, by the way. I put the necklace and the
scarves in my bag. I plan to chuck the whole thing into
the Storm whenever I get word from you guys. (I have
notifications set up on my phone. I doubt I'll be able to
write back once we start, but I can see your posts.)

I'll let you know where Marty and I end up
tomorrow. I don't know how I'm gonna sleep tonight.

That made two of us. Sleep was the furthest thing from my mind,
yet there was nothing left for me to do. Tomorrow was the Day of
Change, and all I had on my docket was a Hail Mary meeting in the
morning and the showdown with the Storm that afternoon. I'd just
have to execute before Deirdre brought *The Little Red House* back, *if*
she could bring it back.

I thought about the people I might want to say goodbye to, but the
few who came to mind would ask too many questions that I wouldn't
be able to answer. I even toyed with the idea of writing a letter to
Bella, but there was nothing I could tell her that she didn't already
know.

It was a scary place to be as a writer, not having anything to say.
But I took it as a good sign, a sign that I was done. That I was ready.

I sat on the bed and watched the city outside the window until,
several hours later, I finally fell asleep.

There were no dreams of little red houses.

CHAPTER 28
DR. BRIGHTWELL

"Is there a kind of magiq that is more dangerous
than the others?"

— GIGIGUE

The Day of Change. Funny how it felt like any other. The sun
still moved along the same path, the birds still chirped, and
my back still ached from sleeping on shitty hotel beds.

I showered and dressed, taking a bit more care to make myself
presentable. I was about to go catch a cab when my phone rang. I
didn't recognize the number.

I answered but waited a moment before speaking. "Hello?"

"Marty?"

"Who's this?"

There was a pause, then the woman said, "It's Benefactor."

"Oh. You're calling. This can't be good."

"I wanted to hear your voice. It's been a while."

"So we've met before?"

"Only the once, about twenty years ago. Bruno's Deli, I think. No,
Bloom's."

"Dr. Brightwell."

"Dr. Brightwell's fine, but you can call me Knatz."

I'd always assumed, or hoped, it had been Knatz who gave me the coin. But after her last message to the Mountaineers, I wasn't sure. I had a thousand questions—what happened the day of the bastard hex in 1998, where'd she been all these years—but now wasn't the time.

"How are you, old friend?" I asked.

"A damn sight better than you, I imagine. You ready for today?"

"More or less. I'm meeting someone this morning who might be able to help. But it's a long shot, to be honest."

"This whole damn thing is a long shot," she said. "I'm calling for a couple of reasons. First is to talk you out of it."

"Talk me out of what?" I asked.

"C'mon. Half of Basecamp knows you're gonna try to offer yourself in exchange for the Book."

"Well . . . shit."

"I think Augustus was the first to figure it out. Not the Roman emperor, obviously. The Mountaineer. Other Mounties agreed it was something you'd be willing to try, so I'm calling to dissuade you from the idea."

Offering myself in exchange for the Book was exactly what I had planned. I found it frustrating that everyone knew, because I didn't want anyone to try to stop me. I especially didn't want Cole to find out. That could cause some problems.

"Thanks," I said, "but if the pendant and scarves don't work, it's the only option. One way or another, come landfall, we're getting The Book of Briars back."

She sighed. It was a tired, heavy sound. "Marty, there's something you should know. About the part of the Storm that used to be Nate, about what it does. I've heard about people being traded before. It doesn't end well. They lose pieces of themselves. It's not Sweeper bad, the complete memory wipe, but in a way it's worse. You still have some of your faculties, enough to know you aren't where you're supposed to be. You just don't know what happened to you or how to undo it. You're lost. To the world, to time, to yourself. It's why

Kemetic Solutions called the project 'Wanderer.' I know that's not the news you wanna hear, but you have to know that if you do this, it's not going to end well for you."

"Duly noted."

"You're a stubborn son of a bitch, aren't you?"

I laughed. "If I was truly stubborn, I would have made you keep that coin twenty years ago."

"Yeah, that's the other reason I'm calling."

"I'm sorry, I don't have it anymore," I said. "Your daughter does."

"I know. I just wanted to know how she is. *Who* she is. The Mountaineers seem to like her, but you've actually seen her, met her in person. I . . . I just want to know if she's well."

"Alison is as well as could be expected. She's been through hell, but so have we all. She's tougher than nails. And competent. There's no one I'd rather have next to me in the foxhole, that's for sure. You should go see her."

"I will. Soon. But not yet. When it's safe."

When it's safe. If it would ever be safe.

"Knatz," I said. "What happened after you said goodbye to the Mountaineers in '98? Why didn't the spell erase your memories?"

Knatz was silent for so long that, for a moment, I thought I had lost the connection. Then she said, "I couldn't go through with it. I couldn't be some mindless, passionless drone and not be able to show my daughter that the world was so much bigger than anybody thought. So, at the last minute, I ran. Well, I came back to my old life once. To see Saberlane. Get him home. He'd used the coin to protect the rest of the '94s long enough for the hex to be cast, and he lost all memory of magiq. I don't blame him for a second. And truth be told, I don't think he did it all out of fear. There were things he wanted to forget . . . Anyway, not my story to tell. But that's how I got the coin back. Brought it to you when I saw you snooping around the old message board. Figured it was the least I could do. I didn't deserve that charm. I ran, and I deserved to keep running for leaving them behind."

"And where would we be right now if you'd gone through with it? I think you made the right decision," I said. "For Alison's sake. For all our sakes."

"I hope so. I would see her, you know. In secret, when it felt safe, being her benefactor from a distance, sharing things with her about her gift, about magiq. She probably would've had a safer life without me, but it is what it is. She's special, Marty. Powerful."

"I can vouch for that."

"The Council came to her when they needed to find a way to teach the Mountaineers about Nate, about Wanderer. But she got too close to KS, and they came for her before I could do anything. But I helped when I could. Requested the spells from the Low, got some unsavories off their backs a couple times. Those damned Devoted were a right pain. But the Mountaineers saved her. *You* saved her."

"I remember it a bit differently. She was the one doing the saving, I was just along for the ride."

Knatz chuckled. It was a pleasant sound, a wistful burr full of pride. "Tell you what. I wish I had that coin at the moment, though."

"Why? You plan on coming to the show?"

"Got a show of my own to perform, I'm afraid. You all taking on the Storm is going to be one hell of a diversion."

"Should I ask?"

"Best you don't."

"Fair enough," I said.

"Speaking of . . ."

"Yeah, big day today. Should get ready for this meeting I've got."

"Good luck, Marty."

"Thanks. You too, Knatz. Talk to you in another twenty years?"

"Sounds like a plan."

I hung up the phone and put on my jacket. As nervous as I was, I didn't want to be late for my meeting.

I arrived in Greenwich Village only a few minutes late. The house was what could only be described as Old New York. It was five stories tall with decorated eaves and a gorgeous facade of wood and brick that should have clashed horribly, but instead worked to create a lovely, if rather ominous, structure.

I walked up the steps to the door and, not seeing a bell, used the grotesque door knocker instead. I could feel the clang shake the entire door. When the reverberations finally fell silent, the door opened.

"Ah! Martin Rank!"

"Hello, Teniman."

"Please, come in, come in."

Teniman was wearing a silk burgundy dressing gown over pinstriped pajamas, looking even more the part of Lord Blackweather than he had in the black-tie finery he'd worn the night of the Translation. His hair was disheveled but in a way that appeared intentional, as if his stylist had spent the past hour mussing his hair just right.

"I must say, Martin, I am quite pleased to know you're alive. I thought for sure Celia and I were the only ones to escape the Translation unscathed. That was quite a do."

"I don't know if I'd say I got out unscathed, but yeah, I'm alive."

If the outside of the house was Old New York, the inside was an eclectic mix of old and new. A grand staircase wound up to the second and third floors; a chandelier hovered high above the foyer. Just as the outside elements of the house flirted with clashing, so did the inside. The walls were paneled with rich mahogany planks, but the floor was a burnished marble. Yet somehow it all worked together to create an atmosphere of utter opulence.

There was a pleasant hint of bergamot, cedar, and the clashing but not unpleasant scent of something else . . . almost a seaside campfire, which had an immediately calming effect on me.

"May I offer you some refreshment? Coffee or tea? Something stronger, perhaps? I certainly wouldn't judge."

"No, thank you. I'm fine—"

There was a terrible ruckus upstairs, followed by a string of colorful curses. Teniman shouted upstairs, "Look in the closet next to the study, dear!" He then turned to me and blushed. "Terribly sorry.

My wife has misplaced her favorite apothecary attaché and has spent the better part of the morning looking for it. It has tremendous sentimental value, you see."

"It isn't there!" Celia's voice rolled down the stairs.

"Did you look under the saddlebags?"

"No, Ten, love, the *closet* isn't there!"

Teniman saw my confused expression and gave me a sheepish grin. He waved his hand in the air above his head and said, "The House of Blackweather is many things, Mr. Rank. Predictable, however, is not among them. It's been a tad skittish this morning, no doubt due to the presence of our distinguished guest."

"She's here?"

"Waiting for you in the library."

I wanted to ask how a house could be skittish and a closet no longer be where it was supposed to be, but my plate was already full enough with magimystical quandaries.

Celia Blackweather appeared at the top of the stairs, looking even more regal than Teniman in her own silk dressing gown. "It has to be in the basement, Ten, and you know I'm not allowed in the basement this year. I—oh!"

Celia, strangely, perked up when she saw me and rushed down the stairs. But instead of embracing me or even saying hello, she came to a halt five feet in front of me, pulled a penny from her pocket, and tossed it to me in a high sweeping arc.

Reflexively, I caught the coin. Celia then squeezed her eyes shut and said, "I wish I could find my apothecary attaché!" She opened her eyes, her face practically glowing.

"Celia, dear, Mr. Rank has important business to attend to. Let's not bother him with our domestic trivialities." He put his arm on her shoulder and began leading her away.

"Doesn't he have a sense of humor?" she asked, looking back at me, winking.

"Martin, the library is on the third floor. You can't miss it," Teniman said.

"It's the room with all the shelves," Celia said as she waved. Then

Lord and Lady Blackweather disappeared down the hallway, bantering as they went.

I made my way up to the third floor and discovered that Teniman was right: I couldn't miss it. As far as I could tell, the library *was* the third floor. Natural light illuminated every corner of the vast, open space. Every wall was filled with bookshelves from floor to ceiling. There were half a dozen sitting areas with various lounge chairs and couches, and a couple of antique desks that could be used for study.

Strangely, the hundreds of shelves were conspicuously empty. Only a few books sat upon them, and at odd angles, as if the library's contents had been cleared in a hurry and the handful of titles that remained were left behind in the rush.

"What do you have there?"

I turned toward the voice. There she was, sitting in a high back leather chair in front of a grand fireplace, her legs casually draped over the arm as if she had been napping. She stood, taller than I remembered and certainly more corporeal than last I saw her. Lauren, the new Cagliostro, was no longer made of snow.

"Oh, I get it," I said, tossing her the coin. "I'm a Well."

"Yes, Martin, you are. But I had no idea you were the wishing kind."

"I think Lady Blackweather was making a joke."

Lauren smiled and gestured for me to sit in the chair opposite her. "Sadly, it won't help her find her attaché," she said, sitting back down. She played with the coin, studied it as she held it between two delicate fingers. "The house is keeping its secrets safe while I'm here. It doesn't know if it can trust me yet."

"So . . . the house is alive?"

"No, the House of Blackweather is . . . something else. And a story for another time."

I shifted in my seat. The fire in the fireplace was pleasingly warm —surprisingly so, considering that it was already sweltering outside. "Cagliostro—"

"Lauren, Martin. Please. Come on . . ."

"Lauren, okay." I took a breath. "How are you? The last I saw you . . ."

Lauren nodded, her eyes still focused on the coin. "I wasn't myself?"

"That's one way to put it. I mean, what happened? Where did you go? If Teniman hadn't told me he could contact you, I'd think you were still . . . not yourself."

Lauren turned her gaze on me, and I became acutely aware of how powerful she was. There was something in the way the firelight glinted in her eyes that left little doubt she had progressed even beyond burning libraries with her mind or sprouting wings to fly. Timelessness swirled about her in a way that I could almost see. The feeling was vertiginous.

"I went back to the beginning. But that's an even longer story and one I am not ready to tell just yet. Maybe someday. For now, let's talk about you. You and the Mountaineers have gotten yourselves into a situation, haven't you?"

I was sure Lauren didn't mean it to sound patronizing, but I couldn't help but feel I was being scolded. "We don't know what else to do. Sullivan Green had a plan, and we're following it the best we can."

"What are you going to try and exchange for the Book?"

"We were hoping to get *The Little Red House* out of Neithernor, but that doesn't look like it's going to happen. Deirdre's gone, and we don't know when, or even if, she's coming back. So Cole has some scarves and a silver pendant he thinks might work."

Lauren said nothing, only stared at me with her timeless eyes.

"They won't be enough, though, will they?" I asked.

"No."

"But I would be."

The corners of her mouth rose in a slim smile. "Yes," she said. "Physical Wells, places still connected to the lost age, to magic, are rare. But *living* Wells, those are something else entirely. And truth be told, calling you a Well is like calling you sober, in that it's far more complicated than it looks on the outside."

She could brush aside all the bluff and bluster and cut right to your heart. I kept talking, like my metaphorical pants weren't hanging around my ankles.

"And if I do this, exchange myself for the Book, it's not going to be pleasant for me, is it?"

She shook her head.

I was still determined to go through with it, but part of me had hoped that Knatz had been wrong. I should have known better. "I can't think of anything else that might be of equal value," I said.

"There are plenty of things, actually, but none of them have been seen in a very long time. Even if they had, they'd be on the far side of the world. *You* could never get them in time, especially with magiq almost faded."

I listened to the crackle of the fire, soaked in its warmth.

"Why do you want to sacrifice yourself so badly?" she asked.

"I don't. But . . . if it could help, change all of this . . . save these kids. They're risking their lives—"

"I don't mean now. Not *just* now. I mean everything. Your addiction. Your isolation. All the risks you've taken. All the dark holes you've crawled into. You've been trying to sacrifice yourself for decades. Do you think any of this will bring him back?"

It took me a minute to steady myself. Finally, I answered, as difficult as it was. "I've been thinking about that a lot lately. There's this dream I have where no matter what I do, I can't get to the little red house. To the piece of him that's missing. I know it's too late save him. Really, there's no reason to, aside for my own selfish needs. He has a wife, kids, he's lived a whole life without me. But losing him, losing them all, my wife, his daughters, it can't just be for nothing, Lauren." It was all I could do to try and choke back the well of tears threatening to overflow. "I don't know what Sullivan's plan is, but all this led me here, to this choice, and that book. We have to bring it back. It's all I have to hold onto. And if it takes my life to make this all mean something . . . well, I have nothing left to lose."

Lauren sat back and twined her fingers together. "You arranged this meeting to ask for my help. As much as I would like to, my powers are somewhat . . . frayed at the moment. I'm still getting my sea legs, as they say. But there is one thing I can do for you." She sat forward, her elbows on her knees, and said, "The Mountaineers are planning to wield some powerful magiq. Dangerous magiq. And they aren't just opening a cookbook and following the recipe. They're customizing the spells, Martin. Tailor-making them to suit their own needs. I know adepts who wouldn't dare risk such a thing. That the Mountaineers are capable of it is a testament to just how clever they really are. Even so, they need to know what's happening on the ground in real time if they want to succeed. And I don't think the Storm is going to observe the Marquess of Queensberry Rules while you take a timeout to send a text. But I can be their eyes and ears on the ground. I can be their liaison."

"You're willing to be there?"

"Not physically, no. I can't. I need to stay here. Lady and Lord Blackweather have allowed me to remain while I . . . finish waking up, so to speak. But I don't need to be there with you. When the time comes, I'll keep the Mountaineers up to speed."

I never really thought about what that afternoon was going to look like. Probably because if I did, I'd run screaming and find a bed to hide under until it was over. Cole and I were planning on drawing the Storm out to a specific location, but once it showed up we had no way of relaying anything to the Mountaineers. Lauren was right. I certainly wasn't going to be on the forums while facing down the Storm.

"That's more than I have a right to ask for. Thank you."

"You saved my life, Martin. That's why I agreed to meet with you. I owe you this one." Lauren came over and stood next to my chair. She held out the coin and said, "You should keep this. It has no magiqal value here, but the ladies of this House have a long and storied history. One should always cherish their gifts, no matter how seemingly mundane."

I took the coin and slipped it into my shirt pocket. I was about to stand when Lauren put her hand on my shoulder and said, "Stay awhile. Enjoy the fire."

"Thanks, but we're having a bit of a heat wave at the moment."

"I built this fire just for you, Martin. It will help you with your sleeping issues. You understand?"

The chills, the nightmares, the endless nights of frigid despair . . .

"Yes," I whispered. "I understand."

Lauren patted my cheek with a kind, warm hand, and then she left me alone with the empty shelves and the gloriously perfect fire.

CHAPTER 29
THE DAY OF CHANGE

"She would not be their victim anymore. Not her,
not anyone else."

— DEYAVI

ENDRI:

 The Corners have been Called. It's time. So this, in a
perfect world, is how I hope things will break
down today.

The Day of Change Schedule:

—Around 4 p.m. Cole will let us know where he's
chosen to open the door to Neithernor.

—Operation Gladitor will begin. Participants will
prepare an offensive "sucker punch" to use against the
Storm to help buy Cole and Marty time. Once
finished, I will cue the lantern bearers to begin casting
The Lantern of Low Hollow. Time will be of the
essence.

—Cole will open a door to Neithernor to lure the Storm out when we're all ready.

—Hopefully the lantern bearers will have some confirmation that they've accessed the Storm, then they'll attempt to override the Silver's controls. A lantern bearer or someone watching them should let me know when the Low Hollow spell is complete. Once completed, I will cue the storytellers here in the Day of Change topic.

—Then the storytellers will begin to convince the Nate part of the Storm to trade the things Cole has brought for The Book of Briars in 1998. Even if you aren't a lantern bearer or storyteller, it's key that we all focus on The Book of Briars. The more attention we put on it, the better chance we have of getting it back (complete conjecture).

—Once the trade is complete, Cole will let us know. He and Marty will either escape to Central Park or Neithernor.

—And then it will up to the storytellers to convince the Storm to disperse.

—Am I missing anything? Thoughts? Alterations?

ROBERT:

 Looks reasonable (in a crazy, this-is-the-new-normal way) to me.

Over the last several months, with Lauren's chill deep in my bones, the heat had never really affected me. I wasn't always cold, but I was never hot. Now that Lauren's fire had removed that chill, I suddenly felt like I was living in a sauna.

Sweat poured out of me; my clothes stuck to me like cling wrap around a squished banana. By the time I got to the Alice in Wonderland statue, I was so dreadfully uncomfortable that I almost stripped off my clothes and jumped in a fountain.

ASCENDER:

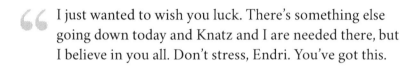 I just wanted to wish you luck. There's something else going down today and Knatz and I are needed there, but I believe in you all. Don't stress, Endri. You've got this.

GINGER:

ASCENDER!!!
    Thank whoever or whatever you want that you're safe. (I mean relatively, considering whatever's going down today.)
    Best of luck to you and Knatz.

READER:

I know next to nothing about magic, but I'm here for moral support. Go team 33.

ENDRI:

Operation Gladitor's ready. Good work, Mounties. We're now waiting to hear from Cole and Marty, and then I'll cue the lantern bearers.

A few minutes before four o'clock, I saw a young man in jeans and a T-shirt with a backpack slung over his shoulder. There were few people milling about, so when he spotted me, he made a beeline.

"Marty?"

"Hey, Cole," I said and shook his hand. He was tall, scruffy, with kind eyes and so terribly young. Of course, everyone under the age of thirty looked like a toddler to me, so I shouldn't have been surprised at how surprised I was. "You're taller than I was expecting."

"You're . . . well, to be honest, you're exactly what I was expecting. I . . . don't mean that as a bad thing."

"Don't worry," I said. "Any sense of vanity I had went out with the Reagan administration. Any news from Deirdre?"

Cole shook his head. "I'm glad she isn't here, though. I just wish I knew she was okay." He patted his backpack and said, "I've got the scarves and the pendant, though. We should be good." From the tone of his voice, I could tell he wasn't thoroughly convinced. I didn't want to tell him that I knew they weren't going to be enough. If I did, he might not be willing to go through with any of it.

He looked at his phone and said, "I think the Mounties are ready. They're just waiting on us."

"It's your show. I'm following you."

COLE:

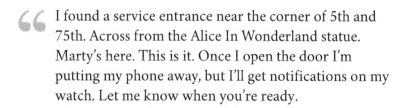 I found a service entrance near the corner of 5th and 75th. Across from the Alice In Wonderland statue. Marty's here. This is it. Once I open the door I'm putting my phone away, but I'll get notifications on my watch. Let me know when you're ready.

The two of us walked out of the park and crossed the street. He glanced at his phone again and smiled.

"What is it?" I asked.
"Alison's back."

ALISONB:

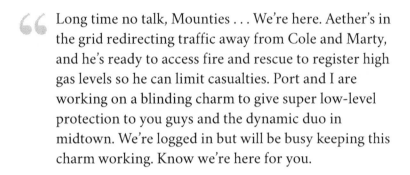

Long time no talk, Mounties . . . We're here. Aether's in
the grid redirecting traffic away from Cole and Marty,
and he's ready to access fire and rescue to register high
gas levels so he can limit casualties. Port and I are
working on a blinding charm to give super low-level
protection to you guys and the dynamic duo in
midtown. We're logged in but will be busy keeping this
charm working. Know we're here for you.

"And . . . Holy shit!" Cole exclaimed.
I looked over his shoulder to see his screen but had a feeling I
knew who'd just showed up.

FKALAUREN:

Surprise. I owe Marty one for saving my life a few
months back (according to him) so . . . here's the one
he's owed. I can't get in the middle of this (long story)
but I can watch what's going down in midtown and be
your eyes. Cool?

"Lauren's online. The frickin' Cagliostro!" His thumbs worked
over his phone screen with a millennial's mastery.

ENDRI:

Lantern bearers, you can start.

Cole pocketed his phone and checked his smartwatch. "It's time, Marty."

I clapped him on the back. "Then let's get ready for some weather. Do your thing."

Cole nodded. He went to the iron door, glanced over each shoulder to make sure no one was close by, then closed his eyes. After a moment there was a small but distinct clanging knock on the other side of the door. And then Cole knocked back. He rapped his knuckles around the door in a specific pattern. There was a click, thick and guttural from deep within the door—a sound like an anchor lightly tapping the hull of a battleship—and Cole pulled the door open.

Inside was the warren. Sullivan's home in Neithernor.

I felt like Dorothy seeing Oz for the first time—the warm little room. The dazzling light coming in from the small window. I could smell grass and trees and spice and decay and a world so completely foreign yet familiar that my knees almost buckled.

"Marty, you all right?"

"Yeah, I . . . Damn, it's unbelievable."

"It takes a little getting used to. But this is nothing. It's even more incredible the farther in you go."

I genuinely lacked the imagination to see how that was possible.

"How long can we keep it open?" I asked.

"Not very. The door gets pretty hot. I meant to bring gloves, but with everything going on, I spaced." Cole glanced down at his watch. "I've got the forum feed here," he said. "Lauren says she can see the Storm. It smells Neithernor. About eleven blocks away. It's coming our way fast . . ."

He trailed off, no longer staring at his watch but at the hairs on his arm. They were standing on end. Mine were as well. I could taste the electricity in the air, acrid in my mouth.

AUGUSTUS_OCTAVIAN:

 Good luck, Marty and Cole.

ENDRI:

 The lanterns are lit. Start the story.

Everything looked normal. Even though no one else was around, thanks to Aether, it seemed like just another ordinary day in New York. If I didn't know what was coming, I could have tricked myself into relaxing.

FKALAUREN:

 Make sure you've got control of it, Mountaineers. It's coming in fast. You've got less than a minute.

Cole heard it first. He cocked his head slightly, listening. Then I heard the unmistakable whine of a distant freight train chugging closer and closer. The air pressure dropped, and the oppressive heat vanished. I could see the trees in the distance, once still, suddenly agitated by the Storm's violent gale—only to become still again as it passed. The sound grew louder, the dancing trees closer, until, too quickly, the Storm was before us.

It was larger than when I'd seen it in Port's aunt's house or when it attacked me at Fallon's. The blackened wall carried a wind of a thousand whispers, bending over us like an accusatory parent. Inside the eye, dark shadows swirled and danced to a music only they could hear.

AUGUSTUS_OCTAVIAN:

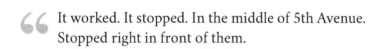 Gladitor, now!

FKALAUREN:

 It worked. It stopped. In the middle of 5th Avenue.
Stopped right in front of them.

"Cole? Cole, you still with me?"

"Yeah, yeah. Jesus . . . okay. Marty, hold the door. Careful, it's getting hot."

"No, you hold it, stay clear. I'll take the backpack."

"Not gonna happen. No way. I have to do it," Cole replied.

I wanted to protest, but he was adamant, steely. It didn't matter. As soon I saw my chance I was going to walk into the black, and no one would stop me.

"Okay." I grabbed the door to keep it from closing. It was already hot to the touch—I wasn't going to be able to hold it for long if it got any warmer.

Cole took two steps toward the Storm. How he managed to do it, I had no idea.

"Cole!"

He turned back to me. A mix of fear and determination in his eyes. I didn't know what to say to him, I just nodded, and for a second he flashed a smile at me, nodded back, then turned to the Storm.

How a parent could reject any kid, I don't know. But a kid like Cole . . .

I was so happy knowing I could keep him safe. Do something with my life.

This was it. Time to go.

FKALAUREN:

 Cole's pulling his backpack off.

He's saying something. He's throwing it in.

ENDRI:

 Focus on the book, guys, everybody focus on The Book of Briars.

FKALAUREN:

 Blinding. White.

Lighting. Everywhere. I can't see.

It's hazy. Hang on . . .

It didn't work. The pack's on the ground.

The Storm's getting bigger.

Shit.

Marty's gone.

NIMUEH

 Oh no. Please no.

SEL:

  It wasn't enough.

FKALAUREN:

  You're losing your grip on it. The Storm's getting free.
    Tell Cole to run.

ENDRI:

  Don't let go of the Storm, guys! Focus!

AUGUSTUS_OCTAVIAN:

  Lantern bearers - Focus! Storytellers - Say it out
  loud again!

FKALAUREN:

  Cole's hurt. Struck by lightning. His left side is bleeding.

He let go of the door. He can't get in.

SEL:

  COLE, YOU NEED TO GET OUT OF THERE. NOW.

FKALAUREN:

 It cut him off. He can't get to the park. I'm sorry. It's done.

Shut the Storm down or it's going to destroy him.

VIVIANE:

 Nate, we know you can hear us. Stop. Stop this.

FKALAUREN:

 No. Wait!

There's something in the air.

Like literally.

It's Deirdre.

DEYAVI:

 In the air?

FKALAUREN:

 She has a stick. And a book.

But something's wrong.

The book is unbinding.

I can feel it. It's not supposed to be here. It's being pulled apart.

DEYAVI:

 It's *The Little Red House*. Has to be.

FKALAUREN:

 I can feel her.

Strong.

She's not scared. She's pissed.

TINKER:

 Come on, guys! Keep holding!

FKALAUREN:

 She's about to throw the book in . . .

This is it.

ENDRI:

 Everyone focus . . .

ORACLESAGE:

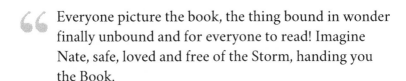 Everyone picture the book, the thing bound in wonder finally unbound and for everyone to read! Imagine Nate, safe, loved and free of the Storm, handing you the Book.

FKALAUREN:

 A piece broke off in her hand. The whole thing's turning to ash.

She just cast something and blew the ash into the Storm.

She's weak. Hurt.

ORACLESAGE:

>> She's just used a ton of magiqal energy! I would
imagine.

FKALAUREN:

>> It's done.

Shut it down.

VIVIANE:

>> Rest. Sleep. Be at peace.

AUGUSTUS_OCTAVIAN:

>> Nathan Fallon. Hear us.
"he finally rested, peaceful and free."

FKALAUREN:

>> Oh God. They know. They know you're inside. The
Silver.

They're making the thing in the eye kill what you were
controlling.
The boy inside the Storm is dead.

The Silver have the Storm. They have control again.

Deirdre is telling Cole to run, to the park. He's not going to make it. He's too hurt. It's coming for him.

I can hear her mind. She won't let it hurt anyone else. This is the thing that kept her family from her.

ORACLESAGE:

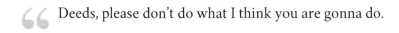 Deeds, please don't do what I think you are gonna do.

FKALAUREN:

66 She just ran into the Storm.

RIMOR:

66 Oh no.

NIMUEH:

66 What is she doing?!

FKALAUREN:

    “ I'm trying to look in.

    It's searing.

    Hold on.

AUGUSTUS_OCTAVIAN:

    “ Our brave, sweet Deirdre. If anyone can do this, it's her.

DEYAVI:

    “ What is she doing? What's going on??

VIVIANE:

    “ Deirdre, you can do it. We're behind you.

FKALAUREN:

    “ In the eye.

CHEYYYME:

 We're all sending all the energy we can muster.

TINKER:

 Come on, Deeds!

FKALAUREN:

 She's standing with something. Some shadow.

Walls of black around them.

Lighting is striking her. But she's covered in some kind of glass. No. Translucent armor. And a helmet.

She has a shield and sword. Holy hell. She's wearing the icons of Elainnor.

I can't stay here without breaking a lot of magiq.

The Silver are in there with her. Commanding the thing in the eye. It's coming for her.

But she's ready.

She's raising Gladitor . . .

> In the old times a witness would be allowed to name someone whose actions they know will live on in stories . . .

May I name her?

CJ_HEIGHTON:

> Do it.

AUGUSTUS_OCTAVIAN:

> Name her, Lauren.

FKALAUREN:

> She is Deirdre of the Isles.

The Mountain's Will.

And Stormslayer.

REMUS:

> Wait. She did it?!

NIMUEH:

 Stormslayer?! She did it!!!

FKALAUREN:

 She's with Cole now.

Ooh, that was fun. Cags never got to name anybody.

DEYAVI:

 Is Cole okay? Can you see Marty anywhere?

FKALAUREN:

 Cole is hurt.

ROBERT:

 AlisonB, now would be a good time for Aether to call in an ambulance.

ALISONB:

 He's on it.

RIMOR:

 What about Marty?!

FKALAUREN:

 I don't see him.

I can't feel him.

An ambulance just pulled up.

Good work, Mountaineers.

I'm sorry about Martin.

AUGUSTUS_OCTAVIAN:

 So are we, Lauren. Many of us knew it would come to this. That he would try and sacrifice himself.

ROBERT:

 Mountaineers, it's back. The Book of Briars is back.

CHAPTER 30
SACRIFICE

"Sounds liking flying is the way to go…"

— FRAXI

Lightning crashed all around us.

The whole of the world was engulfed in the Storm's blinding light. I felt needles in my eyes as my pupils dilated. When I was finally able to see again, I saw the backpack swirling in the winds of the Storm, with the leaves and the twigs and the detritus of a dozen worlds, around and around until, finally, it fell to the cement path, torn to shreds.

Cole stared at the backpack for a moment before turning back to me, terrified. The scarves and the pendant weren't enough for the Book.

I knew what I had to do.

But apparently, so did Cole.

Our eyes met, his brows came down in a fierce scowl, and he charged straight at me. For the briefest moment I thought he was running from the Storm. It swelled behind him, growing wider, towering higher, swirling faster. I was about to run for it, into it, but

Cole was quicker. In that moment I realized why he was determined to offer the pendant and scarves while I held the door.

"Cole . . ."

He dropped his shoulder, body-checked me, and sent me sprawling backward into Neithernor. Right on my ass.

"Sorry, Marty! We're family now!" It was hard to hear him over the roar of the Storm behind him.

"Cole, no!" But he didn't listen. He slammed the door shut, and then all went quiet.

I pounded on the broom closet door until my fists were raw. It wouldn't open, no matter how hard I pushed. I was alone in the warren.

I pulled out my phone, but there was obviously no signal in Neithernor. I was trapped with no way to help. I couldn't save Cole, couldn't save Sebastian. I'd failed to do the one thing I'd come to do because I let myself become part of this insane story. Because I let them care about me.

I collapsed back onto the floor. My hands were bloody from knocking, and my chest burned where Cole had shouldered me. It took a moment to realize it wasn't my chest that was on fire.

It was Lady Blackweather's coin.

I pulled it from my shirt pocket, but as soon as I touched it, it cooled. I examined it, and it was a simple penny on one side—but when I flipped the coin to its other side, I could see through it, like a peephole, straight into New York City.

I stood up and held the penny against the door. I peered through it like a keyhole and saw Cole standing with his back to me, facing the Storm, which had grown so much that I couldn't see any of the park behind it.

Cole was glancing to either side, looking for a way to escape, but the black clouds loomed large around him. There was nowhere he could go. Whatever power the Mountaineers had over the Storm, it was fading or already gone.

And then lightning flashed.

An angry, violet bolt of electricity burst out from the Storm and struck Cole. The force of the impact lifted him off the ground, the concrete beneath him shattering in a cloud of sparks and smoking debris.

Cole landed in an awkward slump. He was alive, but his entire left side was covered in blood and his hair was singed to the scalp. Smoke trailed up from his ruined clothes.

I couldn't believe I'd let this happen. Saw the look in his eyes, knew what I had to do, but didn't. A million ways I could've prevented this flashed through my mind. Didn't this sweet, stupid kid know the young don't die for the old?

That's all I could think through streams of hot tears, tears that clouded my vision and burned my eyes. I clawed at the door, helpless, ashamed. I wanted to look away, drop the coin . . . but if I did, Cole would be alone. I slid to the floor of the warren, one hand holding the coin to the door, the other clearing my eyes.

If I had been stronger, if I had thought to give myself to the Storm the second it appeared, if I had been firm with Sebastian oh so many years ago, this wouldn't be happening. But I hadn't, and now I had to watch another friend lose himself. For me.

What a useless thing to give his life for.

Cole rolled over and started to drag his body, leaving a smear of blood on the broken pavement. Somehow, he managed to get onto his knees. He looked around, searching for a way to escape into the park, but the Storm had him cut off.

Lightning crackled inside the Storm, thick lines of white-hot energy that briefly illuminated the shadowy figures swirling in it depths. It started to inch forward, then stopped. I squinted, wishing Lady Blackweather had given me a quarter instead of a penny, but I could see feet hanging in midair. Someone was hovering just above Cole; they slowly lowered to the ground next to him.

It was Deirdre.

Translucent wings grew out of her back. In one hand she held her father's walking stick, and in the other, a book. *The Little Red House.*

I had been right. I could see the cover, feel the wave of nostalgia that washed over me. It was the unnamed book. *My* book. The book that disappeared, returning long enough to take my son with it. And there was nothing I could do but watch as it disintegrated in her hand, dissolving like tissue in water. It wasn't supposed to be here, in this time, and was crumbling like the original *Guide to Magiq* had.

Deirdre turned to Cole and shouted, "Run!" I couldn't hear her, but there was no mistaking the word her mouth was shaping.

Cole tried to stand but floundered onto one knee. There was nowhere he could go anyway. The Storm was everywhere.

Flecks of the book spun around Deirdre, some drawn into the Storm, some pushed through the coin's peephole. I could feel them stick to my cheeks, settle on my skin. I couldn't bring myself to brush them away.

I'd failed.

Deirdre planted herself between Cole and the Storm. I could swear the Storm flinched under her gaze. The book continued to unbind until it was nothing but ash in her hand. Gone.

She raised the stick and worked some strange gesture in the air with it. She was casting a spell.

Deirdre blew the ash into the air, and I watched it swirl and writhe until the Storm sucked it into itself.

There was another flash of brilliant light. When my eyes adjusted, I could see that Deirdre had been hurt, though not nearly as badly as Cole. And something was happening inside the eye of the Storm. The shadowy figures that I'd seen before were swarming over one another, singling out a figure in their midst. They tore at it viciously, shredding it apart until it was gone.

My heart ached as I realized I was witnessing a murder of sorts.

The Mountaineers had been telling Nate stories to try and control the Storm. That was the essence of how their spell worked. The Silver must have discovered what they were doing and commanded the other beings inside the Storm to stop it. By killing Nate. His spirit, his essence, which had existed inside the Storm, was now dead.

Despite myself, I felt for Fallon. As monstrous as he had been, as complicit in the evils inflicted upon his son and others, he was still a father who, in his own twisted way, had tried to do what he thought was right.

The Storm was now no longer susceptible to the Mountaineers' control. Its swirling winds grew darker and more ominous, spinning faster. Cole collapsed to the ground, cradling his bleeding side. I could see Deirdre shouting, calling his name, demanding he run, but the poor boy was too injured to move.

The Storm lurched forward, but Deirdre swung her stick around and pointed it threateningly. She was speaking, shouting, and though I couldn't make out her words, there was no mistaking their intent: Cole was off limits. The Storm darkened further, and Deirdre's hair whirled about her in its winds.

And then she ran determinedly into the Storm.

I tried to make out what was happening, and just when I thought I'd lost sight of her, the peephole zoomed into the Storm, obeying my wish. I could see her hands move in a variety of deliberate gestures. The walking stick cracked in several places along its length. Blinding light shone from within, bursting out from the cracks and splits. The shadows moved toward her like ants swarming over rotten fruit. And then there was a flash of light so bright that I recoiled and dropped the penny.

My hands were shaking. I fumbled with the coin, trying to pick it up, finally able to get it between my fingers and back up against the door.

I peered through and saw Deirdre in the eye of the Storm, the shadows of the beings within it attacking her like antibodies fighting a virus. Lightning flashed—I could actually see concussion waves rolling out from the eye in concentric circles. But Deirdre remained untouched. Whenever a bolt would strike her, it illuminated a protective barrier around her. It looked as if she was wearing a helmet and armor made of pure-spun glass. And in her hands were a sword and shield of shimmering light that paled the electricity assaulting her. She was wearing the armor and wielding the blade of Elainnor. Like the story Sullivan had read to her.

Deirdre raised the sword. Energy snaked over her arm and along the blade, sparking and spitting in defiance of the Storm. She brought it down in a wide, sweeping arc as time slowed, the sword slicing through bolts of lightning as if they were nothing more than hair-thin wisps of glass.

A searing surge of light burst from the sword. Ripples of heat rolled away from her, a pebble dropped into the surface of the sun. The penny scorched my fingers, and I dropped it again. This time, when I picked it up, its edges were melted and it was slightly warped, like an old CD forgotten on a summer dashboard.

I sat on the cool floor and stared at the misshapen disc in my hand. My only link to the world was gone. I had no idea what was happening. I didn't know if Deirdre and Cole were alive or dead, if the Mountaineers were under attack from the Silver, or if Sullivan Green's plan to bring back The Book of Briars had actually worked.

There was no sound, no movement, just a perfect and tranquil stillness all around me. I lay back and stared up at the ceiling of roots and soil. Sunlight shone in thick bands of light through the small window. I should have been filled with wonderment, with awe for where I was, what I was seeing, but all I could think about was a girl in magical armor wielding a sword of light. Deirdre's fate, Cole's fate, was in their own hands now—just as it had always been. I had failed completely.

There was nothing I wanted more in that moment than for this strange world to consume me until none of me or my failings remained.

CHAPTER 31
THE MOUNTAIN'S WILL

"I still think making tinfoil hats would be a
good idea."

— GOLDTHORN

"Marty? Marty, wake up."

Bella was trying to wake me with a gentle touch on
my shoulder. Her fingers were delicate but strong,
growing more forceful the longer I remained still. But her voice was
strange. She sounded younger, and her Mediterranean accent
sounded . . . Irish?

I opened my eyes. It was dark, but I could see pinpoints of stars
shining through the window. And then I remembered. Neithernor.

It took a moment for my eyes to focus. When they did, I saw her.
Young and pale in the starlight, her hair a frightful mess, but I
instantly recognized her. Even without the magical armor.

"Deirdre?"

"Hi, Marty."

"You're alive." I sat bolt upright and said, "The Storm. The
Mountaineers. Shit, where's Cole?"

"It's okay. He's in the hospital. He just woke up about ten minutes ago. He told me you were here, so I came as soon as I knew he was all right."

She helped me get to my feet. My knees were stiff, and I almost lost my balance until she helped steady me. I was beginning to feel every bit my age.

"Everyone's trying to find you. They think you're either dead or displaced in time."

"No one's getting that lucky today, least of all me." I arched the small of my back, and it cracked. "I saw you inside the Storm, with the armor, the sword. What happened?"

"The Storm is gone," she said matter-of-factly. "Destroyed. The Mountaineers' spells did most of the work."

"You weren't exactly sitting on the sidelines."

She chuckled. "No, I suppose not. Lauren named me. From my understanding, it's old magiq."

"Named you?"

"Stormslayer."

"Now, that's a name," I said.

Deirdre asked, "You ready to head back?"

I took a look around the room, then nodded.

"Sorry it took so long to come. I didn't know what happened and Cole was out for hours."

"It's okay, I knew someone would come looking for me eventually."

Such a small thing to say, but something I couldn't have honestly said before all of this. But here was Deirdre Green, and back home were Cole Sumner, and Knatz, and Lauren, and all the Mountaineers.

I had failed at all the things I thought I had to do. But most of all, I had failed so spectacularly at being alone.

Deirdre led me to the door. She knocked a pattern and opened it. I followed her through, and we found ourselves in a coldly lit hospital room. Cole was there on the bed, wrapped in bandages, with the broadest grin on his face when he saw us.

Deirdre walked over and took his hand. They really were a

beautiful couple—aside from the bandages, wounds, and general dishevelment.

"You look like hell," I told him.

Cole tried to shrug, his bandages pulling against his skin. "It's not too bad. Twenty stitches or so. I am going to have some interesting scars, though. The burns down my side look like lightning."

I shook my head. "If you had just let me—"

"That was never going to happen," he said, stern and resolute. "You all right?"

"I am now that I know you two are okay, relatively speaking. But yeah, I'm good." Outside the window, I could see first light breaking the horizon with hues of pink and orange.

"Did Dee tell you?" Cole asked. "The Book . . . it's back."

I went straight home and checked in on the Mountaineers. I replied to a topic titled "Finding Marty." The Mountaineers were busy conjuring up magic to find me, assuming I'd been swept into another time by the Storm. It was incredibly heartwarming, but I'd had enough of other people putting themselves at risk for me. Though truth be told, I was happy to know that if I ever needed them, they would be there for me.

I WROTE:

 I found Marty. Cole shoved me into the warren and shut the door because he knew I was willing to trade myself for the Book if it came down to it. I spent the better part of the day there, until Cole woke up in the hospital and told Deirdre where I was. Cole is burned and lacerated but he's awake, and when he's feeling better I'm going to buy him a whiskey and shove *him* somewhere. Sorry to scare you guys. Really great work today.

It's a new world.

The Mountaineers had used Deirdre's new name, "Stormslayer," to reveal the fifteenth fragment.

> Gnascorius.
> More commonly referred to as The Dawning Age.
> A time known in classical magimystic parlance as
>   The Book of Light.
> 40.727422 – 74.005961

The next couple of days were slow and restful. My chest ached where Cole had body-checked me, and I had a nice bruise where I'd landed on my ass, but that's what ice packs are for. Still, I thought it best to watch the Mountaineers' progress from the safety of my home.

Deirdre, it turned out, had been put on an IV for a while not long after I left. She was dehydrated and, understandably, exhausted. Spell sickness, the Mountaineers reasoned. She wasn't eager to leave Cole's side. But she did agree to follow up on the coordinates the Mountaineers had found on the Gnascorius page once he fell asleep.

The next day, she posted to her blog.

DEIRDRE: SEPTEMBER 27TH, 2017:

   It turns out 175 Varick Street is where Ackerly Publishing House moved when it changed its name to A&L Printing and became a paperback printer. And where it burned down in the 70s. My father wrote a last entry to me, which the location unlocked, and I'll share anything that seems relevant when I can. It's been hard. Not just everything that happened but knowing this is it. This entry was his goodbye and I'm just . . . It's too much right now.

I knew if we made it here I would have to say goodbye, but I wasn't ready.

I still have to tell you what happened at the vault. I'm working on it. I've just been in a daze. Sleeping beside Cole's bed, or wandering the streets around the hospital. I can't even bear to go back to Neithernor. It feels all the more empty. It's strange to lose a father I never knew and have all those strange feelings, and then get to know him, spend a year with him in a way, then lose him all over again. And finally feel the true grief, the pangs of loss . . .

It's over. For me at least. I know there are wonderful things to look forward to, things to cherish, Cole, the publishing company, actually experiencing my new life . . . I'm just not ready yet. I had this extraordinary last adventure with my father. And now it's over.

The chronocompass didn't work at the address. But it did reveal a letter my father wrote you. His goodbye to you as well.

"Mountaineers,

You have come further than anyone ever has. Done things that most thought were impossible. But you have one final task ahead of you. A difficult task.

Fragment 16.

Shifting through time is a dangerous and traumatic experience. Even for books. The Book of Briars doesn't remember what it is. It doesn't remember its purpose. It is most likely confused, and even afraid (if you believe that books can be afraid).

You have to remind it.

Tell it about the fragments.

Tell it histories of its time with you, and your own memories.

Tell it poems, sing it songs.

Create art and objects that will help it remember what it is and what it's meant to do.

Tell it what all this has meant to you.

It is a ceremony to wake The Book of Briars.

The last fragment and your final assessment.

Create.

Know, once the Book is awakened this time will be over. You will usher in a new age, and nothing will ever be the same.

Though we never met it has been an honor to work alongside you in our common goal. I believe the peak we've sought is now in sight, Mountaineers.

You've reached the final climb.

We all believe in you.

SG"

The Mountaineers began their work on the sixteenth fragment, knowing it was their responsibility to see this through, but also knowing once they did, all this would be finished.

The next day, Deirdre wrote about her experience in the vault, in what would be her final post.

DEIRDRE: SEPTEMBER 30TH, 2017:

 There were maybe 8-10 people in the vault when I got there. They'd been trying to figure out the solution to unlock *The Little Red House.*

I didn't know what they were capable of, or how far they'd come in solving the puzzle, so I hid, trying to think of what to do. It was night outside, but each of them had a light hanging from their hand, like a lantern light without a lantern. They were using them to navigate the dark castle. I realised it was the only light in the vault. The candles hadn't lit for them. Something my father had done?

So I held the stick tightly, and thought of *The Wishing Jar*. The book about a magical jar that catches the last ray of sunlight before the world goes dark. I imagined the stick was like the jar. I told myself a version of the story, feeling the stick resonate when I was getting it right, when I was figurating. The world going dark, the stick catching the only light and hiding it, protecting it. (I'm fully aware of the possibility that I'm only able to figurate because of the stick, btw.)

And suddenly all their lantern lights were pulled from their hands and zapped inside the stick. I didn't know how long it would last or if they'd be able to just cast a new one, so I hurried in the dark, taking the books, using the chaos of the sudden dark and my memory of the castle's layout to solve the puzzle. One of them had conjured some sort of glowing plant by the time I made it back to *The Little Red House*, and they saw me. We were in a silent standoff. They were stunned, not by me, but the appearance of the stick. I heard a knock behind them. I'd summoned a door. I grabbed the book, raced through the bookcases, and ran for the door Cole and I had rehung. I looked back to see the glowing plant had grown up to the ceiling. They could all see me. They were all after me, one within arm's reach. I made it through the door, but the man behind me reached through. I slammed it against his arm, and I'm not proud to say that I gave him a stern promise that I was about to deposit his arm, on its own, in lower Manhattan if he didn't let me go. But he wouldn't. And they all started pulling at the door, trying to get through. I couldn't hold them back.

But then the doorway started to heat up like it had when we'd first come back from the vault. When we left it open too long. His arm was burning. He was screaming, but they kept telling him not to pull his arm back. But he did, and I slammed them out.

I had no idea where Cole was so I checked the forum. Lauren was already watching and telling you what was happening. I was almost too late. I had to do something to get the book to Cole.

There was no way I'd get there in time without magiq . . . so I caterpillowed myself. It was incredibly painful. I could feel invisible wings growing out of my back. But I knew how to use them instinctively. Like I'd always had them. As soon as I grew them, cracks ripped open all over the stick and my stomach turned. The stick was going to break. I had to hurry.

The rest you know. The book started to fall apart, and I used the wings to blow the remains into the Storm. I kept the piece that broke off in my hand. It's sitting on the mantel now. The last piece of my parents.

It's been hard to tell you about my father's last entry. His goodbye to me. I'm not sure why, but I think because once I do, it means this is over. This past year, and this time with you in a way, is finished.

My father planned out everything I had to do to get to here, but he says he also hoped I could create a life after, whether magiq or not, out of the shadow of him and all of this. He wrote in the last letter that he had followed in the shadow of his father, my grandfather Warner Green, for years. He grew up in the old printing house, at my grandfather's heel, and he took on the responsibility of A&L Publishing when his father died. He spent a year there, determined to take the reins of the company and build it in his father's absence, refusing to believe there might be something more out there in the world.

But then the printing house burned down in 1979. My dad got there before the fire department could and found the fire already raging, thousands of paperback books kindling the blaze. He'd tried to put out the fire himself, but it had spread throughout the building, and he'd almost died, lost inside, consumed by the smoke and heat.

Then he saw a man in the fire. A figure that, in his delirium, he swore was his father. He blacked out, and when he came to he was in the back of an ambulance, being treated for smoke inhalation. The fire department had arrived, but there wasn't much they could do as the building collapsed. He thanked them for saving his life, but he was told they found him out on the sidewalk.

He had no idea how he'd gotten out. My dad knew he'd been delirious from the smoke, it couldn't have been his father, but it was in that moment he knew he had to let him go. Let that life die inside the smoldering wreckage of the publishing house.

With his father's footsteps burned away he knew he had to walk his own path. He wandered for years, lost . . . And in that wandering was when he first heard about magiq. He had always been a believer. But in the absence of a purpose, he pursued it.

It was only years later that he learned his father had also believed in magiq. And had pursued it in his own way. My dad would turn a corner, visit a city, or meet someone new, and find familiar footsteps there. Traces of his Warner Green. (He mentions "the materials" my grandfather left him when he died, but I don't know anything about them, and he doesn't mention them again.) Years later in the palace of doors, in the midst of assembling the final steps to open The Book of Briars, knowing his time here was coming to an end, he found his father's pocket watch. The one he remembered his father carrying with him throughout his childhood.

"I had always thought my father had been the force I felt, the force I called my soul's providence. But only now, at the end of all this, have I finally seen the truth. A truth I wish I'd always known. So I want to tell you that I love you, more than I thought I could love, and I hope I have not troubled you so much so that you can't continue on. I am gone now. There are no more clues to riddle. No more puzzles to solve. Nothing now but all the wonders of a life still unwritten. I gave my life for a cause, and if you're reading this, we succeeded. And now I go to a place where you can't. A place where my shadow can't reach you.

It's time for you to blaze a new trail for yourself and leave my shadow once and for all. You don't need to be told what's next. Find where your heart lies out there, my dearest girl, and seek it. I have no doubt you will find it.

Remember, you are your own soul's providence."

That was essentially it. Part of me wanted some last revelation. Some final truth. Some story to continue.

But it's over.

It's why I've been wandering the streets of New York. Why it took me so long to transcribe it. To show it to you makes it true.

I don't know what will happen now, Mountaineers. For you, for me . . . I think we'll be part of each other's lives forever though, in one way or another. We found magiq together. We changed the world. We'll always be a big, weird family.

I imagine I won't be in touch as much as I have been.

I'm really not sure what I'm going to do. I have Ackerly Green Publishing, but part of me feels like that wouldn't honour the sacrifice my father made. To live in that shadow.

Cole should be out in a few days. He's doing well, considering how hurt he was.

The stick is cracked, but not broken. I wouldn't use it again until I know more about it.

Until I know where I'm going.

I guess this is what it's like to climb a mountain.

Most people start looking for a way back down, but I'm up here looking for the next peak to summit.

Deirdre was done, for now, but the final task remained ahead of the Mountaineers. The Book was back in our reality, and the Mountaineers were ready to find the final fragment. All they had to do was work in concert to magiqally call the Book forth and, if everything went well, they'd be able to open it at last. They settled on a time and made their preparations.

If I were still a drinking man, I'd have been preparing a drink to celebrate. But I also knew that nothing was guaranteed—especially in the world of magiq. There was always more going on than we were aware of, and that had certainly been true on the Day of Change, as Endri explained on the day the Mountaineers had planned to wake up the Book.

ENDRI:

 Hey Mounties,

So this is kind of hard to say, but I wanted you to know before we call the Book today.

Ascender sent me a message in the wee hours a couple days ago.

Apparently the "thing" that he and Knatz had to do

on the day we fought the Storm was a sort of house cleaning of Monarch's Mountain. I've gathered that they used the opportunity to lead a mutiny against the more conservative forces of the old houses. And they won.

Monarch's Mountain is in shambles right now, but Ascender and Knatz are determined to rebuild. And Ascender asked if I would join them. There are countless books, scrolls, and coded histories they need help sorting through. And they want me to lead the effort.

I said yes.

This isn't a goodbye. I swear. But let's be honest, you guys haven't needed me for quite some time. And that makes me happy. But it's good to know I am needed somewhere. Somewhere I can make a difference.

I'm proud to be a part of the group we built. Deirdre's right. We're a family. Forever.

And I wouldn't give up a moment of it.

But I think this, now, is what I'm meant to do.

So once we open the Book I'm going to start my new adventure.

But I'm only ever an @ away.

Love you guys,

-Endri

I was glad to hear Ascender and Knatz were okay, especially given the ominous conversation Knatz and I'd had. The Mountaineers had been fighting this war for decades, if not longer. And finally, they were winning it.

Soon after, the Mountaineers began to call The Book of Briars, using their own stories and poems. Together, they reached out with some of the most beautiful and heartfelt messages I'd ever read. I wanted to write something myself, but it felt undeserved. The Book wanted the truth returned to the world, and I'd let that truth turn to ash in front of me. This had worked because of the Mountaineers, not me.

Eventually, after dozens of messages, the Book responded:

> "No one remembered the books but her. That was
> the first sentence in The Book of Briars."
> Mirumagiqum. Tell the heir you found the word.
> The Book of Briars is awake.

The heir could only be one person: Deirdre.

CHAPTER 32
MIRUMAGIQUM

"I think the Mountaineers of this age have proven ourselves."

— FURIA

 The ant almost protested but realized he had to trust his friend. He nodded and carefully climbed onto the bird's foot.

"How are you going to convince her to set me free?" the caterpillow asked.

"You must trust me as well," the ant responded with a smile.

They were getting closer and closer to the cliff, where it seemed Ms. Corvid had decided was a fine place to make a meal of the caterpillow. The ant knew he was running out of time. He climbed up the bird's back and made his way to her head, holding on tight as his little body blew this way and that in the strong winds. Finally, he climbed right onto her black beak, squarely between her eyes.

She gasped. "Just who do you think you are, climbing onto me?"

The ant answered boldly. "I am a fire ant, and if you don't let my friend free, I will bite you right between the eyes."

Ms. Corvid laughed, her beak rattling with glee. "If you bite me, I will tumble from the sky, and what will you do then, you frightened little speck?"

The ant clacked his pinchers and replied, "Well, it's just as you told me, Ms. Corvid. I'll sting and pinch the whole way down."

And with that, the ant bit the bird right between her eyes. She howled and shook her head, throwing the ant into the sky as she dropped the caterpillow from her clutches.

They tumbled back down toward the glade. For the first time, the ant saw the beauty of a brave view such as this. He regretted little, only that he hadn't lived a courageous life and allowed his friend to do the same.

Just as he was about to smash into the ground below, something caught him and lifted him back up into the sky. But it wasn't the hungry bird who'd caught the little ant; it was his best friend, the caterpillow, who now had great big, beautiful wings, their many colors shining brightly in the sun.

The caterpillow set the ant down in a thicket of grass, and they hugged tightly with all their little legs. Then they stepped back and each took a long look at the other. The caterpillow was tall now, lanky like a string bean, but with that same sweet, puffy face. And now he had enormous wings on either side of him. The ant was standing upright, four hands on his hips, his chest puffed out boldly, exhilarated by all the adventure. He smiled at the caterpillow and said, "You look so wonderfully different."

The caterpillow looked back at the ant, and with a proud smile replied, "And so do you, my brave friend. So do you."

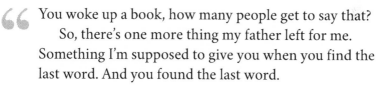

The Mountaineers contacted Deirdre immediately, and despite her recent goodbye, she responded quickly. It was her first posting on the forum.

DEIRDRE:

> You woke up a book, how many people get to say that?
> So, there's one more thing my father left for me. Something I'm supposed to give you when you find the last word. And you found the last word.
> I'm a little indisposed at the moment (I'll explain everything) but I'll come back tonight to give you the last piece myself. It has to do with the Roman numerals.

She was true to her word and, several hours later, responded.

DEIRDRE:

> This was supposed to be the end. I've had about seven endings in the past 12 months. I was supposed to say goodbye. I was supposed to wait for you to wake the Book and get the final word, and then move on with my life.
> But I couldn't.
> I had too many unanswered questions. Too many things still unresolved. I know what my father was

telling me. This wasn't a riddle. It wasn't a test. It was just the end.

But I wasn't done. It wasn't the end for me.

I went to the one place where I had any chance of getting answers to my questions.

I went to Orvin Wallace. My father's attorney. The man who wrote the letter that first brought me to New York. He was surprised to see me, to say the least.

I started rattling off things I'd been wondering the past year: How exactly did my father die? How could he have planned so exactly when he'd die, when the Guide would be found, when I would come to the States? How could he be sure I would come at all? What did he see in the Storm that told him his time was coming to an end? What truth did he learn in his last letter? How could an incorporeal council and one man trapped in a park do all of this?

I had a million questions. Mr. Wallace just sat down and listened to me. He watched me pace his living room for about twenty minutes without a word in response. Finally, I'd run out of steam and was near tears. I sat down across from him and asked him how I was supposed to go on when everything was still so unfinished.

He said I had too much of my father's blood in my veins. I couldn't stop, even when the road had ended. He smiled, offered me tea, and said he'd sit with me and listen as long as I wanted, but sadly there was nothing left to tell.

But then, and I almost didn't register it, when he stood to go to the kitchen he glanced over my shoulder, to the wall of books behind me. And then I saw him realise I saw him. He approached me, but I had already turned to the books and lifted up my father's walking stick.

I don't remember exactly what I thought, what I conjured, but I pulled a thousand books off the wall in a single heartbeat. All except one. A small leather journal that had been hidden behind the others. Weathered. Half-burned. It floated in the air in front of me. I could see almost invisible strings reaching from the book to Mr. Wallace. The book he'd glanced at . . .

I could feel the stick shaking, a crack appearing under the palm of my hand, the wood cutting into me. He snatched the book out of the air before I could.

He held it to his chest. He had tears in his eyes. He said, "He made me promise to burn it. And I tried. It was the one promise I made him that I couldn't keep. And to give it to you now is the second."

I asked him what it was.

He said it was the true ending of *The Monarch Papers*.

I asked for it. He said he would give it to me, but I wasn't prepared for what was inside and that he should explain before I read it. I asked again, and he put it in my hand. I sat with it. Held it. Orvin sat too, with his head bowed. He couldn't bring himself to watch.

It wasn't a final puzzle. My father never wanted me to see what was inside this book. And I almost considered handing it back.

But I'm a Green.

I opened the journal. The first page (which I'm transcribing) read, "It is the end of the 19th century. Your name is Sullivan Green. That might not seem familiar now, but with this book you'll hopefully soon remember most of who you are, and your purpose. You don't belong here. You were swept away in a storm, from another place and time. But it was your choice to go. And now I will tell you why. It's time to wake up."

"Your father didn't die last year." That's what Orvin said as I read the first page.

He then told me everything. My father didn't die last year. The Storm had seen how powerful he'd become when it touched him. And the Silver wanted something in 1898. Something equally powerful. The day he escaped the palace of doors and the Storm touched him, he caught a glimpse of where it planned to send him. It was a blessing and a curse. The only way he and the Council knew their plan would succeed is if they had someone helping it along throughout time. So he decided then that instead of waiting to die in the park, hiding from the world, hoping this plan would work, he would let the Storm take him, and *ensure* the plan would work.

I flipped through the journal. Different years. The journal unlocking decade after decade, revealing more and more to my father. Who he was and what he was meant to do.

The old journal entries that we received from the 1800s were his, before he realised who he was.

I didn't know what to ask. So I asked when he really died. Orvin didn't know. My father would escape for decades into Neithernor, growing older but not old. Slowly remembering who he was, and all the while learning more and more about magiq. Waiting for the right time to emerge, to affect the timeline, to help Monarch's Mountain finish a pamphlet, to encourage a young writer named Fletcher Dawson, to watch himself be born and his father die, to leave himself the materials we needed in his father's will to guide us all to now. To here.

The truth he learned was that he was his own soul's providence. And ours.

Orvin said my dad spent so much time in Neithernor, to guide the timeline, he had become Neithernorian. To come home would mean a quick

death, like jumping onto a speeding carousel. But my
dad discovered that if he came back and left the door to
Neithernor open he could watch the world flicker past,
and guide the plan along its path, still connected to
magiq. But if that door ever closed, he would die. It was
a risk he took over and over to get us all here.

The fire in the printing house was a door left open
too long. The "ghost" my father saw was him, older.
Another moment where my father had created his own
history.

I flipped ahead, to the 90s. The stormswept Sullivan
was the man who took me to the vault, who read me the
stories, while my own father was somewhere looking
for Neithernor. He wanted to be with me one last time
before the entries ended . . . And then sometime after,
he disappeared.

I just sat there. I closed the book and put it down. All
I could do was stare at the walking stick in my lap. My
father's walking stick.

Out of the blue Orvin told me that it didn't belong
here, the stick. It's a magnet for magiq. And the more
you travel, the more stories you make, the more you
experience places rich with magiq, the more it gathers.
It's useful for quickly conjuring, and most skilled
magimystics find their "true stick" at some point in
their lives. But it's breaking because the magiq inside it
that I'm using doesn't belong here. It's a stick on the
outside, but it's held together by magiq on the inside,
and the more I use it here, where it's not supposed to be,
the more I risk breaking it.

And then a thought occurred to me. It doesn't
belong here. The stick. Like my father, it's
Neithernorian. It belongs there.

And I think I do too.

I'm going back.

I'm going to open the warren.

My new peak, my new path, isn't here. It's there. I
need a goal. A purpose. And I think it's going to be
finding the rest of the Lost Collection. Finishing what
my family started.

And if at all possible, I'm going to reunite this
walking stick with its rightful owner.

The Mountaineers were stunned by the revelations. They asked
about Cole.

DEIRDRE:

 I can't ask Cole to come with me.

Watching Deirdre post in real time from the hospital, Cole
responded.

COLE:

 You don't have to ask.

They're releasing me in an hour, and then I'm free
for whatever . . . Neithernor. Pizza.

Well, it looked like I'd have to wait to buy Cole that drink. But I
understood. Completely. My adventure, which started a lifetime ago,
was at an end, and as much as those two had been through, theirs was
just beginning.

Deirdre responded to the Mountaineers.

DEIRDRE:

 I don't know when we'll see you all again. But I'm sure
we will. Someday.

Cole, I'm on my way.

OMG! I forgot the part I was supposed to give you!

So, my dad left an entry in the last journal. That I
should look for something in the vault's copy of *Ant &
Caterpillow*. It would prove useful to the Mountaineers
when they found the last word . . .

It's a foreword. A foreword he wrote.

He said the foreword was all you'd need to open the
Book. So I wrote it down and I'll transcribe it now. And
then I'm going on a pizza date with my guy. (And then
Neithernor.)

FOREWORD:

 "For my dearest girl.

This was your favorite story the last time I saw you.
You would have me read it to you every night before
bed. Do you remember?

Memory, after all, is a very funny friend.

Sometimes he loses the fondest of thoughts and
sometimes the saddest he holds onto forever. I hope
that he has kept for you more fond memories than not,
and I hope that I am somewhere with you, in a memory
held tight.

The way things are can't be undone, only perhaps
rewritten someday. The corvids have come and gone.
It's time to leave the glade.

For now, I go to a place where you can't.
But I am always your caterpillow, and you are
my ant."

It was the last time we heard from Deirdre or Cole.

It was such a bittersweet moment, knowing the two of them had
been such a brief part of my life but that I would miss them terribly.
Still, I was happy for them. I made a cup of tea and raised it in their
honor.

At Basecamp, the Mountaineers were poring over the foreword
that Sullivan had left. All throughout their search for the fragments,
they had been finding strings of Roman numerals, and they were
certain those numbers were the final clue they needed to finally open
The Book of Briars. It took some trial and error, but after Bash had
compiled all the pieces of Ant & Caterpillow and added the foreword in
front, Tinker realized they needed to use the first letter of each word
indicated by the Roman numerals. The race was on to find the hidden
message. Deyavi was the first to cross the finish line and found this:

The Book of the Wild
The Book of Kings
Two worlds rebound
In butterfly wings

And by entering that stanza into the Book's URL, the
Mountaineers had finally unlocked The Book of Briars.

Accessing the new page, touching the final key there, the site
became a sort of portal. The Book was a spell, and we'd finally cast it.

The vision took my breath away. Something inside of me gave
way, like a dam breaking as I watched. As we all watched. It was a
vision of everything we'd put into the Book over the past year. Every
ingredient in the spell we'd cast. We saw images of the dark and
beautiful ruins of Neithernor, of vast vaults of ancient artifacts, and
pieces of the fragments the Mountaineers had spent so much time and
effort finding in their journey to the truth.

And then one final message: "The End," which slowly faded into: "The Beginning."

۞

In the following months, we waited for the truth promised by the Book, but nothing happened. Nothing tangible, at least. Nothing to point at and say, "That's how we changed everything." We had unlocked the Book, seen glimpses of its interior. But it had yet to open. It had yet to show us what it had promised in the tarnished gold-leaf riddle on its cover.

One by one the Mountaineers went back to their everyday lives, keeping in touch when possible, but also trying to reacclimate to the mundane, while knowing without a doubt that magiq wasn't just a figment or a fairy tale. It was a powerful force that together they had uncovered, interacted with, and briefly wielded, before the last of it left this reality. The Mountaineers had done everything asked of them, admirably, and wanted nothing in return but the truth. What the Book had promised. Truth and treasure. They had hoped they would've righted something in our reality that had been wrong. The age we lived in, The Book of Kings, was a lie, born out of a lost age of magiq and wonder. And if we couldn't have that age back, we at least deserved to know why we lost it in the first place.

But I'd accepted that sometimes there is no rhyme or reason for why we lose what we lose. And more painful, there's no promise that it will ever be returned. Not even with magiq.

I'd stopped thinking of losing The Little Red House as my failed last shot at saving Sebastian. Seb was fine. He was happy and loved. I was the one who needed saving, and letting him go had been the thing that finally let me breathe for the first time in decades. It still hurt. It always would. But it was my pain to bear, not his, and that would have to be good enough.

We did learn that Deirdre had followed another rabbit hole of her own before she'd left. When she'd looked into who had registered the Ackerly Green social media accounts, she'd found a familiar name. CJ

Bernstein, the author whose children had originally found the Guide (and who helped me assemble this tangled story). He'd been rightfully fascinated by the Guide and its history and had hoped that by using Ackerly Green's name on social platforms he'd find others who were drawn to this mystery and who might be able to unravel it.

And with those accounts he'd found Deirdre Green. They had kept in touch over the course of unlocking the Book, and when the time came for her to venture back into Neithernor, she asked CJ to manage the company in her stead.

CJ reached out to me about turning everything that happened into the book you're reading now. He felt it was important to share the story, to tell people willing to believe what happened. I agreed, thinking maybe this was the truth promised by the Book. What we did, what we learned. Maybe that's how the change we'd hoped for would come about. Maybe, somehow, that's how we'd make new magiq.

Once we'd finally organized everything into a semi-cohesive narrative and I was left to assemble it myself, CJ created a company calendar to keep track of the important dates on the road to publishing *The Monarch Papers*. It felt good to see, to have a clear plan for the future. We wouldn't wait for the truth. We would be the truth-bringers.

A day later, CJ received a notification on his phone. There was a new entry on the calendar. It was a release date for *The Book of Briars*.

A year from the date we'd unlocked it.

We hadn't undone the lie or changed history. Instead, we'd somehow helped create a new story out of the ashes of this old one. A story we would all read together.

We didn't learn how the world had changed, or why, but we knew how *we* had changed. We had formed a family, and in doing, brought about something akin to a new age. Or as we were told in the final message . . .

Mirumagiqum.

More commonly referred to as The Age of Magiq.

A time known in classical magimystic parlance as
  The Book of Briars.

EPILOGUE

"Go now, but be sure to return. It was a pleasure,
no, an honor, to meet you."

— RICARDO

The air had turned humid, and the city was alive outside my window. I brewed some coffee and then made my way to the central library to do something I hadn't done in too long a time.

Write.

It felt so good to get back into it. The research, the refining a turn of phrase, the simple act of putting words on paper. I was liberated. And I didn't come up for air until late that afternoon.

My mind was running a million miles an hour. I needed to email all my editors, all my old contacts, anyone and everyone I ever knew. After *The Monarch Papers*, there were a million more stories I needed to tell, articles to write, mysteries to solve.

I also, desperately, needed to eat.

I walked down to a deli and grabbed a sandwich, then made my way up to the park to eat it. As I sat down, I got a text notification. It was Bella.

"Where are you?" she asked.

I realized in the aftermath of everything, including asking her to shelter Jeremy, Port, and Alison, I'd never followed up with her. I texted back, telling her all was fine and that I was enjoying the weather in the park before heading back to the library to get some good work done.

I finished my sandwich and sat and watched the people. Joggers ran past, dogs pulled their owners from one smell to another, businessmen took phone calls, and lovers held hands and stole kisses. I thought of Deirdre and Cole, strolling through Neithernor, hand in hand, their smiling faces smeared with pizza grease. It was a lovely thought. I couldn't think of a better day than that. My mind drifted, thinking of the Book, the Mountaineers, Augie, Knatz, Lauren, Lord and Lady Blackweather.

I realized I'd planted myself directly across from the Ramble. Where so much of this had started. Where Sullivan had planned and plotted with the 18 Gates to help us do whatever it is we did. *The Book of Briars* would be out in a few months, and who knew what would happen then. A new age was just being born.

A wave of something washed over me. Not joy, exactly, but akin to it. The preamble of joy. Hope. And then something else happened. I remembered a name. The name of a young girl, not more than ten.

Scarlet.

I could suddenly remember a little girl I hadn't remembered for decades. Well, not suddenly. It was more like a cool, slow-moving wave of memory carried on a current of air, cutting through the heat. Scarlet had been on a trip to the zoo in the park with her brother, her twin, Samuel, and after lunch she had stood in the same grass laid out in front of me now, looking into the Ramble . . .

Inside the thicket of trees Scarlet saw a boy. A boy with toffee-brown skin, who was inexplicably riding a tall white dog with a long, sweet face. The boy's name . . . was Franklin.

She followed the boy into the woods, and that's where she found an old tumble-down cottage.

A flood of goosebumps surged across my neck and forearms.

I was remembering *The Little Red House*.

I stood, overwhelmed. I could almost see them in front of me, the kids from the book. I searched the faces of people in the park to see if I was the only one feeling this. The Guide's reappearance had triggered memories before it turned to ash; maybe *The Little Red House* had done the same.

No one seemed to be experiencing what I was, but as I looked, I found a familiar face approaching me from one of the winding park paths. It was Bella. Her eyes were wet and rimmed with red. She held on tight to the little pink hands of twin girls. Sebastian's girls.

It was too much to bear in the already overwhelming moment. I tried to compose myself, but then I saw who was trailing behind them. Sebastian. My boy.

He approached me, and without thinking, I reached out and held his face in my hands, swept away in the moment. I needed to know he was real. I could feel tears streaming down my face. He reached up and put his hands over mine, and instead of pulling them away, he squeezed. He smiled at me through tears of his own and spoke two words that brought me low with pure, unadulterated joy . . .

"Hi, Dad."

The Story Continues:
The Book of Briars

November, 2018

EXPLORE THE WORLD OF MAGIQ

✦

Discover Your Magimystic Guild:
http://www.magiq.guide

✦

Join the Mountaineers in the Search For Magiq:
http://ackerlygreen.com

✦

Follow @AckerlyGreen to uncover secrets and discover more wondrous mystery:

instagram.com/ackerlygreen

YOU CAN MAKE A BIG DIFFERENCE

Did you enjoy this book? Reviews are the most powerful tools in our arsenal when it comes to getting attention for our books.

I don't have the financial muscle of larger New York publishers. I can't take out full page ads in the newspaper or put posters on the subway.

But I do have something much more powerful and effective than that, and it's something that those publishers would kill to get their hands on. A committed and loyal bunch of readers.

Honest reviews of my books help bring them to the attention of other readers. If you've enjoyed this book I would be very grateful if you could spend just five minutes leaving a review (it can be as short as you like).

Thank you very much.

ABOUT CJ BERNSTEIN

❧

CJ Bernstein spent much of the last decade working as a Hollywood screenwriter, but has had a lifelong obsession with myths, magic, and the mysterious goings on in books.

He lives in New York City (the most magical place in the world) with his husband, kids, and pups.

http://ackerlygreen.com

facebook.com/cjbofficially

instagram.com/cjbofficially

19020305R00283

Made in the USA
Middletown, DE
03 December 2018